ADRIFT

A NOVEL

LISA BRIDEAU

Published by Sourcebooks Landmark, an imprint of Sourcebooks
P.O. Box 4410, Naperville, Illinois 60567–4410
(630) 961-3900
sourcebooks.com

Cataloging-in-Publication Data is on file with the Library of Congress.

Printed and bound in the United States of America.
LSC 10 9 8 7 6 5 4 3 2 1

To Mr. Falcone, Mrs. Palethorpe (now Mrs. McNeil),
and all the other kind teachers who fueled my love for
writing and encouraged me in this joyful foolishness

1

THE BOAT BOBBED IN THE water, going nowhere.

She read the note taped to the counter twice and still didn't understand.

This is the only way out alive.

It felt like sea urchin spikes were being jammed into her temples. Closing her eyes against the headache, she stumbled, slamming against the stove in the minuscule galley. Metal pots clanged together. She flinched. The movement of the boat and the dizziness from her headache intertwined, both eager to push her to her knees.

She willed time to slow so she could sort out what was happening, but the waves lapping against the hull persisted in the same unrelenting rhythm.

Leaning on the counter, she forced her eyes open and stared without recognition at the long fingers and neatly trimmed nails in front of her. The hands weren't hers, weren't familiar at all.

Nothing was familiar.

She felt sick, didn't know why. When she tried to recall the previous day, to remember what she'd done to cause this, her mind served an expanse of blankness. She groped for some recollection beyond waking up and staggering out of bed minutes ago. Anything. But it was all gone: how she'd come to be in the cabin of this little boat, who she was, her name.

She gripped the counter and held on to the edge designed to keep things from sliding off in turbulent waters. Tried to focus on the typed letters marching across the paper. Movement above the sink caught her eye. The note forgotten, she put a finger on the mirror, then on her cheek to confirm what she was seeing.

A stranger's face.

She dropped to her knees. Her body clenched, threatening to vomit but unable to. Dragging the palm of a hand across her dry lips, she sat back, closed her eyes, and shut out the fact that she didn't recognize her own face. She focused on the rocking of the boat. That sensation was familiar. The rigging creaking outside: that sound she knew. She was on a sailboat. She knew boats. *She knew.*

That wisp of familiarity let her breathe. She extended the hands she didn't know, inspecting them through squinted eyes. Turning them palm up, shaking, she saw hardened callouses, evidence of labor she couldn't remember.

Putting the hands—her hands—on the varnished floor, she steadied herself.

"Okay." Her lips tightened into a thin line. The voice was wrong too.

She traced fingers along the back of her neck. Working them through her long hair, she inspected her scalp, hands trembling but methodical. No sign of injury. No reason for the intense throbbing behind her temples, for the blankness. She grabbed the edge of the wooden counter and heaved herself up. A flame flashed across her right shoulder.

"Fuck!" She hugged the arm against her torso. Ribbons of pain reached down to her hands and made her vision fade at the edges. Tears formed but she wiped them away, clenched her jaw, and stood straight. She tore the note off the counter and read it again and again and again.

There are pills in the drawer for the headaches.
You want answers, but this has been done to keep you from them.
This is the only way out alive.
Start over.
Don't make yourself known.
Don't look back.

—

She perched on the bow of the sailboat, her bare feet stuck to the fiberglass hull, keeping her from sliding into the ocean and sinking to the bottom. The headache continued to pulse, enveloping her in a bubble of pain before subsiding and letting her experience the world. In and out, a tide reaching for the shore until finally the stabbing in her temple vanished. She opened her eyes and braced for the pain to return, but it didn't. A sound halfway between a laugh and a cry escaped her. Nearby, a cormorant squawked in reply and took off.

The boat was anchored next to a cluster of forested islands that shot out of the ocean with a sense of urgency. Trees towered at the edge of low cliffs as if they might teeter over into the sea in a strong wind. It was beautiful and empty and unfamiliar.

She watched the closest island disappear bit by bit, erased by the fog. Had her memory loss been like that, or had it all gone at once? Had she felt the emptiness expand and take everything, everyone?

She wrapped her arms around her legs, put her head on her knees, and wished she was a barnacle on the hull.

A scrawny seagull landed clumsily on deck a few meters away. He struggled to stand, favoring one deformed foot. They eyed one another.

She rose. As she walked along the edge of the boat to the cockpit, her legs accommodated the gentle rocking with unsettling ease. She rummaged in the galley and returned with a tin of sardines. The seagull kept his distance as she tossed a chunk of oily fish his way. It hit the deck and the seagull hopped forward, gobbling it down just before it went overboard. Setting the tin on the deck, she backed away. He devoured the fish in less than a minute and flew off.

It was time to face her own situation.

Inside, she downed a glass of water, the tang of plastic and chlorine replacing the stale taste of her dry mouth. She read the note again, hoping to understand better now that her head wasn't killing her. The note implied her memory erasure was deliberate. Impossible—unless that was just another thing she'd forgotten. Putting the note on the counter, she smoothed a ragged edge with the tip of a finger and then turned her back on it and started searching.

The first drawer she checked contained two envelopes marked "Important," which started her heart racing, but she set them on the table unopened. Instead, she emptied every drawer, cubby, and compartment on the boat. Anything that wasn't clothing or boating gear she put on the table as she found it. When the search was complete, she folded herself onto the bench and faced the meager collection of objects. Something here had to explain what was going on.

A library of sailing and navigation books. Blank notebook. Five hundred dollars in twenties, Canadian. A bottle of white pills, unlabeled, each tablet imprinted with a "c" in a square.

Then there were the two envelopes held together with a rubber band, "Important" scribbled on the front in thick black ink. The first contained a sheet of paper with bank account details and a bank card—Bank of Cominotto, Malta. Also a Province of British Columbia driver's license—issued two months ago. The photo showed a woman with a square face, sharp nose, straight black hair. She glanced between the photo and the mirror a few times to confirm it matched. Name: Sarah Jane Song. She'd never heard the name before.

Birth date: January 20, 2004. Leaning over to the boat's instrument panel, she looked at the date: July 5, 2038. The date didn't surprise her, didn't seem wrong, but it also didn't bring up any memories of the previous day or any others. She did the math: thirty-four years old—another thing she should know but didn't.

The second envelope contained documents for the boat, *Sea Dragon*. An operator's license, ownership papers, radio operator license—all in the name of Sarah Song.

She was not Sarah Song. It didn't fit. Shoving all the documents in a drawer, she slammed it shut to avoid the growing temptation to throw Sarah Song into the ocean. She turned to the collection of navigation charts. They were new, still keen to fold shut according to their original shape. A shard of jealousy jabbed her, that the charts had more memory than she did. Spreading the first chart flat, she saw someone had helpfully circled her anchor spot. How kind. She was in the Pacific Northwest, tucked into the remote archipelago of Haida Gwaii off the coast of British Columbia, south of Alaska.

Her ability to read the chart with ease gave her pause. Running a hand across it, she noted all the circles with plus signs clustered around the shoreline. Underwater invisible hazards, she knew. If she stopped and listened for it, she could hear wind whistling through the rigging, the anchor chain clinking as the boat swung around with the tide. None of the sounds scared her; if anything, they comforted her.

Her gaze slid over the rest of the map, reading place names, waiting for something to pop as familiar. T'aanuu, Windy Bay, Gwaii Haanas, Hotspring Island, Hecate Strait.

Nothing.

Looking through the porthole at the wild, forested island nearby, she wondered why they'd chosen this spot. She wanted it to mean something, to be a clue, but if it was, she couldn't see it.

Someone had taken her memories, her very self. Whatever remained of her was supposed to, what, live on this boat forever? Swim to shore and live in the woods?

Start over. It felt impossible.

To quell her unsettled stomach, she filled another cup at the tap, drank it, then went to refill it. The tap gurgled, made a choking noise. She slammed the lever to turn it off. Frozen, hand on the tap, her heart sank. She knew what that sound meant.

"No, no, no." She repeated the word over and over, until it was no longer a word, just an acoustic representation of frustration.

Snatching an empty metal water bottle from the shelf, she held it under the tap and slowly lifted the lever. The tap gurgled, released two spurts of water, then nothing. The boat shifted. The pump caught another bit of water, then it coughed and produced nothing. She closed the tap and put the lid on the bottle. Less than a liter.

Opening cabinets, she calmly pushed aside containers of oatmeal and freeze-dried meal packets. She groped deeper until her hand wrapped around a waxy carton. Relief. She drew out a container of oat milk and put it on the counter next to the water bottle. Less than two liters of drinkable liquid between her and death by dehydration. The water she'd just chugged sloshed around her stomach. Anger flooded her veins. Someone had left her on a boat in the middle of a giant, uninhabited national park without water. She tightened the cap on the bottle with a hard yank, then put it on the counter and turned away, desperate for a distraction.

Hunching over the control panel opposite the galley, she put three fingers on the radio's power knob. There was a slight resistance as she turned it, as if offering her a chance to reconsider this idea. She clicked it on. Loud static filled the cabin. The radio was set to Channel 16, and she knew, somehow, it was the channel to monitor.

While she listened to the static confirming her isolation, she checked the other instrument displays. Her batteries were at 96 percent power and charging, backup fuel cells were full, hydrogen tank to feed the fuel cells was full. She poked buttons until she found a depth meter that reassured her she had adequate clearance. She pulled open the floor panel and checked the bilge. Dry. Everything was okay, everything except the radio that refused to break its vigil of uninterrupted static. No boats calling to each other. No sign of other people nearby. She lifted the radio handset, felt the heft of it, thought about pressing the button, calling out. Calling for help. She put it down and stepped back. Not yet.

Slipping on the jacket she'd found in a cubby earlier, she went on deck. Ignoring the scenery this time, she studied the boat, ran her fingers over each line, checked that the solar panels were secure, made her way to the bow and checked the anchor chain. She couldn't say what she was looking for, but nothing she inspected caused her worry.

A metallic tapping noise caught her attention. She found a loose halyard clanging against the mast and secured it, her mind elsewhere as her hands worked deftly to tie a knot she didn't know she knew. The task complete, she stood, arms hugging her torso, staring at the perfect knot. She studied the lines neatly running from the sails into the cockpit. It was all familiar but unknown.

She could pull anchor, hoist sail, and test herself, discover if she knew how to sail or not, but her hand stayed away from the anchor motor switch. Being anchored was safe. Safe was good.

Movement on the rocky shore of the nearby island caught her eye. She was halfway to standing, arms raised over her head, about to yell for help when she froze. *Don't make yourself known.* Her voice evaporated and she dropped her arms to her sides.

She squinted at the island in the fading light. A fat black bear trundled along the shore, flipping over rocks with its paw. The island was a wall of wild, lush forest. There was no one there to save her.

Maybe there was no one left at all.

2

SHE'D STAYED UP AS LONG as she could, terrified that sleep would act like a reset button and steal her single day's worth of memories, trap her in a cycle of horrific discovery. Hours had dragged by as she'd tried to bring up an image of her parents or the face of a friend, a sibling, anyone. It seemed survivable to have lost events, but to have lost people—she fought against that. In the end though, sleep had pulled her under.

When she woke, head pounding and nauseous, she remembered her one day. Then she remembered that she'd lost everything else, everyone else.

Swallowing a headache pill with a minuscule ration of oat milk, she leaned against the mast and forced down a breakfast bar, squinting in pain as a cloud drifted leisurely by, en route to block the sun. A metallic taste suddenly filled her mouth, replacing the peanut butter of her breakfast. She puzzled over the source, thought about allowing herself a mouthful of water. The sound of water slapping against the boat receded into a muffled whisper and then she jerked, her body spasming like she'd been nudged awake from an unplanned nap. Her hand involuntarily released the breakfast bar wrapper, and the wind carried it off to become another scrap of ocean litter. The sun, which had just been shining, was somehow suddenly behind a cloud, about to emerge from the other side of it. Her eyes were dry as though she'd forgotten to blink for a long time. It was as if the world had skipped ahead five minutes.

Retreating to the safety of the cabin, she tried to fight off this new source of confusion. She'd just been distracted, lost in thought. Dehydration and bad sleep made it hard to focus, that was all. A sip of water washed away the already fading metallic taste.

She rested her head on the cool table and focused on breathing and the ache in her shoulder. Tangible things. When the headache finally relented, she opened the notebook where she'd tried to organize her thoughts in the early hours of the morning, a weak attempt to fend off sleep. The printing was shaky and repeated the same few bare facts, the same questions: who was she, who had wiped her memory, what of family, her family, and what now, what now, what now. How does one start over from here. The questions buzzed in her head still, swirling around the wide emptiness.

She focused on what she did know. She knew what things were: utensils, boats, radios. She could look at the island and name the tree types. The chart said she was in Canada; she knew the capital city was Ottawa. Facts she knew. But anything personal was gone. Name, gone. Memories of loved ones, gone. Memories of any events or life experiences, gone. A lifetime, gone.

A buzzing from outside interrupted this thought spiral. She went out to investigate. On deck, the early-morning sun glinted off the hull of a small metal boat as it came directly toward her. The confirmation that there were other people in the world comforted her marginally; she wasn't the last human on earth, or a figment of her own imagination.

The high-pitched whine from the boat's electric motor increased in intensity as it approached. When it was within a few meters, the engine switched off and the boat coasted alongside silently, the man at the helm raising a hand in greeting. He was alone.

She was frozen on deck, hands balled into fists. Shaking them loose, she tried in vain to think of what a normal person would do with their hands, how a normal person would determine if someone was a threat.

"Hello!" His voice was deep, and he was built like a bear. The brim of a baseball cap hid his face.

"Hello," she echoed.

"Saw you anchored out here… not a usual spot for tourists." He adjusted his hat and squinted up at her. "Thought I'd check in, make sure everything's all right."

He seemed to be waiting for a response. Her brain searched futilely for guidance on the correct thing to say. A new panic crawled up from her stomach and perched in her mouth, making it difficult to answer. "I like it here." She attempted a smile.

He bobbed his head. "You must, been here for over a week. Pretty spot. Most speed by on their way to Burnaby Narrows, don't appreciate it."

She took a step toward him. "How do you know I've been here a week?"

"Ah, well, I'm a Watchman, one of the guardians of the ancient Haida village sites. I'm in the cabin around that island, over at T'aanuu Llnagaay." He spoke without urgency, like he was telling her a story, like they were neighbors who chatted every day. "Saw you drop anchor here last week when I went fishing. It's early in the season for sailors, so I noticed."

The sun brightened. She felt lighter. "Did you see anyone else on this boat? Before?"

He tilted his head. "Didn't really look too close, you know. More focused on things in the water."

Disappointment lapped against the boat's hull. Someone else must have been here. Someone had stranded her here. That person was a thread to pull on that might unravel everything, if she could find some trace of them. If she wanted to pull threads.

As her conversation with the Watchman stalled, it became painfully obvious she had no idea what she should do. She met his gaze, unblinking, and he turned his head to look into the distance. Sunlight sparkled on a bottle of water near the wheel of his sleek fishing boat. The temptation to jump over and chug the entire bottle was so strong that she gripped a nearby line to hold herself in place.

He tugged on his cap. "Uh-huh. So, weather calls for thunderstorms and pretty choppy water starting late tomorrow. Looks to be rough, even by our standards. Hard to know if the forecast is right; Haida Gwaii makes its own mind up about the weather. But it's a full day to Skidegate if you go directly, more if wind isn't on your side. Good time to head to town if you're planning to go. Otherwise, you'll have to hunker down and wait for the weather to pass. Sometimes these storms come to stay for a bit and rough up small boats."

"Shit."

This made him grin. "Yeah, shit. Well, radio us on Channel 6 if you want to come visit or if you find yourself in trouble."

It was unclear what she should say to this. Tears welled up.

"You're good?" he asked, not looking at her.

One word, just one word and she could push off her water problem by another day. She opened her mouth but couldn't get her voice to work, so she nodded and looked away.

He zipped his jacket, waved. A few minutes later he was a speck in the distance, and she could move again.

Frustrated with herself for failing so terribly with the first person she'd ever met, she replayed the conversation over in her head, torturing herself with all the ways she could have done it better.

"Shit," she repeated.

The coming storm forced her to face the fact that she'd been waiting for someone to come get her. Whoever put her here, surely they wouldn't go to so much trouble and then leave it to chance if she survived.

Except apparently they had.

She needed to get to safe harbor. She needed water. She also needed to learn how to be among people without giving herself away as broken, and she wasn't going to learn that out here. Piling the sailing books and equipment manuals on the table inside, she got to work.

—

After the Watchman left, she spent the rest of the day and night learning how to use the autopilot and GPS systems, testing equipment, testing herself, furling and unfurling sails, referring to the sailing books, doing her best to remember the details, the right order to do things. She fell asleep slumped over a manual, her cheek pressed against a diagram explaining the difference between true and apparent wind.

When the mystery pills released her from the morning headache the following day, she studied the storm clouds gathering in the distance, feeling a new chill on the wind. Her head seemed clearer, her thoughts no longer flitting nonstop from one worry to the next. Encouraged by this new ability to focus, she slipped on worn sailing gloves she'd found in a drawer, noticing their perfect fit, then raised anchor and tried to apply what she'd read and practiced.

Instead of easy progress, she kept stalling, her sails billowing uselessly as the boat faced the wrong way. The motor saved her, kept her away from the rocky shore, but every time she started it, the weight of failure dragged at her a little more.

A small part of her had been sure she knew how to sail. She thought despite the memories being gone that the knowledge, the skill, would remain. How else to explain the knots she could tie, that she knew a bilge pump even existed, much less where it would be?

It was like trying to dance when you couldn't explain the steps. If she could get into a zone, it worked. But as soon as she thought analytically about it, things went sideways. Her brain would skip around, searching for previous experiences to inform her actions, interrupting her instinctive movements. She'd get the mainsail up, boat angled into the wind, have a moment of smooth sailing, and then the wind would shift. Instinctively she'd know what to do to adjust and sometimes her body would do it. But sometimes she'd hesitate and the thread of instinct would snap, leaving her staring at a bunch of lines with no idea which to winch.

After hours of mis-starts and failures she stood in the cockpit, sails flapping, and let out a full-body sigh. She rolled her injured shoulder a few times while doubt and uncertainty swirled around her. The wind shifted. Kneeling on the bench seat, she scanned the water, her gut urging her to watch out for something. Four seconds later, the main boom struck her and she went overboard.

The cold cut through her. With an involuntary gasp, she went under.

Frigid water wrapped around her, made it hard to think. She kicked, broke the surface, took a breath, and coughed.

She needed to get to the ladder at the back of the boat, and *Sea Dragon* suddenly seemed enormous. She didn't feel particularly in control of her limbs in the cold water, but she tried thinking about moving them, hoping some neural pathways would spark and get the job done.

She flipped onto her back, managed to orient herself the right way. Her muscles clenched against the cold, but she kicked as best she could. *Sea Dragon* was drifting toward a rocky shore. Small waves splashed icy water over her head and up her nose. Panicking, she broke form and her head dunked under. She pictured her life jacket where she'd left it, draped over the cabin door.

A current tugged her under, insistent, strong. The pressure on her chest grew. Everything slowed. She stopped fighting.

How strange that something so empty could possibly sink. If she was swept away, what would really be lost?

A hot pain shot up her left arm. She almost gasped in surprise but managed to keep her mouth shut. Jerking her arm in against her body, she kicked to stop her descent. Kicked again, harder, toward the surface. Now her left ankle joined with its own shooting, burning sensation. She focused on getting her head above water. The urge to inhale expanded to fill every brain cell, and she broke the surface just as her lungs demanded she breathe. The pain in her left arm and her already-injured right shoulder made swimming an ugly, lurching affair, but she kept trying, kept struggling. *Sea Dragon*'s stern swung toward her, bringing the ladder closer. Good *Dragon*.

After an eternity of swimming, she reached the ladder without any other parts of her catching fire, only swallowing half the ocean in the process. Throwing her body at the metal rungs with her last scrap of energy, she hauled herself up. As she summoned the energy to climb, she saw the plume of the monster jellyfish in the water, a cloud of thin tentacles trailing gracefully behind it for several meters.

Crawling to the cockpit, she pulled on a line without thinking— the correct one—and furled the loose sail to stop *Sea Dragon* from catching any wind. She decided they were far enough from any shoreline that she could risk drifting for a bit longer. In the cabin, she cranked the heater on, stripped off wet clothes, and wrapped herself in a wool blanket, lungs trying to cough out the ocean.

When the violent shivering subsided, she forced herself to the tiller to program the autopilot to hold position. Then she slipped the blanket off and saw the red welt running elbow to shoulder, skin blistering like a burn. Another line of stings wrapped around her ankle. Wiping her eyes, she grabbed the first-aid kit she'd found earlier and applied the jellyfish-sting spray. She tried to dry-swallow painkillers, but her raw throat choked and she had to use her remaining ration of water to get them down.

Tugging on dry clothes, crying out as fabric scraped over her welts, she smeared fresh sunscreen on her face, buckled her life jacket around her waist, and stood at the cabin door. Her head was pounding and her throat was raw from the seawater. A wave of shame washed over her for getting knocked overboard. She thought about the moment of calm underwater, the pull to give in to the current. And the choice not to.

Standing straighter, she pushed her hair back and went to turn off the autopilot.

3

THE NEXT DAY, DARK CLOUDS hung over T'aanuu in the distance, marking how far she'd managed to travel despite her struggles. She'd have to work to stay ahead of the stormy weather, but it was a relief to have a task. The drugs took the edge off the morning headache so she could bear daylight, but the dehydration meant the stabbing pain and light nausea stuck around. A lotion calmed the jellyfish stings marginally.

She scraped dried blood from her shin and applied a bandage over the gash caused by slamming into a cleat late the previous day. This was a new day, no need for reminders of her blunders. This day would go better.

Once she stopped trying so hard to sail and just trusted her instincts, things clicked into place. Throwing caution overboard, she sailed outside the chain of islands, in the Hecate Strait, the steady winds in her favor. Gripping the tiller with white-knuckled hands, she refused to retreat to the calmer sheltered channels. A glimpse of a motorboat she'd seen yesterday gave her courage; other boaters charting the same course was a good sign.

Her sails set perfectly, she sped along, legs braced, hand on the tiller, wind sucking the moisture from her eyes. While standing at the helm, she didn't think about her missing pieces, her thirst, her loneliness. Something else took control and she danced over the water.

For lunch, she forced down a protein bar and the last dregs of gritty oat milk and pushed on, sailing all day and doing her best to ignore the dizziness that dogged her, the constant pull to try to fill a cup at the tap.

When boat traffic increased and her GPS showed she was approaching town, she furled her sails and turned on the motor to navigate Maude Channel. She passed the village of Skidegate, marked by a constellation of towering wooden poles carved and painted with striking animal figures. Bald eagles perched on trees and power poles everywhere she looked. Solar panels on roofs sparkled in the sun. She rounded a point with a beautiful Haida longhouse set safely behind a dike.

Tearing her gaze away from the scenery, she checked her GPS screen over and over to confirm she was passing Skidegate and heading west, dehydration scrambling her ability to think spatially.

According to the "Welcome to Haida Gwaii" brochure in *Sea Dragon*'s library, there were two towns of note in this area. Skidegate was the cultural hub and Daajing Giids had most of the commercial services. Indigenous Haida people made up the majority of both town populations. She sailed past a dock crammed full of old, neglected fishing boats and steered toward Daajing Giids's Sunrise Marina, which had a scattered population of pleasure boats and several open berths. It took twenty minutes to sort out how to position her boat correctly to sidle up to an empty spot and get lines tied to the dock.

Once she had *Sea Dragon* secure, tying knots she could only tie because she was too exhausted to interfere with what her hands were doing, she ran to the spigot on the dock and filled her water bottle. She chugged the water, nearly choking as she laughed with relief. Cold, perfect, potable water. She refilled her bottle, her gaze resting on a sign conveying a zero-tolerance policy on diesel fuel use. Having quenched the thirst that had been fogging her head for two days, she felt her brain spin with new worries.

She retreated to the safety of her cabin, shutting the door behind her with a gentle click. Watching the dock through the small window, she scanned for any sign of other people. She wanted to hear something other than her own voice, to be distracted from her thought spirals, her constant flow of unanswerable questions. What a gift that would be! Also, a strangely terrifying prospect.

The note admonished her from the drawer: *Don't make yourself known.*

Pulling the note out, she smoothed the paper and read it over. She had it memorized by now, but she studied it anyway, willing it to help her understand and do the right thing. Was she safe, or was she in danger?

There are pills in the drawer for the headaches.
You want answers, but this has been done to keep you from them.
This is the only way out alive.
Start over.
Don't make yourself known.
Don't look back.

She thought of the documents insisting she was Sarah. Was it time to be Sarah?

Flipping open her notebook, she wrote the name. She wrote it over and over, but it felt awkward each time and her pen strokes got heavier and heavier until she tore the paper. As she yanked out the page, a frustrated cry caught in her throat. She wasn't Sarah Song. She blacked the name out letter by letter, leaving only one S at the top of the wrinkled paper.

Ess.

Movement drew her eye to the dock outside, where a figure approached her boat.

Gripping the countertop, she thought about how far she'd come from being crumpled on the floor in pain and confusion. She picked up her jacket and climbed the stairs to stand on deck.

"Hello!" The woman on the dock waved.

"Hello." Shrugging on her jacket, she wondered how a nonamnesiac would stand and tried to mirror the pose of the woman on the dock: hands in pockets, standing tall, big smile. Not an impostor in sailor's clothes, but a real person.

"Sii.ngaay 'laa. Welcome to Daajing Giids! I saw you tie up, thought I'd come welcome you. Have you been to our marina before?"

The word *welcome* washed over her. Smiling for real, she shook her head.

"Well, we should have everything you need. Laundry and showers are next to the office. We can top up hydrogen tanks if needed, swap batteries, all that. How long are you looking to stay?"

"How long can I stay?"

"Long as you want, really. Not as many pleasure sailors this season, given everything that's happening. But it's a nice time to be here; warm weather is coming; we have amazing seafood you can't get further south anymore. You can pay your rental fee online if you like, or in the office."

"I have cash?"

"Well, come on over to the office when you're ready. I can get you registered and paid up." She smiled again. Ess appreciated all her smiles, wanted to collect them. "Nice to meet you—ah, I didn't actually get your name. I'm X̲uuya, or Raven, your choice."

"Oh, I'm—" She paused, not wanting to say it. "Sarah." She frowned. It was fourteen kinds of wrong. "But I go by, uh, Ess." She waited for Raven to accuse her of being a fraud.

But Raven smiled. "Ess for Sarah, easy enough. Lovely to meet you."

Ess felt ten feet tall as Raven walked away. She'd had a human interaction and hadn't blown it, hadn't given herself away as a mere hull of a person.

Now that she was safe from the coming storm, she realized there was another advantage in getting to town: she could perhaps find out who Sarah Song was. Safely docked away from the storm, no more sailing to do, the crushing weight of questions couldn't be avoided anymore.

Ducking inside, she went to the sink with her water bottle to clean up. Ess didn't want to enter the world encrusted in salt and sweat.

4

SHE MADE IT A FEW meters down the dock before stopping to look back at her home, tucked in with the other boats. It didn't seem bothered by her leaving it, but she felt like a hermit crab without its protective shell. She forced herself to walk away.

The marina office had a hand-lettered sign on the door welcoming visitors in a beautiful script she assumed was Haida, with smaller English print beneath.

Register and pay, a straightforward transaction, nothing to stress over.

Inside smelled like cedar and fresh rain. The walls of the small office were lined with wood, and light slipped in from the skylights set between thick roof beams.

Raven smiled widely. "Hello, hello, I'm glad you're here. It's been so quiet this week. The entire universe is over at Skidegate today for a salmon barbecue, and I'm sitting here hoping someone remembers to bring me food." She took Ess by the elbow to guide her to a seat in the office area.

Ess's sudden inability to move halted their forward motion. All that existed at the moment was her arm and the first human contact she had any memory of. She stared at Raven's delicately tattooed fingers resting on her arm, caught in the sensation.

Raven's hand moved from Ess's elbow to her shoulder, her silver bracelets clinking together. "Are you okay? Did you have a rough trip? You're solo sailing, aren't you? Poor thing, it probably wiped you out. There's no easy sailing around here. Let's sit. I'll get you a drink. Tea? Water?"

She encouraged Ess forward with a gentle pressure on her shoulder. Ess rediscovered her legs and let Raven settle her in a chair.

"It's usually busier here. All the recent crazy weather's put people off, I think." Raven kept talking as she filled a mug with water from a cooler. "I heard from the Watchmen that the southern part of Gwaii Haanas is drowning in rain right now. I always say you don't come to Haida Gwaii if you want to stay dry, but every year it gets more extreme. And it's supposed to hit twenty-nine degrees this week in Skidegate! Mideighties Fahrenheit, it's unheard of. When I was a kid, twenty was a hot summer day. No wonder all the poor cedar trees are dying, going from waterlogged to summer heat wave."

Happy to let Raven talk, Ess tried to project an air of calm. Her shoulder tingled where Raven's fingers had gently squeezed it.

Pressing the mug into Ess's hand, Raven dropped into the chair behind the desk and gathered her long, dark hair over one shoulder, smoothing it. "Wish I could offer you something stronger. Are you hungry? I've got pilot biscuits and thimbleberry jam made by my sister."

Ess shook her head, gripped the mug, running her fingertip over a ridge in the pottery.

"So. You're here for a bit?" Raven made a waving gesture at her computer and the screen flickered on.

"I don't know—"

"Playing it by ear... That's lovely. Well, let's get you settled. Just need your boat registration and ID."

"Oh, I–I didn't bring it, I'm sorry, I can get—" Ess's cheeks burned at her error. She put the mug down and stood to return to the safety of her boat, but Raven waved her back into her seat.

"We can fill in those details later. Sit, sit. We'll put in your name and the boat name and sort out the rest later. We're not that fussed here." She hesitated, midkeystroke. "You're registered in Canada, yes?"

Ess nodded and Raven relaxed. "Good, easy then. So many regulations around foreign visitors, Americans, it's a huge headache. Put your proper name—if it's Sarah—on your documents." She slid the keyboard over to Ess to type in her name and her boat name.

"Ah, Song, what a pretty name." Raven took the keyboard back. "My mother says I came out of the womb such a chatty baby they had no choice but to name me after the talkative raven."

The note said to keep a low profile. Ess drank, but the water sat heavy in her stomach at the thought that registering in whatever system Raven was typing into might trigger some alarm, expose her.

A frown creased Raven's face. "Awaaya!" She made some quick swiping gestures, typed, frowned further. "This doesn't make sense."

The instinct to flee flooded Ess, but she forced herself to stay where she was, hooked a foot around the leg of the chair. She focused on a large digital map on the wall that shifted with changing weather patterns, the animated white trails of wind arrows like brushstrokes over the islands.

Raven ignored Ess, reading something on her screen and muttering under her breath. Then she hit a few keys and smiled triumphantly. "Ah. There we go! At least twice a week the system loses its connection and gives us grief. All better now. You can pay for just today or a few days at a time, whatever you like. All in, it's seventy dollars a day. Covers power, drinking water up to the limit, free pump out, showers, laundry, and access to our library of marine charts, all that stuff."

With shaking hands, Ess removed money from her messenger bag and counted off two hundred and twenty, the plastic bills sticking to her sweaty hands. She put money on the desk, shoved the remaining cash in her bag, and stood to leave, transaction complete.

"Wow. That's a lot of cash. We don't, you know—don't see that every day. Most people e-transfer or pay with a wrist tap." Raven laughed, counted the bills. "So, you're good for three nights." She handed Ess ten dollars in change. "I'll send you a copy of the invoice." She looked at the screen. "Oh, you forgot your email."

"I don't have an email," Ess said, sweat rolling down her back.

Raven's smile changed to some other expression Ess couldn't read. "Oh. Ooh, did you ghost?"

"What?"

"Toast all your accounts, quit everything, and start over somewhere new." She raised an eyebrow at Sarah-goes-by-Ess. "New name."

"Uh. I can't—"

Raven grinned, waved dismissively. "We've been getting ghosts up here more frequently in the past few years. It's fine; we keep a printer here. Sailors who come this way often have strong antitech feelings. We're remote; we get a certain slice of the market. I'll print your invoice." She hit a button on the keyboard and pushed herself out of her chair.

Ess swallowed, mouth dry. "Is there somewhere I can get online?"

"Oh, our network code will be on your invoice."

"But I don't have any equipment."

"Wow, you really ditched it all, didn't you? There's a VR gaming café in town with terminals the off-grid people use when they must relent and connect. Should do the trick." She handed Ess the printed invoice and tore a paper map off a pad on the desk, circling a street not far from the marina. "Jacked is the gaming place. If you're hungry, go to Crow's Nest. Good food, good people."

"Thanks." Ess took the map.

"Sure, just pop in tomorrow with your registration and ID. Folks coming down from Alaska since the Pacific cod collapse have made things difficult. Border Services has new patrols up north to try and

25

stop folks, but they insist on checking the marina's records regularly in case someone squeaked by. Don't want you getting hassled because of some empty fields on the form."

It seemed the transaction was done, so Ess spilled out onto the dock, echoing Raven's see-you-laters. She put a hand to her face, feeling hot and flushed. If she turned her head, she could check on *Sea Dragon*, make sure it was okay.

Biting the inside of her cheek, she stopped that stream of thought. Walking away from the office, away from *Sea Dragon*, she went up the gangway on shaky legs, pushed open the security gate, and stepped onto solid ground. Born at sea but only now making landfall. It felt anticlimactic.

She stood on the path that ran between a small parking lot and a chain-link enclosure of recycling bins overflowing with bottles and cans. Papers fluttered, scattered over the ground nearby. Annoyed at the idea they might blow into the ocean, she bent over and collected them. Mixed in with the scrap paper were old photographs with delicate, scalloped edges. A sepia-tone smiling bride. Awkward families posed in uncomfortable formal wear. A portrait of a woman still in its cardboard oval mat, stained with coffee on one corner. It was old, the woman long dead, but the photographer had captured her young and smiling in her starched nurse's uniform. Ess struggled to understand how the photos could have ended up discarded alongside empty beer cans. She dropped the papers in the recycling bin but slipped the photos into her bag to contemplate later.

Walking up Wharf Way to Oceanview Drive, past worn wooden buildings set at odd angles to the street, she felt conspicuous, a flashing beacon of wrongness. A woman with no memory of walking along a street before. Effectively had never gone into a shop and purchased a thing. Never eaten at a restaurant. She was a collection of nevers assembled into human form. Surely everyone could tell she was missing all normal experiences. A burly man stood outside the fishing gear shop, his thick arms crossed, head turning to follow her progress down the road. She hurried past, wanted to break into a run and keep running forever.

On the outside, Ess appeared normal. She needed to remember that. She thought about Raven's welcoming smile and warm hand on her arm, and her heart rate slowed.

The road running along the shore had been raised to defend against the rising ocean, so she had to cross to the other side, where the buildings were scattered. It was quiet except for the electric motors of cars and scooters cruising leisurely along Oceanview Drive. A bald eagle swooped overhead and landed on a sign for the Northern Savings Credit Union. The bank machine by the entrance was shiny and new, out of place in the little town where everything seemed repurposed and comfortable. Digging the card from her bag, she slid it in the machine and typed the PIN she'd memorized from the document on the boat. The machine demanded her fingerprint. She put a finger on the flashing scanner and held her breath.

It worked. The bank knew who she was, biometrically speaking. She requested her account balance.

Her eyes struggled to make out the tiny print on the screen, the glare of the sun dazzling her. This was all she had in the world, whatever this balance was. This and *Sea Dragon*.

$10,014. She did quick math using the only price she knew. Four months of moorage. She'd need a job at some point, a thought she wasn't remotely ready to face. But for now, a weight was lifted. She had time; she wasn't going to starve.

After withdrawing a few hundred dollars, she requested the list of recent transactions. There was a deposit of $10,114 five weeks ago, a service charge of $100, then nothing until today. At the end of the transaction it took a hard tug to free her card from the machine.

When she succeeded in extracting it, a blood-red exclamation mark appeared on the screen. Ess flinched. Then she leaned in to read a warning that her account had "suspicious activity or characteristics." The Northern Savings Credit Union recommended speaking to a banking professional about the importance of banking with an accredited institution.

Ess shoved everything in her bag, feeling like a thief. Another question in her ocean of questions. Time to try to find a few answers.

5

Ten minutes later, she had made her way to Jacked. She studied it while standing in the meager shade of a half-brown cedar tree. The single-story wooden building looked abandoned except for the blinking "Open" sign. Two teenagers skateboarded up, ignored Ess, and went in. Ess wished she could peer inside, study how things worked for a few minutes, but the window was papered over with sun-faded ads for energy drinks and drones. She mentally mapped the route back to the marina, past the long-vacant gas station with wildflowers poking through cracks in the pavement. A quick stop at the store and she could be cozy in *Sea Dragon* in half an hour with food.

She pushed the door open.

Inside, glowing screens threw everything into shadow. Ess's eyes took a moment to adjust enough to see a guy at a counter next to a price sign. He had black hair sculpted into a gravity-defying wave.

He yawned. "Do you need a computer or directions?"

"A computer," Ess said, relieved he'd asked a direct question she could answer.

"VR or old school?"

"Uh. Not VR." She started to sweat.

"How much time do you want?" He poked his screen a few times, then his hand froze in the air, waiting for her. "An hour?" he suggested when she didn't reply. She nodded and he completed his screen tapping, handed her a plastic fob, and pointed at a panel for tap payment. "Ten bucks."

Ess handed him cash, which he cocked an eyebrow at but accepted. A woman in a cubicle in the far corner swore loudly and stood, her chair rolling away until it hit someone else. She yanked off her VR headset and swore again.

"Hey! Chill, Sands." The counter guy turned his head, and Ess noticed his towering wave of hair didn't move. She wanted to reach out and touch it but shoved her hands in her pockets instead.

"Some moron on my own fucking team just blew me away in the middle of a raid, Jaalen! Fucking newb."

Jaalen pointed at the dark room divided into little cubicles, half of them equipped with monitors, a few of them in use. "Grab any machine you want," he said to Ess.

"Could you show me?"

The eyebrow went up again at the request, but he slid off his stool with a shrug and walked to a machine away from the other patrons. He showed her how to log in using exaggerated, slow movements. He held the fob against the bottom of the screen, tapped the touchscreen to open a search window, and left Ess to it.

The clock in the corner of Ess's screen counted down each second of her allotted time. She eased into the seat and looked around. A large woman three cubicles over sniffled and coughed. A squeaky ceiling fan whirred. And the search box stared at her, the blinking cursor waiting for her question.

She had so many questions but struggled to think of one a search engine could help with.

She raised a hand to rub her eyes and accidentally opened a new window that autoloaded a news feed. At the top, a carbon pollution ticker showed the weekly global measurement: 485ppm. Images of a catastrophic flood in Calgary filled the page; the Bow and Elbow

Rivers were both at new record-high levels. Twenty-eight neighborhoods were under mandatory evacuation orders, and five people were dead. The National Disaster Response Team had been flown in. Ess moved her hand and scrolled to the next article. It announced skyrocketing global grain prices based on the U.S. Midwest failing to get crops in the ground for the third year in a row because of flooding. Experts were calling it the end of the U.S. Corn Belt. The UN had elevated the Global Food Security Risk Level to seven and was urging global cooperation to prevent famine.

Ess closed her eyes. This wasn't what she'd come for. Flicking the news screen shut, she went back to the search window and typed in the name, her name. Her pinkie hovered over the enter key and the words of the note came to her: *Don't look back.*

Fuck it. She could at least look forward, couldn't she? The note couldn't begrudge her that basic knowledge if she was to embrace a new life as Sarah. She punched the key and a page of results appeared immediately.

Sarah Song was a Scottish news reporter, actual name Sarah Scrymgeour.

Sarah Song was a professor of political science at Berkeley with a special interest in citizenship and immigration.

Sarah Song was a Chinese-Australian actress and the 2030 Miss Chinese International winner.

Sarah Song was a stroke rehab specialist at the Seoul National University Hospital.

Then a kindergarten teacher, then a perpetrator of investment fraud, then an Olympic medal-winning epee fencer.

Sarah Jane Song, played by Yang Mi, was a massively popular character from a TV show that ran for nine seasons in the 2020s.

None of the faces matched hers, as far as she could tell. Not that she'd expected them to. But she had hoped for some easy answer, had hoped there had been a mistake somehow.

Leaning back in the hard plastic chair, Ess contemplated the many versions of Sarah in front of her. Was the plan to hide behind these myriad Sarah Songs and make sure no trace she might make would ever rise to the surface? She flicked the windows closed one by one, jealous of each Sarah Song who knew who she was, each one surrounded by family and friends, smiling, complete.

Pushing a hand against the new ache in her chest, Ess flipped to the page of data she'd copied into her notebook. She opened the Canadian Register of Vessels site. The government of Canada logo stretched across the top of the page, boxy and official. She carefully typed *Sea Dragon*'s license number into the query box but hesitated and deleted it. She tightened her ponytail, cracked her knuckles. Hearing the floor behind her creak, she closed the window with a flick and swiveled her head. A slim man in a baseball cap dropped into the cubicle behind her, but he was busy logging in, uninterested in what she was doing.

Swearing under her breath at her ridiculous paranoia, she sat up straight, reopened the window. She wasn't going to get anywhere if she was afraid of a website, startled by creaking floors. Looking up her own boat wasn't digging into the past, wasn't violating the note. She was fine.

Typing quickly, she hit Enter and the results page opened immediately. Boat owner: Sarah Song. Address: 6 Sun Street, Old Massett, British Columbia.

Celebratory yelling came from several cubicles over. Someone in a VR headset pumped their fist in the air.

Hunching over her notebook, Ess traced her finger down the page to the address copied from Sarah's driver's license: 6 Sun Road, Old Massett. She searched for it, one hand still pressing on her chest.

The map zoomed in to show Old Massett, a small town on a spit of land between a river and the ocean a hundred kilometers north of where she was. She pressed a knee against the underside of the desk, pinned herself in place.

Would people there know her, recognize her? A smile started but was interrupted by the exclamation point next to the address on the map. Looking more closely at the red dot marking where her house should be, she realized the problem. It was in the water.

Turning on the satellite view, she gestured to zoom in. Sun Road branched off Shark Street and ran straight into the ocean.

Smile gone, she looked up the street name and found an article on the *Haida Gwaii Observer* website from five years ago about relocating the Council of the Haida Nation office to a new building on higher ground. The article mentioned the abandonment of low-lying Raven Road and parts of Sun Road. She turned the satellite images back through the years and watched the ocean retreat to reveal a small red-roofed building that definitely did not exist anymore and hadn't for many years.

Frustrated, she moved on to the last piece of data in her notebook, all caution gone. Without hesitating, she searched for the Bank of Cominotto and her screen filled with news reports of international banking fraud. Stories of European attempts to get the Maltese bank to release customer information to assist in major fraud investigations. International calls to comply with basic banking regulations. Bank of Cominotto was named in a case against an American health insurance CEO who had allegedly squirreled away half a billion dollars in company money while denying basic health treatment to clients. The bank was refusing to provide information. Ess thought of the warning screen on the bank machine, wondered just how dodgy the Bank of Cominotto was. How dodgy she was.

The woman to her right shifted in her seat, started a wet coughing fit. The room suddenly felt airless and stifling.

Staring at the screen, Ess felt a sharp metallic taste creep over her tongue, as if she'd just sprinted at top speed. The phlegmy coughing noise faded into the distance. A flutter of panic rippled through her. Then she jerked, her body spasming like it had on *Sea Dragon*.

Except this time, she had a clock in front of her. She saw that she'd lost four minutes in what felt like one second.

Logging off as fast as she could, she left Jacked, wanting to run but not able to bear the attention.

On the side of the road, she wiped her hands on her pants over and over while looking for a place of refuge. She'd been so sure she would find something that would tell her who she was supposed to be, what she was supposed to do. But she had no answers, and something was clearly physically wrong with her beyond just not knowing who she was.

The sun had set and she couldn't see much of her surroundings, but a bar sign lit up the darkness down the road. Approaching and looking in the window, she saw it was dim and mostly empty, the kind of place where people sat, immobile, staring into their drinks while one day melted into the next. She didn't know if she was a drinker, but she desperately needed to numb the feelings overwhelming her, so she stepped in.

The bartender was wrestling a keg out from under the counter when she approached. She abandoned the task and stood, squinting at Ess. Tucking thin strands of long hair behind her ear, the bartender used the interruption as a chance to take a swig from a mug on the counter. "Need a drink?"

Ess nodded. She crossed her arms and stood a few feet away from the bar. Dug her fingernails into her arms to get her brain to stop spiraling and focus.

"Okay." The bartender waited, brushing debris off the counter onto the floor. "Should I guess?"

Ess hazarded another nod.

"Rum and Coke it is." The bartender put a glass on the counter. "Bathroom?"

One hand pointed to the back of the bar while the other reached for a liquor bottle. Ess appreciated that the bartender was ignoring her as much as possible. The tension running through her body relaxed a notch.

In the bathroom, Ess avoided looking in the mirror and scrubbed her hands roughly with hot water. She held her hands under the dented, ineffective air dryer, trying to think of her favorite drink, trying to picture her favorite bar, to picture any bar. She gave up on both futile tasks, wiped her hands dry on her shirt, and went to claim her drink. The rum and Coke was dark and the first sip went down easily, obliterating the lingering memory of the metallic taste on her tongue.

She thanked the bartender and went to find a table in a dark corner.

An hour later, she felt better. The few people who came into the bar didn't even look at her. She could study people without worrying about being wrong and attracting attention. The drinks that kept coming helped tremendously in moving her problems to a distance.

She tried to review, in her increasingly fuzzy head, what the results of her research had been, to piece the scraps into something that made sense. Her bank was sketchy, her address bogus, but *Sea Dragon* was licensed in her name and seemed to be legally hers.

The question circled in her brain; why was this insanity better than whatever she'd been facing before? She ran a finger around the table's worn no-smoking, no-vaping sticker.

Just as she was about to circle through the string of thoughts again, a shadow fell over her table, which seemed strange given how dark her corner was to begin with.

"Hey, mind if I join you?"

6

Ess LIFTED HER GAZE TO the man standing by her table. The realization that she had not actually achieved invisibility over the past hour took a moment to process.

The guy was of average height, but he cast a big shadow. He looked sturdy, had an uncertain smile she liked. His clothes were like what everyone else wore, but some feature she couldn't put a finger on made him stand out subtly from the other people in the bar. He was like a maple leaf on the floor of a cedar forest.

She was surprised at being addressed, but not scared like she would have been three drinks ago. It took a second to mentally flip through possible responses to his question and evaluate why each was wrong. In the end she shrugged, hoping the ambiguity of the gesture worked. He sat next to her and extended a hand.

"I'm Rene." A slight French accent tinged his voice.

"Ess." She shook his hand quickly and drank, her mouth completely dry. Now that he was sitting there, staring at her, studying her, she felt uneasy.

He adjusted his chair and picked up a cardboard coaster, tapping it on the table with a rapid, staccato beat. "Ess? Unusual name, is it short for something?"

"No." She took in his brown hair, the crow's-feet by his eyes. "It's just Ess."

He nodded, absorbing this information as though it were significant. "Thanks for letting me join you. I've been traveling alone for a while and could use some conversation."

Loneliness. That was something she knew. "Oh?"

"Found myself telling the grocery store clerk my deep-seated guilt over not calling my mother often enough, figured that was a warning sign I should seek company."

The mention of a mother cut her, but it was a dull ache. She liked this, having emotions and then watching them float by rather than sinking into them. She finished her drink, keen to obliterate all remaining feelings. He raised an eyebrow at her, and his smile shifted. She liked the diversity of his smiles. A server came and they ordered new drinks.

"You've been a negligent son?" she asked, slurring the last two words together, suddenly concerned she wasn't using real words. *Negligent.* It didn't sound like a real word.

He scrubbed a hand over his face before answering. "Life has gotten complicated, and I don't know how to explain it to her. And I can't bear chitchatting."

"Isn't this chitchat?"

He laughed. "You're quite funny," he said, as though he'd expected something different. "I'm making an exception. Also, this feels more like a confessional than chitchat. Sorry. I don't do this, you know, chat up strangers in a pub. I just… Yeah, I don't know." He turned away from her, smiles gone, mind off somewhere else.

Ess saw a rope burn on the back of his hand—sure sign of a boater. She almost reached over and put her hand on his, but kept her fingers wrapped around her empty glass. His gaze snapped back to her.

The drinks arrived. Ess swallowed a mouthful.

"Would it help if you explained your complications to me?" she offered. "I can sympathize with complicated."

"Merde, no." He laughed, but Ess didn't believe it this time. "I want to hear your story, how you ended up here."

The question was like a splash of ice water. She mirrored his posture, back straight, hands resting on thighs. Strained to think clearly. "In Daajing Giids? Came to see the sights. Get away."

"Get away from what? What do you do?"

Ess thought about how to answer. She looked into Rene's eyes and tried to glean some sense of who he was. It was dark so she couldn't even tell what color his eyes were, but his expression encouraged her, the careful, neutral set of his mouth. Her fingers tingled like she was standing on the edge of a cliff as she contemplated letting out the secret clawing at her insides.

"Oh, fuck it. Do you want the truth? I mean, are you looking for a fun chat or a real answer?"

His shoulders relaxed. "Let's go for real."

"Okay." She emptied her glass and sucked on an ice chip. "I–I... Fuck. This is the first time I've said it out loud." She crunched the ice and swallowed, scraped her fingers against her jeans. "I have amnesia. I guess. I don't remember anything before a few days ago. I have no idea who I am, why I'm here. I woke up on a sailboat by T'aanuu a complete blank and just managed to sail myself here today. I don't know why I'm here. No idea what to do next."

Having said it aloud, she felt split down the middle, wide open. His gaze dropped to the table, then looked at her with an expression she read as pity.

"You're serious?"

She nodded.

"There must be something left. Some childhood memory or..."

"If I could convey the depth of nothingness to you—" Her voice caught and her vision liquefied. She put a napkin to her eyes, surprised.

He touched her hand, a kindness that only encouraged the flood of emotion. She reclaimed her hand and walked out of the bar, bouncing off a table and a server on the way. Around the side of the pub, she leaned against the wall of rough-hewn siding, trying but failing to keep the waves of rum-fueled despair from pulling her under completely.

A hand touched her shoulder. She jerked away, then saw it was Rene and relaxed, managed to breathe normally a few times. She wiped her nose with the napkin crunched in her fist and, when that was used up, her sleeve.

He leaned on the wall next to her. "Let's take a walk."

"I have to—" She gestured to the bar.

"I settled the bill. Got your stuff." He put her jacket and bag in her hands.

They walked in the direction of the dock, the crisp evening air helping dry Ess's eyes. She felt raw and heavy.

"Sorry—"

"Like I said, I hate chitchat."

"Apparently I can't do chitchat. I don't even know how to have a normal conversation with you right now. How do you know what's normal when you don't have any experiences to draw from? I spent the day worrying I'd attract attention by being weird. I can't attract attention. I have instructions—" She put a hand to her mouth. "Apparently I ramble when drunk. I'm drunk, right? Not losing my mind, just drunk?"

"Yeah, pretty sure this is you drunk," he said.

She bumped into him gently and apologized, tried to straighten her trajectory. "I'm terrible company, I think. It's just hard to accept that you've been erased, that you're gone, you know?"

"I don't know about amnesia"—he spoke so softly Ess had to lean in to hear—"but even without long-term memories, I think you're still you. The experiences that formed you still formed you, even if you don't remember them."

Ess thought about this, turning the idea over like a pebble, wanted it to be true. "Aren't we our memories? Don't all those experiences layer on top of each other, form us like a cake? Or a pearl? Or something else with layers. Without the memories, what's left?"

They approached the dock and stopped, looking down on it from the main road.

"I'm sorry you're in pain," he said after a pause. His voice caught and he coughed.

She didn't trust herself to respond, so she started walking again instead.

"What're you going to do?" he asked. "Put your face on the national news feeds, see if anyone recognizes you? 'Do you know this woman' headlines? Talk show circuits?"

She shook her head vigorously. "No. No, none of that." Another bit of truth clawed its way out. "I do want to know if I have family, people who miss me. I'm desperate to know. But I can't."

Her strange statement hung awkwardly in the air. He didn't ask what she meant.

"If you wanted some unsolicited advice from a stranger..." She didn't stop him. "One way to look at your situation is as the ultimate fresh start. Think of all those miserable people in the pub, most of them drinking to forget their problems. We ruminate over our fuckups, the thousand ways we've been burned, the people who have screwed us, the disasters we've seen, the people we've lost to pointless tragedy. You're free of all that. You're free of the baggage that makes most of us bitter, jaded assholes."

"If you had the choice, would you wipe everything to be free of that? Your childhood, your first love? Your mom? Your knowledge of the proper thing to say in this moment or any moment?"

He took a long time before answering. "There are things I'd love to not remember. People I've hurt."

"I remember every morning that I've forgotten my past, forgotten everyone I ever knew. That realization will be how I start every day of my life now." Tendrils of the familiar morning panic reached out for her as she said this. She felt suddenly, unpleasantly sober. "When it first happened—when I woke up like this, trapped on a boat in the wilderness—I was terrified to go to sleep. Thought I would start every day blank, that my life would be a loop of living that same awful moment over and over."

"Shit," he said, looking away.

Ess wanted to tell him to look at her, to see her for the broken mess she was.

"But they stick... The new days? The new memories?"

"Yes. The new ones stay," she said. "And I can read, type, walk. I know what things are. I can tie complicated sailing knots. But don't ask me who my parents are. Don't ask me how I spent my last birthday, if I had a happy childhood, if I was loved." Her voice, tight with anger and hurt, rose in pitch.

The streetlights on the road spread farther apart, leaving inky blackness ahead. Without speaking, they turned to retrace their steps back toward the dock.

"I think you're going to be all right, Ess."

These ridiculous words buoyed her. "Why on earth would you think that?"

She saw he had his uncertain smile on again.

"Just a feeling."

"I was a drunk, sobbing mess next to a dumpster half an hour ago."

"Yes, well, blame that on the poor company. You were fine before I came along."

Ess didn't reply to this, busy wondering what "fine" was, if she had ever known it. At the entrance to her marina, she stopped, pointed. "My boat's down there."

He faced the darkness. "Ah. I'm back at the inn by the pub."

The way he pronounced *pub* with his accent made her smile. Seeing his face in profile, she felt a flicker of familiarity. Is this what having conversations did, created these warm sparks of familiarity so quickly? She closed her eyes and luxuriated in the feeling. When she opened them, he'd moved next to her, close enough she could see a puckered star-shaped scar on his neck. Her alcohol-soaked brain urged her to kiss him, then sowed doubt that she knew how to. She imagined kissing him, imagined herself melting, becoming a pool on the dock reflecting moonlight.

And then he stepped back. His fingers rested protectively on his lips, like he was warning her to stay quiet. He studied her with an expression she couldn't read as he retreated another step. "I should go."

They stood like two buoys in the water, the world moving around them.

"What if—"

"Do you want to come onboard?" she asked.

His posture softened, his shoulders rolling forward as he nodded, making him seem less imposing. She unlocked the marina gate. The clomp of his heavy steps on the wooden dock behind her made Ess realize what care she took to avoid making noise.

They stood in *Sea Dragon*'s cabin, Rene leaning against the galley counter, hands in pockets, Ess by the radio, arms crossed. Having another person onboard felt like breaking a rule.

"Tea?" he asked.

"Tea? Yes, I have loads of tea." Ess moved toward the galley but Rene had already opened the right cabinet and pulled out the canister. "How'd you know—"

He looked at the canister in his hand. "All boat galleys are the same, I guess."

"It's all Earl Grey." She stood close to him, unhooked two mugs from the rack over the sink, and put them on the counter.

Finding the kettle in the lower cabinet, he went to fill it at the sink but Ess handed him a large water bottle.

"Water tank isn't working," she said in response to his raised eyebrow.

"What do you mean?"

She shrugged. "Tank doesn't hold water, which I found out while pretty far from a water source, unfortunately."

He looked surprised at this little story of hardship. "That's strange. For a boat so well kept," he said casually, squeezing past Ess to sit at the table. The scent of black tea, beer, and rust followed him. She perched on the bench next to him, not knowing what else to do.

"Ess, you should know you aren't the only amnesiac around."

The wake from a passing motorboat shifted the floor beneath them. Ess had to remind herself to keep breathing. "What?"

Rene pulled a thin newspaper from his back pocket, unfolding it as he spoke. "There have been two cases reported in the last week. People adrift in boats in waters down by Vancouver, no idea who they are, no identification." He paused, his long fingers pressing the newspaper crease flat. "I'm telling you this because the authorities are involved, taking the amnesiacs into custody and trying to identify them, confirm they're legally allowed to be in the country." He flipped the paper over and put his finger on two photos at the bottom of a small article below the fold. "They've enlisted the media to show their photos to try and identify them. These faces have been everywhere."

"Oh." Ess couldn't find anything more coherent to say. She was busy berating herself for not thinking to check for other amnesia cases when she'd been online. And she'd just told this stranger everything, laid herself bare in front of him. She was dizzy with the stupidity of it.

He was studying her and she wondered what he was looking for, what she was failing to say or be. "Are you going to tell the authorities about me?" she asked.

His voice was soft. "No, no. I'm warning you so you're careful who else you tell."

Sliding the paper closer, she quickly skimmed the text. "Second Strange Amnesia Case in BC Waters," the headline read. A resident of Skidegate, down south for work the week before, reported finding a man in a small boat between Vancouver Island and the mainland with no identification, claiming to have no idea who he was or how he got there. The amnesiac could speak English and function perfectly, recount facts like the names of capital cities, but all autobiographical information appeared to be missing.

Ess shivered.

Authorities were investigating, confirmed this case was similar to the one reported on Monday but had no information to share. Both amnesia cases were in custody, and the police reassured the public that they would be detained until their identities could be confirmed.

Ess couldn't bear to look at the faces at the bottom of the page, their eyes filled with a confusion she knew too intimately.

Two cases. Both men found on barely seaworthy boats with no identification, no money, just the clothes on their backs. She thought about the note in her drawer, the ownership papers for *Sea Dragon*, her Sarah Song identification.

"How did they lose their memories?"

Rene shrugged, looked away. "Don't think they know. Isn't it usually a head injury?"

The pull to haul anchor immediately and sail south toward these other cases was powerful like a riptide. Ess wasn't supposed to go trawling for answers, but…her mind started grasping for excuses, some contorted logic that would make it okay despite the instructions, despite the warning.

The whistle of the kettle pierced the air, and they both leaped up to unplug it. Ess got there first and distracted herself with tea bags and mugs.

"Hey. Uh, I have an idea. A proposal," he said.

She handed him a mug, which he took and set aside.

"We should sail away together. Go on an adventure, get lost in the world. No plan. No expectations. No obligations." His words spilled out, tumbling against each other until he closed his mouth.

She understood from his nervousness this wasn't an ordinary suggestion, and she felt the vast nothingness where there should have been experience to draw on to form a proper response. "You don't even know me."

"I don't. But I don't mind. I'm tired of being alone, if I'm honest," he said, his voice low.

"Why have you been alone?"

"Oh god, out of habit? My work requires a lot of travel, sudden departures from places I never return to. I don't stay anywhere long enough to connect with anyone. I stopped trying to connect. I'm here to finish my last job. I want to start fresh."

She wanted to let his excitement power the boat and take them away. Being alone with her blankness filled her with dread. He could help her understand how to be in the world. He could look at her every day with recognition, reassuring her she was known.

"The sailing season is just getting started, so we've got months of exploring weather ahead. We could start with a trip to Hotspring Island. It's not far."

She slipped the newspaper under the chart on the table, traced her finger along the chain of islands that made up Haida Gwaii until it landed on Hotspring Island. She'd noticed it on the map before, drawn to the promise of relaxation it held out. "I did wonder about that place."

Maybe the safest way to avoid the temptation of looking for answers was to be with someone who didn't care about the questions. "Let's do it. Let's get supplies and go," she said. "Tomorrow."

He grinned and squeezed her arm. Ess didn't melt at his touch as she expected to. Instead she froze in place, aware of all her awkward limbs and sharp elbows and a twist in her gut. His hand moved down her arm, and she flinched as he touched her jellyfish blisters.

Retracting his hand, Rene rubbed his face like someone just sitting up from a nap. Wind passing through the rigging of nearby boats created a strange howl, and they both turned their head to the window. Rene backed toward the door. "I should go. I have to go. I'll be at the Misty Harbour Inn by the pub for another night. If you think, with a clear head tomorrow, you still want to go, come find me. If not, no hard feelings."

"I—"

He held up a hand and shook his head. "Decisions like this should be made in the fresh light of morning. Just, whatever you do, be careful who you tell about the amnesia thing."

Without waiting for a reply, he left. Ess felt the boat shift as he stepped onto the dock.

A cool breeze blew through the open door. Closing it, Ess picked up her mug of unwanted tea and stared at the second mug sitting on the table, trying to understand the unease that was coiling around her. She locked the door and pulled on a sweater to fight off the chill.

7

THAT NIGHT, WIND AND CHOPPY water turned the boat into an echo chamber of creaking and banging. Plates and mugs and cutlery clinked in the cabinets all night long. Proper sleep never came. Ess tossed and turned with *Sea Dragon*, going over her encounter with Rene and growing angry with herself for risking exposure so wantonly.

When the sun peeked through the porthole, she gave up on sleep, took her headache drugs, and lay on the dining-table bench for a change in scenery while she waited for the pain to recede. When she closed her eyes, she was on the dock with Rene, feeling him step away from her, remembering the inexplicable urge she'd had to reach out and hold him in place. Annoyed by the unrequested memory, she forced herself to open her eyes and squint against the light.

From her vantage point, she spotted an edge of white paper wedged between the bench seat and the wall. She slid to the floor, gave her head and stomach a moment to protest the change in orientation, and crouched under the table, pulling at the card with her finger. It wiggled but wouldn't come out. Backing out from under the table, she got a knife and stabbed the paper, dragging it free millimeter by millimeter. It came loose suddenly and she narrowly avoided slicing her leg.

Wiping the dust off, she sat under the table and studied the card, her headache protesting the small font. It was a business card for

Ballast Boat Shop and Repair Center in Nanaimo. Flipping it over revealed the name *Sam* scribbled on the back.

The tension headache released, and she exhaled with relief. She read the card again. Nanaimo. Crawling out from under the table, she found the chart showing the whole coast of British Columbia, stretching from Alaska to Washington, and ran a finger down it until she found the city of Nanaimo. It was on the coast of Vancouver Island, across the Georgia Strait from Vancouver.

"One thousand kilometers," she said, looking at the scale. "Fuck."

All she needed was her real name. With her name, she could start to unravel the rest. Sam could perhaps give her that.

The card fit in the palm of her hand but represented something much larger. Every fiber of her wanted to find answers, to fill the enormous void inside.

And the note said not to.

Shoving the chart off the table, she collapsed into the seat, held her head in her hands, and faced what getting her name really meant: cracking open the protective shell she'd somehow been given.

Viewing the theft of her memories as a thing she should be grateful for made her want to vomit.

The problem was, the lack of memories was something she felt viscerally, constantly. The threat the note spoke of, in contrast, was a vague situation that had apparently required this drastic action to save her life. An abstraction. She couldn't feel relieved to be safe from a threat she didn't remember, a threat she couldn't even confirm was real.

Yanking her notebook from the cupboard, she extracted the typewritten note and placed it on the table, its sparse smattering of words bobbing in a sea of white space.

If she'd been in trouble so bad that someone wiped her memory to save her from it, then the note's instructions were a lifeline she'd be a fool to ignore.

But she couldn't go through life never knowing. Couldn't exist with everything important missing. Cut off from family—

She pinched her arm to stop the thought spirals that were taking off.

"Enough."

No more flapping uselessly like a loose sail.

She tore the business card in half, tucked the pieces between the pages of the notebook, and shoved it in the back of a cabinet under a stack of radio operating manuals. She left the note on the table, decided she would have breakfast and then go to the Misty Harbour Inn. Decided that's what Sarah Song would do to start a new life.

———

"Good morning, *Sea Dragon!*"

Still trying to feel at peace with her decision, Ess swept her hair into a ponytail and went outside. "Good morning, Raven."

"Sii.ngaay 'laa, Ess. Rough night, eh? Unsettled waters. Hope you're not too rattled."

Ess thought about how welcoming Raven had been yesterday. "Would you like something to drink? Tea?"

Raven smiled. "Tea would be lovely." She stepped onboard gracefully and joined Ess in the cabin.

Ess filled the kettle from a water bottle and plugged it in.

"Problem with your water tank?" Raven observed, tapping one of the water bottles lined up on the counter.

"Yes. A leak, I think."

"My aunt does boat repairs if you need something fixed. I can have her come over later today and take a look." Raven sat. "We had a leak in a skylight at the marina office last year, and she was on the roof ten minutes after I called her, had it all sorted that afternoon. I think she keeps half this island shipshape all by herself. Not sure when she sleeps."

Ess put the tea canister on the counter and wondered if it would be weird to hug Raven. She'd no idea how she was going to get the water tank sorted out. "That's very kind, Raven. I would love to have her fix it."

She waved away the thanks. "I actually came by to get your registration info. I should do that before I forget."

"Right." Ess spun around and dug through the drawer for her documents. "I was going to come to the office. Got distracted last night." As she put the boat registration paper on the table, Ess realized the warning note was sitting in plain view. Raven put her small notebook on the edge of it, pinning it in place. Ess hovered while she slowly copied the registration information.

"Done! Now the authorities will be kept happy and we can return to tea." Raven put her notebook in her pocket. "I don't mean to be nosy, but I saw you made a friend last night. He wasn't giving you trouble, I hope?"

Putting tea bags in mugs, Ess looked over to see an expression on Raven's face she couldn't read. "Trouble?"

"He's not a local, so I worried when I saw him going aboard your boat. I was on my way to check, make sure he wasn't troubling you, but then he left in a hurry." She paused. "You're all right?"

"We met at the pub, were talking about sailing." Ess hesitated but continued, feeling like she was missing a piece of a puzzle. "Why were you worried?"

Raven leaned back in her seat. "Well, have to be careful who we trust, don't we? I learned that as a very young girl, thanks to my aunties' warnings. It's not so bad here where most folks know each other, but strangers passing through… You never know what kind of people they might turn out to be. I try to keep an eye out. We have to take care of each other."

Standing suddenly, Raven looked at *Sea Dragon*'s control panel. She whistled and pointed at a black box on top of the instrument panel, peeking from behind a tide chart that had been taped up. "Is that a G2000 satellite signal box?"

Ess grabbed the note from the table and shoved it in the cabinet, feeling slightly less exposed. "A what?"

"Top-of-the-line satellite ping box? Sends your location every minute no matter where in the world you are. It's the most powerful nonmilitary-grade unit there is. Top of the line. Are you planning an ocean crossing?" She laughed but stood on her tiptoes to get a better look.

It was an unremarkable black box with a single tiny, green LED glowing to confirm it was operational. Ess hadn't noticed it.

"I don't know what that is. You're saying it's sending my location somewhere?"

"Yeah. Superprecise location. Usually used on race boats or expeditions where people are really concerned with knowing location at all times. All the automated cargo ships have a version so the Coast Guard can map them in real time. Don't usually see them on pleasure craft. Transponders do the job for us if we get into a pickle. That beauty is usually for people on land who want to keep track of something on the water and are willing to pay big bucks for it. Must be an annoying drain on your batteries though, yeah?"

The kettle whistled. Ess turned it off and absentmindedly made two cups of Earl Grey.

Someone knew her location.

Instead of being hidden, she was exposed.

"Haawa," Raven said, approaching and taking her mug of tea. "Do you have overprotective family that wants to be able to drop in anytime? My auntie would do that if she knew the technology existed." She chuckled.

Ess muddled through a conversation with Raven, doing her best to appear normal and unconcerned about the fact that her location was at that very moment being sent to someone. The note was yelling at her from the cabinet to hide. She may have been in a remote corner of the world, a place most hadn't heard of, but whatever protection that had been intended to bestow seemed blown.

Halfway through tea, the conversation ground to a halt as Ess fell further into her own worries. Raven twisted a silver cuff bracelet on her wrist to access a display screen and excused herself to deal with an issue in the office.

After Raven disembarked, Ess forced herself to count to twenty before ripping the tide chart down and attacking the black box with her hands. It wouldn't budge. She couldn't find an off button; there were no switches or exposed power connections. Taking a breath, she got a screwdriver from the toolbox and worked on the tiny screws mounting the box to the boat. Her shaking hands made progress agonizingly slow. In frustration, she hit the box with the screwdriver handle, denting it but not helping her cause at all.

Trying the screws again, she got the box loose and could see the wires connecting it to her power system. She thought about how best to go about unhooking it and then positioned herself to just yank it and snap the wires. She wanted it off the boat, wanted to sink it to the bottom of the ocean.

But if someone was on the receiving end and the signal died… She clenched her teeth and put the box on the shelf for a second, the thin wires taunt but safe.

"Fuck."

She paced the tiny cabin.

Someone was tracking her. And that felt invasive and chilling. It felt like the safety that the note said had been bought by obliterating her precious memories had just burned away like an early-morning fog.

How could she be safe with her location being broadcast to space?

With her having no idea what possible trouble was heading her way as a result. Her ignorance was a massive liability.

If sailing off to start a quiet new life had been an option, it didn't feel like one anymore. She needed to get that thing off her boat and get far away.

She needed to map a route to Nanaimo. Get supplies. Get the water tank fixed. Get that box onto someone else's boat.

She needed to find out what was going on.

8

Ess HOLED UP AT THE marina office and spent hours looking at weather reports and navigation charts, getting advice from Raven. Sailing solo to Nanaimo was risky. One look at the charts made that clear.

Haida Gwaii was an island group surrounded by the fury of the Pacific Ocean. The only safe way to get south to the city of Nanaimo was to sail down along the more sheltered coast of the mainland, which meant the first step was to get across the Hecate Strait. Eighty nautical miles of complex currents and a tendency for unexpected gale-force winds. It was a sixteen-hour crossing on a good day, an exhausting shot of continuous sailing where the autopilot would likely be overpowered. If she made it to the coast of the mainland, she faced a thousand-kilometer meandering sailing route through tiny island chains, trying to stay shielded from the wrath of open sea. Plenty of opportunities to misread a tide chart and wreck her boat on craggy rocks with no one nearby to rescue her.

The consensus was it would take three weeks to reach Nanaimo if weather was on her side and she didn't have any mechanical issues. Four weeks or more (or never) if she was unlucky.

She thought about Rene as she walked past the Misty Harbour Inn on her way to purchase supplies, thought about his invitation. Everything was different now. She forced herself to keep her eyes ahead, pretend the inn didn't exist.

Two days later, every cabinet on *Sea Dragon* was crammed with supplies. Raven's aunt had repaired the water tank. And Ess was burning to put distance between her and the location the tracking box was transmitting, but sailing into a squall in the strait wasn't an option. She was stuck until a window of decent weather released her. She found a pair of broken-in running shoes onboard and started jogging to avoid going stir-crazy. Going slowly at first and then speeding up when she found her body could handle more. She trusted her body knew what to do, trusted that because these shoes had been packed, it meant she was a runner. She put this bit of info into her sparse lexicon of known facts: sailor, runner, hates oatmeal. She wanted the rest, all the stolen details, all the more important parts.

Raven offered to go sailing with Ess one day, show her all her tricks. Slow-moving when on land, Raven turned into a powerhouse on the boat, unfurling sails and hauling on lines like a racing captain. They went to the open waters south of the Hecate Array wind farm. The giant turbine blades turning languidly in the same winds that Ess struggled to manage with her sails made her feel grossly incompetent. But Raven's shouted instructions got her out of her head. One thing at a time. Don't be distracted by windmills in the distance. Raven showed Ess how she liked to handle a boat when sailing alone, taught Ess how to read the currents, drilled her on technique.

"You'll be fine," Raven said to Ess as she left *Sea Dragon* after their long day on the water. "The Haida went further down the coast than Nanaimo back in the day, and they did it in canoes. Just don't get cocky. Nature is always in charge."

In exchange for the sailing lesson, Ess carefully disconnected the G2000 box and quickly installed it on Raven's boat, hoping the five minutes without power wouldn't be noticed by whomever was watching. Raven promised to let the box continue operating as it was for a few weeks before wiping and resetting it.

Finally, the winds in Hecate Strait calmed. It was time to go. Raven agreed with Ess's assessment. She gave a tight goodbye hug that Ess received gratefully. Her last human contact for the foreseeable future, she knew. When Ess asked that Raven not reveal where she went, in the unlikely case someone showed up asking about her, Raven just nodded as though keeping that confidence was assumed.

"Ising dang hll king gas ga," Raven told her as they parted. "I will see you again."

There wasn't a word in her Haida dialect for *goodbye*, she'd explained.

At five thirty, under a dark sky tinted with a hint of orange sunrise, Ess motored away from the marina, feeling better with every bit of distance she put between herself and the location the tracking device was now sending from the cockpit of one of Raven's boats. She scanned the diked road along the shore for Rene futilely, letting herself wonder for a moment where they'd be if things had been different. Increasing speed, she turned away and motored out of the harbor.

At the entrance to Hecate Strait, she flicked off the motor. Shards of wood jutted out of the water, remnants of a building set too close to the old shoreline, now left to the ravages of the rising ocean. A warning to others not to try to fight nature.

She unfurled her foresail and surged forward.

9

CROSSING THE STRAIT WAS EXHAUSTING, as advertised. Ess had to constantly be on the lookout for logs in the water that could destroy her keel, wreck the propeller, or punch a hole in her hull. Sixteen hours of solo day sailing provided too much time to think over the meager supply of memories she'd gathered over eight days, to analyze every interaction for errors. When the sun set at ten, the wind picked up. The water turned choppy and her engine stepped up to power through it. Unable to see hazards in the water directly, Ess watched the screens of her GPS and radar. Motoring in the dark by sensors alone tied her stomach in knots and obliterated all thoughts except those needed for the task.

After two hours of nonstop vigilance in the dark of night, she was going inside for water when she heard—felt—a sickening thud against the hull, and her heart fell out of her chest. Rushing on deck with a flashlight, she peered over the edge, salt water splashing in her face. A log. She froze, listening to see if it was scraping underneath her hull on its way to mangle her propeller.

It bumped against the hull once, twice. Then nothing but the sound of wind and waves. She resumed breathing. Her gut told her it didn't sound like a hull-breaking hit, but only time would tell.

It was another three hours before her GPS showed the shoreline of Banks Island. The clouds cleared and a scrap of moonlight gave her a blue-black sense of where she was. She navigated into a cove in uninhabited Byers Bay and dropped anchor, relaxing only when it hit bottom and she could go inside to check her bilge. She lifted the access hatch to see if the log encounter had damaged the hull. It was dry.

She'd survived the first step.

The weather that followed the crossing was gentle, let her get her sea legs on the first few days. The toughest thing she faced early on was lack of sleep that made her cranky, but her body handled it, so she kept pushing.

Sometimes she'd catch a glimpse of a sleek silver motorboat in the distance or a Coast Guard drone overhead. She knew if she activated her distress beacon, the Coast Guard drone might arrive in time to document her peril, but nothing would be likely to reach her in time to actually assist. Unless that motorboat behind her was heading where she was and kept up with the relentless pace she had planned, she was alone.

Eight days after the crossing from Haida Gwaii, on course for a marina in Bella Bella where she could resupply, she made a choice. Rather than take the sheltered inside channel, she chose the more exposed and direct route. The weather sounded manageable and she could shave off an entire day this way.

Every morning she woke and was reminded of everything taken from her, and she struggled to get up, to brush her teeth and get on with living. She wasn't sure how much longer she could manage it. The business card for the boat shop in Nanaimo was pinned next to the radio, urging her on.

As she set her new course, Ess glanced at the silver boat in the distance, the boat that appeared every few days but never got closer, never passed her. She started to think it was a figment of her imagination, maybe a ghost boat haunting her.

As she came out from behind a group of islands, the wind hit *Sea*

Dragon with a force that took Ess's breath away. Angry whitecapped waves extended to the horizon. Energy built up over thousands of kilometers of uninterrupted ocean hammered against her hull. She kept *Sea Dragon* under control, thought about turning back—possibly the most challenging maneuver there was under these conditions—but pressed on. She was terrified but glad for the test, a chance to know what she was capable of.

Lightning flashed, showing her open ocean in every direction. She was utterly alone. Thunder rolled over the water, echoing in her chest. She left the cockpit to furl her sails, triple reefing the main, her hands pulling on sheets with confidence. Moving around the boat when it was heeled over sideways terrified her if she thought about it, but she maneuvered effortlessly if she didn't. She chose to believe she could handle this and let her instincts take over.

She kept a scrap of jib sail out for stability. Batteries at 85 percent; enough to motor her way through the weather to the shelter of the next island without even needing her hydrogen converter to kick in. Which was good since the converter didn't work tilted sideways.

Rolling thunder and raging winds made Ess's ears ring. Strands of hair kept getting loose, whipping her in the face as she worked to keep *Sea Dragon*'s bow pointing at the correct angle to the waves to minimize the risk of overturning. Cold sea spray drenched her within the first ten minutes.

Bracing the tiller with her arm, she wiped her hair back and redid her ponytail, fingers already stiff with cold. An unexpectedly huge wave broke over the boat. *Sea Dragon* rolled sideways, ripped the tiller from under her arm. Untethered, she flew across the cockpit, slamming against the deck. Before she could pull herself up, everything tilted the other way. The lifeline, the aptly named band of wire around the edge of the boat, caught her and kept her from falling overboard. A never-ending wall of water slammed down on her as she held on. She kept trying to inhale at the wrong time. Her throat burned with salt water.

Time slowed, let her contemplate how she felt about this as an ending to her short, rebooted life. Her tether, the cord dangling from her life preserver that she was supposed to clip to the jackline on deck, was unhelpfully tangled around her wrist and she wondered if she had been more diligent about safety pre–memory wipe. Another wave hit, sweeping her legs over the lifeline, leaving a one-handed grip between her and a drop into the frigid water. Her shoulder burned. She struggled to get a hold with her other arm, but the water kept coming. She held her breath, waiting for the end, feeling her tired hand slipping, slipping.

The boat hit the bottom of the wave trough and shuddered. *Sea Dragon* righted herself, slamming Ess against fiberglass. Her hip took the brunt of the impact. Ignoring that pain, she got her second hand wrapped around the lifeline and heaved herself onto the deck, her shoulder protesting with sparks of pain that made her eyes water. She scrambled to the helm and clipped her safety tether to the jackline. Pushing the engine to max, she gripped the tiller with all the power left in her exhausted, mangled hands and angled *Sea Dragon* to cut through the waves again.

Holding the tiller in position required the same shoulder muscle she'd just reinjured. Maybe this was how she hurt it pre–memory wipe, by almost dying at sea. She coughed violently, then retched, her body trying to clear the ocean from her lungs.

Ess rode out the bad weather for another half hour, shivering at the helm. When she arrived in waters calm enough to switch on the autopilot, she sat for a minute staring blankly at the horizon, which was now staying delightfully horizontal. Her legs trembled with adrenaline and exhaustion. Part of her wanted to take time to process how close she'd come to being tossed overboard, but the part of her she'd decided to trust to carry out the journey told her to get up and drink water and choke down food. She forced herself to check her position on GPS, listen to the weather report, and adjust the autopilot. She would make the sheltered bay at Price Island in an hour, leaving plenty of time to relive each terrifying moment of the storm before bed.

Ess failed to sleep that night as scenes from the storm ran through her mind. She rolled out of bed in the morning more worn out than when she'd fallen into it. But during the night, she'd reached the conclusion that the storm had given her something in its attempt to throw her overboard. Perspective. The time and energy she'd spent in Haida Gwaii worrying about people thinking she was strange, worrying about screwing up, embarrassing herself: none of that mattered. It had never mattered.

The two weeks that followed were smooth sailing in comparison. Keeping to more sensible routes, she maintained a grueling schedule, the emptiness in her that constantly called for answers pushing her on whenever she wanted to stop or rest. She wasn't sleeping properly, had to set alarms to remind her to eat. The ghost boat haunted her, following and hovering just out of sight like a mirage. She was decently certain she was hallucinating it just for the vague sense of companionship it provided.

Three weeks after hugging Raven goodbye, a thousand kilometers traveled, she finally furled her sails to motor toward downtown Nanaimo. A handful of twenty-story buildings marked the downtown; everything else was low and hugged the gently rising topography. Development sprawled over everything she could see, a dramatic change from Haida Gwaii and the tiny towns along the coast, where a few single-story buildings clustered near each other constituted urban development.

Ess inched through the busy harbor, wiping sweat from her face and missing the cool open-ocean air she'd left behind a few days ago. Her water tanks were low and she needed to figure out where to fill up, but first she had to stop and rest. The last leg had required constant manual navigation, the waters complicated by heavy traffic: big car ferries, giant luxury yachts, and enormous autonomous cargo ships. Coast Guard and Harbour Authority drones buzzing overhead had frayed her nerves, and the oppressive heat sapped her meager energy reserves. All she wanted was to sit still with her eyes closed and a cool cloth against her neck.

Cruising toward a cluster of small pleasure boats moored to buoys near downtown, she turned off the engine to get her bearings. Drifting and staring at the city skyline, it hit her—the journey was over. Sleep-deprived and completely drained, battered and bruised and dogged by uncertainty about whether this was the right thing to do, she felt this accomplishment tip her over an edge, and she started crying. Then the now-familiar metallic taste flooded her mouth and she moaned in protest, but sound faded into the distance.

When she spasmed back into reality sometime later, her GPS was beeping. Scanning the water to see if she had drifted close to any hazards, she moved a hand to wipe the tears from her cheek, but they'd already dried.

A voice boomed through a megaphone. "*Sea Dragon*. This is Nanaimo Harbour Authority. You are on course for a restricted zone. Change course now."

10

Ess FLINCHED AT THE WORDS echoing off the water. A Harbour Authority patrol boat coasted a few meters off her stern. Two people in uniform stood at the helm looking at her, one with a mic held to their mouth. She couldn't make out any features; they were just uniforms. She stood, wiping her nose with her arm. Mechanically, she engaged her motor and turned from the port, inching away. Harbour Authority followed at a careful distance. Once she had repositioned herself, the megaphone blasted another message.

"*Sea Dragon*, prepare to be boarded. All hands on deck."

She stood next to the tiller and waited. Her *Sailing BC* book had explained Harbour Authority as a type of marine police force and emphasized the obligation to comply with their orders. They angled their boat ninety degrees to *Sea Dragon*, and a uniformed man stepped over onto her deck. He was tall, torso thick with protective gear. A second Harbour Authority agent stood watching from the patrol boat, hand near her holster. The uniform on *Sea Dragon* studied Ess, his hands at his sides. His black baseball cap put most of his face in shadow.

"Hello, ma'am. Are you alone onboard?" Waves of authority emanated from him.

Ess nodded slowly, weighed down with exhaustion and worry. She thought of the newspaper article Rene had shown her weeks ago.

Authorities had reassured the public they were watching for amnesia cases. And now authorities were on her boat.

"Do you have any weapons, firearms?"

"Weapons?" Ess took a second to think, suddenly worried she might have overlooked something packed into a cubby somewhere. "No. I mean, I have a few knives in the galley."

"And where have you come from?"

The question surprised her. "Why?"

"Excuse me?" His voice was sharp. He slouched to see her face under her hat brim, then gestured at the marks on her arms, the bruises on her legs and lowered his voice. "Are you okay?"

Ess studied her body for a moment, the memories of the mishap that had caused each mark flickering through her mind. He cleared his throat and she looked up at him. "Yes, I'm just... I've been sailing down the coast from Haida Gwaii. But why does it matter where I've come from?" Ess wiped her eyes with the back of her hand, the dried tears from earlier marking her face, sweat and misapplied sunscreen crusted in her eyebrows.

"We're watching for smugglers. Obviously." Leaning over, he peered into the cabin. "You're alone?"

Ess nodded.

"You were sailing into restricted Port waters; your GPS should've alerted you."

"Oh." She turned her head toward her GPS, vaguely recalling it beeping. "It may have. I was... I was distracted. Saw the skyline and, um, got lost in thought, didn't realize I was—" Tripping over her words, she decided to stop.

Studying Ess for a second, he gave a small encouraging smile. "Okay, no harm done. Just pay more attention in future, yeah?" He pointed at her helm. "I've got to scan your boat license. And I'll need your photo ID."

While he scanned the laminated documentation posted on the control panel, she ducked inside and got Sarah Song's license from the cabinet. She took a moment to wipe a wet cloth over her face to steady herself before returning to the deck.

"Boat license was updated very recently." He looked over at Ess. She didn't respond to the nonquestion, didn't know how to. She held out her ID, hand shaking only slightly.

"You said you came down from Haida Gwaii?" His eyes flicked between the photo and her face a few times before tapping the ID against his wrist comm.

They were standing close enough now that Ess could see black stubble on his face and a thick, jagged scar on his chin, the skin puckered and discolored. She stared at it, wondering if it was a childhood scar, if he remembered getting it, recalled the incident every morning when he shaved. She started to lift her hand to touch it, then caught herself, froze.

"Hey. I need you to answer my questions, okay?" Voice and expression suddenly serious, he crouched to look at her face.

Dropping her arm, cheeks flushed, she moved her eyes off his scar and up to his sunglasses, forced herself to gather the energy to focus. "Yes, Haida Gwaii, through Bella Bella."

"You sailed that alone?"

Ess nodded, wiped at the sweat trickling down her temple. Wished for a cool Haida Gwaii breeze.

"That's impressive. Tough waters up that way." Returning his attention to his comm, he extended the screen and made a dissatisfied noise.

Ess's heart stopped.

"ID isn't scanning." He manually typed in her identification info. "Have to do a manual check against the database. It's going to take a while." He pulled a piece of equipment from his belt and pointed into

LISA BRIDEAU

the cabin. "Meantime, let's have the grand tour. I need to conduct a search."

After making a hand signal to his partner, he moved down into the cabin and pointed at the bottom stair. "Please stand here."

Ess complied, suddenly viscerally aware of how big he was compared to her. Big and armed. Her ID wasn't working. She tried to think of how she might get away from him once he realized what she was.

He scanned the boat with a device that showed surfaces in a rainbow of colors. Pulling off her hat, she took out her ponytail and tried to untangle her salt-encrusted hair. She suddenly felt every bit of her three weeks of hard labor. Her brain just didn't have the energy to find a way out of this situation.

"Thermal imaging clear," he reported into his wrist comm.

"Is it an amnesia case? Tell me it's an—" He punched the screen of his wrist comm, cutting off the audio from his partner.

"Negative. Conducting standard search," he said.

Ess found herself leaning in, wanting to hear more. She got close enough to feel the heat radiating off his black uniform. He smelled of sunscreen and sweat.

"Hey!" His voice was loud and firm. He pointed at the step. "Back it up."

He added the word *please* but it was not a request.

Once she was back in position, eyes locked on the floor, he proceeded to search every compartment on the boat, only making as much of a mess as the task required. She took the liberty of sitting on the stairs while he worked, the hot sun on her back providing an excuse for the sweat dripping off her nose. She glanced at her control panel and the marks on the wood above it where she'd unscrewed the tracking device, tried to assess how suspicious it looked.

"How long have you been traveling?" he asked, elbow deep in the storage space under her dinette seat.

She jerked upright, tried to focus. "I left July 13, been working my way here since."

Pausing his search to wipe his forehead with a handkerchief, he reassembled her dinette seat and opened the cabinet holding her notebook and the typed note. He pulled the notebook out and she stood to stop him from opening it. If he read the note, she was done. She kicked herself for not hiding it or destroying it. Being alone and sleep-deprived for so long hadn't prepared her for this encounter. Glued to her step, she crossed her arms to keep from reaching out and snatching the notebook.

He rifled through the boxes of spare boat parts in the cabinet and shoved it all back in place, notebook on top. Then he pointed to the sleeping cabin, asking for permission he probably didn't need. She nodded.

"What kind of smugglers are you looking for?" she asked when he'd finished with her sleeping cabin and moved to search the galley.

At this, he stopped rummaging through her food, put down her container of oatmeal, and leaned against the counter with arms crossed. His expression made it clear that instead of harmless small talk, she'd asked about something obvious. She felt sick.

He squinted at her, head tilted as if she were a puzzle to be pieced together. "People. We're looking for people who smuggle people," he said. "Or drugs."

She studied the floor. Sweat rolled down her side.

"How long have you been up in Haida Gwaii?"

Ess's stomach tightened. "Oh. As long as I can remember."

A loud ding provided relief from his scrutiny. He extended the display on his wrist comm, read a message, shook his head. "Huh. ID is clear. Your boat license has a C-status flag. That means kid-glove treatment. No searches. You should have said." He reached up and closed the cabinet gently.

Another ding. He glanced at his wrist comm again, raised his arm. "Yeah, I'm almost done. All clear. C-status."

He leaned against the counter and contemplated Ess with a raised eyebrow. "What's your plan here?"

Her ID clearing had dropped her stress from stratospheric levels to something manageable. "Is this an official question?"

"Hey." He put his hands in a don't-shoot position. "I would never interrogate you now that I know you're C-status. I could offer some friendly advice if you want it."

Ess uncrossed her arms. "Advice is welcome."

"Your setup is weird. It's going to attract attention." He waited, looked at her expectantly, then continued. "We're pretty relaxed here. If you go to Victoria though, I don't know how they'll react to you. They get a lot of Americans sneaking up the coast who forget to stop in for passport control, forget they need visas now, so the officials lean toward being paranoid. Usually C-status boats have their own helicopters, so they'll raise an eyebrow at the status on a boat this modest. The C-status is supposed to smooth things, but Victoria has been on edge since the California fires sent that wave of Americans our way. And now the floods and crop failures in the Midwest have visa applications through the roof."

"Thanks." Ess was tired at the thought of all the things she needed to learn. "I haven't been paying attention lately, don't really know…" Her voice trailed off. This guy, who could haul her in on an infraction of some kind and abruptly end her journey, was instead trying to help her. Thinking about Raven and what Raven would do in this moment, Ess wiped her hand on her shorts and extended it, did her best to hold it steady. "My documents say Sarah, but I actually go by Ess."

After a pause, he gripped her hand and gave it a firm shake. The comm on his wrist dinged and his eyes rolled upward for a moment before looking at the display and replying. "Yeah, got it, Dash. Two minutes."

He adjusted his hat and made eye contact. "I'm Hitomu, but everyone calls me Hito."

"Hi, Hito."

"Hi, Ess."

"Oh, uh, would you like some tea?" Ess offered.

The wrinkles at the corner of his eyes deepened as he smiled. "Bit hot for tea, but thanks. Kind of you to offer."

"I'm not sure I have enough water for tea anyway." Ess frowned.

"One more bit of advice then," he said. "Fill up at the National Parks water station at Saysutshun Island. The private marina water suppliers may be cheaper, but their standards are all over the place and you might get some bonus *E. coli.*"

"That's really helpful. I wasn't sure…" Ess was caught off guard at having a pressing issue resolved so easily. "I'm glad you boarded me."

"Not something I hear often." Hito grinned.

The bumpers between *Sea Dragon* and the Harbour Authority boat squeaked and seemed to remind him why he was there. Standing tall again, he shifted his weight and moved toward the stairs. Ess stepped out of the way, and they rotated around each other in the small space.

Stopping with one foot on a stair, he paused, looking outside then back at her. "If you want…" He took his foot off the stair, looked like he didn't know what to do with his hands. "I could show you around Nanaimo later, get you oriented. No pressure; it's fine if you don't want to. But if it's helpful…"

A bead of sweat rolled down his temple and Ess watched it, wondered if turning him down would have repercussions. If Raven would caution her.

"Is there someplace to get fish and chips?" she asked finally, her stomach making itself known in the decision-making process.

He laughed, wiped his forehead with the back of a hand. "Sure, that's easy."

"I've been craving fish and chips for a few hundred kilometers. Let's do it."

Her quick, decisive response elicited an amused smile. She found herself reflecting it.

"Great. That's great. I'll pick you up from your boat at six. If you change your mind, just anchor somewhere else and I'll leave you alone."

A moment later, sunlight poured down the steps. The boat bobbed as he disembarked, and she heard his partner swearing at him for taking so long. Their motor switched on, then faded away.

Mechanically stowing the oatmeal Hito had left on the counter, Ess went through *Sea Dragon*, putting things back the way she liked them. When the boat was in order, she peeled the taped-together business card off the wall and held it by its edges. Ballast Boat Shop and Repair Center, Nanaimo. On the map, her finger traced the distance between her location and Ballast. Possible answers waited for her just a kilometer up the passage.

11

BALLAST BOAT SHOP WAS BY the water in an area left unprotected by the system of dikes and seawalls around Nanaimo's shore. A low wall of sandbags curved around the entrance, an inadequate effort if the old watermarks on the building were any indication. Behind the shop, a busy dry-dock held boats in various states of repair. The air was thick with the chemical smell of paint and polyurethane.

Ess stepped inside the shop and walked up to the counter, sweat dripping down her back from the short trip down the channel in her dinghy under the blazing sun. She desperately needed to eat a proper meal, shower, and have a daylong nap, but that all had to wait. Even if she had to fight off vertigo and stand on trembling legs threatening to collapse, she was going to get the answers she'd come for.

A woman stood behind the counter, fingers deftly moving over disassembled electronics spread on her worktable. She paused to wipe her forehead and noticed Ess. "Oh, hey," she said, a smile brightening her face.

"Hi." Ess had been thinking about this moment for so long but couldn't think of what to say now.

The woman put down her screwdriver and approached. "How's the *Dragon*? No problems, I hope?"

Ess couldn't speak around the sudden lump in her throat.

The woman tilted her head, her easy smile wavering. "Are you okay? You look... Do you need to sit?" She steered Ess to a chair in the corner next to a solar-panel display. "It's the heat, yeah? It's rough. Man, I was reading about Phoenix; their heat wave is going on two weeks. Hit 122 Fahrenheit a few days ago. The letters are melting off street signs, two hundred people are dead, it's crazy. Puts this heat wave in perspective." She adjusted an ancient fan so it blew in their direction and sat in a rickety folding chair across from Ess. Her chitchat petered out.

"I... Are you Sam?" Ess finally managed.

"Uh, yeah." Sam looked confused.

"We've met?"

Sam's eyes darted to the office door. "Yeah. Sarah, what's going on?"

Sarah. Sam knew her as Sarah. The lump in her throat grew. She tried to process this information. She'd just found someone who knew her.

Worried that if she moved too much Sam would disappear or turn out to be a figment of her imagination, she held still. "I had an accident—" Her voice caught but she forced herself on. "A head injury from a car crash. I'm having trouble with my memory. I'm trying to retrace my steps for the past few months, fill in some gaps."

"Whoa." Sam sat back at this explanation, stopped looking at the office, and focused on Ess. "That's heavy shit. I'm sorry. Head injuries are no joke. My friend fell while rock climbing, had a concussion it took months to recover from. Can I help?"

"If you could tell me how we met, what I came here for, anything you remember." She gestured at the shop. "This is all missing. I know I was here..."

"Yeah, sure. Okay. It was end of May when you and your friend—"

"My friend?"

"Yeah, imposing guy. He didn't say much. I didn't really talk to him. Anyway, you came in with this guy and had specific upgrades you wanted for your boat. Sweet forty-two-footer, classic twenty-teens in immaculate condition. Beauty with a beast of an engine. I installed the skookum autopilot and GPS system, top-of-the-line stuff. It was pretty clear you wanted the boat to be easily handled solo, but I didn't think it was for you. Why did I think that?" She put her chin in her hand, striking the classic thinking pose.

"Ah, yeah, your friend pushed to add a kick-ass radar to the upgrades and you were against it, were insulted at the suggestion actually. But he convinced you pretty quickly. The whole thing was a bit weird, if I'm honest. But I don't ask questions and you paid well. You haven't had any issues with the gear, have you? Because you didn't want any documentation, so the shop doesn't have records." Her brow furrowed with worry.

Ess leaned forward, hands on knees, staring at Sam, dying to peer into her brain and see these scenes. She'd been here, had conversations with this woman. This was a specific thing that had been stolen from her. Anger bubbled out from the marrow of her bones. She studied Sam, her not-quite-symmetrical face, her hands, pores caked with black grease, her beefy arms that looked like they could effortlessly hoist a sail in bad conditions. Ess took it in, waiting for some glimmer of recognition.

Nothing. Always nothing.

"No issues," Ess said finally. "Did you know me before I came in for this work? Had we met before?"

"No, you were a new customer."

There must be more. "What—what was I like?"

Sam shifted in her seat and cleared her throat. "Oh. Um. You were very clear in what you wanted done. You were polite. I mean, I don't—"

"It's okay, I won't be insulted." Ess tried to be reassuring, but her eyes were filling with tears at hearing herself described, at the idea that Sam knew her better than she did.

Standing, Sam backed away, shaking her head. "No, you were fine. You hired me for a job. We got it done. You were fine."

Ess wiped her eyes. Waited for Sam to make eye contact. Watched her fixate on her shoes, lift limp hair from her neck and wipe at the sweat trickling down. The silence stretched on. Ess had waited four weeks for answers; she could easily wait Sam out now.

With a sigh, Sam sank into the chair. "We never had a chat, never talked except about the work. You made it clear you weren't interested in talking about the weather, if you know what I mean. You were on a schedule and you were the kind of person to keep to schedule. Methodical."

"And this friend of mine?"

"That dude, I have no idea. Sometimes he seemed like an employee, but other times it was like he called the shots. 'Friend' is probably the wrong word. I dunno. He always watched to make sure we installed stuff properly. Skulked around in the shadows."

Ess didn't know what to do with this puzzle piece, this unexpected "friend." "What did he look like?"

"White guy in his midthirties. Brown hair. Average height. In good shape. Nothing particularly remarkable about him. Bit out of place in the marina with his nice clothes, except he looked like he could handle himself if trouble came up. Saw him scare off a guy at the marina who tried hitting on you, but he didn't even say anything, just, like, intimidated the guy with his physical presence. Pretty badass to watch."

"Did you catch his name?"

"No. Dude was weirdly quiet around me, would pull you aside to talk. Always watching for who might overhear. Didn't say anything if it didn't have to be said, you know. I tried to chat with him the first day, learned that wasn't his thing. You both seemed on edge and in a hurry."

Ess sat on the edge of the chair, her knees almost touching Sam's, as if proximity would get her closer to her memories. A bell chimed and Sam stood, head swiveling to the entrance.

"I have to—"

Ess nodded and Sam stepped away to greet someone. Ess dropped her head into her hands. This place should be familiar, Sam should be familiar, the smell of grease and stale pot should be familiar. She negotiated with her brain: one memory, just one small memory. That would be enough; she wouldn't ask for more right now.

Nothing.

She got up and paced the store, desperate for something to spark the flood of memories she'd come for. Turning away from a shelf of emergency flare sticks, she returned to the counter, pressing on it with her calloused, rope-burned hands. All the effort to get to this place, all the abuse she'd put her body through, and she'd gotten nothing. She hit the counter, suppressing an urge to scream and tear through the shop like a hurricane.

"Whoa," Sam said, appearing through the door behind the counter. "Don't trash the place. The owners are sensitive about that kind of thing." She glanced up at a security camera mounted on the wall, its red light blinking, then handed Ess a glass of water in a tumbler smudged with grease.

The sensation of the cool water slipping down her throat was a welcome distraction. Ess's anger subsided enough for a thought to form.

"Does that camera record?"

"Yeah. But one punch to the counter per customer is allowed, so you're okay."

"What if we looked at footage from May to get an image of the guy I was here with." Ess grabbed Sam's arm, clutched it tightly.

Sam extracted herself from Ess's grip and stepped back a few paces, holding out her hands to keep Ess from following. When Ess stayed put, Sam studied her, considered the request with a frown.

"No way, man. Sorry. Not risking my job poking around in my boss's security stuff." She picked up a box of parts and headed to the back, clearly done with Ess.

"Would your boss be interested in the work you did on *Sea Dragon* off the books?" she asked. "Do you think?"

Sam froze.

Ess pushed on with her hunch. "No documentation of the work, right? You pocketed some funds?"

The box of parts hit the table with a clatter. Sam crossed her arms. "Thought your memory was a problem."

"Memory is weird," Ess bluffed. "I don't want to cause trouble. I just want some images from the security footage. It can't be that hard to look at the files and make some copies. And we can avoid any awkwardness with your boss."

Sam swore softly to herself. "I've got a backlog of work I have to take care of or there will be people loudly expressing their unhappiness in my face tomorrow. Come back day after tomorrow. Wednesday."

Ess thought by then she would have died of impatience, but she let a frowning Sam shuffle her out the door. She sat on a concrete wall in a pocket of shade cast by a yacht named *Fish & Chics,* balanced her notebook on her thigh, and wrote the scraps of information she'd acquired. She'd been in Nanaimo with *Sea Dragon* in May. With a white guy with brown hair who was nondescript but intimidating. She was Sarah, or had been then. She'd been bossy and confident. Maybe even an asshole.

Putting the facts on paper didn't make them any more fruitful. And the chemicals from the boat varnish made her head throb. She shoved her notebook into her bag and walked to her dinghy. That was Ballast. That was the information she'd traveled a thousand kilometers to get.

12

ESS EMERGED ON DECK, WIPING sleep from her eyes just as Hito pulled a small motorboat alongside and tied up exactly at six. A breeze blew over *Sea Dragon*, bringing a tiny moment of relief from the oppressive heat.

She'd intended to rethink whether it was a good idea to do this thing with Hito, but after Ballast she'd filled her water tank, taken a shower, and fallen into a dead slumber. Now here he was. And she was starving.

The uniform and armor were gone but Hito still cut a substantial figure, tall, fit, and carrying himself with easy confidence. Without his hat and shades, Ess could get a good look at him as he came on deck. His short black hair, asymmetrically cut, had a bit of gray shot through it. A tattoo peeked out from the left sleeve of his T-shirt, the trunk of a tree. Seeing him standing there as a person instead of an imposing uniform made her breathe easier. She reminded herself that her ID had come through clean. As far as Hito knew, she was normal. She just had to maintain that facade. And after three weeks alone, she was giddy at the thought of company.

"Hi, Hito."

"Hey. You're still here." He grinned.

Her heart kicked an extra beat. Seeing someone so happy at the sight of her threw her off-balance. He steadied her with a hand on her arm. She closed her eyes for a second, let the touch anchor her.

"Ready?" He extended an arm to welcome her on his small motorboat.

Throwing the messenger bag she'd found onboard over her shoulder, she stepped deftly from her boat to his. "Yes. I'm starving."

With a practiced motion, he untied from *Sea Dragon* and started them toward shore. "Yeah, I saw your supplies, pretty dire. Something deep-fried should help make up for all the oatmeal and protein bars. I know the perfect place."

When they were a few boat lengths away, Ess gave in to the urge to look back. Seeing *Sea Dragon* from a distance, she cringed.

Hito slowed the boat. "Everything okay?"

"Yeah, yes, fine." Ess forced her gaze toward land.

He looked back at *Sea Dragon*. "Ah, mainsail?"

It was poorly flaked and missing the sail cover. A disorganized mess she'd meant to fix earlier, but after the trip to Ballast, it hadn't seemed important. "It's fine. I can fix it when I get back."

A few seconds passed, then he moved them forward again. She mentally apologized to *Sea Dragon* and faced the city.

Nanaimo, while far larger than any of the tiny towns Ess had stopped in on her way down the coast, was still a modest place. A few boarded-up buildings sat low by the water where the docks and marinas were, but most of the city was situated on a small escarpment above the water. Six or so twenty-story towers stuck out like rude interruptions to sprawling low-rise development that crept up the hill. The mountain backdrop helped make the city look tiny and insignificant. She'd studied images in Raven's office while waiting to start her trip, but it looked so much smaller in person.

Navigating the harbor, Hito took them to a wooden dock that had seen better days. He hopped out and tied up, seemed to trust the structure, so Ess followed.

"Welcome to Nanaimo, officially," he said. "Nanaimo: the 'Harbour

City,' semibustling quasimetropolis of seventy thousand people, once a booming coal town contributing to catastrophic climate change, briefly a hub of virtual-reality tech development until the global tech crash, famous primarily for the dessert bar."

"Dessert bar?"

"Nanaimo bars? More widely known and celebrated than the city itself? Sugary concoction topped with chocolate?"

Ess tensed, decided to be honest and confess ignorance. She shook her head.

"Haida Gwaii doesn't have Nanaimo bars? I'm shocked. We'll have to find a café and get you one. Then I'll write a strongly worded letter to the mayor of whatever the big town is in Haida Gwaii to let them know of this culinary oversight."

Relieved that lack of knowledge was amusing rather than flag-raising, Ess turned her attention to the building perched on pilings over the water next to the dock. Boarded-up windows and a facade covered in layers of graffiti tags made it clear it hadn't been a happy, active place in many years.

"What happened?" She gestured to the building.

He led her down the rickety dock to the gangway. "Yeah, it's sad. Used to be the lively waterfront destination. When I was a kid, my mom would bring me to a great teahouse here. It was always bustling with vacationing people. It flooded a few times in bad storms—Odette in '27 was the worst, then there were insurance problems since it's in the floodplain, and here we are. Cheaper to let it rot than to fix it. Especially since it's just a matter of time before the rising ocean claims it. The city's official adaptation plan is to let this bit of shoreline go, save the part of downtown on higher ground. Have to pick your battles with nature when you have a limited budget."

Ess walked up the gangway, holding tightly to the hot handrail. Pausing, she studied the boarded-up building, draped in overgrowing greenery, willing a memory to come forward. She'd been in Nanaimo before—Sam had confirmed it—so she should remember this. Should remember something of this place.

"The rest of Nanaimo looks less like a dystopian film set, I promise."

Realizing she was being weird for studying the eyesore, she stepped back and bumped into Hito. They apologized in unison, Hito moving back quickly and inviting her to go first.

"This is not the most flattering approach to the city. Think of this as the back door and don't judge harshly."

"I just came from a place that considers it fancy to gut the fish before selling it to you from the back of the boat."

"Yeah, well... I mean, that is some pretty good service. You may not get that here."

They reached a narrow set of crumbling concrete stairs, climbing the natural grade that protected downtown Nanaimo from the rising ocean.

"Have you always lived here?" She'd decided to ask him all the questions, to ask so many questions he wouldn't notice she had no answers about herself.

"Yeah. A born-and-raised Nanaimo boy. Went to Vancouver for a few years of university, but it didn't work out."

"What did you study?"

"Coastal engineering, flood protection stuff. Seemed like a safe career choice, given all the coastline we've got and our propensity for perching cities on the edge."

They reached the top of the hill, and Ess turned to face him. "So, what happened?"

Hito's half smile faltered. "Let's save that for later. I'm obligated as a Nanaimoite to point out that we are standing in the shadow of the glorious historic Bastion. A majestic, intimidating wooden structure built by the Hudson's Bay Company in 1850-something to protect the town when it was a fur-trading outpost or something. Don't quote me."

They were standing next to a three-story, octagon-shaped structure with a quaint peaked roof. "*This* defended Nanaimo?" she asked, suppressing a smile.

"I don't think it's ever been tested. Potential attackers are presumably put off by its massive stature and impenetrable, uh, wooden structure. If you came here to launch an attack, I assume you are now seriously reconsidering."

He kept a straight face as he delivered this ridiculous statement and Ess nodded solemnly.

Crossing Front Street, they moved into the town center and Ess felt her thread of connection to the water stretching thin. She ignored the pull to get back to the familiar. Hito steered them onto a tidy street lined with shops, with wide sidewalks and the occasional mature tree. He noticed Ess looking at the stumps of the many missing trees.

"Our downtown street trees took a hit during the Japanese beetle infestation when it came up from Oregon years ago. Entire blocks of trees were wiped out downtown. The rest of the city was spared by virtue of not having many street trees to begin with. The dead trees here were a hazard, so the city cut them down. Only recently started planting replacements."

"It must have been so lovely before," Ess said, stopping under a survivor, the cool shade of its wide canopy a welcome gift. Hito glanced up, like he hadn't properly appreciated it in a long time. She guessed he was recalling a memory of what the street used to look like, filling in the gaps of reality with what once was. So easy for him.

A group of scooters raced down the street, the whine of their electric motors interrupting the quiet moment.

"You know what I miss?" Hito asked. "Birds. I remember birds chirping on this street when I was a kid. I mean, they were loud enough to hear over the gas cars spewing fumes. Now"—he paused to listen—"nothing. You have to go to the woods to hear birds, can't just stand in a street and enjoy birdsong anymore."

Ess found the urban environment overwhelming after all her time alone on *Sea Dragon*. Now that Hito pointed out what was missing, she felt the absence of wildlife and greenery compared to Haida Gwaii, where dolphins swam alongside her as she sailed and bears trundled along shorelines snacking on crabs.

"Sorry, that was depressing. This concludes our catastrophic environmental disasters portion of the tour; you'll have to come back if you want to learn about the flash floods of '29 or '33 or the run of record droughts. In less depressing news, there's a good marine supply shop ahead if you need equipment. It's next to the strip club, because we're classy here in Nanaimo."

They strolled down the street, past cannabis shops, bookstores, and restaurants offering both authentic Canadian and Chinese food. Ess laughed at Hito's jokes and watched the other people walking and cycling by, people just living life. It seemed so easy for everyone.

—

After a quick loop of the small downtown area, they'd claimed one of the tables by the water with an umbrella for shade. Hito had also offered a restaurant with air-conditioning but Ess liked being in view of the water, even with the sticky, unrelenting heat.

Fish and chips remnants were spread in front of them, the paper trays stained with grease. People strolled by along the waterfront dike, and the food truck behind them played sad country music on tinny speakers.

Hito leaned back, beer in hand, staring at Ess with his head tilted.

"You're studying me?" she asked, eating a french fry soggy with vinegar and trying to appear at ease.

"You've managed to go"—he checked his watch—"one hour without telling me anything about yourself."

"Think I can make it to two?"

"I have no doubt. But I will start to wonder what you've got to hide. Professional hazard."

Ess tensed. "At least you know I'm not a smuggler."

He raised an eyebrow. "Could be an assassin?"

"Do you get a lot of assassins in Nanaimo?"

"Wondering how much competition you'll have here?" His voice took on a professional curtness and his expression was serious.

She gambled and smiled, saw him break into a smile too.

Exhaling, she ate another fry to buy herself a few seconds. "Okay. Uh. Not much to tell. My parents died when I was young. Don't really remember them. I grew up in some pretty remote places with various relatives. Nanaimo is the biggest city I've ever been in. I'm used to trees and infinite horizons." She rushed through it, the preplanned words falling clumsily, inadequately off her tongue. "It's a sad and ultimately boring tale."

"I'm sorry about your parents," Hito said softly, his voice almost lost in the music of a nearby busker singing off-key, "I know what that's like. So why Nanaimo? Why now?"

"Oh, I don't know. Time to see more than the islands and forests I've spent my life in? Get some answers to what life is about. Hear new stories, meet new people."

"Cheers to new people. Even if they are assassins." Hito raised his beer can and tapped hers.

"Okay, so now you know I'm an assassin. Your turn. Coastal engineer to Harbour Authority?"

The smile disappeared. He drank his beer. "Mom got sick when I was halfway through my degree. I came home to take care of things. After we lost her, I had my sister to look after, so I found a decent job here so I'd qualify as her guardian. Eventually joined Harbour Authority. Now I rummage through the personal possessions of law-abiding citizens who happen to drift into the wrong bit of harbor. On exciting days I issue tickets for improper discharge of sewage."

"And watch for amnesiacs, apparently?" Ess hazarded, holding her breath. She reminded herself that he'd checked her ID; she wasn't suspect.

"Finding one of the amnesia people would definitely make the day more interesting, but no such luck yet."

He excused himself and went to the chip truck to get them more beer. Ess was disappointed, having nurtured a small hope he might know something about the amnesia refugees that would help her understand how they were coming to be and how she might be connected to them.

"I'm sorry about your mom," she said when he sat.

"Oh. Thanks." He seemed surprised that Ess was still thinking about what he'd said. "It was a long time ago—" He started to dismiss the topic, then stopped. "I think the worst part is how the memories have faded. The sting of missing her is there, still sharp, but the detailed memories of her slip away." He sat up straight, opened a new beer. "Shit, I'm sorry. That's depressing as fuck. New topic."

Her chest tightened. Ess wanted to share with Hito how she understood the misery of being unable to remember loved ones.

"I've been thinking a lot about memory lately," she ventured, taking the beer he offered and pressing the cold metal against her neck. "How there are things you want to remember, but your brain just doesn't cooperate. And does it change who we are, if we can't remember things? My memories of my parents… Their faces are blank spaces. But I remember every sailing knot they taught me."

Hito leaned on the table, chin in hand, focused on her words. Ess picked at her food, self-conscious. She'd said too much.

"I know exactly what you mean. My mom's voice. I used to remember it so clearly, but now I have to rely on videos. If she doesn't live in my memories anymore..." He took a drink, staring into the distance.

They sat in a comfortable silence for a while.

"Have you read the news reports about the amnesia cases? The amnesia refugees?" Hito asked, putting air quotes around *refugees*. "Speaking of weird memory things."

Ess shook her head, gripped her forearm tightly.

"In the past few weeks there have been a bunch of people found, all claiming amnesia. Each discovered alone in a boat floating not far from the border with no identification, no idea who they are. They can walk, speak English, know how to tie a shoe, but they claim all their personal memories are gone. Apparently it's a bit sketch—normal retrograde amnesia is super rare and usually affects memories closest to the damaging event. These folks are claiming to be 100 percent missing all personal memories with no sign of head injury, and there's a bunch of them. It's very, very weird."

"How many?" Ess asked quietly, unsure what she wanted the answer to be.

"Twenty-five cases reported."

Ess kept her face neutral while she tried to sort out the implications of the big number Hito quoted. Clearly the world hadn't been on pause while she sailed here.

"The first theory was that the amnesia was a side effect of some new virus. But since it became clear the cases were all showing up in barely seaworthy boats within fifty klicks of the border, that idea died and the explanation the media loves now is a story that they're paying to have their memories wiped as part of being smuggled into the country. Hence 'amnesia refugees.' And while it's true you can't deport someone back to a country if you can't tell where they came from, lack of documentation isn't a free pass. It just dumps them into immigration limbo, so I'm skeptical."

"So, no one knows what's causing it?"

"It is a juicy mystery," Hito said. He raised his beer to her. "Yours for the solving, if you like. Whatever the explanation, the worry is that the ones found so far are just the tip, and the rest of the iceberg is heading our way. With us only forty kilometers from U.S. waters, I guess we're on watch duty."

The beers had loosened Hito's tongue, and he continued without any prompting. "Imagine a wave of people appearing with no resources, no skills they're aware of. Unknown laundry lists of bad deeds, or good ones. Are we obligated to take care of them? If we don't, who does? Do we hold them in custody like criminals while we argue about it forever? It's a hot mess in progress."

Ess processed this ocean of information. "Is it a problem to let in refugees?"

"Shouldn't be, but always seems to be, doesn't it? We're not the warm, welcoming place we once were. If we ever really were. What's it been like in Haida Gwaii? You must get loads of people from Alaska looking to relocate with the fisheries' collapse and all the land they've lost from permafrost melt."

"I—I guess I've been too removed to pay proper attention." Ess scrambled to pull together a better answer, thought of her conversations with Raven. "The Haida Nation has a lot of experience dealing with foreigners on their lands. They probably don't see it as much different from the past few hundred years of Canadian settlers showing up."

Hito nodded. "We're so fucking lucky to have been born here. We just get to enjoy it without having to struggle for it. We can take it all for granted and look down on people who want it." He stared out at the water for a moment. "I still can't imagine what would push someone to wipe their entire past. I mean, doesn't the essence of who you are go with the memories? I just can't see who would volunteer to give that up. I think it's happening to people against their will. That's my worry."

She nodded along, feeling sick but trying to look thoughtful, hoped he would shut up before she fell to pieces in front of him. They sat in silence for a few more minutes.

He shifted in his seat, flattened his napkin on the table. "If I'm honest, I was a bit worried about you when I boarded *Sea Dragon*."

Jolted from her thoughts, she looked up at him. "Why?"

Hito raised one eyebrow briefly. "Well, you... I'm not judging, but you'd clearly been crying. Were a bit out of it. For a second when I boarded, I thought you might be an amnesia case." He reached out a hand and grazed her forearm with his fingertips. "You're also covered in bruises. Shoulder is injured, I think?"

His light caress banished any coherent thoughts Ess had formed, and she felt her face turning red. "Oh."

"I know you're not an amnesia case. Your boat's too nice"—he smiled briefly—"but, you're okay though?"

Ess nodded, not trusting herself to voice an answer to that loaded question.

"Didn't get attacked by pirates?" he pushed.

"There are pirates here?"

He laughed. "No. No pirates. Joking, sorry." Hito pointed to the darkest bruise on her arm. "Can I ask?"

She looked at the constellation of fading bruises as if she hadn't noticed them before, ran a hand over the faint trail of blister scars from her jellyfish sting. "Sailing mishaps. Around Bella Bella, I almost flipped overboard in rough water, swallowed a decent portion of the ocean, and got knocked around. The recent ones are because I tend to zone out after twelve hours of solo sailing and things whack me—tillers, boom, galley counter, drawers." She paused. "I should come up with a better story, one with more derring-do and skulduggery."

His posture softened with her answer. He ate the last cold french fry. "Sailing alone from Haida Gwaii to Nanaimo in three weeks is pretty fucking daring. My friend went the other way one summer, only made it as far as Bella Bella, and that took him four and a half weeks. He still talks about how many years going around Cape Caution took off his life."

"I didn't fully grasp how hard it was when I started."

The conversation moved on to other topics. They lingered even when the food truck closed and their beers were done. The busker packed up and left. They watched the sun set, wispy clouds turning cotton-candy pink. Cutting through all her turmoil for a moment, the sight left Ess just feeling grateful. For this place, for the beauty of sunsets, for the kindness of a stranger.

"Thanks for dinner, Hito. I appreciate—"

He didn't let her finish. "Thank *you* for not objecting when I inappropriately asked you out while on the job. It's been nice to have new company."

A loud group of people strolled down the path, their laughter trailing behind them.

Hito tugged his shirt and looked off into the distance, then at Ess. "Want to get back to your boat?"

"Not even a little."

Hito's smile at her reply made her blush.

13

They walked around the city for another hour, Hito telling Ess stories about the place. Useful things like where to get good food, and sentimental things like the library where he'd hid as a kid when his mom and stepdad fought.

Ess gave Hito a few more crumbs from the backstory she'd sketched during her long days of sailing, tried to make it generic but authentic sounding. He seemed okay with her reluctance to talk about herself, satisfied with her scraps of history. She let herself relax, be herself as much as she knew how to be, and enjoy the satisfaction she got from making Hito smile and laugh.

"Best tacos in the city at Gina's," he said, stopping by a small rain garden filled with flowers, pointing across the street at a house painted bright blue with pink trim. "I eat here more often than I should. It's so close to home and so damn good, a deadly combination."

Not looking at the taco shop, Ess touched his outstretched arm and slowly pushed up his sleeve. A spotlight from the convenience store nearby illuminated his arm. He watched her trace a finger along the trunk of the slender tree tattoo that reached toward his shoulder. She'd been wondering all night about his ink, fighting the urge to touch it.

"There's a Sitka tree in Haida Gwaii that's over six hundred years old," she said, remembering something Raven had said. Ess's hand ran back down Hito's arm, then dropped to her side. "Apparently."

Looking up, she saw him studying her with an expression she couldn't read. She'd been too weird. Ruined things just to satisfy her curiosity. She shoved her hands in her pockets and glanced at the taco place he'd been pointing out. "You live near here?"

He fixed his sleeve. "Yeah, the tall building there, with the balconies."

"Is that part of the tour?"

His serious expression dissolved, a smile returning. "The tour is à la carte. Whatever you want is on the tour."

"Mayor's office?" she joked.

"Of course. Coincidentally, the nighttime mayor's office tour comes bundled with an inside look at the jail. Very exclusive."

Dimples appeared in each cheek as he tried to stay serious.

Wiping sweat from her eyebrow, Ess wished she could take a breath of cool sea air. The heat made it hard to think. "Well, since it's late, we should end the tour with your place. Don't want to get greedy and try to see the whole town in one night."

"Very prudent," Hito agreed.

Hito's building was modest, though taller than anything around it. It took several tries before the entrance would recognize his fob and open the door. "This has been a headache for years," he said. "Sometimes I miss keys. Sometimes I feel old for saying things like 'I miss keys.'"

When they stepped into the lobby, the temperature dropped ten degrees and Ess shivered. The elevator filled with awkward silence as they rode up. At his apartment, Hito tapped his fob to unlock the door and turned the handle, then paused. "I wasn't expecting guests. For the record."

Before Ess could say anything, he'd entered and removed his shoes. Soft lights flickered on as he made his way down the hall. She copied him, slipping off her sneakers by the door. After his comment, she expected to enter a disaster of a space, but instead stepped into a tidy, cozy living room. VR equipment and a thick first-aid reference book covered the coffee table. Hito collected some boxing gear from the floor and tossed it in a closet. He tapped the screen of a control panel in the hall, and quiet piano music came on.

The apartment felt like a home more than any place Ess had been. She wanted to bottle up the feeling and take it back to *Sea Dragon*. She ran a finger along the spines of a manga collection that filled several shelves. The top shelf held a photo set in a gold frame, a portrait of a serious-faced Japanese woman, her hair gathered in a loose bun, expression questioning.

"Welcome," Hito said, motioning for her to sit on the couch as he went into the kitchen.

She lowered herself onto the couch, wondering what Hito remembered of his mother, how often those memories comforted him and how often they pained him. Then she turned her head and saw the painting, and the world stopped existing. The artwork filled the wall opposite the couch. It started as a soothing swirl of saturated pigment that intensified as it spiraled tighter and tighter, the paint growing chunky and chaotic as it circled closer and closer to the ominous blue-black center. A tiny shadow figure cowered in the bottom left corner, their back to the violent swirl above, ridiculously out of scale, fragile.

Someone had reached into Ess's soul and smeared her deep-seated feeling of overwhelm on a canvas.

When she remembered where she was, Ess sprang up and looked around. Hito was in the doorway to the kitchen, watching her, a drink in each hand. She wondered how long they'd been configured like that, each lost in a different view. She put a hand on her cheek, felt flushed. He shoved aside electronics and books to set the drinks on the table. He stood next to her, close but not touching.

"What did you see?" he asked, carefully looking at the painting, giving her space to compose herself.

It took a minute to choose what to say aloud. "I'm trying to decide if they're in danger or not."

"The figure?" He looked at her now.

She nodded.

He sat. "Ah. Not everyone notices the figure."

She perched on the couch next to him, looked to see if he was joking.

"Really. I had the painting for two days before I noticed it. I think most of us are experts at looking and not seeing. Or maybe we see what we expect to see. She never put figures or people in her paintings before, so I wasn't looking for it."

He shifted next to her and their legs touched. Her complex mess of a life faded into background noise. He leaned toward her, created a short eternity where she wasn't sure if they would kiss, wasn't sure she'd do it right, wasn't sure it was the right thing to do.

And then Hito kissed her, impossibly lightly, grazing her lips, giving her room to change her mind. He ran a finger along her temple and behind her ear, down her neck until he ran out of skin. A shiver ran through her and she was aware of every centimeter of skin on her body. She touched the jagged scar on his chin, finally, leaned into him, wanted to stay forever in this place where problems didn't matter.

A faint chiming sound interrupted the music briefly.

They kissed again, less softly, and she felt herself falling under a wave of feelings, felt a current tugging her off course. He kissed her neck. She took a deep breath to try to stay afloat.

Something fell on the floor. Ess came back to herself and put a hand on his chest. She tried to think of the right words, to explain wanting to continue and needing not to because she couldn't get distracted from her task, didn't want to get lost, was already so lost. He ran a hand along her arm, leaving a trail of electrified skin, obliterating any rational thoughts. Her hand gathered his shirt, pulled him in so she could kiss him. She'd sailed a thousand kilometers from the tracking device; that must buy her some room to relax.

Another noise from the hallway jerked them both out of the moment.

Hito pulled back from Ess, his hand gripping her arm while his head swiveled toward the noise, his brow furrowed. Then he let her go and rushed to the door. Ess heard him swear, heard strange scuffling noises. She tried to put herself back together, to smother the sparks running through her blood. Hito reentered the living room carrying a small woman in his arms. One of her legs was streaked with blood. A dotted trail of blood on the floor traced the path back to the door and probably into the hallway and who knew how far beyond.

Ess jumped out of the way, knees wobbly. She opened her mouth but too many questions crowded on her tongue so she said nothing. Lowering the woman onto the couch, Hito slipped a pillow under her head, gathering her tangled long black hair to one side, a practiced motion. Ess could see the woman was lovely, even in this disheveled, bloody state.

"Red bottle in the fridge, get it now," Hito commanded, attention focused on the woman on the couch.

Jerking out of her contemplation of the woman's face, Ess ran to the kitchen, gave herself a second in the cool air of the fridge, then brought him the red bottle. He propped up the woman, who was out of it but not entirely unconscious, and put the bottle to her lips, making her drink. Most of it went down her chin and wet her shirt, a red stain blossoming across the silky white fabric. A gash on her thigh bled steadily. Ess grabbed a towel from the kitchen and applied pressure to the wound. The woman smelled of expensive perfume and cheap pot.

"Hey! Hey!" Hito patted the woman's cheek. "What'd you take, Im? Tell me. What was it?"

She opened her eyes and smiled a slow, languid smile. She let her head roll back to rest on Hito's arm. "Aw, Hito. You're the best."

"What'd you take, Im?"

"Everything and the sun!"

"Really not helpful." He put the bottle to her lips again. "Drink this."

She swallowed a few times, then pushed the drink away, frowning. "Don't you have any whiskey?"

"Did you test it? Before taking it?"

A nod, sort of. Ess watched Hito's face furrow with concern and annoyance and felt her heart ache, knowing there was no one to look at her that way.

"Were you with Jessie?" he asked, his thumb gently pressing under her eye where a bruise was forming. "Is this from her?"

She pushed away Hito's probing hand. "She called me 'exotic.' She *knows* that bullshit triggers me. I may have started something, but she deserved it."

"Oh, Im." Hito put a hand on her cheek, seemed lost in thought for a moment. He put the bottle on the coffee table and turned to look at the thigh wound. Placing a hand over Ess's, he lifted the towel and assessed the injury, then put it back.

"Can you hold—"

"Yeah, I've got it."

Hito disappeared and returned holding a huge first-aid bag and a bowl of water. He washed the wound, ignoring his patient's halfhearted protests. His actions were sure and methodical, but Ess could see tension in his movements. She stayed back, handing him tape when he needed it and stealing glances at the woman. Her makeup was sliding off. Lipstick smeared. Mascara on her cheeks. A scatter of freckles over her nose made her seem young and innocent. Ess wondered how someone so slight had gotten into such trouble.

With the leg wound bandaged, Hito looked like he was about to interrogate her, but she was out. He checked her breathing, lifted an eyelid, and blocked the light with his hand. He rolled her onto her side and adjusted the pillow under her head. Putting his hands on his knees, he studied her for a moment, picked up one of her hands, and rested it on his palm. Glancing over at the painting, then finally over at Ess, he released the hand, stood, and motioned for Ess to follow him. By the door, a pair of small, black sneakers and a purse lay on the floor next to the trail of blood droplets.

Hito kicked the sneakers toward the closet and leaned against the wall. He put his head back, took a deep breath. Ess waited, no idea what she should do. The distress caused by the woman's appearance was evident on his face. Distress mixed with something else.

"I'm sorry—" he started.

Ess wanted to rub her palm on his forehead to erase the creases of worry. "You don't have to apologize—"

"Yeah, I do. I... Shit. I'm sorry. I can't get you back to your boat tonight. I can't leave her alone like this." He gestured to the living room. "I don't know what she's taken."

"Oh." Ess assessed her situation. She had cash but no idea how to get to *Sea Dragon* anchored in the harbor. She slipped her shoes on. "Yeah, no, of course."

Hito's jaw tensed, his hands fists at his side. "I haven't seen her in months, had no idea she'd show up. I never would've brought you if I'd... Shit. In any other situation I'd get you back to your boat safely. I just... I—"

Ess opened the door. She didn't want to go, needed to go. "It's fine."

They abruptly said goodbye and then she was in the hallway, bag in hand. Alone. Turning away from his apartment, she hurried to the stairwell. She took a deep breath and exhaled loudly, and the stairwell breathed with her. She descended slowly, her body still buzzing with expectation.

Sinking onto a wobbly bench in the deserted lobby, eyes closed, she let herself enjoy the new memories she'd made. The feeling of being wanted. She sat for a long time, enjoying the safety of the lobby and memories.

It had worked out for the best. A definite and sudden stop from going down a path Ess knew was a distraction. Even if Hito could make her laugh, make her insides melt with a touch, she needed to find out what had happened to her. She had a life to get back to, and she felt a million miles from where she meant to be.

The sound of traffic outside faded, and Ess opened her eyes in panic as the metallic taste flooded her mouth. She gripped the bench.

The full-body spasm that rippled through her as she returned was becoming too familiar. She looked around, relieved to find she was still alone. She swallowed to try to rid her tongue of the sharp metallic taste.

At the front door, she pressed her forehead against the cool glass, trying not to think of what would have happened if she'd frozen in front of Hito. Pushing the door open, she felt the hot night wrapping around her as she walked back the way she and Hito had come, unwinding the thread, retreating.

14

Ess sat on the edge of the bed, breathing in jagged intervals.

Smoky, swirling shadows had been chasing her, larger than life and looming around every corner. She wasn't fast enough to escape them, and they were intent on erasing the rest of her, the bits the memory wipe had left behind.

"Just a fucking dream," she assured herself, unclenching her fingers and smoothing the duvet, fingertips catching on a tear in the worn fabric. The feeling that someone was after her persisted even though she was fully awake and aware she was safe in a dingy hotel room.

She staggered to the bathroom. Her shower steamed up the room until the excessive water use warning went off, the high-pitched trilling impossible to ignore. By the time she'd dressed, the dream had faded and she could think rationally enough to remind herself that whoever installed the tracking device had no way to know where she really was. And once she had the answers about what had happened to her, she could protect herself properly.

Clean and with a few hours of sleep in a real bed, she felt as ready as she could be to face a new day. She shoved her few belongings into her bag and went downstairs. A woman in a sickly green shirt and matching tie scowled at her from behind the check-in desk, waited for her to speak. When Ess had arrived late last night, the woman had been fixated on her lack of luggage, had hesitated to give her a room. Ess hadn't noticed then, but the clerk's outfit matched the lobby wallpaper.

They stood staring at each other. Ess sensed she was annoying the woman with her silence, but she kind of enjoyed it.

The hotel clerk relented, rolling her eyes to the ceiling before speaking. "Checking out? I'll need your key card," she said, scowling harder.

Ess fished the card from her bag, put it on the counter, and asked how one would get a ride to a boat anchored in the harbor. After looking at Ess through narrowed eyes, the clerk tore a tourist map off a pad and circled the hotel, then circled a marina. She pushed the map across the chipped laminate countertop.

"You'd have to ask at the marina." She turned to her computer, clearly at her limit of providing assistance for the day.

Ess picked up a pen, mentally retraced her evening walk, and made a small mark to note Hito's building.

Outside, the humid air slid over her skin and seeped into her pores. Pedestrians sped past. Ess pressed her back against the wall and tried not to be pulled under by the sense of being outside everything she saw. On *Sea Dragon*, she could pretend she was coping well with her situation. But now, surrounded by so many people striding purposefully to work, she felt alone in a way she never had before.

She'd sailed a thousand kilometers for answers. But Ballast Boat Shop wasn't the only place answers could live. Wiping sweat from her temple, she scanned the map for the street name she remembered from Hito's tour, her finger landing on a spot downtown, not far away. She stepped into the flow of people on the sidewalk and pretended to be one of them.

The public library was a big brick building with a small plaza in front. Neglected flower boxes flanked the entrance, filled with drooping daisies and forget-me-nots. A sign on the door advertised it as a designated cooling center, and it was busy inside.

Ess loitered just inside the door, pretended to study a display of new mystery novels while she breathed in the cool, conditioned air and watched people, studied them to know how to act.

The librarian at the information counter nodded eagerly when Ess finally asked for help, apparently happy someone was there for more than just cool air. He set her up at an old computer and demonstrated how to log in without her asking.

She read every article and post she could find on the amnesia cases. Hito's number was a bit off; there were actually twenty-seven cases of amnesia refugees now. The two additional cases had been reported just yesterday, the first time two had been found in one boat.

Experts quoted in the news debated the source of the amnesia cases. The theory that the amnesia was a result of a virus or other medical condition was dead, and the arguments were now around whether the memory wiping was forced or voluntary. Was it terrorists torturing people? Criminals looking to escape punishment for unspeakable crimes? Or folks who wanted an extreme version of a new start?

The refugee theory seemed to resonate with most, tugged at some heartstring, and the name *amnesia refugees* was sticking. With refugee camps around the world bursting with the millions displaced by war and famine and the climate disasters that caused or compounded everything, it was easy to believe that paying smugglers to wipe your memories for even a sliver of a chance to get refugee status in Canada was a thing some folks might contemplate. The director of the refugee advocacy group interviewed in one article pointed out that if Canada wouldn't support proper relocation of more refugees, it was inevitable that people would try to find alternate paths, if that's what the amnesia cases were.

Whatever the cause, the authorities were isolating the amnesiacs until more was known. Every article ended with a stern line directing the public to watch for amnesia cases and report any to police.

Ess resisted the urge to look around and see if anyone was staring at her, reminded herself that she was not wearing a flashing neon sign that advertised her memory issues.

She flipped through the cases found during her weeks at sea. Article after article, each one with photos of the amnesiac found. She studied their faces, wondering if she was connected to them in some way, wondering why her situation was so similar but so different.

She imagined being turned in, her photo posted everywhere and family coming forward to tearfully claim her, her loneliness instantly erased. Then the terror from her dream seeped in, of someone stepping forward to claim her who was not a friend. *"This is the only way out alive."*

Rene's warning to stay quiet about her amnesia had been more relevant than he could have guessed.

Slipping her notebook in her bag, she pressed a button to reboot the machine and erase her search history. Head down, shoulders hunched, she hurried out of the library as unobtrusively as possible. Thinking through the previous night, she tried to reassure herself she hadn't said anything that would make Hito suspicious.

The vivid memory of Hito running his finger down her neck stopped her on the sidewalk. She drew in a breath of hot air, her skin tingling, her face flushed. She wasn't used to being overwhelmed by vivid memories and wanted to sink into this one, but a man hurrying toward her on the sidewalk, his gaze locked on her face, pulled her back. He turned his head to keep staring at her after he passed. Feeling exposed, she started running and kept running all the way to the marina, only relaxing when she was onboard *Sea Dragon* with the door locked where no one could see her.

15

AFTER HER LIBRARY PANIC EPISODE, Ess had taken time to tidy *Sea Dragon*, finally wrapping her mainsail properly and giving the deck a good scrub. The oppressive heat made it slow work but she persisted. Her shoulder throbbed from the effort, which brought memories of the storm and facing the possibility of the end out there alone. She'd survived that. She could handle walking down public streets in Nanaimo.

Fortified, she did go back to shore, went into public to get to an electronics store. And no one pointed any fingers at her or ran in fear screaming, "Amnesia refugee." Now she was the owner of a cheap tablet with an unregistered cloud data plan. She'd bought the essentials the saleswoman said she needed, rejecting the wrist-comm interface and all other wearables, rejecting all virtual interface equipment. The woman had pointed at a sign advertising appointments to insert bio interfaces but didn't seem shocked when Ess shook her head. She'd set Ess up with a voice over internet protocol account; if Ess ever had anyone to call, she could do it from the tablet. No alarms had gone off when Ess used Sarah Song's bank card to pay, and she'd been free to return to the seclusion of the *Sea Dragon*.

Night came but brought no relief from the heat. Unable to sleep, she sat in bed in the dark and read about memory loss to try to understand what had been done to her. She started with fluffy simple explanations about how memory worked, then quickly graduated to more technical medical sources. The technical words gave her comfort. Memory was a neurological system with rules and order. Malfunctions had causes. But nothing she read even hinted at how one might intentionally wipe someone's episodic, autobiographical memory. Retrograde amnesia was rare, caused by messy head trauma or brain surgery mishaps, nothing that could be done intentionally and addressed with a short note.

She summarized in her notebook:

Declarative memory is the memory of facts and events. Can be subdivided into semantic and episodic memory.

Semantic memory is a record of facts, meanings, concepts, and knowledge about the external world that we have acquired. It refers to general factual knowledge independent of personal experience and of the spatial/temporal context in which it was acquired. It includes such things as types of food, capital cities, functions of objects, vocabulary.

Episodic memory represents our memory of experiences and specific events in time (places, associated emotions, other contextual who, what, when, where, why knowledge). It is the memory of autobiographical events, the collection of past personal experiences that occurred at a particular time and place.

Things known to affect episodic memory: trauma, hydrocephalus, tumors, vitamin B1 deficiency, Alzheimer's disease.

She added her own conclusion:

Things that do not exist in current medical science: deliberate, intentional wiping of someone's episodic memory.

Tossing her tablet and notebook to the side, she closed her eyes, listened for the comforting whistle of wind racing through rigging. But the air didn't stir. Nanaimo was stuck in a dead calm, a troubling place for a sailor.

Shouts from a boat at a nearby mooring buoy drifted in the window, a disagreement in progress, half the couple desperate to put down roots, half with itchy feet needing to explore. Ess listened to them hurl ugly words at each other until a sudden quiet fell over the water, the issue unresolved.

What to do with one life and the luxury of many possible paths.

Turning back to her tablet, Ess started the daunting task of getting up to speed on current events so she could handle small talk and pass as a normal person.

Taking stock of the world all at once felt like drinking a large quantity of expired milk. Storms and drought and forest fires, Arctic ice shelves collapsing. Extreme weather hammering everyone worse every year, leaving no time for communities to recover from one storm, flood, or fire before the next one hit. Florida losing land mass more quickly than expected. The ocean was swallowing Prince Edward Island too, but residents were moving to the mainland with government support rather than fighting an unwinnable battle.

All the articles made it clear that little of this was new. It was all just a degree worse, a bit more extreme, a bit more frequent. The world seemed to be fracturing. The old ways weren't working anymore, but people were desperate to stick to what had once made them prosperous and so many stubbornly refused to adapt. Refused to change.

Maybe Rene was right, maybe one of the benefits of being wiped was being free of all this baggage. It felt so heavy and hopeless. She supposed she'd grown up watching the world creep closer and closer to this tipping point. Like watching an inevitable car crash happen in slow motion, the driver refusing to turn the wheel.

Trying to digest it all at once made clear how much trouble was ahead if the world didn't dramatically alter its ways. Quickly. At that depressing thought, Ess got out of bed and turned on the Environment Canada weather forecast for company. The broadcast was about massive forest fires burning in central British Columbia— three hundred fires, two towns burned to the ground so far—but the monotone delivery was soothing.

Suddenly a bright spotlight blazed through the porthole, blinding her. She shielded her eyes and groped her way to the main cabin, stumbling as the boat shifted. Footsteps on the deck above made her heart stutter. Two quick, sharp raps on the door echoed in the cabin. She squinted against the blinding light. She hadn't latched the door. Why hadn't she latched the door? He'd been joking, but her mind went to Hito's pirate warning and she panicked.

She grabbed a can of peaches and stood, arm raised, facing the door and expecting it to explode open.

Instead, someone called her name.

She lowered the can. "*Hito?*"

Hand shaking, she opened the door.

"Hey," he said, his soft voice filling the cabin. "Can I come in?"

Stepping back, she nodded, her heart hammering. She shielded her eyes futilely.

At the bottom of the stairs, he spoke into his wrist comm. "Nordell, turn the lights down. This isn't a raid." The bright light dimmed, then swung across the cabin and disappeared. Ess closed her eyes in relief and put the can on the counter.

"Sorry—" Hito started.

"I thought you were a pirate." Ess groped her way to the table and let her legs give out. She opened her eyes a sliver to look at Hito but could only see darkness.

She sensed him crouch in front of her. He smelled of

coconut-scented sunscreen and stale sweat, bringing back the memory of their first encounter and a flood of feelings. The adrenaline rush was fading but her chest was still tight.

"Are you okay?" She wished she could see his expression.

"Me? I'm fine. Ess, I… When I came by your boat yesterday, your mainsail was still a mess, and I couldn't find anyone who had seen you at the public marina. I kicked you out at night… Nanaimo isn't the safest place. I thought—I thought a lot of terrible things. Are *you* okay?"

"Yes. I got a hotel room. I had things to do in the city."

He exhaled. Ess's eyes had adjusted to the dark enough to see his head drop. His wrist comm dinged but he ignored it.

She wanted to take his hand, say a clever thing to bring back the laughing Hito from their night out, but she forced herself to be still. "How's your guest?"

"She's okay. I mean, she's fucked, right? That's… She's… I don't know. It's complicated. It shouldn't be, but." He shrugged, like his ability to care had diminished significantly over the past forty-eight hours. "She shows up like this sometimes, unexpectedly, in crisis and I have to…"

A moment of silence passed, Hito's mind elsewhere. His wrist comm dinged again.

He gestured at the door. "I've got to go. I'm actually on shift. I'm glad you're okay," he said. She thought she saw him lift an arm to touch her, but the touch never landed. "I'm sorry for the other night. I had no idea she'd… I was such an asshole. It's not how I… I'm sorry."

Ess stood as a wave rocked the boat, causing them both to sway in an impromptu dance. "It was a good night. But better that she arrived when she did, I think."

A thump on the side of the boat.

"Sorry," he said. "It's not my usual partner. This one doesn't like personal stops. She's probably composing a sternly worded complaint right now."

He moved toward the stairs, and Ess wanted to grab his arm and hold him in place a while longer.

"Hang on." Ess squeezed past him and got her new tablet from the bed. "It's possible to contact me without a floodlight, if you want to." It took her a few tries to unlock the device, her fingers fumbling. Hito took it and quickly tapped his wrist comm before handing it back, holding on for a second, their fingers touching, resetting Ess's human contact counter.

"Good night, Ess." He fixed his posture into its cop form. In a minute his boat was motoring away into the night.

Ess sat at the table, raising her hand to look at it in the dim glow of her tablet, her skin tingling. All her days alone on the boat since Haida Gwaii, missing human contact hadn't bothered her and now it affected her so powerfully. It struck her how much one experience could tempt a person to change course. Her entire library of erased experiences that made her who she was before... If she had those now, would she even notice Hito's hand touching hers?

16

IT WAS THE DAY SAM was due to have the images from the security cameras ready. Ess didn't love the idea of being out in public, but it couldn't be avoided. She jammed a brimmed hat low on her head, realizing rationally that it made no difference, and was glad the route to Ballast Boat Shop was along unpopulated industrial streets.

The shop door jingled as she opened it, and an older woman at the counter glanced up.

As Ess opened her mouth to ask for Sam, the woman raised a hand. "Just a sec. Trying to do six things at once." She ducked into a back room with a box under her arm.

Ess adjusted her hat and ran her finger along the worn wooden counter, tracing the grain, glancing up at the security camera.

The woman emerged and grabbed the phone, transferred a call to someone else, then ran a hand over her face and looked at Ess.

"I'm looking for Sam," Ess said abruptly, barely resisting the urge to crawl over the counter and find her.

"Yeah, I'd like to talk to Sam too. This is the third shift she's missed. All her accounts are dead." She gathered her gray hair into a twist on her head, fixed it in place with a pen, and sighed. "She's the second employee to ghost on me in two years. Explain to me why it's impossible to give notice before ghosting. Fine, take off and move to a cabin in the woods to raise sheep because the modern world is too much, if you need to, but why do you have to leave people in the lurch?"

The floor of the shop shifted under Ess as the woman spat the words out. Ess gripped the counter, her knuckles white. "Sam is gone?" she asked, aware it was a useless, redundant question.

"Was she doing work for you? I can find the order in our system, but I'll be honest—there'll be a delay now that we're shorthanded. We're still sorting through it."

If the world would stop spinning, Ess could figure out what it meant that Sam was suddenly gone. "No. I just… She was going to look at shop security footage, help me identify someone. Are you surprised she ghosted?"

"Well, she didn't say boo to me about it. But neither did Amir until he deleted all his accounts and moved north two years ago, so what do I know. Sam was just talking about her August vacation plans in Banff, though, asking for leads on good campsites." She threw up her hands in frustration.

Ess's stomach knotted. "I don't suppose she left a message for Sarah?"

The woman glanced at the computer. "I'm trying to figure out her systems for documenting her jobs. I can't find half of the things I know should be there. She walked away in the middle of our busy season. I'm so pissed." She rested her hands on the counter, took a breath, exhaled slowly through her nose, and focused on Ess properly for the first time. "Sorry. What did she say she would do for you?"

"She said she'd review the shop's security camera footage from May to see if there was an image of a person I'm trying to find."

The woman shook her head. "Well, that's easy. Our security system reuses the same cloud space, and it reset the other day, wiped everything. Might have footage from Tuesday, definitely not from May."

"Nothing?"

"Yeah. No chance. The system messaged about the reset, saw it when I logged in this morning."

Ess hung her head, lost on how else she might trace this mystery man. Her only connection to pre-memory-wipe Sarah had just evaporated.

The woman took a step toward the worktable covered in half-assembled parts. "Look, I'm sorry Sam promised you something she couldn't deliver. She left a lot of us in the lurch. It's not how Ballast normally does business. I gotta go. People are waiting for things to be fixed, you know?"

She waited a second for Ess to respond, then went through the door.

"People are waiting for things to be fixed," Ess repeated softly.

Two women entered the shop, laughing and talking loudly. Ess glanced at them flipping through the navigation charts, then resumed staring blankly at the counter, irritated by their bubbly lighthearted chatter. One of the women was considering buying a boat and complained about how long the Transport Canada office was taking to produce the ownership and registry history she'd requested.

Ess stood straight, like she'd been poked with something sharp. According to the document on the boat, Sarah Song was the registered owner of *Sea Dragon*. She must have purchased it from someone before the memory wipe. Someone who would remember her.

17

THE TRANSPORT CANADA OFFICE WAS in a squat concrete building in downtown Nanaimo across from the library. Ess stood in the lobby at an ancient kiosk, tapping the screen to submit her request. The sensor was misaligned, so she had to tap half a finger-width to the right of whatever she actually wanted to select. Finally, the machine spit out a printed receipt acknowledging her request for records for *Sea Dragon*: all prior owners and registered ports of call for the past year. Her fingers tingled with anticipation. Then she read the delivery estimate printed at the bottom: three weeks.

"Fuck."

As quickly as frustration set in, an alternate path came to mind. Someone who could probably access the same data instantly.

Exiting the cool government office, she wandered Nanaimo in the heat, circling downtown in a spiral centered on Hito's apartment while she weighed the risks of the idea.

She found herself loitering outside his building, still undecided. Someone tapped her on the shoulder from behind and she jumped, heart racing.

"Are you waiting for someone? Lost?" the young woman asked, staying a few steps away from Ess, a cigarette in hand. "You've been hovering by our entrance for ages."

Ess tried to calm her flight instinct and reply like a normal person.

"I'm thinking of visiting someone," Ess said quietly. "Not sure if it's... right to."

The woman's posture relaxed, and she laughed. "That's all?"

Ess nodded. "I–I was here the other night but we..." She struggled to summarize the night. "I'm not sure if I'm welcome."

"I see." The woman looked at the door along with Ess. "Well, if you've got questions, best to go try and get answers, yeah? Unanswered questions will for sure drive you crazy."

She put her cigarette to her lips, drew in a long breath, and watched Ess approach the entrance.

It didn't take long to find Hito in the building directory. She buzzed his unit and within a few seconds the door unlocked, no questions asked. She lunged to get the door before it locked again and stood holding it for a second before passing through.

The door to Unit 502 stood ajar. She stepped over the threshold. "Hello?" she called into the apartment. She couldn't help but scan the entrance for a small pair of black sneakers. Nothing.

"Just leave it by the door!"

Not Hito's voice. Ess retreated out of the apartment, froze in the hall.

A small figure met her at the door. A sober, clean version of the woman whose blood Ess had mopped up so recently. She wore shorts and an old, oversized T-shirt hand stenciled with "No human is illegal." A bandage wrapped around one thigh, neatly taped. Her long, black hair was gathered into a messy bun. She had a smattering of freckles across her cheekbones, a purple bruise under one eye, and a frown on her lips.

"What's the problem? I paid and tipped when I ordered." Her gaze dropped to Ess's empty hands. "You don't have my noodles, do you?" she asked with a sigh.

Ess shook her head. Her brain offered zero suggestions on how to behave in this situation.

"I'm so fucking hungry. If they forgot my order again, I'm going to set that restaurant on fire." She turned her back on Ess and stormed toward the living room. "How hard is it to deliver some noodles, for fuck's sake?"

After a moment of indecision, Ess slipped off her shoes and followed.

Stabbing at the control panel screen, Hito's guest sighed dramatically. "Hi, yeah, I ordered noodles ages ago and they aren't here. What's up?" She gave Hito's address.

"Order status: out for delivery. Estimated arrival: one to ten minutes," an automated voice replied.

Waving her hand at the panel to disconnect, she went to the kitchen. Ess followed and watched her get a drink from the fridge. A knock at the door echoed down the hall.

"Ah!"

She returned to the kitchen, smiling, opened the metal takeout container and got chopsticks from a drawer. Ess stood by the counter, no idea what to do with herself.

"Okay, so who are you?" The small woman pushed noodles in her mouth and looked at Ess as if it was a struggle to remain interested.

"Uh, I'm Ess."

She stopped chewing for a second. "Ess, like the letter?"

"Yeah. I'm a friend of Hito's. I mean, not friend—we just met, but—"

The woman watched Ess struggle, calmly eating her noodles and not rescuing her.

Taking a breath, Ess stopped the flow of words and started over. "Who are you?"

"If we're going by letters, I'm Y." She carried her takeout container into the living room and sat on the couch.

Ess followed again, sitting on the other end of the couch, thinking it would be less awkward than standing. As soon as she sat, the painting on the wall opposite captivated her. She couldn't take her eyes off the figure crouching under the swirling vortex of color.

"You like it?" Y asked, voice tinged with scorn, chopsticks pointing at the painting.

"It's incredible. I don't know how Hito has it in his living room."

"Why's that?"

"I get lost in it so easily, I'm not sure I'd do anything else if this was in front of me. It's entrancing, don't you think?"

Y shrugged and glared at the painting, tilting her head. "I feel differently about it every time I see it. Sometimes I hate it, sometimes I love it. Sometimes I hate that I love it." She returned her attention to her food.

"Do you know where Hito got it?"

"He didn't tell you? He usually won't shut up about it."

"We didn't get a chance to talk—" Ess stopped and blushed as Y looked over at her with one eyebrow raised.

She put the takeout container on the table and wiped sauce from her lips with the back of her hand. "Hito's at his boxing gym. You can set your watch by his workout schedule. He'll be home in fifteen minutes. You can wait if you want, if you think he'll be happy to find you here."

Y stood and stretched. "I'm gonna go take a nap." She picked up a flyer from a stack on the table, handed it to Ess. "There's a protest next week in Maffeo Sutton Park. Bring some friends. It's going to be big."

Taking the paper automatically, Ess glanced at it. Angry text demanding the government create new immigration pathways for people displaced by climate crises. "150 million climate migrants need help!"

Ess watched Y saunter down the hall, clearly at home in Hito's apartment.

Not wanting to see Hito's reaction at finding her in his home uninvited, she'd scribbled a note and put it on his fridge. Now she sat at a table in his favorite taco shop and waited for her order to arrive, trying to go at least five minutes before checking the time again. It was stuffy and hot in the tiny restaurant, the air infused with the sharp scent of hot sauce.

She contemplated the Help Wanted sign on the counter next to a white ceramic cat with its left paw raised and thought about her shrinking bank balance. Withdrawal fees from her Maltese bank were enormous, and some online browsing had clarified they were typical for offshore bank accounts that offered specialized services like handling money for people who wanted their identities hidden. She needed to sort out moving her money to a Canadian bank. Best to wait until she could do it using her real name, once she was back in her real life.

A plate with three small tacos arrived. She lifted one and got some of it in her mouth, half the filling falling on her plate. With a sigh, she wiped her hands on several napkins.

To add to her frustration, her brain kept circling back to the news about Sam. The security system *happened* to reset this week. Sam *happened* to ghost. She didn't want to face it, didn't want to determine what it meant.

"Hey, Ess."

She turned, a smile escaping despite her desire to be unaffected. "Hey, Hito."

He still had his workout clothes on, hair wet with sweat. He was slightly out of breath but trying to hide it. "Good or what?" he said, sitting next to her, pointing at her tacos.

"I've heard good things about this place."

A server greeted Hito by name and took his order.

Hito gestured at the protest flyer on the counter. "I see you met Yori." He paused. "She can be… Did she say anything inappropriate?"

"She was just disappointed I wasn't her noodle delivery." Ess tore her napkin in half and put it on the counter and just blurted out the question that was on her mind. "Who is she?"

Hito's eyes narrowed in confusion. They were dark brown, Ess noticed.

"She's my sister," he said slowly. "My half sister, if we're being really accurate. But I explained when she—"

Ess tried to hold it back, but a bubble of laughter escaped and kicked off a laughing fit. She tried to get her breath and regain a sense of decorum, but the laughing continued and she didn't really want to stop it.

"You didn't tell me… I thought—I thought—" She couldn't finish. His horrified expression made Ess laugh harder.

"You thought I had you over and my girlfriend showed up?"

She shrugged, enjoying this new buoyant feeling. Someone put a plate of tacos in front of Hito that he ignored as he joined Ess, shaking his head and laughing.

"She's Yori? Not Im?"

"Ah, Im's a nickname. I used to misuse Japanese words to bug my mom, mashed up Japanese and English. *Imouto* is the Japanese word for little sister. I've called her Im since we were little. I called her Emily for a few years for reasons that seemed witty to a teenager." He paused his flustered rambling.

Ess wanted to hug Hito for making her feel fifty pounds lighter. She'd needed this laugh. When she could breathe again, she took a bite of a taco and watched most of the crumbly tofu fall on the plate.

"Um. I don't know what topic of conversation typically follows clearing up that the woman passed out in one's apartment is a sibling, not a lover." He ran a hand through his hair, then his face lit up. "Oh, this might interest you. I was on shift with a guy yesterday who was one of the agents who found and brought in one of those amnesia cases we were talking about. He escorted them to the hospital to be seen by the big-shot neurologist on the case, so he now considers himself an authority on the subject of amnesia refugees, which is really delightful to hear about nonstop for a whole shift. But he did say something interesting that made me think of our chat about memory the other day. He said the amnesiac was inconsolable over their lost memories, but when 'Summer of '69' came on the radio on the way to the hospital, the guy sang along, knew the lyrics by heart. Isn't it funny that such a detail could stick when you can't remember your own parents?"

He drizzled hot sauce over his food and ate a taco in three quick bites.

The story hit too close to home, and Ess didn't trust herself to respond so she also busied herself with her taco, copying Hito's technique. Observe and copy. Pretend to be normal. She tried to think of a safe thing to say, something a normal person would say. "Is the neurologist someone who understands this bizarre amnesia, how it happens?"

"Maybe. All the amnesia cases get sent to the same brain doctor, so hopefully they know all about it by now. Would be interesting to hear an explanation, wouldn't it?"

A muscular guy wearing a T-shirt stretched to capacity appeared next to Hito and clapped him on the shoulder, cutting off any further digging on the topic.

"Hitomu! Congrats on the invite letter! Have you scheduled your interview and assessment? I'm so pumped you finally applied; you're going to crush it. We should schedule an extra workout session this week to prep you." The guy took a moment to clue in that Hito had company. "Oh, hey, sorry. I didn't mean to interrupt. Hi."

"Hi." Ess responded after a second, still thinking about the neurologist.

"Ess, this is my buddy Will. Will, this is Ess; she's new to Nanaimo."

"Welcome to town, Ess. You've met the nicest local we have. Sorry for interrupting, I just need this guy to tell me when his interview is so I can swing by afterward to celebrate with him."

Hito shifted on his seat, looked at the door. "Ah, Will, I haven't—"

"No. You are not going to tell me you aren't doing it, I know you aren't. We've been training to get you through the physical, and you've been talking about this since I met you. This is the moment. You're doing it."

"Yeah. Okay, yeah, I'll schedule it."

Will frowned but nodded. "Okay, cool. I'm going to call you tomorrow to find out what your time slot is, so you better get it booked." He grabbed his box of tacos from the counter and left, the bells on the door jingling merrily with his exit.

"He seemed really happy for you."

Hito was looking at the door and replied somewhat absentmindedly. "I've been invited to apply for a job. Something I've wanted to do for years. Kind of an elite thing."

"What's the job?"

His attention returned to Ess. "It's with NDRT, on-the-ground work in hot spots."

"Sorry, NDRT?"

"National Disaster Response Team?"

Ess vaguely recalled reading about that somewhere recently. "What do they do, exactly?"

He looked a bit surprised. "They're sent in during disasters when local resources are overwhelmed. Flooding, hurricanes, ice storms, all over the country. In Ottawa when the ice storm hit a few years ago, it was NDRT on the ground who helped triage, helped get critical systems running again. I'm trying to think of an event when they were deployed up your way but I'm drawing a blank." He paused and dropped the twisted napkin he'd been crumpling. "I haven't told anyone about applying. Will's been training with me to make sure I pass muster on the physical, but no one else knows."

"Well, I don't have anyone to tell."

Hito relaxed when she said this, leaned back. "I've been wanting to do this for years, but it means being called away for weeks at a time on short notice and I kind of need to be here for Yori. I'm not sure there's much point in being tested and interviewed."

"Sounds like the accepting part is a decision you can put off until you've been offered the job."

"You make a point. Though being offered and having to turn it down might be harder than just walking away now."

"Is Will going to let you walk away?"

Hito laughed, breaking his own tension. "Good question."

There was a lull in the conversation. Hito picked up some scraps of taco filling and ate it.

"I have something I wonder if you can help with," Ess ventured, eyes locked on her empty plate. "I'm trying to find some history on *Sea Dragon*, trying to track down a previous owner. Wondering if you can get that data, if it's allowed?"

"Sure. Easy. I mean, you could do it yourself but it can take a few weeks. They're federal records we access all the time, pretty standard search. Didn't do it with you because of your C-status. With that, you get minimal scrutiny. You still haven't explained your C-status to me, actually."

"I like to maintain my mysterious aura," Ess said, face flushing.

"Mission accomplished." He looked at his watch and jumped from his seat. "I'll get the records for you, no problem. I have to clean up and get to work. But, ah, if you're not busy, Yori and I are grabbing dinner out tonight. It would be great to have you join us and meet Yori, my sister, properly. Did I mention she's my sister?"

Ess couldn't prevent her smile. "I'm definitely not busy."

"Great. Cool." He told her the name of the restaurant, and they arranged to meet there at seven. Ess watched him break into a run once outside, clearly late.

18

THE CASINO WAS SET AWKWARDLY between a derelict mall and a busy intersection. Its facade was a shade of chrysanthemum yellow that hurt the eyes. The map on Ess's tablet confirmed this was the place Hito had named, a blinking dot cheerily celebrating her arrival. She watched a few people enter the tired casino, tried to get a sense of how to behave, how to fit in, but the blacked-out windows didn't give anything away, so she gave up observing and went through the door. Pushing aside threadbare velvet drapes, she emerged into the main casino and froze, dazzled by blinking and flashing lights. The cacophony of sound nearly pushed her back out the door. Loud pop music clashed with excited gambling machines talking and dinging.

A slim woman in black, almost invisible, approached with a glassy smile and asked Ess if she needed help, offered to take her to the cashier to buy chips, recommended the roulette table. When Ess mentioned the restaurant name, the woman pointed straight to the back and faded away into the dark lobby.

The maze of blinking, chiming slot machines assaulted Ess as she walked. Automated sultry voices started as she passed, tried to lure her to stop at each machine and created a wave of pleading ads in her wake. She had to stop and shut her eyes, just for a second, just until the dizziness passed. When she reopened them, she realized she'd gotten turned around and lost track of where the restaurant was. She tilted her head to work out a sudden tightness in her neck, wished she had a drink to wash away the sharp, metallic taste on her tongue. Then the racket of the casino faded into muffled, almost soothing, background noise.

She felt the full-body spasm and flushed red as she looked at the small crowd of concerned faces that now surrounded her.

"Oh, I think she's okay! Are you okay?"

Ess couldn't answer, horrified at all the people staring at her.

Someone handed her water in a martini glass. She drank mechanically.

"So strange! You just froze, like a statue. Wouldn't respond at all—"

Ess forced a smile, desperately needing all the faces to go away. "It happens sometimes."

The woman frowned, squinted her eyes like Ess was a puzzling specimen. "Should we take you to a hospital?"

An older man stepped forward, waved the crowd away with his cane. "Everyone get lost. Bunch of lookie-loos. She had a little seizure, it's hardly front-page news."

People dispersed.

The man held out a small paper box. "Gum," he said, "I find it helps after seizures. Can't say why; it just feels better."

Ess took a piece from the box, hand shaking slightly, and started chewing, glad for the overpowering mint flavor.

"I've had tonic seizures since I was a kid so I'm used to staring crowds," he said taking care not to look at Ess. "Your seizure was a bit different, but no one needs a nosy audience."

Twisting the gum wrapper in her hands, Ess thought she saw side glances directed her way from the nearby gambling tables and imagined everyone discussing her. She handed the man her empty wrapper and thanked him, and hurried off down the aisle lined with the fewest slot machines.

Following signs to the washroom, she eventually exited the gaming floor, passed through faded velvet curtains, and pushed the door open. Finding the washroom empty, she leaned against the wall, exhaling in relief at finding a scrap of privacy.

She focused on the news report playing and tried to stop her thoughts from spiraling.

Nanaimo had hit a new record-high temperature. Fifty-eight heat wave deaths so far. Hotter temps expected tomorrow. Cooling centers extending hours.

The news switched.

Dramatic increase in the number of people ghosting. Record number of people cut digital ties and walked away from their lives in 2037. The government reminding people that requests to delete social insurance numbers would be universally refused.

Ess thought about Sam. Thought about a world where the drive to abandon everything and start fresh was on the rise. An overwhelming longing filled her for the simplicity of life when it had been just her and *Sea Dragon* surrounded by the wild forests of Haida Gwaii. No one to stare at her. Just ocean breezes and cedar-scented air.

At the sink, she scrubbed her hands under hot water. She'd shown up at Hito's door that morning because he held the possibility of distraction and the possibility of answers, and Ess wanted both badly even though they were pathways in opposite directions. She wanted the name of the neurologist he'd mentioned. To get it, she had to hide who she was, hide the only salient fact about herself that she knew: her amnesia. At a dinner whose purpose was to get to know each other better. And if she gave herself away for what she really was, she'd get thrown in a cell, get her face plastered on the news, attract whoever was after her before she could even find out why she was in this mess.

There was a narrow channel ahead with rocky shores on either side, and she had to find a way to slip smoothly down the center without a tide chart.

Pulling out her ponytail, she ran her hand through her long hair and studied her reflection, tried to believe it was the face of someone who could pull this off. Walking down the hall back to the casino floor, she heard a familiar voice. She paused behind the curtains, not wanting to interrupt.

"...is like an escape from all the shit going on," Hito said.

"You can't hide from the real world, especially not with another person. Trust me, I've tried."

"Yeah, still trying, I see."

"Don't give me grief this early," Yori said.

There was a pause. Ess looked around but saw no other exit.

"So, this one," Yori continued, "who lets you forget all the bad things in life, are you planning to just have horizontal fun or get serious?"

"Stop it, Yori. Not here."

"Hey, you're the one working all the crazy hours. Otherwise, I would have asked this before in a less embarrassing setting. Though we both know you'd be blushing no matter where we were."

"Why don't you tell me what happened to the rehab program."

Yori took a long time before answering. "I didn't go."

"Yori—"

"Yeah, I don't need to hear it. You're disappointed. It's a great program. I know. I'm managing fine on my own right now. Let's move on."

There was a long silence. Ess lifted her hand to push the curtain aside but Hito spoke again so she retreated.

"What's your plan then?"

"I don't bother making plans. I live in the moment. I'm like a really excellent Buddhist monk."

"Right." A pause. "Want to talk about what brought you home the other night? The cut on your leg?"

"I just wanted to see my brother. Is that cool?"

Hito's voice softened. "Yeah, it's always cool to visit your brother, Im. You know I want you to stay."

"Okay then. Back to your love life. What's your wooing plan? Do you know how to woo? When did you split from your last girlfriend, like a year ago, two? Do you remember how all this works?"

"God. One mortifying question at a time."

Hito's phone buzzed. "Search and Rescue HQ. I have to take this. If she arrives before I get back, be nice, Yori. Please."

"I am always nice! I'm better than nice, I'm delightful."

Waiting a bit, Ess pushed the curtain aside and walked over to Yori, who was leaning against a wall, eyes locked on a bar nearby. She jerked to a standing position when Ess said her name.

"Hi." Yori forced a smile that survived a few seconds. "Hito will be relieved you're here. He thought I'd made us so insanely late you'd've left. He's outside on a call." She flopped into a chair at the nearest slot machine. "Please tell me you and Hito are sleeping together."

Ess stood by the slot machine, tried to tune out all the chiming and dinging. "Why?"

"Seriously, he's wound so tight. I keep telling him he needs to embrace the one-night stand. There are loads of women who would hook up with him. He just needs to load his social profile on the right app. But he hasn't embraced sex as a recreational thing. He has these notions." Her voice faded as she waved her hands dismissively. She fidgeted with the slot-machine buttons. She seemed to be fighting an urge to dance or run a marathon.

"So, uh. Sorry about the other day." Yori shrugged, glanced at the next row of machines and back, to the nearby restaurant door, her lap. "I probably should have introduced myself like a normal person instead of watching you squirm." Her gaze landed on Ess briefly before continuing its scan of the room.

The conversation stalled. Ess watched Yori fidget for a minute, then checked to see if Hito was approaching before asking, "Do you know about ghosting?"

Yori's attention snapped to Ess. "What?"

Sitting on the chair at the slot machine next to Yori's, Ess repeated her question. "Ghosting? Why do people do it?"

"Did we just dramatically change subjects?"

Ess sensed she was being weird but she continued, betting on Yori taking it in stride. "Yes."

Swiveling her chair to face Ess, Yori stopped fiddling with the slot-machine buttons. "Why are you asking?"

"It keeps coming up. People mention it to me, usually when they find out about my lack of tech."

"I was wondering if your no-wearables thing was a statement or what." She twisted her bracelet. "Ghosting is complicated. What did Hito say?"

"I haven't talked to him about it."

Yori narrowed her eyes. "Why?"

The noise in the casino made it hard to think straight and Ess found herself being honest, unable to judge how risky that was with Yori. "I don't want the black-and-white answer; it seems like a gray thing. You seem like you'd know gray."

"Huh." Yori nodded and her gaze fixed on Ess like she was seeing her for the first time. "Okay. I mean, you're right. Hito is chronically unwilling to see the advantages or necessity of ducking underneath the system. He's very stuck on rules and law. Ghosting is definitely a gray area thing. You scrub what you can, delete the accounts that are deletable and then go off-grid. That's real ghosting. Finding a way to live off network is hard and getting harder. My favorite sushi place, run by an eighty-five-year-old woman who handwrites receipts, stopped taking cash years ago. You basically have to be a hermit homesteader to survive without participating in digital life."

"Who does it then? Why take such an extreme step?"

Yori shrugged. "People who have been burned. People running away from something. People who have fucked up life in this world too much to continue on the same path. Thirty years ago, people would move to Bangkok, be an expat distorting the Thai economy. Well, that's not a great option anymore unless you're a really good swimmer, so, ghosting. For most folks, it doesn't stick. Seems like a nice idea, a fresh start, a do-over, but reality is messier. Exiting one's life is…" She took a second to try to find the right word, then shrugged. "It's hard."

Yori opened her mouth to say more, but Hito returned. He was wearing a crisp button-down shirt decorated with ridiculous tiny anchors. Something happened when Ess saw Hito, saw how happy he was to see her. It made her feel more three-dimensional.

He was smiling widely, running a hand through his hair. He stood between their chairs, his gaze bouncing between Yori and Ess, trying to read them, worry creasing his brow. "Glad we didn't miss you, Ess. So, uh, ever dined in a sad casino restaurant that hasn't been updated since 2020?"

"First time," Ess said, happy to have a safe conversation topic. "But according to the sign, the restaurant doesn't open for ten minutes."

Hito verified and returned, glaring at Yori.

"My bad," Yori said. "This is the casino that time forgot. I didn't think it ever changed. Guess being late wasn't an issue, eh?" She jumped off her chair and reached up to Hito's shoulders, digging in to massage as best she could from her height. "Relax. We can get drinks, show Ess the exciting Casino Nanaimo in more detail, then get food."

He lowered his voice but Ess still heard him. "No drinks, Yori."

Yori frowned, stopped massaging him, and crossed her arms. They stared at each other, expressions unreadable to Ess, a silent subtle negotiation underway. Hito tilted his head and Yori dropped her arms, rolled her eyes. "Fine. Your party."

She reclaimed her slot-machine stool.

"So, Ess… It's Ess, right? Just the letter? Why visit Nanaimo of all places? I mean, why not go to Victoria or shiny Vancouver?"

"I like Nanaimo." Thinking about all the things that had made her smile since arriving, Ess added, "The library is great, and there's this grocery store near the marina with amazing fresh produce."

Yori raised her eyebrows. "I admit I haven't been in the library in a long time, have perhaps failed to consider it for the civic asset it is."

"And I've often taken for granted the fresh produce," Hito added, a half smile pulling at his lips.

"Oh. Haida Gwaii, you know, doesn't have the same amenities," Ess stuttered, sensing her response had landed weird. She quickly turned attention away by asking about Vancouver, which triggered a lengthy rant from Yori about a favorite café being replaced by a store selling nothing but champagne-filled, gold-flecked gummy candies. By the time she was done, the restaurant sign had flickered on and the door opened.

The hostess showed them to a table in the middle of the enormous empty space. The restaurant was carpeted and upholstered and draped entirely in red fabrics, making it feel like they were inside a tomato. Yori sat first and, while shielded from view by the hostess, reached over and shifted the cutlery of the other place settings so they were askew.

Hito sat and immediately straightened his cutlery. Yori grinned.

Once the server left, Hito apologized. "Despite appearances, the food's actually pretty good. Yori's been making me come here for years. I've almost gotten to the point where I don't notice how weird it is."

"C'mon, this pit of despair is the best way to feel better about your own life choices. I mean, look." Yori pointed through one of the arched windows overlooking the casino floor. On the other side, a middle-aged man sat hunched over a slot machine pressing buttons with all the enthusiasm of a janitor mopping a bathroom floor.

"It's the lure of hope," Ess said quietly. "Even if you know the odds are astronomically against you, when everything else is dark, a tiny spark of hope has immense power." Ess turned away from the sad man at the slot machine and saw Hito and Yori staring at her. Averting her gaze to her menu, Ess tried to stamp down her feelings. The long list of salad options blurred for a moment, but she blinked a few times and got it under control.

"As the experts here, if you two want to order for me, I'd appreciate it," Ess said, putting aside her menu.

Yori and Hito looked at each other. Hito suggested a dish, Yori nodded. They put their menus aside in unison. The waitress arrived and took their order, then an uncomfortable silence settled over the table. The red fabric walls muted the din of the casino, making it feel like they were just outside a party, like uninvited neighbors.

"How's life in Haida Gwaii?" Yori asked, eyes darting to Hito as if she wanted to be sure he witnessed her efforts.

Ess wished she could thank Yori for asking a question she could answer honestly without having to fabricate and remember lies. "Beautiful. I've spent a lot of time on *Sea Dragon* recently. Just *Sea Dragon* and me and the ocean." She leaned forward and rested her elbows on the table. "There were days when I would sit, anchored next to forested islands pulled from a storybook and watch the mist roll in, obscuring everything. Like I'd been plucked from the world and moved to a void. The air dead, the ocean calm and still as a lake. The birds would quiet. Then"—she snapped her fingers—"the spell would break. A drone would fly overhead, or a seagull would squawk and I'd be returned to this world, disoriented and cold. There's something about the place, like magic slips in through a crack and wraps around it."

Yori had stopped her fidgeting while Ess talked, her hands resting on the table. Hito looked at Yori, a strange expression on his face that Ess couldn't read. Shifting in her seat, Ess tried to steer the conversation away from her. "Did you two grow up together? You're stepsiblings, right?"

He shook his head. "Yori's my sister. Half sister is a technicality I only bring up on very bad days. Yori's dad, Cormac, and our mom got together when I was six. Yori arrived when I was seven."

"Hito was a happy only child, the center of Mom's universe, and then I came along and took away the spotlight," Yori said, a slight edge back in her voice, fingers pulling at the frayed hem of the tablecloth.

"Hardly. As far as I remember, Yori was always there. No memories of pre-Yori years exist; therefore, there never was a time without Yori. Mom did say that I pestered her for a sibling on every occasion where I had a chance to request gifts. Though perhaps I confused 'sibling' with 'puppy.'"

"Well, Mom always went on about Hito, the academic awards, the track championships—"

Hito reached over and put a hand on Yori's arm, forcing her shifting gaze to land on him for a second. "Im, Mom fucking doted on you, hey? She called her best friends every day and talked about how smart you were, how talented."

Yori held his gaze and gave a slight nod, looked away. The waitress arrived with their food, ending the moment.

After they'd sorted out the food, Hito explained. "Our mom died when Yori was pretty young and Cormac had left—"

"Oh god, don't ruin dinner by mentioning Dad. She doesn't need to hear our sad orphan tale. Tell her about the insane yacht you boarded last year, the one with the helicopter and half the population of Russia onboard."

Ess wished she'd brought her notebook so she could try to sketch the connection between Hito and Yori. It was a tangible, living thing, sometimes tense and vibrating with resentment, other times gentle and glowing with love. Seeing it highlighted her solitude, but she didn't mind. She laughed as Hito told a ridiculous tale about a giant yacht that arrived in Nanaimo looking for a luxury hot-spring spa that didn't exist. She forgot about the empty parts inside for a moment.

—

Dinner lasted two hours, but the time blinked by. As Hito waved away Ess's cash to pay, Yori excused herself to make a call. Outside, Hito and Ess were reminded by a wall of sticky air that Nanaimo was still in the grip of a gross heat wave. The sun had set but there was no evening relief.

They found Yori opening the door of a cab. She waved. "I'm off to see some friends. Hito, you'll get Ess home, yeah? Good. Bye!"

Hito shook his head as the cab drove off. "Sorry. That's—that's typical, actually. Do you want to walk or cab?"

Ess thought of the cabin walls closing in on her, and her chest got tight. The feeling surprised her, that her boat wasn't where she wanted to be.

"Let's walk. I always prefer to walk," she said.

"Sounds good. Where's your dinghy tied up?"

"Public dock by the floatplane terminal."

They strolled side by side down the cracked sidewalk toward the city center, Hito setting a slow, easy pace. Ess brushed against him as she veered to avoid startling a pair of pigeons in her path.

She'd spent dinner enjoying herself and hadn't found any opportunities to steer the conversation to amnesia refugees and neurologists.

She hadn't wanted to spoil things. But now she was running out of time. "Hito, I've been thinking about the amnesia refugees you talked about before."

"Oh?"

"Do you know what happens to the cases that officials find?"

"They aren't telling us much about it, to be honest. They're all in custody, if that's your worry. Not good to have people wandering around who can't remember their own name, who could be here for any reason. Risky, right? There's a neurologist, a specialist who scans them to confirm the nature of the brain damage causing the amnesia. I assume they're also sorting out if their brains have been altered in other ways we don't understand that might make them dangerous. Who knows who they were before—war criminals, terrorists, people who put pineapple on pizza."

Ess's throat closed, preventing a response.

Hito continued. "They're keeping the cases in custody to do whatever medical testing is necessary to figure out what's going on. I imagine they'll keep doing that until they have answers. That's what I'd do."

An image of Hito flashed in Ess's mind—in his uniform and body armor, looming over her, exuding authority and power. His mirrored sunglasses hiding the softness in his eyes.

"Oh, no." Her voice broke and she coughed to hide it, struggled to regain her composure. Took a minute. "It must be so terrifying to have lost all sense of who you are, to have it all replaced with nothingness. To wake up every day and rediscover that you don't know who you are." She needed to shut up but couldn't. "They must feel so lost. How do they rebuild a life from there? Without memories, are they just lost forever?"

There was a long pause as they walked, the silence cutting deeper into Ess with every step. They automatically turned toward the waterfront, walking down a steeply sloped street. Eventually Hito replied. "I'll be honest. I hadn't given any thought to what they must be going through—"

Despite her efforts to suppress it, a shiver escaped. "I didn't mean to—"

Hito put a hand on her arm. "Don't apologize. I appreciate your ability to cut right to the heart of things. Working for Harbour Authority is turning me into an asshole, slower than some other people, I think, but still, I need to get out before the transformation is complete."

She forced herself to take a breath, to hide the fact that she was crumbling to pieces in front of him about people she shouldn't have any connection to.

"Is that what the NDRT interview is about?" she asked.

"Yeah." Hito sighed. "I want to help people, not fine them for bylaw infractions or for failure to renew a permit. You may be surprised to know that most of the boats that come to Nanaimo do not contain assassins such as yourself. It's more likely to be vacationing Americans who failed to get proper paperwork to be here. Usually they're older and they forgot the border is different now, that the rules have changed."

"You help people. I've experienced it."

"Last week I took a couple into custody. Two ladies in their seventies celebrating their twenty-fifth wedding anniversary, recreating their honeymoon trip by sailing here from Seattle. They hadn't been to Canada since that trip, forgot they needed visas, didn't stop in Sidney for customs, so they spent the day in custody and then got escorted back to American waters. Hard to see how detaining them helped anyone."

Ess didn't have an answer. "What would you do with NDRT?"

Even in the dark Ess could see Hito's slumped shoulders lift. "Get flown into the center of a disaster and try to pick up the pieces. Set up shelters, rescue people trapped in hazardous places, coordinate repair of damaged critical infrastructure. Get my hands dirty. Be useful."

Hito turned them off the main street onto a quieter, darker side street where chain-link fencing surrounded anonymous beige commercial properties. Down one side of the street a row of freshly planted saplings stood proud, water bags strapped around their bases. The scent of the ocean washed over them and Ess relaxed.

"I wouldn't have the guts to run toward a disaster."

"Disaster is part of life," Hito said. "Like storms. You do what you can to prepare, but you can't stop it happening."

They arrived at the dock. Side by side at the railing, they looked at Ess's small rubber dinghy tied up below but made no effort to go there.

"Thanks for dinner," Ess said. "I enjoyed meeting Yori. She's…"

"I'm dying to know how you're going to finish that sentence," he said after a pause, half smile in place.

"She is who she is. Doesn't pretend just to make others comfortable."

"She is who she is," he repeated. "Yes."

"She has problems."

He made an ambiguous head movement. "I think her drinking is a problem; she doesn't. She'd say she likes to have a good time. When she stays with me, she has to be clean. That's the rule. She's here now because she's got a gig she has to be sober for, but when that's done, I don't know. Usually she disappears, doesn't let me see that side of her life. Before the other day, I hadn't seen her for ninety-nine days." Hito paused as the engine of an electric floatplane roared over the water, climbing into the sky. "I try to help her, but she can't find her way out, or doesn't want to, or…"

Ess waited for him to emerge from his thoughts. The uniform that had alarmed her earlier was gone, replaced by a worried brother struggling to help his sister. Ess stared at the water and enjoyed being quietly in someone's company with nothing required of her, no risk of saying the wrong thing.

"Sorry," he said, returning. "Sorry. What I meant to say is thanks for joining us for dinner. Sorry for the oddball venue. It's Yori's thing. But it was great to have you. I want to hear more about your trip from Haida Gwaii; your description makes it seem like another world."

"It was a memorable trip," she said, glancing over at him. He smiled at her as though he got her joke, and she couldn't resist smiling back.

"I'm glad you sailed into Nanaimo on my shift, and sailed into a restricted zone."

"I'm glad you didn't arrest me."

"People tend not to let me take them out for fish and chips when I arrest them."

Ess wanted to make a witty reply, to make him laugh. She could feel the emptiness of her boat from here. Her home, her refuge, and her solitary confinement. Hito stared at the harbor with her, letting her be lost in her thoughts. If she closed her eyes, she still felt him next to her. He was solid and tangible, in sharp contrast to the ghost people she spent her time with on the boat, the idea of family and friends that might exist. He was a calm harbor she wanted to take shelter in.

"Do you want to go somewhere—"

"Yes." Ess turned her back to the water. "Yes. Let's go somewhere."

Hito laughed. "All right. I like the enthusiasm for an unknown destination."

19

THE AREA HITO TOOK THEM to was a hodgepodge of rusted and patched metal industrial buildings. He dropped the rental scooter in a designated spot and swiped his wrist comm over the control panel to finish their trip. They walked down the street and stopped in front of a building painted a vibrant patchwork of colors. A four-foot-tall metal dragon sat on a plinth just behind the chain-link gate, welded together from scrap metal and holding a blinking security camera in its mouth.

Ess pulled her shirt from her back and tried to generate some air flow, but it was hopeless.

Rain started to fall, hitting the metal roof of the building with a gentle patter that quickly escalated to an angry downpour. Hito tapped his wrist comm against the security panel and the gate clicked open. They jogged for the tiny awning over the front door, not really in a hurry for cover. A crack of thunder rolled in the distance. Ess could feel the air changing around her as the heat wave broke.

They stared at the water driving against the ground like they hadn't seen rain before, both grinning.

Ess shook her head, flinging off droplets of water. "What is this place?"

"It's an artist co-op. C'mon inside." He placed his hand on the small of her back.

Lights blinked on ahead of them as they moved through the

building. They passed through a central open space, half gallery, half shipping yard with crates piled in one corner. A giant canvas leaned against a wall next to a table holding a dozen oversize plaster heads.

Hito led them down a wide hallway toward the back of the building. They skirted a pile of smashed pottery. At the end of the corridor, he unlocked a door and stepped back, signaled for Ess to go in. Pale street light streamed in through the window that took up an entire wall of the little studio. Hito clicked on a floor lamp with a fringed shade.

A worktable, easels, and a shelf piled with canvases and other supplies were all shoved into the corner. A sofa huddled under a drop cloth by the window. Ess sat on it, falling back into its softness. Hito passed her a clean rag to dry off with as he sank into the sofa next to her.

She gestured at the easel. "You're a painter?"

"Me? No. I have no artistic talent. This is Yori's studio. Or it was. She hasn't used it in ten years. I keep it in the hope she'll come back to her painting. Usually I rent it out, but it's not being used now." He sighed. "I love the energy of all these artists making things from nothing."

"Why doesn't Yori paint anymore?"

Hito tipped his head to the side. "That is an excellent question. I wish I had a clear answer. She was a prodigy. I can't remember a time when she didn't draw or paint." He paused, lost in some memory. "Mom saw her talent, poured money into her lessons, pushed her, kept pushing her. By fifteen, Yori was getting significant exposure, multiple big galleries wanting to show her work, a steady flow of commissions. After Mom died, she changed. It became mechanical for her. Then one day she torched her career and walked away from it all. The pressure got to her, I think. She would say something like she simply had nothing more to say. Which is poetic as fuck and hard to argue with."

Ess sat up straight. "She—she did the painting in your apartment. That's Yori's!"

Hito smiled widely and nodded. Ess looked at him, her mouth open.

"Yeah."

Adjusting her mental image of Yori to incorporate this new information, Ess was quiet for a minute. "How many did she do before she walked away?"

"I have just the one at home. And the unfinished one here." He pointed to the canvas on the easel nearby. "There are eleven other big ones in private collections and a series of smaller paintings—maybe forty, all of those were sold to private collectors. I've been trying to buy one for years but they're hard to find."

"She doesn't have any?"

"No, thank god. She would burn them to ashes if she did. I'm sometimes worried about leaving her alone in the apartment with mine. I've made her swear in blood she won't touch it."

Ess sat back. "I'm jealous of people who have a craft. People who have spent years training and studying and developing a skill. I–I don't have anything like that. I feel like all the years it took to get to this point in my life, and I don't have any special thing to show for it."

"Well, you appear to have somehow survived in this world without letting it make you jaded or bitter or suspicious of people. That's incredible. Really incredible."

"Are you jaded and bitter?" Ess asked, surprised.

"Find me anyone who works in law enforcement who still holds any hope for mankind, and I will give you ten thousand dollars."

They listened to the rain on the window. Hito's words reminded Ess of Rene, and she wondered where she'd be now if she had sailed away with him.

"These amnesia refugees," Hito said suddenly. "That's the latest

LISA BRIDEAU

thing. We're supposed to hunt them, cuff them, take them into custody like they're criminals." He sighed. "All of Harbour Authority is on high alert, all the agents sniffing around hoping to find the next one like it's some kind of fox hunt."

The hair on Ess's arms stood up.

"Maybe they are criminals," he continued. "Maybe they're the victims. I don't know. I guess I want a job where it's clear who needs help."

He reached over and picked up her hand from the couch between them, paused, then intertwined their fingers. "The world is so complicated, but you manage to maintain an open, unguarded way of seeing things. I admire that. You're like an antidote to it all."

She studied their hands, all the unfamiliar fingers mixed together. The pressure of his palm on hers was comforting as long as she ignored what he'd just said, pushed away the image of the uniform he would put on in the morning to go hunting people like her.

Her mouth was dry and all she could picture was Hito in his mirrored sunglasses and body armor, hand on his Taser. Slowly pulling her hand away, she levered herself off the couch and walked to the other side of the studio, where an easel held Yori's unfinished painting. She needed Hito to get her closer to answers but didn't want to use him, manipulate him. Didn't want to be constantly on edge about passing for normal.

It had all been easier alone on *Sea Dragon* when her wants had been clear: find out what had happened, figure out how to be safe.

She squeezed her eyes shut, pulled in too many directions, wanting too many things.

He didn't make any noise, but she could feel him standing next to her. His cologne filled her head.

"Before I forget." Hito held out a data stick. "*Sea Dragon* history, as requested. I was in a hurry so didn't actually read it, but I hope it helps."

138

It took Ess a moment to register what the slender metal stick was and what it might lead her to. "This is very kind of you, Hito." She choked up at this willingness to help her.

When he rested a hand on her shoulder, she nearly collapsed into it.

"Hey." His voice bounced off the walls in the quiet room. "Hey. You okay?"

She tried to push away the ugly mess of conflicting feelings coiling around her, but it was like trying to put fog in a box. She wanted to fall into the comfort Hito offered, to be wrapped up in it. Leaning forward, she felt his arm tighten around her and they kissed. It felt like warm sunlight on an early spring day.

She remembered sinking in the water by T'aanuu weeks ago, thinking she should let go, let the current take her; this was a warmer version of that.

Hito touched her lightly with his fingertips, but his kisses felt like he'd been waiting a lifetime to do it, like he might not have another chance. The power of that attention focused so entirely on her made Ess's head swim.

He went to caress her arm and a shock of static electricity passed between them with an audible pop, causing them both to flinch in surprise. Ess pulled away and looked at her arm, thought of the jellyfish sting that had saved her last time she found herself sinking under. She remembered crawling onto the boat after almost drowning, determined that she would figure it out, that nothing—not even the ocean itself—would stop her. Then the memories flooded in, the hard weeks of sailing to get to Nanaimo to get answers, to get her life back.

And Hito the Harbour Authority agent, the amnesia refugee hunter, was he worth the risk?

"Oh no. Oh." She couldn't form any proper words. But she could will her legs to move, like she had before, not controlling them as much as thinking about moving in a certain direction and hoping they would find a way to make it happen. Backing toward the door, she stumbled over her bag. Hito stepped forward to help but she recovered, threw the bag over her shoulder, and crossed her arms, squeezing the data stick in her fist. He retracted his hand, put it in his pocket.

"I have to go." She wanted to say more but accidentally glanced at him, saw his expression of confusion—maybe tinged with suspicion—and knew there weren't any words to explain. She hurried out of the studio into the hallway, following it until she found a fire exit. Spilling into the night, she sucked in a breath, drawing it in deep and replacing the heat inside her with moist air. She walked for a bit, turned the corner, and leaned against the corrugated siding.

Realizing that running away was not a good way to pass as normal, she turned back, but the sound of dripping water on the metal roof above her faded and the sharp, metallic taste came. She spit, trying to get rid of the taste, as if that would prevent the seizure.

The spasm combined with a shiver when she came back. Goose bumps covered her wet skin. Her phone dinged and she finally had the presence of mind to take it from her pocket and look at it. Saw two missed calls from Hito and a new message.

> **Hito:** I've called a cab for you. It will be out front of the art building in a few minutes. Please take it, be safe.

She'd been out for almost five minutes. She pressed her forehead against the rusty metal siding as her body continued to shiver, and her brain forced her to imagine what might have happened if she'd had her seizure in front of Hito.

Turning to her phone, she typed *I'm sorry*, with shaking fingers, then deleted it for being so inadequate and pathetic and went to take the cab back to the safety of *Sea Dragon*.

20

THE SHRIEK OF SIRENS PIERCED the air. Ess jumped out of bed and scrambled to get on deck. It was late morning, but there was an eerie orange glow over the city, and the air was gritty. Two Harbour Authority boats emerged from the haze, speeding toward her. She wanted to hide or do something to look more innocent, but she froze. Hito must have realized what she was after she ran off last night. He'd pieced together her weirdness, finally. Can't risk having people with no memories walking around; they might be damaged, a risk to the public.

The boats slowed, their wake rippling, reaching out for Ess. They pulled up on either side of a small yacht that had tied up to the mooring buoy near *Sea Dragon* last night. The commotion played out only a few boat lengths away.

"Vessel *Paradise Found*, prepare to be boarded."

Two Harbour Authority officers in face masks boarded the motorboat while two officers stayed behind, rifles ready. Ess coughed and slid into her cabin, moving slowly and locking the door behind her. She watched events unfold through a porthole. It didn't take long before the officers reappeared with a man and woman, each in handcuffs. The woman spoke to the officer escorting her, but the officer shook her head and passed her into a waiting Harbour Authority boat.

Within minutes, it was over.

The HA boats were gone and the stillness in their wake was unsettling. Ess flicked on the weather report to break the silence. The monotone voice reported that the smoke choking Nanaimo was from new forest fires raging south of the city.

She checked her tablet for news, looking for mentions of what had just happened. Scrolling past the hazardous air quality warnings, announcements of clean air shelter locations, and the N95 face mask advisory, she scanned the news sites over and over. It took twenty minutes before news appeared, a perfunctory report of an American arrested by Nanaimo Harbour Authority for smuggling someone into Canada without proper visas. The article expressed some sympathy for the Americans, listing the most recent disasters and towns destroyed by extreme weather and associated infrastructure failures. Then it moved on to theories about where exactly the "illegal" person was from and how lucrative illegal transport across the border could be.

A wave of vertigo hit Ess. Had sneaking across a border been part of her process? Hito's scan of her ID hadn't gone smoothly. What if someone looked more closely?

She wiped grit from the corners of her eyes. She hadn't slept much. The memory of the previous night washed over her, leaving a trail of goose bumps. There Hito was. The scent of his cologne. The feeling of his fingertips on her arm.

She snapped back to her boat, shaking her head to will the memories away.

The problem was obvious. Hito had physical presence, and she was happy in his company. Content.

She needed to be realistic about the threat Agent Hito represented, no matter how much she enjoyed being with Off-Duty Hito. Picking up her tablet, she read details about what Nanaimo Harbour Authority did, and her stomach started to ache. Originally tasked with ensuring boats had appropriate permits and didn't illegally dump waste or violate marine laws, they'd started acting as backup to Canada Border Services a few years ago. It was a move to prepare for the increase in migrants arriving in Canadian waters that everyone expected. Thailand had formally announced plans to abandon most of Bangkok to rising waters. Indonesia had started the relocation of their capital from inundated and sinking Jakarta to East Kalimantan back in 2022 but their resettlement program, scaled to accommodate one million people, was failing under the strain of the estimated five million people fleeing floodwaters. Articles suggested it was only a matter of *when* smugglers would load desperate people onto rusty ships and try to get them to stable northern places, like Canada.

Ess closed the international news windows and sat back. Unclenched her jaw. Everything was bigger and worse than expected. Canada was expecting a tsunami of migrants to hit. A great humanitarian response was needed to answer the global pain being experienced, but the reports all talked about the tide turning another way. Resettlement of migrants in Canada was waning, and border security budgets were ballooning. The biggest rise in immigrants granted status was not refugees, but Americans who wanted to preemptively exit before trouble hit, people choosing to relocate instead of those who needed to because of desperate circumstances.

Harbour Authority was busy trying to separate credentialed vacationers from people slipping over the border with no intention of returning home. They had broad powers to take people into custody for suspected immigration violations. Ess shivered. If she'd been a hair weirder, or Hito a bit less nice… She didn't finish the thought.

Taking a deep breath that triggered a cough, Ess tilted her head back and stared at the orange sky outside. The air smelled of woodsmoke and ash. She had to shut the door on Hito. That's just how it was. It was too risky, and he was too distracting.

He'd mentioned a neurologist that the amnesia refugees were

being taken to for testing, for a scan that confirmed the amnesia. Ess would find the neurologist, without Hito, somehow. They'd know what was going on. Hito could just be a nice memory from this weird, temporary interlude when all other memories were gone.

She typed an inadequate message and held her finger over the Send button, hoping the universe would intervene and show her she didn't need to do this. But everything was quiet. She hit Send.

Hito, you've been so kind. Life is complicated right now, so I can't see you again. I'm sorry.

That done, Ess jammed the data stick into her tablet and loaded the files Hito had given her, silently pleading for just one reference to her name pre–memory wipe.

Two files. One for ownership history, one for registered ports of call.

The ownership file had two lines: Sarah Jane Song, who became the owner in May of this year, and the original owner, Kala Winter of Victoria, who had purchased the sailboat new twenty years earlier.

"Kala Winter." Ess tested the name for familiarity but, as always, there was nothing.

She opened the other file. It showed her arrival in Nanaimo four days ago, and before that, Sunrise Marina in Haida Gwaii. That was all her. She put her finger on the screen on the next entry—a June date in Sandspit, Haida Gwaii. That was before she'd woken up in this life. That was pre–memory wipe. The next entry was Nanaimo in May, just as Sam had said.

Sarah Song bought *Sea Dragon* in Victoria from Kala Winter and sailed her to Nanaimo for off-the-books upgrades. And then she'd gone to Haida Gwaii immediately.

She'd been operating under the freshly created Sarah Song identity while in Nanaimo in May. And she'd been in a hurry to sail to Haida Gwaii. Had she been running from something? Is that why she'd been operating under a fake identity? Or had she just tried to ghost, to sail off to a simpler life, and things had gone sideways?

Staring at the printed warning note that had been left for her, Ess tried to detect some personality in it—something that would give away the writer. But the words sat dully on the worn, wrinkled paper and revealed nothing.

Trying to reconcile the note with her going around using the Sarah Song identity before the memory wipe always tied Ess in knots. Ever since her first visit to Ballast, an ugly thought kept trying to crawl to the front of her brain. An idea that managed to make everything worse. Maybe all of this—the new ID, the memory wipe—wasn't coming from somewhere else. Maybe she'd done this to herself.

21

Ess HATED WAITING; ADD THAT to the list of personality quirks she'd discovered.

She'd messaged Kala Winter the day she'd found her name on the ownership records but it took Kala two days to reply. Ess spent those days in limbo, lying on deck in her N95 mask listening to reports of worsening forest fires and getting to know just how long twenty-four hours could take.

After scrubbing her spotless deck and inspecting all her sails, Ess ran out of things to do before the scheduled call with Kala. She was cleaning the storage compartment under her dinette seat when something banged on the side of the boat. Ignoring it wasn't making it go away, so Ess put on her face mask and went out in the haze to investigate. On her port side, she found a rubber dinghy bobbing in the water. Yori sat in it, pounding on the sailboat with her fist.

Seeing Ess, she pushed her mask down, let it hang around her neck. "Oh, thank god. Help me over. I hate boats."

Ess helped Yori tie up and climb onboard. Yori's knuckles were white by the time she peeled her fingers off the lifeline, slouching on a seat at the back of *Sea Dragon*.

She coughed. "I have a killer headache from this gross wildfire smoke and I hate boats."

Ess adjusted her face mask and wondered if she was supposed to reply to this.

Yori studied Ess, her eyes squinting. "Okay, I've things to discuss and they're face-to-face things, hence my voyage here in a dinghy of questionable quality from my friend Joe, who just loaned it to me instead of captaining me here like a true friend would have done. Can we go inside? Do you have an air filter going?"

Following Yori inside, Ess automatically scanned the cabin looking for things that might give her away. She picked up her library book, *The Self Illusion*, and hid it next to the sailing manuals on her shelf. Then she forced herself to stop. There was no way to discern her brokenness by looking at *Sea Dragon*.

Flopping on the bench, Yori yanked her mask over her head and threw it on the table. "Well, a bit more breathable in here, yeah?" She coughed.

Ess took off her mask and was about to offer tea.

"Right. So, what the fuck happened with you and Hito? He was all hot for you and talking about you and being weirdly upbeat, and now I'm not allowed to even say your name and he's stress exercising, which is exhausting to watch."

Running a hand over her face, Ess thought about how to answer. Yori waited, her leg bouncing.

"I don't want to create trouble between you and Hito," Ess said.

"What?"

"I can't see him. He can't know why. If I tell you, you'll either tell him or be forced to have secrets from him," Ess said.

"But you'd tell me otherwise?"

Ess nodded.

"Why?" Eyes narrowed, Yori leaned back.

"You, I think, take weird stuff in stride. It doesn't upset your worldview."

Yori shrugged. "Weird doesn't faze me. If anything, normal freaks me out. That's why I can't stay with Hito for more than a few weeks."

"Hito wants to do the right thing. Needs to, I think."

The whir of Ess's tiny air-filtration unit filled the cabin while Yori digested that.

"Yeah. I get it. You don't want to drag him into a place of grayness when his world is delightfully black and white. Good guys, bad guys. Honest people, liars." Slipping gum into her mouth, Yori chewed for a few seconds before continuing. "If you want to tell me something, I can keep it from him. That's not a problem. You've made me curious as shit, but you do you. I don't have to know."

She picked up a tiny puzzle piece from the table. "Should I ask?"

The puzzle was a half-complete image of an elephant in a lush green jungle. "I got it from the secondhand store by the library. To pass the time."

Yori tried the piece in a few spots before tossing it on the table. "You know a used puzzle is going to be missing pieces, right?"

"Still worth putting it together, I think," Ess said, her voice barely audible.

Yori crossed her arms. "I don't know what went sideways between you and Hito, but look, I'm sorry I interrupted your first date the way I did at his apartment. I know I was a total mood killer and not at my best. Don't judge Hito based on me, yeah? He's got his shit together more than anyone I know. He's a good guy, deserves good things. Sometimes I fuck it up for him. This is me trying to unfuck it."

Ess didn't understand why Yori was saying this, but she was waiting for a response so Ess hazarded a nod.

"Okay. Good. That's sorted."

Yori stood suddenly and Ess leaned back, expecting her to vomit.

"Glad we had this chat." Yori started to move toward the stairs, then turned back to Ess, then to the stairs again. She sighed. "So, I also came to ask for a favor."

"Oh?"

Yori turned and lifted her chin, meeting Ess's eyes. "I need to hide someone here tonight. Just one night. She'll arrive late and be taken away early tomorrow. You'll barely notice her."

"I don't understand."

"I help out, finding temporary way stations for people who are running from bad things. The best places are ones unconnected to anyone, places no one would think to check." She gestured at *Sea Dragon*. "Seriously, it'll just be one night, eight, ten hours of your life, max."

"She's in trouble."

"Yeah."

"Do you know what from?"

"Yeah, her husband." Yori's words were clipped and vibrated with anger.

Ess nodded.

"Is that... Are you saying yes?"

"Yes." Ess didn't let herself overthink it.

"Huh. I'll be honest. I didn't think you'd do it. Almost didn't ask."

"Oh." Ess didn't know what to say.

"Anyway, okay, I'll message you details tonight. At some point a boat will show up, drop her off. Then another will pick her up in the morning."

"Okay." Ess passed Yori her tablet so she could transfer contact info. "Do you do this a lot?"

Yori shrugged, fingers swiping on her wrist screen, her easy manner back. "I have a thing for underdogs." She handed Ess her tablet and moved toward the stairs. "I gotta go, gotta get to land and someplace with clean air before I hurl."

Ess helped Yori into her small dinghy, where she took two wobbly steps before grabbing the side and positioning herself on the seat by the electric motor. Putting her mask on, she saluted. "Goodbye, Captain."

Saluting back, Ess watched Yori motor off until she couldn't see her through the haze and traffic in the harbor. Yori, she suspected, had no small number of secrets from Hito.

—

At exactly the scheduled time, Ess pressed the connect button. She ran a hand through her hair and straightened her shirt, waiting for Kala to join the meetup.

The meetup window expanded. Kala's curly silver hair filled the frame, and a smile lit her face as if Ess was an old friend. "Hi, you must be Sarah!" Kala's singsong voice shattered the quiet.

Kala didn't know her. Ess resisted the urge to exit the meeting and throw her tablet into the ocean. "Yes, hi."

"How's *Sea Dragon*? Treating you well, I hope."

"She's great. She's home." Ess forced a smile. "Feels like I've never known another."

"I'm glad to hear it. She was in storage with me. It's good she's on the water full time again. Your message said you had some questions about the sale of *Sea Dragon*?"

"Yeah. I've lost some of my files to a virus and I'm trying to track down info from the past few months. My memory is terrible, and there was just a lot going on then. Do you remember the details of selling her?"

Kala looked skeptical but maintained a tight smile. "Happy to help fill in any blanks. I'll be honest; it worried me when you sent your representative to check her out. That was strange for me, dealing with someone's representative. But it all went smoothly in the end. Do you need me to find my copies of the paperwork?"

Ess shivered and reached for her sweater. "Copies would be helpful. Can you describe the guy I sent? I had a few scouts out."

"Hang on, let me find my files. What was his name? Bob? Bob, ah, I'm forgetting his last name. Something Scottish or Irish. O'something. He was very professional. Not a chatty, friendly guy, kept to himself."

Pulling the sweater tightly around herself, Ess sat forward. "What did he look like?"

Kala glanced at the ceiling, a motion Ess noticed people did when trying to access specific memories. "Oh, average guy. Nothing noteworthy. Medium height, in good shape. Brown hair. White. Pretty pale actually. But he knew how to sail, took *Dragon* through her paces."

"Did you have contact details for him?" Ess asked.

"Yes, but it stopped working. I realized after he had the boat hauled off that I'd forgotten to install the new life preserver I had in my garage. I tried contacting both of you but the messages bounced back. Seemed weird. I worried the payment was going to bounce and the whole thing had been a scam. But the money stayed in my bank account, thank goodness."

Kala looked off-screen again. "Ah, here we go. An old message from you, 'My representative, Bob McDonald—sorry, no O after all—will be in Victoria on Friday at 8:00 a.m. to take the boat for a test sail if that's compatible with your schedule.'"

This man in the shadows had a name. Ess did her best to be cordial while ending the call quickly. She should have been happy, but she couldn't shake the feeling that she had played her big card and won a booby prize.

—

A speedboat operated by a woman with long red hair and thick biceps arrived at ten with a single passenger. Ess helped an older woman onboard. Ess's guest stayed on deck until the speedboat disappeared, her mask dangling around her neck while she coughed and surveyed her new surroundings.

She came inside eventually, stepping lightly as if she hoped she could erase her own presence. Handing her a mug of tea and some cookies, Ess converted the dining area into a bunk, showed her the bathroom facilities and food supplies. The woman nodded at everything Ess said, murmured words of appreciation, but seemed to be operating on autopilot, like she was fully occupied trying to process how she had come to this place in her life.

Seeing this woman, so broken and lost, felt like too much of a mirror. Ess gave her a blanket she wouldn't need in the summer heat and said good night, shutting the thin wooden door between them. Ess listened to her guest sighing and ruminated on running away, how many varied reasons there were for doing it, how it was easy for some people, how it took a great deal of courage for others. Eventually, Ess heard light snoring and felt gratified the woman had found enough peace to fall asleep.

Unable to sleep herself, Ess switched on the weather report, volume low. The monotone voice whispered about the two-hundred-acre wildfire that had triggered the closure of the Nanaimo airport as crews struggled to establish a control line around it. Air quality in the region was a ten on the ten-point scale and considered hazardous.

Turning that off, Ess closed her eyes, pretended she was back in Haida Gwaii breathing in the crisp pine-scented air, thought about how little she'd appreciated it while surrounded by it.

Restless and unsettled, she picked up her latest library book and tried reading. She'd moved on from medical books about memory impairment to more philosophical texts, wanting reassurance of another kind. She opened her notebook, forced herself to be detached and clinical, and started making notes.

Self: an illusion the brain uses to process, organize, and interpret the world based on past experiences.

Sense of self is both an illusion created by neural circuits and real as far as the brain is concerned. It satisfies the pattern-seeking structures of the brain. It creates order.

Self provides a focal point to hang experiences together in the here and now and to join those events together over a lifetime. Experiences are fragmented episodes unless woven together in a meaningful narrative. The self pulls it all together.

Episodic memories, particularly autobiographical memories, are crucial for constructing the self story. Without these memories, there is no self.

22

"I CAN'T BELIEVE YOU MADE me come here," Yori said, towering over Ess, her body vibrating with tension.

Ess stood and stretched, stiff from sitting on the floor of the artist co-op atrium for an hour. Yori was late, but Ess was relieved that she'd shown up at all. After Yori's guest had been collected from *Sea Dragon*, Ess had messaged her, insisting they meet in person the next day.

"We needed somewhere private to talk, someplace on land so you don't vomit."

"Yeah, well, this place, it's—" A group of artists came out of another work space, laughing. Yori turned away, her shoulders hunched as they passed. "Whatever." She fussed with unlocking the studio door, hands shaking.

Ess hovered at the door as Yori went in.

Strong winds from the Pacific Ocean had pushed the wildfire smoke off Nanaimo, bringing back blue skies and clean air. Bright, clear light spilled in the big window and bounced off the studio's white walls, making Ess squint. The unfinished canvas sat on the easel where Hito had left it. Yori stopped in front of it, arms crossed, and it suddenly occurred to Ess that bringing Yori to her artwork might have been a mistake.

Without taking her eyes off the canvas, Yori grabbed a tube of old paint from the table, unscrewing the cap with her teeth and spitting it out. She squirted green pigment over the canvas with such violence that it splattered on the wall behind like a spray of algae. She threw the empty tube, a growl building in her throat. Ess stepped forward, thinking she should intervene, then froze, thinking she should stay out of it.

Yori grabbed a palette knife and scratched and stabbed at the canvas, shouting and swearing. The canvas tore and the knife slipped from her hands, everything slick with paint. She attacked the canvas with her hands, yanking it off the easel and throwing it against the wall, slipping and falling to the floor, making no effort to cushion her landing.

Crumpled on the floor, she wrapped her arms around her legs and cried. Ess joined her, put an arm around her. She expected to be pushed away but wasn't. Yori's ragged intakes of air punctuated the quiet of the studio. When her bony shoulders stopped shaking in Ess's arms, Ess let go and found a clean cloth for her to blow her nose with. Yori inhaled and exhaled normally once, then again. She sat with her head on her knees like a child sent to the corner.

"I was painting that for Hito," Yori said, her voice wavering.

Ess looked at the canvas carnage on the floor. "Why did you stop?"

"I choked. I broke...."

Yori's breath caught. She lifted her head, dragged the rag under her nose, and tossed it aside. When she spoke again, her voice wasn't full of hurt anymore. It was sharp with anger.

"I was a kid and my mom died. I didn't know how to exist without her."

Ess reached over and wiped a splotch of paint off Yori's arm while she waited for her to continue.

Yori scrubbed her hand roughly but there was no way to get clean. "I tried to produce as much as I could after she died. We needed to pay the mortgage on the apartment. For two years, I painted and painted.

But I was empty. I was a human-shaped shell around a void. The gallery harassed me about deadlines and taking on more. More. More. More. I had a recurring nightmare where I was a vending machine. I snapped. Told the gallery to fuck off and I came here every day for months trying to paint that for Hito, to do something for us to see if it would fix me. But that damn canvas never got any further. I thought I destroyed it—drowned myself and it in a few liters of vodka and set it on fire."

"Hito said he had it in storage."

"Of course he did." She picked at the scab on her thigh. "My memory of those days is admittedly fuzzy. I know he went through my room looking for sketches, trying to save them before I could get at them."

"He told me you destroyed everything you could get your hands on."

"Fuck, yes. I wanted it all gone. All the reminders. I didn't *want* to stop. I just couldn't do it anymore. I was as surprised as anyone. It wrecked me, being amputated like that, left without my..." She waved her hand, unable to find the word. "Without a way to get my thoughts out. Hito couldn't understand. Fuck, he loved my art so much, I had to take his loss on top of my own."

"What did you do?"

"I got away in every way I could think of. Got drunk and high and avoided Hito and the gallery and anyone who expected anything of me other than a good time. Ended up crashing in a sty of a house full of people who didn't know anything about me, didn't care. Didn't have any expectations of me. It took a lot of alcohol to drown out Mom's voice telling me to live up to my potential, to stop squandering my talent. A year later I landed in the hospital with alcohol poisoning and they called Hito as my emergency contact. I was living on Doritos and questionable onigiri from the Asian grocery on Terminal Avenue. He took me home, got me kind of functional, and then I took off again. Found I didn't quite fit in his neat life anymore. Don't fit. I've been some variety of a mess ever since. All I knew was painting, art. I'm no good for anything else."

"Bullshit."

Yori lifted her eyes to Ess, her expression dark, voice brittle. "Yeah, you know something about this? About losing the thing that defines you, your very identity?"

Ess laughed, tried to stop. Only laughed harder. She gripped Yori's arm to prevent her from standing and stalking out.

"Don't go. Just—" Struggling, Ess calmed the laughter and wiped her watering eyes. "That's why I wanted to meet you, to tell you. I wasn't trying to ambush you about your art. I didn't know this place was so complicated. I'm sorry. Really."

She met Yori's gaze, waiting for confirmation that Yori would stay, wouldn't punch her in the face.

Yori nodded, lips tight. "Better be good. I don't have a lot of fucks to give right now."

"Okay." Ess took a deep breath, all mirth gone. "This is going to sound like something I've made up, but it's the truth." Ess studied her hands, green paint settling into her pores. "You won't tell Hito?"

Yori bobbed her head slightly. It wasn't a particularly reassuring vow of secrecy but the words were already pressing against Ess's lips. "I woke up on my sailboat in Haida Gwaii a month ago. I have no memories from before that." The rest spilled out. Headaches and pills. Sarah Jane Song. The note. The tracking device as a sign she was exposed and in danger. Deciding to find answers. Sailing and almost drowning.

"This is the thing I can't tell Hito. No one else knows. Well, some random guy in a pub in Haida Gwaii knows. And now you." Ess paused, feeling empty and vulnerable. She thought she'd feel lighter.

"Amnesia refugees," Yori said.

This time Ess bobbed her head vaguely. "Same but different," Ess said, watching Yori's face for disbelief or disgust. "I'm trying to figure out the connection."

"Holy shit, Ess. I need a drink." She looked at Ess and narrowed her eyes. "Why are you telling *me* this?"

"Because I'm going crazy. Because I'm scared and I don't want to do this alone. And because Hito's link to these other amnesia cases is the only hope I have of finding out what was done to me."

Yori wiped at the paint on her arm, then threw the rag on the floor. "Were you hooking up with my brother just to use him?"

Ess flinched at the sharp words. "No."

"Why didn't you just tell him?"

"He's Harbour Authority, and they're basically hunting amnesia refugees. He said if he came across one, he'd lock them up, let the doctors do their tests and sort it out."

Yori groaned. "Yeah, okay, fair. But the way he talks about you, I promise he's not looking to put you in a cell. Handcuffs, maybe, but fuzzy ones."

"Hito doesn't seem like he has different rules for friends and strangers. Locking people like me up is the right thing. It's his job. Black and white, right?" She waited for Yori to disagree. She didn't. "I can't risk it. I need *your* help. Please."

"I've met a lot of people in trouble. They usually make big promises when they ask for help."

Ess held her hands wide. "What should I offer?"

Yori shook her head and stood. "No, I mean, the fact that you aren't offering me bullshit makes me inclined to trust you." She extended a hand and pulled Ess off the floor. "What's your plan?"

They stood facing each other, Yori's attention focused on Ess, her fidgeting quieted.

"Hito mentioned a neurologist that they take all the amnesia refugees to for testing, to confirm they're the real deal. I want to find the neurologist, find out if I'm the same as the others."

"You think you might be different?"

"I don't know. They were found with nothing, in stolen boats. I have a bank account, ID, a boat in my name. A note that hints at what was done to me. But the amnesia seems the same, based on the descriptions. Unnatural. Impossible."

Yori didn't look convinced but she nodded. "Okay. I can ask Hito, try to get him to say more about what they do with amnesia refugees they find, where they take them, who they see." She crossed the room, pulled a bottle off the shelf of art supplies and wet a rag. A sharp citrus fragrance filled the room.

"That won't seem weird, you asking about it?"

"Everything I do is weird to Hito." She held the rag against her paint-stained hand, wiping gently. "Besides, I intend to employ subtlety here so he doesn't catch on."

This time Ess failed to look convinced.

"Hey, don't look so forlorn. Hopeless projects are my jam." Tossing the rag aside, Yori clapped. "Oh! I have a genius idea! I know a faster way to get answers that won't make Hito suspicious at all." She looked at her watch. "But we have to do it now."

⌣

When they exited the elevator on the fifth floor, Ess turned left instead of right. Pressing her back against the wall by the elevator, she shook her head.

"I'm allowed to have guests you know; I own half the apartment." Ess shook her head again.

"He's at boxing, I promise. He never misses it. Look, I'll go confirm." Without waiting for a response, Yori turned the corner and Ess heard the chirp of her fob opening the door. Shifting her messenger bag on her shoulder, Ess tried to relax while the minutes passed.

Finally, a door creaked open down the hall, and Ess peeled herself off the wall. She was about to turn the corner when she heard Hito's voice and froze.

"I'm late. Can you run the dishwasher for once, Yori?"

Ess didn't hear the reply. Her ears were ringing as blood rushed to her head. She pressed the elevator call button eight times. Turning in a circle, she confirmed there was nowhere to hide. She pressed the elevator button twice more, knowing Hito was about to come around the corner and fix his stern, questioning gaze on her.

Instead, she heard another door open and slam shut. He'd taken the stairs. The elevator dinged, the doors sliding open and offering an unneeded sanctuary.

The door to Unit 502 popped open as she approached.

"Did he see you?" Yori asked.

"No."

"Lucky. He'll be gone for an hour, so we're good. Come in; I'll show you my brain wave."

Yori wrapped a warm hand around Ess's wrist and pulled her to the apartment control screen. She tapped it, but it would only display a log-on screen.

"Biometric log-on," she said to Ess, who was taking off her shoes. "Old system. It broke years ago and now only holds one profile of bio data in memory. Which is obviously Hito's since I'm a bit inconsistent in my residence here. I can't, like, change the lighting schedule or use the network or other basic stuff. So, he created a work-around for me."

Yori put her hand out and slowly uncurled her fingers, revealing a life-size blue plastic thumb. With a grin, she pressed it against the sensor, and the control panel recognized her as Hito and gave her access to the full menu.

Ess nodded but didn't follow how this was helpful.

"Hang on, we haven't hit the brilliant part yet."

Hurrying into the living room, Yori looked around, went to a black duffel bag on the ottoman and rummaged around in it. She raised an eyebrow at Ess as she pulled out Hito's Harbour Authority wrist comm. Ess backed up several steps.

"What are you—"

"Just going to look at some files and find the neurologist name you're after. It's probably not even sensitive information, barely breaks any rules." Yori extended the comm display screen and pressed the blue finger against the sensor. She tapped in a code and raised her arm in a fist pump. "Hito has used the same pass code since my days sneaking into the HA boathouse."

"Yori, don't—"

"It's fine." Yori quickly tapped the screen, scrolled, searching. "No one will ever know. I'm just looking."

Ess stayed in the hallway as if that made her less complicit. She looked over her shoulder at the door, worried Hito would walk in and arrest them both.

"Aha! Score! So easy. Dr. Saravanamuttoo." Yori spoke to her wrist comm, had it record the name.

Ess held her breath, waiting for Yori to put the Harbour Authority equipment away so it couldn't harm anyone. It felt like watching someone play with a bomb.

"Oh, gross." Yori froze her scrolling.

"What?" Ess stepped into the living room.

"An all-agent bulletin from last week. Instructions to continue to be on alert for people with severe memory problems, most likely exhibiting confusion and panic and lacking identification. Concern there are more cases that have escaped detection. Blah, blah, procedures. Blah, blah, duty, security. Immediate detainment of any suspected cases followed by transport under guard to Nanaimo General Hospital for testing. Federal task force assembled to investigate. Media blackout." She paused. "They are very serious about this."

Now standing by Yori's side, Ess read over her shoulder. She knew Hito had these orders, but reading them stated so plainly was chilling.

Yori closed the bulletin, resumed scrolling, but Ess was done. She went into the kitchen, put a mug with Yori's lipstick on the rim into the dishwasher, and started the clean cycle. She wiped the counter despite it being already immaculate. Rinsed the cloth and hung it from a hook.

Yori leaned in the doorway. "Why're you upset? We got the info; we're golden."

Ess took a breath, straightened the cloth imperceptibly. "Reading bulletins instructing agents to treat the amnesia refugees like hostile criminals, instructing agents to hunt them down... I just—" Ess couldn't finish.

"Okay, fair, that is a lot." Striding into the kitchen, Yori opened a cupboard filled with boxes of Pop Tarts and studied them. "You know, Hito doesn't even eat these. But there's always a million of them here. Like he's trying to summon me with the gravitational weight of Pop Tarts." She picked a box. "You know what pisses me off about the amnesia refugee thing?"

Ess shrugged.

"I don't think they're refugees. It's bullshit that they're using that word. I think they're people jumping the queue."

"What queue?"

Reaching across the counter, Yori fanned out a stack of flyers for a protest against proposed new restrictive immigration policies. "Compared to a lot of the world, we live like kings. Abundant clean water, universal health care, we did a decent job switching to clean power if you ignore Saskatchewan. We have poutine."

Ess leaned against the counter, sensing Yori was launching into something.

"We also have all these rules about who gets to come here. A fixed number of immigrant spots, fixed number of refugee claims we allow each year. Don't want to overwhelm our systems, you understand." Yori's tone dripped with faux-earnest patronizing concern.

"Okay, so?" The familiar pressure of a headache settled into Ess's left temple.

"So," Yori gestured in frustration. "All these people who see the crumbling infrastructure around them and realize climate change is real despite all the effort to deny it, and they finally realize it's going to get extremely shitty. Maybe it's already gotten shitty for them. So, they look up and see Canada and think, 'Hey, that's a good fallback position.' But they're forty-five or fifty and there are literally a million younger people applying, with higher scores on the immigration point system, beating them out because everyone else has also realized that in a world of rising temperatures, Canada is going to be maybe livable for longer. These people have resources, they're motivated, and they know the regular immigration pathway is never going to work for them. I think this is their alternate route. Americans, others who come through via the States." Stacking the protest flyers into a neat pile, Yori flipped them facedown.

Ess took a second to digest this. She hadn't given much thought to who the other amnesia cases were, just that their situation might help her understand hers. "But all the amnesia refugees are being detained. It's not a free pass into the country and a new life. It's a trip straight to custody and immigration limbo, isn't it?"

Yori raised an eyebrow, spoke slowly. "All the amnesia refugees the border service people *have caught* are in custody."

For some reason, that made Ess's guts twist. That there might be more cases, who knew how many more. She shook her head.

"You think people would wipe their memory for a chance at skirting immigration processes?"

Yori shrugged. Tearing the metallic wrapping off two pastries, she put them in the toaster. "Most people, no. But I think there are those who would." Yori ran a hand down her hair, smoothing tangles, lost in thought for a second. "Hito thinks they're just signing up for the smuggling and the memory wipe is a surprise. But he underestimates people's desire to get away from pasts that torture them."

Yori's words reminded Ess of Rene's "fresh start" silver lining. People seemed to focus on being free of bad memories, never on the pain of losing the good ones, or losing all sense of self, or losing any understanding of how they fit into the world. "Why does this make you pissed off about amnesia refugees?"

"Because. It begs the question: Is an actual refugee, fleeing persecution or disaster, missing out on their chance to come here now because these amnesia folks are taking space?" She suddenly sounded worn out, like she'd been having this argument with people for years. "Climate disasters have multiplied the global refugee crisis tenfold, as everyone fucking told us it would for the past twenty fucking years." Yori took a breath. "We should be resettling loads more refugees but somehow don't have capacity or some bullshit. There are island nations completely underwater now. I don't understand why we aren't offering to resettle *those* people, people who have lost everything because of us, because *we* were carbon pigs, because *we* dug out the tar sands. We should be prioritizing based on need."

When she was done, Yori sighed deeply, her hands crumpling the crinkly pastry wrapper.

"So why help me?" Ess asked quietly. "If I'm one of these people who jumped the queue."

Yori let the wrapper go, watched it flutter to the counter. "Well, first, I'm not Hito. I don't think things are that black and white.

Second, you helped me when I asked." She paused. "Also, maybe I sympathize with people who feel like they don't fit in. Being Japanese-Irish in Nanaimo does that."

Yori and Ess locked eyes, each trying to understand the other. Eventually the toaster popped and Ess flinched. Yori dropped the browned pastries onto plates and slid one over.

"You're different, Ess. Somehow. I mean, I'm only five minutes into your shit, so hardly an expert, but your story isn't the same as the other amnesia weirdos. Notably, you've got an ID and aren't clogging up the immigration system."

Ess looked at the pastry covered in hard pink icing, intending to ask Yori to elaborate. Instead, the hum of the dishwasher faded and the metallic taste of copper filled her mouth. She had enough time to wonder when Hito was due to return and then she felt the full-body spasm ripple through. Her arm jerked and knocked the plate off the counter, sending it crashing, uneaten pastry jumbling with shards of white ceramic on Hito's floor.

"Oh my god. Ess. What the fuck is going on?" Yori was next to her, a hand squeezing her shoulder. Her perfectly shaped eyebrows were raised, eyes wide.

"How long was I…" Ess shivered, folded her arms in against her body.

"Forever. You just wouldn't respond. Like, for minutes. You freaked me the fuck out. What—"

The panel buzzed. Yori's head jerked like she'd been shocked. She went to the hall.

"Yeah?"

"Im, buzz me in, please. My fob is buried in my bag."

Yori turned to Ess and waved her arm in a big circle at the door. "Stairs. They'll dump you out the side exit," she said, shoving Hito's comm back in his duffel bag. "I'll stall him. Go!"

Ess ran past Yori, crammed her shoes on, and left. The fire door clanged shut behind her and her feet pounded down the concrete stairs. She hoped Yori would give her enough time.

23

Ess walked from Hito's place to the public dock, needing physical activity to dissipate the tension vibrating through her. Stopping for a moment under a tree in a little park squeezed in between buildings, she took a breath, savoring the clean air and the ability to draw it in deep. While blanketed in forest-fire smoke, she'd missed deep cleansing breaths, had missed the smell of living trees.

Calmer, she continued on, keen to get home and find out what she could about Dr. Saravanamuttoo.

At the dock, she struggled to untie her little dinghy, had to pause to shake out her hands. Her joints were always stiff after an episode. She squinted into the thick fog rolling into the harbor, trying to make out *Sea Dragon* among the sea of bobbing lights but couldn't. Once underway, she kept the engine on low, alert for obstacles and other boats. A foghorn blasted from a ship by the port.

Navigating around the boats she recognized as her neighbors, she approached *Sea Dragon*. Her hand slipped off the motor and she half stood, rocking her dinghy. A figure stood under the canopy by the cabin door on *Sea Dragon*.

Blood rushed to her head. Her dinghy veered in the wrong direction. She twisted to watch the figure on her boat. Someone was meddling with *her* boat. She yelled before she could think better of it. "Hey!"

The figure jerked. As she got her dinghy oriented the right way, the shadow leaped into their own motorboat and took off.

Ess cranked her motor, the electric whine reaching an urgent pitch. The other boat sped away, weaving between boats attached to mooring buoys. Torn between chasing them and checking on *Sea Dragon*, she froze with indecision, and then it was too late. The intruder's boat was swallowed by fog. Ess tied up, went to her cabin door.

Locked.

She dropped onto the bench and exhaled a long breath. Something on the boat creaked and she jumped, scanning for a threat. The neighboring boats were all quiet. Even the water was still.

Quickly checking the exterior control panel for damage, she made sure her hydrogen tank was still in place before she allowed herself to slip inside, like a kid hiding under blankets for safety. Shutting the door behind her, she ran a hand along the wooden table.

Digging out her tablet, annoyed by her shaking hand, she called Yori, who answered sounding groggy.

"Yori. It's Ess."

"Uh-huh, yes. I know it's you," she grunted. "Why are you calling? I just started an excellent nap."

"Sorry. I just… There was a guy on my boat, and I don't know what to do."

"Like, you've replaced Hito with a new guy, and you need me to walk you through seduction tips?"

"No. No! Someone was here—tried to break into my boat. I chased him off." Ess couldn't bring herself to voice her real fear. That she'd been found.

"Oh. That's a much less interesting man-on-boat scenario. Okay. I just woke up. What was the question? Right, are you safe. Well, welcome to Nanaimo. We've got high unemployment and expensive housing, so there are desperate folks around. Did he get your stuff? You don't own anything, so he couldn't have gotten much."

Ess checked the cabinet where she kept her cash, rummaged through drawers to reassure herself everything was still there. "He didn't take anything." In the cabinet where she kept her notebook, she paused. The notebook was tucked under the envelope with her boat operator's license. She always put the notebook on top. Extracting it, she flipped to the note, ran her finger along the crinkled paper.

"Well, lucky you. And you're sure you're alone?"

Ess peeked into the sleeping cabin and the bathroom and exhaled. She pressed her forehead against the doorframe. "I'm alone."

"Cool. You can call Harbour Authority if you want, file a report. Or you could ask Hito to arrange some patrols."

"No, definitely no patrols."

"Right. Right, HA bad. Well, maybe move to a marina with some security? Oh, I have a friend who runs his family's marina. I'll send you his info. He's a weird dude. You two will get on like paper and glue."

"Thanks. Sorry to bother you."

"Uh-huh. Are we going to talk about your frozen-statue thing?"

"Not now."

"Okay. I'm going back to sleep then."

Yori disconnected and left Ess alone in the cabin. A boat passed and she turned her head, following the sound until it moved off. Her eyes landed on the marks on the wall where the tracking box had been mounted. She locked the cabin door and searched for something to barricade it further.

———

Ess sat bolt upright in bed, clutching the blanket like a shield. Her ears strained to detect a repeat of the noise she thought she'd heard— someone tapping on the cabin door. All she could hear now were seagulls squawking overhead, but she pictured a figure skulking on deck, looking for a way in.

Her tablet dinged, the sound bouncing off the cabin walls. Catching a glimpse of herself in the mirror, huddled under a sheet in fear, Ess hung her head and got out of bed. She slipped into her boat shoes, grabbed the screwdriver from under her pillow, and went into the main cabin to check the door. Secure. With only a slight hesitation, she unlocked it and yanked it open. The morning sun fell across her, but nothing else. On deck she turned in a circle, confirmed she was totally alone. It was just her brain trying to do her in.

Tossing the screwdriver on the table inside, she picked up her tablet and saw Yori's message:

Joe the Philosopher. Escape Marina. Tell him I say Aristotle was a bitch and remind him he owes me a jar of pickles.

Ess immediately abandoned her mooring buoy and motored up Newcastle Passage, past the posh Nanaimo Yacht Club to a simple two-prong dock with a third of its berths occupied by a ragtag collection of boats, some of which looked a few months away from a trip to the bottom of the ocean. She tied up at an open berth, noted the hefty gate with barbed-wire fencing at the entrance, and went down the dock to see what it would cost to stay.

The office was a modular building with a greenhouse made of salvaged materials perched on the roof. A large dog lying in front of the office door got to its feet as Ess approached, ears alert, head tilted. Ess slowed, watching it, letting it pick up her scent. She was some kind of German shepherd mix, all muscle and fur and ears.

When Ess was within arm's length, the dog barked once, sharply, loudly. A warning.

Ess stopped and the dog moved toward her. She lifted her hand instinctively, her palm flat. "Sit!" Her voice was clear and commanding. The dog sat immediately.

They stared at each other, both rather surprised.

Ess pushed her hand down, palm flat. The dog lay down.

"Huh. I'm impressed."

Turning away from the dog, Ess saw a man descending the ladder on the side of the building. He was a young Indian guy with dark skin and thick hair that flopped into his eyes when he nodded at the dog.

"Leeloo isn't usually so quick to obey strangers."

Ess avoided looking at the dog and thinking about what it meant that she could command it. She tucked that away for later. "Are you Joe?"

"Yeah. You're looking to dock for a while?" He didn't look particularly excited at the idea, glancing up at the greenhouse. He wore a personal flotation device, a compact thing around the waist that would inflate automatically in water.

"I had a break-in on my boat moored over at Saysutshun Island. Looking for some place more secure."

His hair flopped over his eye and he pushed it aside. "We've got a gate, cameras. I'm here every day, sadly for me, Leeloo too. Never had any issues. Pretty dull actually."

"Dull sounds perfect."

Joe signaled to Leeloo to go inside. Ess followed them into the office.

"Do you have a dog?" Joe asked, sitting at the desk. "Leeloo is friendly with most dogs, except Chihuahuas. She mistakes Chihuahuas for squirrels and goes a bit nuts."

"No dog," Ess said quietly.

She registered and paid for a week in cash, hesitating briefly before giving *Sea Dragon*'s info. The mooring buoy by Saysutshun Island had required a permit, so if anyone was looking, she was already in a system. Her clock was already ticking.

Joe didn't say much, just raised an eyebrow at the cash payment and handed her the codes to the gate and laundry room.

"What made you choose Escape Marina?" he asked in a monotone voice, fingers hovering over a keyboard.

"Yori suggested it."

At this he typed something quickly, then closed out of his computer with a slashing gesture and turned to look at Ess, suddenly alert and paying attention. "I didn't think Yori knew anyone with a boat, given her opinion of boats."

"Well, she still hates boats."

Business done, Joe stood to go out and Ess did the same. Leeloo trotted over to her, tail wagging, having determined she was a friend. Ess rested a hand on her head, stroked her thick fur, felt comforted. "Is she a guard dog?"

Joe snickered and shook his head. "In appearance only. She'll bark convincingly at strangers, but offer her one morsel of food and all loyalty is lost."

Leeloo stayed by Ess's side as they all stepped outside.

"Can I ask about the personal flotation belt?" she asked, pointing.

His hand went to the PFD around his waist, adjusting it. A gesture he'd clearly done a million times. "I have a small phobia about drowning."

The overabundance of life preservers posted along the dock suddenly made sense. "I got knocked off my sailboat a few weeks ago," Ess said quietly. "No life jacket, swallowed half the ocean. Thought I was going to sink to the bottom."

He nodded solemnly. "I had an incident in a pool as a kid. It stays with you. Me more than others, apparently. You're still a sailor, even after the ocean tried to grab you?"

"I had somewhere I really needed to be. Stopping wasn't an option."

"It's a rather inconvenient phobia if you live in a coastal town.

Particularly if the family business is on the water. I don't recommend it." He smiled sadly, moved to the side of the building, and started up the ladder. "Let me know if you need anything. Welcome to Escape."

Ess spent the afternoon purchasing and installing a security camera above the door to her cabin. If it detected movement, it would send a video alert to her tablet showing her what was happening. *Sea Dragon* was home again, safe and secure. Leeloo padded down the dock a few times to watch her work and Ess liked the company.

To distract herself from worrying about who had attempted to break into *Sea Dragon*, she settled in with her tablet and read the profile summary for Dr. Saravanamuttoo. She was head of neuroscience in the Department of Brain and Cognitive Sciences at the University of British Columbia and lead researcher with the University of Victoria's neuroscience lab. The author of two textbooks on memory systems, she was the one to call with a case of something weird happening with memory.

Ess devoured everything she could find about the doctor, and the more she read, the more excited she got that Dr. Saravanamuttoo would be able to fix things.

24

THE GIANT MURAL IN THE atrium of the art collective building bothered Ess. She sat on the floor studying the painting of the wooden schooner being chased by a giant wave, so busy trying to puzzle out what was off about it that she almost missed seeing Yori walk by.

Yori was an hour late. She had her head ducked low and ignored everyone as she made her way through. She paused at the door to her studio, put her shoulders back, set her jaw, and went in. Ess walked over but stopped in the doorway when she saw Yori pick up her torn artwork slashed with green paint. A small flap of the canvas had folded over on itself, dried paint layered on top of the old delicate line work, gouge marks from the palette knife crisscrossing it all. The canvas had been transformed into something sculptural. It had captured the energy of Yori's outburst in a way that made you want to reach out and comfort it. Yori placed it on an easel and retreated a step, head tilted.

After a few minutes of studying Yori as she contemplated her work, Ess stepped in the room and cleared her throat. Yori wiped her eyes but didn't turn, didn't speak.

"It's very compelling," Ess hazarded softly.

"I"—Yori's voice broke—"don't hate it."

"So, just to be clear"—Ess positioned herself between Yori and the canvas—"you're not going to set this on fire?"

Yori hesitated, then finally shook her head.

"Will you give it to Hito like you originally planned?"

A snort escaped. "No way."

"Why?"

"God, because he'll think I've started painting again, and I can't explain. Hito can't know. Even if I do paint again, it won't be like before. It will be something different."

They both looked over at the torn canvas.

Yori ran a finger under each eye to tidy her eyeliner, then smoothed her hair and set her shoulders, tucking away the vulnerable part of herself she'd let slip out. "Enough of that." She turned her back on the easel and sank into the couch, fingers drumming on her leg. "Where'd you go? Hito said you aren't anchored in the harbor anymore."

The question threw Ess. "I'm at Joe's marina. Escape Marina."

"Right, right. Joe's. I forgot." Yori's leg started bouncing. "Has he talked to you about moral relativism or the dilemma of determinism yet? He did philosophy in university and was gutted he had to ditch his degree for the family business. He will go on for hours if you give him the slightest opening to start."

Unsure how to reply, Ess shifted topics. "I read up on Dr. Saravanamuttoo."

"Ah, and is she the shit?"

"She's the leading academic on memory impairment in North America. I found an interesting paper she wrote on patterns of autobiographical memory loss in medial temporal lobe amnesiac patients—"

"Yeah, sounds like a fun read. You should send that to me." Yori stood and paced around the edge of the room, picking up an old paintbrush and rolling it between her fingers. "Assuming the authorities and this doctor have a way to distinguish fakers from real cases, if they looked at your brain scan, you'd know for sure if your memory weirdness is the same as the others." She paused her pacing for a second. "Though I don't see how that helps you."

"It's everything," Ess said in a rush. "The doctor is the key to understanding what was done and how to undo it. How to get myself back."

Yori stopped fidgeting and looked at Ess. "You think this can be undone?"

Ess's head was throbbing suddenly. She hadn't meant to say that. "The alternative is to accept that my life is gone forever, that I'm gone forever."

Throwing the paintbrush on the table next to the pallet knife encrusted with green paint, Yori responded with her back to Ess. "My experience is that fucking things up is super easy; fixing them is a bitch."

The room filled with the smell of solvent as Yori started cleaning the pallet knife. Ess opened a window. Outside, a photographer was doing a shoot, their model perched on top of a rusted truck, setting off a bright-blue smoke bomb and holding it overhead triumphantly. The dense smoke billowed into the sky like a signal for help.

"So how do we get to the good doctor?" Yori asked.

Gathering her thoughts, Ess turned her back on the window. "She lives in Victoria but comes to Nanaimo every two weeks to consult at the hospital. She arrives on an early Monday morning train and stays until Tuesday evening. She's here now, leaves tonight."

"Guess we should just go to the train station and wait for her there then."

"You'd come with me?" Ess asked.

"One of the perks of not having a proper job is I'm available for clandestine activities on short notice. And you need a wingman on this. Dr. Saravanamuttoo might turn you in to the authorities one hot second after you tell her what you are."

Ess's palms started to sweat. "If you're willing to help, I've got an idea."

The train station was a glass box with a central waiting area and a spacious Tim Hortons café. Ess and Yori stood across from the entrance, scanning the crowd, the doctor's image on Yori's wrist screen for reference. The last train to Victoria departed in half an hour.

Ess was just thinking they should check the café and restrooms again when the main entrance doors swished apart and the doctor walked in, easily spotted with her silver hair swept up on her head and a bright-patterned scarf draped elegantly around her neck, just like her profile photos.

Following at a distance, they watched her enter the café and drop into a seat at the back with a coffee. Yori let her hair down and combed through it with her fingers. She instantly looked younger and more vulnerable, like she had when Hito had carried her to his couch. She rested a hand on Ess's arm, pulling her from the memory. Ess nodded, ready.

They entered, and Yori sat across from the doctor while Ess pulled over a chair from another table and sat awkwardly at the corner.

The doctor's eyes narrowed, and she started to stand.

"Dr. Saravanamuttoo, I'm sorry, please don't leave. I just need two minutes of your time. You're the only person that can help. Please." Yori smiled a tiny, fragile smile.

Ess was astonished at the transformation from the usual attitude-filled Yori to this fragile shrinking violet. But the doctor seemed unmoved, mouth creased with a frown.

This woman knew more about what was going on than anyone. Ess opened her mouth to ask one of the questions that had been pressing for weeks, then she caught herself and clamped her lips together.

"I don't know where to start," Yori said, her soft voice wavering.

Ess wanted Yori to get on with it, to stop playing, but she noticed the doctor's posture relax as she settled back into her seat.

Yori stood as if she was going to run away. Ess followed automatically.

"God, this was a mistake. I'm so sorry," Yori said, her words choked.

The doctor waved a hand to get Yori back in her seat. "Tell me what the issue is. I don't bite." Her voice was tinged with a faint British accent, and she spoke sedately, like there was no rush, like there was time for tea and scones if one were so inclined.

Glancing between the exit and the doctor's face, Yori did a convincing job of looking unsure, then perched on the edge of her chair, hands gripping each other. She took a deep breath and pushed out in a rushed whisper, "I have amnesia. Like the amnesia refugees."

The older woman frowned, her posture stiffening. "You need to see your family doctor and tell them your concerns. They'll help you."

"I'm afraid to tell anyone. I don't want to be put in jail like the amnesia refugees. But I'm scared. I don't know what's wrong with me. I had these terrible headaches when I first woke up," Yori's voice caught. "I can remember facts and how to do things, names of things, but anything personal is gone. Everything—recent stuff, old stuff. How is that possible? All the books say it's not possible, that's not how amnesia works."

The doctor drank her coffee and stood. "I can't help you. See your family doctor." She grasped her suitcase handle and turned to walk away.

"Then there are the seizures," Ess said loudly. "Lost time."

The doctor let go of her suitcase and slowly turned to look at Ess, her eyes bright.

"Tell her about your seizures," Ess said to Yori. "Where time seems to pass in an instant but to the outside world, you're frozen and unresponsive for minutes."

"Yes, seizures," Yori said slowly, growing excited. "I, uh, freeze with my eyes open like I'm lost in thought and people can poke me, yell, none of it does anything, I'm totally not home. Then"—Yori snapped her fingers and everyone flinched—"I'm back as if nothing happened."

Dr. Saravanamuttoo sat. "Do you have a name? Something I can call you?"

"Amy," Yori said. "And my friend doesn't need to be introduced."

"Okay. Amy. And friend." She adjusted her scarf. "So, what's your story then?"

"Look, I know you work with the authorities who are keeping all the amnesia cases locked up. I can't be one of those cases. If I tell you my story, what will you do with me?"

The doctor sat up straight, wiped invisible dirt off her pants. "I do get called in when the authorities find a case, and I try to advocate for the patients as best I can medically, but I'm not out hunting them, I assure you."

Yori glanced at Ess but the answer hadn't brought a lot of comfort.

"You haven't been to a doctor at all, have you?" Dr. Saravanamuttoo rubbed the bridge of her nose when Yori shook her head. "You need to get a physical exam done, diagnostic scans. You could have untreated head trauma or other urgent issues that need to be addressed."

"And the scans will show you if I have the same markers as the other cases, the same cause for my memory loss?"

The doctor hesitated, looking Yori up and down, evaluating. "Yes."

This confirmation made Ess's heart swell. She put a hand on her chest, fighting back a smile.

"How are you now? Any issues, ongoing problems?"

"Like what?" Yori asked.

"Trouble sleeping?"

"Uh, no, not really. Not usually."

"Headaches?"

"After I woke up, they were bad. Every morning for about three weeks."

Ess bit her tongue to stop from elaborating on Yori's answer and more fully conveying the dramatic, debilitating pain.

"Do you have difficulty recalling new memories, memories made since you woke up?"

Ess made a tiny side gesture with her hand.

"No," Yori said.

An announcement interrupted them and the doctor stood again, preparing to catch her train. "Look, Amy. We need to assess you, make sure you don't have trauma that needs treating. I have students in Victoria doing double-blind brain scans for a study; we can slip you in that way and maintain your anonymity. I can arrange to meet you in a colleague's medical office for a physical exam outside the normal system of record keeping. That's the best I can offer."

"I have a whole bunch more questions," Yori said.

Dr. Saravanamuttoo handed Yori a business card. "Tell me when you can be in Victoria for the tests. That's the only way this can work."

Yori tried to stall her. "I—"

"Message me when you're ready. Within reason, I am at your disposal."

"What about the others?" Ess said before the doctor walked away. "Are they okay?"

The doctor contemplated Ess. "I can't speak about that."

"Are they in jail? Are they okay?"

"They've lost all their personal memories, their very sense of self. They are utterly alone in the world. How do you think they are?"

The answer landed like a punch to the gut for Ess, and she couldn't look up. She heard the doctor say a curt goodbye. When they were alone, Ess dragged a hand against her eyes. It didn't help to feel sorry for the others; she couldn't help them.

"Huh," Yori said. "So, the seizure you had the other day wasn't a one-off then."

Ess stood, needing to move. "I thought it might be something all the amnesia cases suffer from that they haven't made public."

"Apparently you are brilliant," Yori said, a bounce in her step. "She was definitely hooked when you brought that up. I went from rando crazy to person of interest."

"Can I trust her?"

Yori shrugged. "Trusting anyone is a gamble. She doesn't seem like she's funneling victims into the jail cells of the authorities. Give it a few days to see if she somehow sends authorities after me, after Amy. If she doesn't, then it's up to you."

25

Yori: Tell me ur in the belly of the dragon right now.

Ess: If you mean on my boat, yes. Why?

Yori: I'm at the gate, lemme in and I'll tell you.

Ess STEPPED QUIETLY DOWN THE dock, admiring the dramatic slash of pink clouds to the west. She'd seen a lot of sunsets on her sailing trip but hadn't stopped to appreciate many since getting to Nanaimo.

Despite being as unobtrusive as possible, Joe shouted her name from his greenhouse as soon as she approached the office. He clambered down the ladder and came over, adjusting the flotation device around his waist.

"Have you heard the latest, or do I get to tell you?"

"Haven't heard," Ess managed. Leeloo trotted over and sat by Ess's feet, leaning against her. There was something comforting in the dog's weight. Ess absentmindedly scratched Leeloo's head as she glanced at the gate.

Joe lifted his wrist, extended the display of his comm, and crowded next to Ess so she could see. A few flicks and he had a news site up with a headline: "New Amnesia Refugee Identifier."

"These amnesia cases, I've been waiting all day for someone to talk to about it. The philosophical aspects are..." He made a chef's kiss motion. "Like, without a sense of self, memories have no meaning, yet the self is a product of our memories. But memories are fluid and easily modified, just the act of recalling a memory reshapes it, so how can they be the basis for sense of self—" He looked at Ess, pushed his hair out of his face. "Sorry. Rambling."

"Here." He scrolled. "So, more of these amnesia cases have come up and apparently, new weird bit, they all suffer from some kind of seizure where they freeze in place for a few minutes."

Ess took a step to the side as he talked, tucking herself against the office. She put a hand on the wall, suddenly unsteady.

Joe collapsed his screen, oblivious to the discomfort he was causing. "I just find the whole amnesia thing fascinating. The number of cases is up to thirty. I mean, it's terrible, but I'd love to find one of these people and take them for coffee, find out if they feel like a full person. It'd be such an interesting philosophical discussion, right?"

Forcing a nod, Ess kept her eyes on the dock. It was as if someone had stripped layers of clothing off, leaving her close to naked. She crossed her arms.

A buzzing noise came from the greenhouse, pulling Joe's attention away. He swung himself up the ladder. "If you're going out, keep watch for people freezing in place—a dead giveaway you've got an amnesiac on your hands. If you find one, bring them over for coffee and philosophical investigations!"

Released, Ess walked to the gate in silence, thinking of Dr. Saravanamuttoo. Was it coincidence that seizures were public knowledge now, making it harder for "Amy" to hide?

Opening the gate, she found Yori sitting on the pavement against the fence.

Yori lifted her head but stayed on the ground. Her makeup was smudged, heavy eyeliner making black sockets of her eyes. A smear of something else black streaked across her chin. Her face looked gaunt and worried.

Trying to stand, she flailed for assistance. Ess stepped in to help her up and was hit with the smell of booze and gasoline.

"Is Joe there?" Yori asked in a loud whisper.

A truck pulled into the parking lot, and both Ess and Yori turned their face away from it.

"Yeah, he stopped to tell me something worrying just now—"

"Fuck." Yori's gaze darted toward the greenhouse, to the road away from the marina, to Ess. "I can't let him see me all gross like this."

Standing tall, Yori pulled the fallen strap of her dress up and put her shoulders back. "We'll have to run for it."

She bolted past Ess through the marina gate and down the dock. Surprised, Ess jogged behind her, cringing as Yori veered close to the water's edge and had to contort herself to stay upright and on the dock. Leeloo barked, her tail wagging at the possibility of a game, but Ess signaled for her to stay as she hurried by.

Yori ran past *Sea Dragon* and stopped, clearly confused, at an algae-streaked derelict boat that was only floating out of sheer stubbornness.

Ess caught up and pointed to *Sea Dragon*. Onboard, Yori fell down the stairs into the cabin and stayed in a heap on the floor.

Waving away Ess's attempt to help her up, Yori pointed at the tablet on the table. "Can you check the news feeds, tell me if there's anything local? Any incidents?"

Grabbing her tablet, Ess started scanning, forcing herself to flick past the amnesia refugee article Joe had shown her. She was annoyed at Yori for demanding her attention at that moment and also intensely grateful for it. "What am I looking for?"

Grunting as she levered herself onto the bottom step, Yori massaged the knee she'd slammed on the floor but didn't answer. She got up and paced the cabin with an exaggerated limp, hands wiping ineffectually at dirt on her dress.

"Anything?" Yori asked.

"I don't know. Car crash on the highway? Seasonal stage four water restrictions starting tomorrow? A fist fight outside a Korean fried chicken restaurant on opening day?"

"No, no." Yori yanked the tablet from Ess's hands and flicked a few times, her jerky movements smoothing out with each screen she skimmed. After a minute, she put the tablet down and laughed. "Okay, yeah. Good."

"Good?"

Yori's posture relaxed and she started poking through Ess's galley cabinets. "Aces. What snacks do you have?"

Ess offered an apple. Yori snorted. "No. Real snacks. Chips?"

She found a chocolate-flavored protein bar and shrugged, unwrapping it. "Right, I can crash here tonight, yeah? Hito gets all wiggy when I've had some drinks. I need to stay on his good side a bit longer, don't have my next landing pad lined up yet. Besides, you must be spinning in circles waiting to go to Victoria for your brain scans, and I am very excellent at distracting."

"What just happened? Why are you so ragged and sooty?"

Yori looked down at her dress, then turned and squinted in the mirror over the sink. "I may have gotten a little drunk." She rubbed at the black smear on her chin. "And a little revengey. My ex, the one who cut me... I mean, I can't let that kind of thing go without repercussions, so, I may have set the tiniest of fires in her backyard."

Someone walked by on the dock, their shadow falling across the porthole. Ess dropped onto the bench, heart thudding in her chest. Yori pressed her back against the wall and peeked out, staying behind the curtain.

The footsteps on the dock had a distinctive cadence and canine component that let Ess resume breathing. She pulled the curtain from Yori's hand and shut it. "It's just Joe. He does a walk-through with Leeloo every night before leaving."

Yori looked out the window. "He's a good guy, isn't he? Boring but, like, stable."

"What did you set on fire?" Ess asked, trying to get Yori back on track.

She turned away from the window and tapped her wrist comm. "A shed. Nothing of consequence."

Music started playing. The sound quality from Yori's wrist was tinny but she started grooving and resumed eating her bar. "The fire grew somewhat larger than I anticipated—"

"Gasoline will do that."

"Well. Look who knows all about arson. I had to get lost when the fire attracted spectators, and then I had a bit of a worry that we're still in a drought and it was rather vigorous and maybe sparks or something spread and did more damage than I intended. But no news reports of fires, so I'm good!"

Ess stared at Yori. Even without previous experience to call on, Ess was confident it wasn't well-adjusted behavior to go setting things on fire. "Do you do this a lot?"

"If I did, I'd be much better at it. And more chill."

Ess almost laughed at that. She leaned her head back and enjoyed the music, enjoyed being not alone. Worked at relaxing.

"Ess?" Yori said, drawing out the syllable like a deflating balloon.

Yori was standing next to Ess's collection of old photos stuck to the wall over the radio.

"Who are these people?"

"Oh. I found those," Ess said. "Found them by a recycling bin in Haida Gwaii. Someone's trash. It didn't seem right to leave them there."

Yori traced a finger around the wedding couple. "Oh. Oh, Ess."

Ess contemplated her photo collection, straightened the image of the couple on the porch. "Is it weird? To have someone else's photos up?"

"Yes, but, I mean, not bad weird. It's just... Someone threw these out? God. Someone must have died all alone with no one to give a shit about family history. That's brutal. Look at all the kids this couple had." She put her finger on the photo of the mom with four kids on a couch. "And in the end, there wasn't anyone to care."

Yori sighed, then abruptly turned away. Ess took a bit longer to tuck away the feelings the photos generated.

"Have you been to the studio?" Ess asked.

Yori busied herself with putting her bag on the table and working to open a stuck zipper, but she eventually nodded. And reddened slightly.

"Painting?" Ess prompted.

"Yes, but just exercises to see what I remember, to see what I can do. I'm not producing or anything."

"How does it feel?"

"How does what feel?"

"To be painting? After all that time?"

The music stopped between songs, punctuating the long wait for Yori's answer. "It's a relief," she said. "I built it up to be this huge thing, this impossible thing. Now I remember it's just work. It's a thing that takes practice and effort. I'm rusty and my technique is shit and I don't know if I'll get back to it like before. But I don't think it'll haunt me anymore, not the way it did." She faced Ess, finally. "Yeah, okay, you grinning like an idiot is not the encouragement I need." She pulled a bottle of wine from her bag and unscrewed the cap.

"We shouldn't," Ess said.

"Why?" Yori waited, but Ess took too long choosing her words. "Because Hito has a rule that says I'm not supposed to drink? Too late for that tonight. Anyway, the best way to keep me steady is to give me a relief valve. And if you drink half, it'll hardly even impact me."

She threw the cap on the floor, filled a glass, then waggled the bottle at Ess, who accepted her assigned portion.

"So, Victoria, day after tomorrow," Yori said, settling onto the bench. "I can go with you. I've got a sweet modeling gig for an art photographer later, but my day is free."

"Are you sure? If you've got a job—"

"It's fine."

Ess frowned. "If the doctor has arranged for the authorities to take away a stray amnesia refugee, they'll take you when we arrive. You'll miss your job."

Waving her wineglass in the air, Yori dismissed the concern. "I didn't get the snitch vibe from the doctor. She's a nerd to the core, and you and your brain are a juicy data point. Getting taken by the fuzz is a small risk I deem not worth stressing about."

Ess picked up her glass and drank, doing her best to wash away an image of her brain in a petri dish.

Settling into her seat, Ess let Yori describe how she imagined her ex reacting to the shed fire while her own thoughts focused on the next day, the leap forward she was about to make in understanding what had been done to her. They drank more wine. Ess did enjoy how wine made her feel less present and three-dimensional, like she was more of an abstract concept of an Ess. It took the pressure off. Made her think she should always just be a concept instead of a person.

"When you woke up, what did you think about yourself?" Yori asked suddenly.

"What did I think of myself?"

"Yeah." Yori shifted to lie back, eyes fixed on the roof of the cabin. "Every day I wake up and thoughts run through my head immediately.

Such as: I am fucking beautiful. And: I am a cowardly failure that should hide in shame. God, what would I think if I was free of the memories of all the fuckups, all the racist bullying and bullshit, if I could erase all the times Hito looked at me with his disappointed expression."

It took Ess a second to focus on the question, unsure if she wanted her pain to be Yori's drunken entertainment. "Well, you couldn't feel like a failure because you wouldn't know you tried to do anything. You wouldn't know you had any ability to do anything special. You wouldn't know Hito. You wouldn't know your own face." Ess stopped, knowing tears would come if she didn't.

Yori savored a mouthful of wine. "I see the shitty bits, I do. But, oh, the beauty of being freed from all your regrets, from the weight of a life of bad decisions and causing pain. Free from a lifetime of being conditioned to think you're unlovable because of the shape of your eyes. So much freedom. And a chance to do it over. The ultimate fresh start."

"You're the second person to say that." Ess was back with Rene, standing next to him in the cool night air as he told her she'd be okay, his slight French accent making the words more believable somehow. "It's hard to appreciate being liberated from the weight of bad life choices when you have no memory of the weight ever having been there."

Yori digested that with more wine. "You know what Joe said to me once, on one of his philosophical rants. That identity is a reflection of those around us. We become who we think people expect us to be. 'I am not who I think I am, I am not who you think I am, I am who I think you think I am.'"

"Who said that?" Ess asked.

"No idea. But I hate it. I don't want to be who I think I need to be to meet expectations. I want to be some truer version of myself. Just haven't quite figured out how." She glanced at Ess. "Maybe you've got a path to get there."

In the awkward silence that followed, Yori picked up the wine bottle and drained the last drops into her glass. She straightened Ess's notebook to lie parallel to the table edge.

"Hey, did you see Hito recently?"

Grateful for the abrupt subject change, Ess looked at Yori with a puzzled expression. "No. Why?"

Yori frowned. "He's being weird. I can't figure out why."

"Maybe it's about his interview?"

"What interview?"

Ess closed her mouth and swore, making a muffled noise. She busied herself by getting an apple, rinsing and slicing it, arranging it symmetrically on a plate.

"What interview?" Yori repeated when Ess sat.

"Nothing." She tried to tidy away the wine bottle but Yori held tight. "Maybe he's not doing it. He wasn't sure he could right now. I'm probably just confused."

"Nope, too late. You're going to tell me, Ess. Come on."

Ess shifted her weight, her elbow knocking a pile of charts onto the floor. She gathered them, took care to stack them neatly. Yori's attention was locked on her. Waiting.

"He was invited to apply to NDRT?" Ess finally whispered.

Yori put a hand to her mouth and chewed on a fingernail. "Really? Are you sure?"

"Yes. No."

"Well, fuck, why wouldn't he do it? It's a big deal. They're super elite and hard-core, it's exactly his thing. He's made for that shit."

"He said it required him to be called out of town for weeks on short notice; that seemed to be a problem."

"Why?"

"He didn't say. Can we stop talking about this?"

Yori pulled her lips into a thin line and reached for her wine, took a long drink, finishing it like it was water. "Time to crash, I guess."

Ess quickly converted the dining area into a bed while Yori stared out a porthole at the dark, her arms crossed, her posture slumped.

Unable to tell if Yori was angry with her or Hito or the world, Ess quietly retreated to her bedroom, softly closing the door and lying back on the bed, arms splayed.

Her tablet dinged, and she automatically turned to look. A new message, one that made her arm hairs stand on end. She sat bolt upright.

"View Immediately. Message from Sarah Jane Song." Ess's eyes fixated on the word *from*.

She tapped the message to open it. There were only two words.

Watch video.

26

STANDING, ESS WENT TO THE door to get Yori. Then she stopped, sat, and looked at the screen again. The unsigned message came from a random address, a jumble of numbers and letters. She tried taking a deep breath, but there wasn't enough air in the cabin. She cracked the hatch. Then closed it, needing privacy.

When the hair on her arms relaxed, she put her earbuds in and, hand hovering over the link for an age, finally clicked the video. She had to tell her tablet twice it was okay to play the mystery file, though she shared its doubts.

The video started with an empty chair at a table in a dark room lit by an old desk lamp; then a woman stepped into view. She sat, posture rigid, chin tucked, hands folded neatly on the table in front of her. Ess stopped breathing when she saw the face.

"If you're seeing this, then something has gone wrong or is at risk of going wrong." The woman looked down at her hands, then at the camera. "I'm trying to imagine what this must be like, how confusing it must be. The pull to know about your past must be strong. But you *can't* know. The whole point is not to know." She tilted her head for a moment, listening, then corrected her perfect posture, returned her gaze to the camera. Focused, unwavering. She tugged her blazer to straighten it, an unconscious, practiced motion. Her hair was pulled into a tight bun. Crisp eye makeup made it hard to look anywhere else but her eyes.

"Maybe it will help if I tell you that you were alone before. I—you—had a handful of friends, but none of them close. Colleagues mostly. You—" She stopped and smiled to herself, "I don't know what pronoun to use. I've been told I'm self-centered, so let's go with 'I.' I focused my life on my work, my research. I've done well, made breakthroughs others in my field only dream about, don't even know about—" She stopped and ran a hand along her perfect hair.

"In any case, to accomplish my professional ambitions I missed out on certain things. No marriage, no family. My parents died when I was"—she paused to filter herself—"a young adult. No siblings. Only distant family in another country that I've never met. I'm hoping it will help to know you aren't leaving anyone behind. There is no bereft family wondering what happened to you, waiting for your return. No spouse covering your hometown with missing posters. That's not how it will be. I've been alone for a long time. My absence won't be noticed. But it can be different for you."

She turned her head to look off camera again, listening. Ess strained to listen with her.

"In short. I'm in danger and this is my escape. I've found this one chance to buy a way out. I learned about something I wasn't meant to, thought I could... Well, I was cocky and wrong." She looked to the side as she said this, her head slightly bowed, the earlier arrogance gone. "But you are my escape. My second chance."

"Whatever you're doing, stop it. If you're digging for answers, stop it. Find something that makes you happy. Someone who makes you happy. Find a way to do good in the world. Make friends. Opening the door you're trying to open will land you where I am, and it's not a place you want to be. My work, my breakthrough, was stolen and twisted and used in ways I didn't know about. I thought I could fight that. Trust me when I say we can't. It's too big now, can't be put back in the box. Think of what I went through to get away from this..."

She waved her hand at the camera, unable to put it into words. "Don't walk back into it if you have any other choice."

A door opened and a shadow walked in, breathing hard, standing off camera. "We're out of time—" She lifted a hand and silenced him, gesturing at the camera.

"What you do from here is up to you. You're smart. Do the right thing, for both of us. Take care of yourself. Tell your doctor to watch for heart disease; runs in the family. Good luck."

While she stared into the lens, eyes piercing, someone lifted the camera. The world tilted ninety degrees and she stood, picked up a black case from the desk, and held it close to her chest. The video ended.

When Ess recovered her ability to move, she played the video again. On the second viewing, she watched her face, every frown and twitch of the eye, every tilt of the head. She had to remind herself that this was her own face she was watching. Had to remind herself to breathe.

On the third viewing, she could focus on what was being said. Pulling over her notebook, she transcribed it, studying the words. The words she had chosen. Ess circled "*I've been alone for a long time.*" A weight settled on her chest. She pressed her hands against her eyes, then played the video again. And again.

A touch on her shoulder made her flinch, knocking the tablet onto the floor.

"Whoa," Yori said, picking the tablet up and checking for damage. "What's wrong? You were making a weird noise."

There weren't any words to explain so Ess just took the tablet, disconnected her earbuds, and played the video, closing her eyes and listening.

After the "good luck," Ess opened her eyes and looked at Yori. She seemed unmoved by the video. She took the tablet and left the room. When she returned, she handed Ess a glass of water and a pill.

"What—"

"How many times have you watched that?"

"A couple."

Yori looked skeptical. "Take this. It's a mild sleeping pill."

Ess hesitated.

"You will torture yourself all night otherwise. The video will be here when you wake up."

Ess took the pill and downed it with water.

That done, Yori crawled onto the bed and made herself comfortable, gathering pillows to prop herself up. "I'm going to tell you a story about the time teenage-me stole Hito's work pass and used it to break into HA's auxiliary boat-dock facility so I could make out with some guy in a rubber speedboat."

Looking around, Ess realized Yori had taken the tablet away, stashed it somewhere. She thought about looking for it. Instead, she lay down next to Yori, who smelled faintly of gasoline and smoke, and tried to focus on her words about an earnest Hito, the fresh-faced HA recruit who Yori thought was ridiculous at the time. The words spooled out like a creek, gently flowing on their way to join some larger story stream, Ess thought as she fell asleep.

27

SHE WAS BEING HELD BY her shoulders, immobilized. A shadowed figure sat at a table in the bright lobby of an impossibly tall office building. He was waiting for her. He knew her. He knew everything about her. And he was standing, putting on a fedora, leaving.

She screamed to stop him, screamed with body and spirit, but he walked away. If she could just figure out a way to move forward and leave her shoulders and arms behind, it would be okay.

"Ess!"

Eyes open, she found Yori holding her shoulders, shaking her. She saw the wood paneling of *Sea Dragon* and moaned in dismay. Every bit of her wanted to get back to the dream, to catch the guy, pry answers from him.

Letting go, Yori sat back. "Holy shit," she said, wiping hair out of her face, "you were having a fucker of a nightmare."

Filled with overwhelming disappointment, Ess couldn't speak. She crawled out of bed and stumbled to the sink, waited to vomit, couldn't, then slid to the floor when that relief wouldn't come.

Yori gave her a minute before pulling the door open.

"You okay?" Yori asked, kneeling and brushing Ess's hair out of her face.

Ess shook her head without lifting it. Yori rested her hand on Ess's shoulder.

"You've got heavy shit going on," Yori said. "I'm going to find us something for breakfast while you piece yourself together."

Ess allowed herself two minutes on the floor to marinate in her feelings, then hauled herself upright. The main cabin had been transformed back into a dining area, though there was a leftover cushion tucked under the table whose proper location had apparently stymied Yori.

Taking the plate of fruit Yori handed her, Ess mechanically put a few blueberries in her mouth. She picked up a loose puzzle piece from the table and flipped it image side down, half-heartedly tried to fit it into place that way.

Yori's watch dinged and she stood. "Shit. I'm late for my run through with the photographer. I cannot afford to piss her off. I'll meet you at the train station tomorrow morning and we'll pin Dr. S. down for answers, yeah?"

Yori slicked her hair back into a ponytail, and with her freshly scrubbed face, she suddenly looked remarkably chic and functional despite her pathetic state the night before. Ess could only produce a nod, head thick with hangover.

Sticking her hand into the cabinet over the sink, Yori pulled out Ess's tablet and put it on the counter, holding her hand on it for a moment as though she thought Ess might leap over the table and grab it like an animal. But Ess wasn't ready to face the video again, to face *her* again. She waited to see what Yori was going to say, but in the end Yori just lifted her hand from the tablet and shrugged, waved goodbye, and left.

With the whirlwind of Yori gone, the cabin was oppressively quiet. A sunbeam cutting through the porthole illuminated a small scar stretched across the web between Ess's thumb and finger, a visible marker of an event she didn't remember. The things that shaped her, formed her physically, were all gone.

Resting her head on the table, she listened to her boat creaking. Listened to someone on the dock complaining about the eyesore derelict boat next door. Flicking on the radio, she listened to the forecast. Forest fires on the island and the mainland were largely contained, but now a big storm was gathering energy in the Pacific, heading north, far further north than normal. Early projections had it hitting Vancouver Island in a few days, but that was being dismissed as unprecedented.

28

THE CLINIC WAITING ROOM WAS quiet except for the sound of coughing. There were pictures of calm ocean scenes on the walls that agitated Ess. The puffy clouds dabbed in the sky were meant to be picturesque but were really a sign of coming trouble. Any sailor knew that.

Ess and Yori had caught a morning train to the city of Victoria, Yori arriving at the last possible moment, clearly having not gone to bed at all.

Deep down, Ess had suspected since talking to Sam that she'd done this to herself. She'd avoided the idea as hard as she could, but Sam knew her as Sarah Song. She'd bought the boat as Sarah Song. The few times she thought about it, she'd tried to believe that maybe she'd set up the identity as part of a getaway scheme someone had interrupted, but that had just been a flimsy defense against a harsher truth she couldn't avoid anymore. She'd orchestrated it all; she'd voluntarily erased herself.

Letting go of the idea that someone had done this *to* her wasn't easy.

She'd done it to herself because she'd thought it was the only way out of some life-or-death situation. That's why she'd stashed her money in an offshore bank that never revealed client identities—even when international law said they should.

But the tracking device on *Sea Dragon* implied she hadn't gotten out. The version of her in the video hadn't anticipated being found and tracked. The version of her in the video telling her to stop assumed everything had gone to plan and she was safely cocooned away.

If she wanted any hope of being safe, Ess needed to know what the fuck she'd been running from in the first place. Yori shrugged at this line of reasoning, unusually quiet and lacking in opinions. They'd watched the scenery fly by in silence for the last half hour of the trip.

An assistant entered the clinic waiting room and everyone looked up hopefully.

"Amy?"

Yori stood. It took Ess a moment to remember who Amy was and join her in following the man to an exam room. Ess and Yori stood in the small room, staring at posters of internal organs, feeling out of place under the harsh bright lights. A minute later Dr. Saravanamuttoo entered.

"Amy."

Yori turned. "Hi, Doc."

But the doctor focused her attention on Ess. "How are you?"

Tears sprang to Ess's eyes unexpectedly at the question. The doctor handed her a box of tissues from the counter and pointed at a chair.

"Let's sit, shall we? It's often a loaded question, that one. Seems so innocent. You must be under a lot of strain. Take a moment."

The kindness made Ess want to cry harder, but she held it in. "You know."

"I suspected at the café. Your knowledge of absence seizures sounded personal. But it was when you walked by just now. You have the mark."

Ess's hand went to her neck. "Mark?"

The doctor extended a hand toward Ess's ear. Yori leaned in as the doctor pointed to a small dark spot. "Small scar behind the ear, an injection site."

"Huh," Yori said. "Looks like a mole."

The door opened and a woman with a stethoscope around her neck entered. "Holly, good to see you."

"Danielle, you too. This is our patient, Amy." Dr. Saravanamuttoo said, gesturing to Ess.

Ess backed away as far as the small room would allow. "What's this?"

Dr. Saravanamuttoo adjusted her scarf, unmoved by Ess's obvious discomfort. "I asked Dr. Basko to do the physical exam. I'm a neuro-scientist. I do research and academic work these days. Dr. Basko is a general practitioner, doing this as a favor to me."

Yori positioned herself in front of Ess, arms crossed.

"We need to know if you're okay physically," Dr. Saravanamuttoo said. "No records, no DNA scans. We won't force you, obviously, but I can't proceed without it."

"If it helps, Amy, I don't know any details of your case other than you're generally having memory issues. Dr. Saravanamuttoo wanted me unbiased in my examination. We'll give you a general physical, test for concussion, standard blood tests. I'll give the results to you and won't keep any records. It's unusual, but I owe Holly."

Ess weighed her options. "No blood tests. And my friend stays."

Dr. Saravanamuttoo frowned and tried to convince Ess of the importance of the blood tests, but Ess wouldn't budge. With a shrug, Dr. Saravanamuttoo gestured to her colleague to start. The physical didn't take long. Dr. Basko gave Ess a clean bill of health. The two doctors talked about head trauma for a minute, with Dr. Basko shaking her head in response to all the questions.

Then it was done and Dr. Saravanamuttoo was leading them outside.

—

On the tree-lined street in front of the clinic, Yori pulled Ess away from Dr. Saravanamuttoo. "Um. Amy. A word."

Ess looked over her shoulder. The doctor was waiting for the cab to take them to the university hospital for a battery of brain scans.

Yori was fidgety, her gaze bouncing off Ess to scan the street, then looking at her phone. "Look, you don't need me here anymore, right? You're good? The doctor checks out, not an evil villain. The Amy cover is toast. I'm just deadweight slowing you down."

Ess didn't relish the idea of going to the hospital alone, but she swallowed that answer and nodded. She'd stepped into uncertainty alone before. She preferred having Yori there with her, but she could do it.

"Great, okay. Cool. So, I need to go. I may have screwed up a smidge on photo-shoot scheduling so I'm going to get the next train back—" Yori stopped abruptly, looking at Ess properly and apparently seeing something in her face that gave her pause. "Don't be your usual trusting self," she said. "Be paranoid and skeptical for once. Be me." She seemed to be on the verge of saying more but instead turned and hurried to the bike-share stand by the office building, pulled out a bike, and pedaled in the direction of the train station.

"Your friend had somewhere else to be?" Doctor Saravanamuttoo asked when Ess joined her.

Ess didn't answer. She had no claim to Yori's time or assistance, but losing it still hurt. Somehow the doctor witnessing the loss made it worse.

The cab pulled up, sensing the doctor's phone and stopping in front of them. They got in, and it eased away from the curb and headed to the university.

"Does it worry you," Ess said, "as someone who studies memory and the brain, that someone has found a way to do this to people?"

Dr. Saravanamuttoo focused on Ess as if surprised her test subject would think of such a question. "As a researcher, I'm interested in the how. This is a significant leap in the field, targeted modifications like this. But yes, I worry." Her shoulders drooped. "To see an advancement like this outside the medical research community being used on people without proper testing, without proper ethical oversight..."

The doctor adjusted her scarf and fixed her posture, the exhaustion she'd revealed hidden away again. "Are you ready to tell me your story?"

Ess looked over in surprise. "My story?"

"We need to see the scans to know for sure, but so far we have every reason to think you are like the others, except here you are pretending to be normal and blending in. You've eluded detection. The particulars of your case may provide clues to how this is happening, who's doing it."

It hadn't occurred to Ess that she might be of value. Minding Yori's warning, she recounted a bare-bones version of her story, avoiding any mention of locations and dates.

They arrived at the university as Ess finished, and the doctor led the way to the diagnostic equipment without commenting. Ess didn't know how to interpret that reaction.

It took three hours for all the scans Dr. Saravanamuttoo wanted, including ones where she had Ess in the machine recounting what she did the day before and the day she woke up after the memory wipe. She'd had Ess attempt to remember a childhood event, which had turned into a humiliating exercise as a room full of technicians watched her fail over and over while the scanner made bone-rattling thunking noises.

After the scans came memory and cognitive tests, and after an hour of that, Ess parked herself in a folding chair in a hallway, crossed her arms, and refused to do any more or go anywhere other than to see Dr. Saravanamuttoo.

Someone escorted her to an office building adjacent to the

university hospital. It was around dinnertime when the doctor's assistant deposited Ess in a large office overlooking the parking lot. She handed Ess a sandwich wrapped in paper and a bundle of condiment packets and said the doctor would be in soon. While Ess had been exhausting herself by lying as still as possible for several hours, it had started raining. The weather seemed ominous, like a washing away of the existing world to replace it with something new. She watched the water pooling on the asphalt, wondering if she'd closed the hatch on *Sea Dragon* or if she was going to return and find her home transformed into a swimming pool. It struck her as strange that she could be so far away from her *Sea Dragon* and still function.

Ravenously hungry, Ess looked at the sandwich and collection of little packets clenched in her hands. Ketchup, mustard, mayo. She had no clue if she wanted any of them. She tossed them on the floor in a flash of anger, sick of these constant reminders of what she didn't know. She mechanically consumed the sandwich plain, tasting nothing.

Dr. Saravanamuttoo cleared her throat, and Ess turned to find her sitting down at her desk. Leaving the window, Ess perched on the edge of the chair across from her, gripping her half-finished sandwich in one hand. Shivers kept running through her body.

The doctor put a napkin on the desk and gestured for Ess to put her sandwich down. "Dr. Basko sent a summary of your physical for your records. She notes that the scan of your birth control implant was inconclusive so she can't be sure how long it's good for, and she recommends you get it replaced so you have clarity."

"Thank you." Another shiver.

"Now. The scans." She turned her monitor so Ess could see and dragged two images side by side using quick hand gestures. "Left is a confirmed amnesia refugee patient. Right is you."

Ess's gaze went back and forth between them but she was lost.

Dr. Saravanamuttoo put a finger on each screen. "Here and here. Same anomaly. Hard to tell on this scan what it is exactly. Scar tissue? Missing tissue? The 3D scan gives a different look." She brought up new images that were equally impossible for Ess to make any sense of. The doctor pointed to a dark spot with ragged edges. "This is your scan. See the damage here? This general area of the brain is the temporal lobe. The ability to store and retrieve autobiographical memories that are detailed and vivid always depends on the hippocampal system, whereas remembering facts and general information does not. I can confirm you match our other patients exactly. You all have an insult to the temporal lobe with damage to the hippocampus on both sides. The precision of the match between your scans and the others is unambiguous. The same technique was used on all of you."

Ess needed the doctor to get to the point. "What's your guess on how?"

"Off the record—"

"I don't exist; this whole thing is off the record."

Dr. Saravanamuttoo's answer came quickly once she decided to give it. "There's no evidence of surgery, no other brain impairments. It's very precise damage. It must be nanotech in combination with drugs. PTSD researchers have used propranolol and propofol to disrupt memory reconsolidation, to impair recall of traumatic memories. I've wondered what would happen if—" She caught herself, her gaze landing on Ess. "In any case, this would be a huge breakthrough in nanotech application. It's not my field, but passing the—"

Ess said the next words along with her. They came automatically like tying a knot she didn't know she knew. "Blood-brain barrier..."

"Remains a challenge," Dr Saravanamuttoo finished, looking surprised. "Yes. People have been researching it for years. Currently, nanotech has to be delivered directly to the brain, mechanically bypassing the skull and blood-brain barrier. There has been great success with nano research that directly accesses the brain, the Bliss Alzheimer's treatment, for example. But this…" She studied her screens and frowned. "I suppose it is always easier to destroy than repair."

"Why erase autobiographical memories? What value does that have?"

"Quite right. The nearest comparison is the work on PTSD. Existing treatments focus on interrupting memory reconsolidation and they're crude and see mixed results. The ultimate objective has always been a way to destroy the memory recall ability entirely for the problematic memory. This"—she gestured at the scans on her monitor—"looks like an attempt to do that that hit too widely and destroyed all autobiographical recall. A nanotech encoding error perhaps. The question is why it didn't stay in the lab as a failed line of investigation."

The answer didn't move Ess. She was tired, and she suddenly realized it didn't matter to her *how* it had been done. This wasn't why she was here.

"What did it do to me? Destroy the memories or destroy the recall ability?"

The doctor sat back in her chair. "A good question." She adjusted her glasses, taking her time, choosing her words. "Memory is a big word. It encompasses a host of different capacities mediated by functionally distinct subsystems that collectively produce the performances we call memory. Memory of events, autobiographical information, is dispersed. When we recall a specific event, we think our brains pull together threads of information that overlap—smell, sight, feelings—all things that are housed in different areas of the brain. The memory is like an index that points to the constituent memory bits, a shortcut to assembling the memory.

"That's how we think about it today. Therefore, it's most likely you can't recall memories before this trauma because your index files have been disrupted, so to speak. Your procedural memory is intact. Your semantic memory, your memory of general facts, is intact, which indicates the knowledge is there. Semantic memory recall uses different functionality, so it is unimpeded despite the damage done. Organic retrograde amnesia is never this clean. Typically, more recent memories are impacted and older ones less so—"

Ess cut off the lecture. The doctor was badly missing the point. "So, if the memories are there, how do we rebuild the pointers?"

"What do you mean?"

"I mean, how do we fix it?"

29

THE DOCTOR RUBBED HER NOSE. "It's possible to retrieve facts, like, humans first walked on the moon in 1969, without the hippocampal system, but it's not possible to retrieve any specific unique experiences, such as how you celebrated your sixteenth birthday, unless the hippocampal circuits can communicate with the cortical circuits. Your communication pathways have been disrupted. There is physical damage to your brain, Amy. It can't be fixed."

The deep, pulsing sound of the scanner seemed to have returned, drowning out the doctor and making the room wobbly.

"I should have inferred that's what you were hoping. The brain is a complex machine. When damage is this complete… The good news is you're able to form new long-term memories, so moving forward this won't be an issue."

Ess almost slapped her. The idea that her complete disconnect from her past, from who she was, *wouldn't be an issue moving forward* was insulting. She held it together and pivoted to her last hope. "But some memories, intense emotional ones, are encoded using different pathways, right? So, if I can get back to other familiar things, they could come back?" Ess gripped the arms of her chair, holding on.

"Well. Like any amnesia case, there is a small chance that new connections to stored memories could be established if the conditions were right. Put you in a situation where you're surrounded by faces and places and sounds and experiences that are familiar and emotionally resonant, your brain might be able to rebuild some connections, and the rush of dopamine that would hit when it did, your euphoria at remembering, would create a new index pointer that might stick. It might help, but I don't want to get your hopes up. It would be confusing bits and pieces at best, flashes, not a flooding back of everything, not like in the movies. And it might not happen at all."

Ess laughed. She tried to keep it in, but it burst out, followed by tears. Dr. Saravanamuttoo pushed a box of tissues across the desk. It was clear she wanted Ess to gather herself together, but Ess was forever split. She carried within her all the bits of her previous life but was unable to access them.

There was a slim chance she could get some memories back, but only if she could do the impossible and slip into her old life to jiggle them loose.

The doctor was saying more. Ess nodded automatically, her mind elsewhere. Something had snapped. She felt detached. Rudderless. Entirely adrift.

She'd been justifying digging into her past based on needing to know the danger she was in to protect herself from it, but she faced the bald truth now. She just wanted it all back. At any cost. The bottomless pit of not knowing wasn't something she was strong enough to bear. She didn't have the courage to face staring into the abyss every day and continue on. That was why she'd been ignoring the note and digging and putting so much at risk. Even when she warned herself to stop.

So where did that leave her now?

Suddenly, the doctor's words cut through and demanded attention. "My advice to you is to submit yourself into care. Stop hiding and start taking care of yourself."

Ess sat up straight in her chair, a rock of worry settling in her belly.

"You have serious brain trauma, and you should be in the care of a professional. The petit mal seizures, the absence seizures, are unusually long and rare in adults and may warrant medication to control. We don't know enough about that yet. You need to treat this like the trauma it is." A long pause. "You should contact the authorities. They have systems in place to treat people like you."

The hair on Ess's arms stood on end. She forced herself to nod. She evaluated her exit options. One door. They were on the ground floor, but it wasn't clear if the windows opened.

Dr. Saravanamuttoo gestured at her computer. "Your brain trauma is the same as the others, but how you came to be this way is clearly different." Her voice was quiet and low, as if she was trying to avoid spooking a wild horse. "An investigation into your situation might uncover who is doing this. Someone set up your new identity and delivered you to a location where your memory wipe was done. Any of these facts could lead investigators to the people behind all this. If people are having their memories wiped against their will, you may be able to help stop it from happening to others."

She scrutinized Ess across the desk. "Will you help? Can I make that call for you?"

Ess pictured herself sprinting from the room. Instead, she stood slowly, feeling that any sudden movements might break her wide open. She walked to the window, tried to think straight. Her brain wanted to swirl in self-pity around the news of what was forever lost to her. It also wanted her to smash the window and run before she was locked in a cage.

The phone on the desk buzzed, making Ess jump. Dr. Saravanamuttoo answered it and said a few words Ess couldn't hear over the blood rushing in her ears. Three police cruisers had just pulled into the parking lot. And the window did not open.

She turned and studied Saravanamuttoo, tried to discern the

woman's intentions, but her face was unreadable, her professional mask impenetrable. Ess put a hand on the cool glass behind her, a worry that she was already caged creeping up her spine.

What would Yori do?

Ess bolted for the door and heaved on the handle. It didn't move. They were locked in. She turned to face the doctor, who approached, hands out. "Please calm down. There is a greater good here to consider."

A memory flashed in Ess's mind, so fresh and vivid it made her reach out for the wall behind her: Yori disheveled, dress marred with soot. Ess could smell gasoline and smoke as if it filled her nostrils now.

"I'm asking you to think of others," the doctor said, her British accent thicker now. "If you can stop this from happening to others, don't you want to do that?"

Ess's hand rested next to the fire alarm. She hesitated, those words cutting deeper than she wanted to admit. "I trusted you."

Dr. Saravanamuttoo's expression didn't change. Not a glimmer of remorse.

Ess pulled the alarm, flinching at the deafening ringing that started.

The red light on the lock disappeared, and when she turned the handle, it opened.

The doctor wrapped a hand around Ess's arm but Ess pulled away with a jerk and fell into the hallway where a wave of confused people wrapped around her and swept her toward an exit.

Three uniformed officers were clustered at the far end of the hall. Ess shuffled toward them, craning her head looking for a path out that didn't go by police, but everyone was in the hallway now and the only way out was through.

As she approached, the officer by the door reached out a hand, rested it on Ess's shoulder. Ess stiffened, wondered if she knew how to fight, if she had the capacity for physical violence. But the officer just firmly guided Ess through the door, thanked everyone for remaining calm. Fire safety apparently trumped the threat of a rogue amnesiac. For now.

Outside, everyone seemed to suck in a deep breath of fresh air in unison. Ess walked with them into the parking lot, then inched her way to the back of the crowd. Most people were watching the building for any signs of actual fire. Ess glanced at a scraggly patch of woods on the other side of the parking lot. Best to be subtle, slip away, avoid attracting attention.

She bolted instead. Someone shouted after her. She thought of her runs in Haida Gwaii and pushed herself to go faster and faster, trusted that she had it in her.

She made it to the cover of the woods quickly, feet tripping on roots and discarded beer cans. Kept running. She needed to put an ocean of distance between her and the doctor.

Branches scraped against her cheeks, snagged her hair, slowing her, but she kept going, wishing for an unending forest of giant, ancient trees to protect her. Instead, after five minutes the woods ended abruptly at a sidewalk on a commercial street. She leaned against a tree at the edge and sucked in air. Her legs burned. The taste of iron filled her mouth but no seizure came; this was just runner's lung. She almost cried in relief at that mercy.

She needed to go, to move, to be far away, but she was stuck, thinking over how easily the doctor had turned her in. The first betrayal Ess had any memory of. It felt like tissue had been cauterized out of her heart in a way that would never heal.

Eventually, she emerged from the woods, stepping onto the sidewalk with leaves in her hair, changed; some things permanently lost in her encounter with the doctor.

Now she just wanted to go home, an impossible wish. An

impossibility she couldn't turn away from anymore. She forced herself to walk in the direction of the bus terminal, knowing she'd have to settle for her dragon.

30

DROPPING HER WET JACKET ON the floor, Ess stood in *Sea Dragon*'s cabin and felt a bit of the paranoia that had haunted her on the trip home slide off with it. She closed her eyes and inhaled deeply. The cabin smelled of grease, varnish, and salt water, comfortingly familiar. She double-checked that the door was locked and her security camera was on.

"It is very, very good to be home," she told *Sea Dragon*.

Water streaked the windows, obscuring any view of outside. The storm the news had been warning about for days was building strength and gathering moisture as it barreled over the ocean toward Vancouver Island. It would hit the western side of the island, then head overland to Nanaimo. The word *unprecedented* was a standard part of every weather report now. This rain was nothing compared to what was coming.

Ess rummaged through cabinets. She wanted to forget the video warning message, forget that she'd done this horrible thing to herself. Even if it had been for a good reason, she didn't care. She was still furious at what had been taken. Furious at the doctor for trying to lock her up when she was just trying to live her fucked-up life.

"God, why don't I have whiskey or something? What kind of sailor am I? And why was this boat stocked with so much goddamn tea? Who drinks this much tea?"

Her tablet dinged. She was expecting a message from Yori in response to her report on what had gone down, so it took a second for her tired brain to understand what this really was.

A message from the email address that had sent the warning video. It was short.

You are in danger. Meet at following address tomorrow at 6:00 a.m. Your safety depends on it.

—

After a fitful night where sleep came only in half-hour increments, Ess left *Sea Dragon* to walk to the meeting spot in the dark of early morning. The address was a twenty-minute trip into winding residential streets up the hill from the marina. Ess flipped her hood up to keep the mark behind her ear covered, as if anyone out that early was inspecting the heads of random people.

Nearing her destination, Ess turned on to a dimly lit street. She had to slow to avoid tripping on the uneven pavement. The light pollution from the city center was only enough to make alarming shadows of the trees and bushes that lined the road in increasing density. This wasn't the typical wide-open streetscape of Nanaimo. Here, greenery seemed to be winning. Occasional driveways turned off the street and disappeared behind tall hedges. Ess couldn't see what they led to.

She tried to hold tight to the fact that the message had come from whomever she'd entrusted with sending her the warning video. Pre-memory-wipe her had trusted this person to some degree.

The wind whipped the scent of lilacs over her, stopping her in her tracks. Something about that scent. It mattered. She froze, trying to figure out why, but the memory wouldn't come. Only a vague feeling of comfort. The wind shifted, leaving her in the middle of the dark road, grasping for a thing forever out of reach.

She resumed walking, putting the lilacs in the corner of her brain with Leeloo and the fact that she knew dogs, liked dogs. These fragments of who she was were all she had to build herself from. A hopeless task.

On her left, a wall of hedge started, an expanse of black. A wooden sign painted with numbers was just visible, the foliage wrapping around it, claiming it. This was the address. Ess pushed her hood down and walked through the narrow gap in the hedge.

Her footsteps crunched on gravel as she went up the drive to the hulk of a house illuminated by one weak bulb at the front entrance. Climbing the porch stairs, she stood at the door. Aside from the spiderweb-covered bulb, there was no sign anyone was home. It was dark and secluded.

Turning her back on the door, Ess walked away, her gut protesting everything about the situation. Before she could go more than a few steps, an arm snaked around her neck and pulled her back. She was pressed against the body of the person restraining her, their arm firmly over her windpipe, a threat rather than a choking. Her hands scrabbled at the wooden siding of the house as panic flooded her.

"Please be calm," he said, voice low. "I'm not here to hurt you. I'm here to help."

His arm relaxed and he put a hand on each of her shoulders, kept her facing away from him.

She tried to swallow her fear, but it caught in her throat, filled her mouth.

"I'm going to blindfold you and take you inside."

"Why?" Ess choked out.

"We need to have a private conversation, and it's better that you not see me, that's all."

A strip of soft fabric slid over Ess's eyes. In the darkness, she focused on keeping calm.

Hinges squeaked. "We're going inside now. Take a step up." He guided her by her shoulders through a door, down a narrow corridor where her elbows grazed the wall, then into a room where their footsteps echoed. It smelled of damp old wood.

A folding chair creaked as he guided her onto it. She could hear his clothing rustling behind her, his steady breathing. Her hands were shaking.

"Sorry about this. We didn't anticipate this wrinkle—"

Ess cut him off, too many questions pressing on her lips. "You're the guy who was with me at Ballast Boat Shop in May, getting *Sea Dragon* upgraded."

She heard him sigh.

"You need to stop asking questions like that, stop digging. Let's be clear. This is not a jaunt down memory lane. My objective is to tell you as little as possible to get through this. Here's the situation. We used the services of some smugglers to get you over the border. Unfortunately, they want to meet with you. They're after more of the item you used as payment for your passage and ID. Since they obtained your Sarah Song ID, they know all your new info. They contacted me first as a professional courtesy, but you need to ditch this identity and get lost before they decide to just find you in the system. I can only stall them for so long."

These morsels of information felt like life being injected into her veins. "How did they find me? What do they want from me?"

"Your mooring buoy permit, the marina registry, both easy to hack. And they want something you don't have."

"What?"

His shoes scuffed on the floor behind her. She started to turn and immediately felt a hand on her head to stop her.

"Face forward." He moved his hand to her neck, his touch light but ready. She tried to pull away but he didn't let go.

Once she stopped moving, he continued. "You paid for your passage with unique drugs, and they want to purchase more. They'll do what they have to do to extract from you where they can get more."

Ess tried to process the idea that she was a drug dealer. It was so far from anything she'd pictured, a puzzle piece that she couldn't fit. The fingers on her neck moved as the shadow shifted position. A chill rippled over her skin. This guy knew her pre–memory wipe. He knew her real name. He could unlock everything and explain her to herself, draw a portrait so she could understand. She waited to see if he would say more. Pigeons cooed somewhere above them.

He sighed. "Do you understand?"

"The smugglers I used to get here want drugs from me."

"And you need to go. Sarah Song has to disappear. I mean it—the smallest ping on any network and these guys can find you. They are not people to mess with."

"Why did I have this special drug?"

"Doesn't matter."

"Who are you?"

"Also doesn't matter. Sarah, you need to take this seriously and you need to get gone. No calling Yori to say goodbye—"

She instinctively tried to turn when he said Yori's name, but his hand squeezed her neck so she clenched her teeth and obeyed, facing forward.

He continued. "Leave *Sea Dragon* for now, pull out as much cash as you can and get lost. Today."

"Stop," she said loudly, her voice and frustration echoing in the room. "You knew me before the memory wipe, but I'm blindfolded in an abandoned house with a guy who won't even tell me his name. You could be one of the people I'm running from for all I know. So, frankly, fuck off with the orders."

Holding her breath after her outburst, Ess cringed, waited for retaliation. Instead, he laughed. Not a sinister villain laugh, but one of sincere amusement.

His hot hand left her neck and his shoes scuffed the floor behind her. There was a creak of a second folding chair opening, and she flinched when he cleared his throat because he was now sitting next to her.

"I should have known you'd require more," he said, his tone softer, speech slower.

She tilted her head and the sliver of the floor she could see under her blindfold showed his feet as dark shadows. Jerking suddenly as the taste of copper filled her mouth, she swore and reached up to pull off the blindfold. Not now.

She returned to find herself still in darkness. He was holding her shoulders, held tightly until the spasm passed, kept her from falling onto the floor. Then his chair creaked as he let her go and shifted back. "You okay?"

She never knew the answer to that question. Leaning forward, she spit.

"Here."

Peppermint. She reached out greedily, felt the gum he put in her hand. Chewing, she relaxed a degree as the metallic taste receded.

They sat next to each other in the dark in silence for a while. Then he drew in a deep breath and spoke. "You gave the smugglers the memory-wiping drug."

Ess turned to him even though she couldn't see. He didn't stop her. A denial pressed against her lips but didn't make it out. The repercussions of this new fact came hard and fast, and Ess didn't like any of them. But it fit, slotted in tidily. She was connected to the other amnesia cases but not like them. "No," she said softly—not an expression of denial, just a wish it wasn't so.

"They use it to wipe their clients' memories so they can rob them."

He paused. "I'm telling you this because I need you to trust me and to know what kind of people these are. The smugglers find people who are motivated to relocate to Canada outside of official channels. They take a large fee to provide new Canadian identities and get them over the border. With the drug they can skip the identity creation headache and instead rob their clients of everything, on top of the usual smuggling fee."

"Why would I give them drugs to do that? What was I?"

The sound of an animal scurrying on the far side of the room filled the space left by his hesitation. "Your life was in danger. You needed a new identity and relocation as a rush order. They jacked their usual fee, and it was more than you could afford." He sounded pissed off as he recounted this. "So, you gave them the only other thing in your possession that had value." After a few seconds, he added, "It wasn't your plan to give them the drug. You had other intentions."

"Besides using it on myself?"

"Yes."

Dizzy, Ess put a hand to her head. He caught her hand, moved it away from her blindfold. She teetered in the chair, suddenly unsure in the darkness which way was up. The ground beneath her feet seemed to have disappeared.

He squeezed her hand before letting go. "Steady."

After a few breaths, Ess crossed her arms, sat up straight. She wasn't going to let this opportunity slip by, even if the room was upside down. She still needed answers.

"You know what I was running from."

"I do," he said slowly. His chair creaked.

"They're after me," she said, "whoever they are. I found a fancy tracking system installed in *Sea Dragon* back in Haida Gwaii."

"I know. That was *my* tracking system. Very expensive. I hope Raven is making good use of it."

"What?"

"Sarah, so far you are not on the radar of the people you ran from. Your death was faked and that story is holding. You're okay on that front right now."

"No one is after me?" Ess said the words aloud but didn't yet believe them.

"Not the people you think, no. But the smugglers are, and they will kill you in a heartbeat if you screw with them."

"I sailed a thousand kilometers because I thought I was in danger. Are you saying I could have just stayed in a pub in Haida Gwaii and that would have been fine?"

He didn't answer right away. "Do you regret the experiences you've had?"

Fuck his philosophical questions. "Who was I running from?"

No answer.

"Who was I?"

No answer. There was only the sound of his chair creaking.

Ess wanted to ask what kind of person she was, but she was too scared he might answer that. She was the kind of person who handed over memory-wiping drugs to smugglers who destroyed lives and then continued on her merry way.

"Answers to questions are rarely satisfying," he said. "Probably an important lesson."

"Fuck you," Ess said.

She heard him fold his chair and drop it on the floor. "Time's up. You need to get packing and get lost. I can stall the smugglers but at some point they'll find you without me and show up at Escape Marina. Go today. Off-grid completely. If something requires you to give your name or pay with a card, avoid it. Get somewhere rural, fast, and stay there until you hear from me."

"Why won't you tell me the rest? Who made you the arbiter of what I'm allowed to know? Who the hell are you?"

Ess reached for her blindfold and ripped it off just in time to be blinded by morning light streaming in the open door as he left. She ran after him but tripped on the folded chair he'd left in her path and face-planted on the dusty floor. By the time she got up and to the door, he was gone.

She stared out at the yard, adjusting to the sunny day she found outside, all the shadows gone. On autopilot, she walked down the stairs into the backyard, pacing as question after question circled through her. Eventually the questions settled into statements, distilled themselves into facts that she knew she would carry around forever like ballast.

The yard was a beautiful garden gone wild, an explosion of tall grasses and flowers. Ess walked through it, breathing in the smell of soil and crushing lavender buds in her hands as she tried to accept this new reality. The amnesia refugees that had just seemed like an odd parallel to her own experience were so much more. They were her fault. And she was supposed to run away from it all. Again.

31

AFTER HER MEETING, ESS WENT home, put on her running shoes, and set off, heading to the forest. She tried to outrun the thoughts. She'd done it to herself. The memory loss was permanent. She was responsible for all the amnesia refugees. It couldn't be fixed. Smugglers were coming for her.

Five kilometers later, when she arrived at the entrance to Colliery Dam Park, the smell of cedar trees and the promise of cool shade drew her in. Her steps and breathing slowed. She stood still to enjoy the clean forest air, to listen to the birds, to try to be in the moment. Branches rustled soothingly overhead. Then a voice startled her by calling her name.

Hito stood a few meters away, his running shirt drenched with sweat. He wiped his face with his forearm. Standing among the towering Douglas fir trees, he looked small for the first time.

It took Ess a second to remember she was not in Hito's good graces after her weirdness at the art studio and her pathetic text. She didn't know what to say. She also didn't know what to do with her hands, which she left hanging limply at her sides although she was sure that was conspicuously the wrong thing to do.

He'd smiled when he first saw her, but as he got closer, his expression became a combination of sadness, stress, and possibly annoyance. Or maybe she was reading too much into it.

"Out for a run?" he asked finally.

"Yeah. You too?"

"Making up for all the runs I missed while we were choked with wildfire smoke. It's good to be able to breathe again."

A black-capped chickadee filled the space left by their lack of conversation with its high-pitched, somewhat forlorn sound. Ess forgot Hito as she was hit with the fact she recognized the bird by its call, could picture the tiny creature in her mind. Its name sat on her tongue. Tears sprang to her eyes. This random bit of factual knowledge that she didn't know she owned washed over her, an unexpected gift. She wiped her eyes with her arm, made it look like she was trying to wipe away sweat, glancing at Hito to see if he had noticed her loss of composure.

"You ran here all the way from the marina?" he asked.

"Yeah."

"I didn't know you were a serious runner. Funny thing for a sailor, isn't it?"

"I hadn't thought of what a contradiction it is." She found it amusing now that he pointed it out. "I guess I get antsy on land."

"I know that feeling."

Ess followed his gaze up the main trail. There was a man in the distance, in the woods. She couldn't see what he was doing, but Hito kept an eye on him.

"How's the NDRT interview process going?" Ess asked, searching for a topic to fill the quiet, not wanting Hito to leave.

His head jerked back to look at her. "How do you... Right, yeah, uh—" He ran a hand through his hair, taking a moment to compose a reply. "I passed the physical test last week; Will is very proud. My interview is in a few hours."

She smiled. "That's great!" Hito's expression was hard to read. "Isn't it?"

"It… Yeah, it is, I guess. No, it is, it's great."

"A chance to run toward disaster," Ess said, remembering his words. "To help." Her shadow's instructions to run away suddenly looked pathetic.

A glimmer of sparkling green caught her eye on the ground. She knelt, cleared away leaves, and found a tiny hummingbird with bright-pink plumage around the neck and shimmering emerald feathers on his body.

"An Anna's hummingbird," Ess said.

Hito crouched next to her.

"They once only lived in California," Ess said quietly, the factual knowledge coming to mind effortlessly. "Now they live as far north as Alaska." She stroked the bird's feathers with a finger, expecting it to startle and fly away even though the unnatural spread of his wings made it clear that wouldn't be happening. It was strange to see the normally fast-moving creature so still. Like time had paused. She brushed dirt off its wing.

Down the path, the man in the woods shouted something indistinct and a second man stepped onto the trail. Hito stood, shifted to place himself between Ess and the two strangers, who were now walking toward them. "Were you going to run around the lower lake?"

"I don't really have a plan," Ess replied, covering the hummingbird with a cedar bough and standing.

Hito moved closer to her, keeping an arm's length of distance between them.

She swayed in place, full of conflicting desires to step closer and move away. Hito reached out to steady her but stopped his hand a few centimeters short, left it hanging in midair like an abandoned handshake.

"Should we loop around the lake together?"

They jogged side by side away from the men on the trail, Ess setting the pace. Once they were out of the woods and running along the lake with an open view around them, Hito's posture relaxed. Another birdcall rang out and a name and image popped into Ess's head. She was more prepared for it this time and aside from a twist of the guts, she was fine, kept running without missing a step. "Northern flicker," she said.

"What?"

"Hear the drumming? It's a woodpecker, a northern flicker."

"Really?" Hito stopped running and listened. "I've never seen a woodpecker."

Ess stood next to him, scanning for a standing dead tree that might have attracted the bird. "You still haven't, actually."

"Hey, don't spoil my nature moment."

"Right, sorry."

"What else can you hear in there?"

She closed her eyes, waited for her brain to identify something. "Lot of red-winged blackbirds, some squeaking hummingbirds." She smiled. This new fact about herself, that she knew birds, lifted her spirits. It meant she'd valued wildlife, thought it worth knowing about. She thought of Leeloo and her apparent experience with dogs. There was more to her than drugs and smugglers and causing woe.

"Hito, why do you feel compelled to help people?" she asked abruptly, her voice startling a few birds into flight.

"Oh. Wow. Uh—"

"Is it rude to ask that? I'm sorry—"

"No, it's fine. It just, it cuts to the core. No beating around the bush." He looked at the branches overhead, took a second. "I guess because I can, so I feel I should. I think it's how most people are, feel a responsibility to others, to do what we can."

Taking her gaze off his profile, Ess looked toward the canopy too, watched the trees swaying.

Hito's wrist comm dinged, yanking their attention back to earth.

"HA is on alert because another amnesia case was found this morning north of Denman Island by Comox. Not far up the coast." He swiped at his comm display, read it, frowned.

Ess clenched her teeth, cutting her cheek. The metallic tang of blood made Ess back away a few steps, suddenly reminded of the danger of a seizure in front of Hito. She needed to go. Now.

"I have to get back, prep for the interview." Looking up from his wrist, he shook his head as if he was trying to fling away an unwanted idea like raindrops from his eyelashes. "If you're a bird nerd, Buttertubs Marsh is a bird sanctuary. It's not far from here, a kilometer to the east."

Ess looked the way he was pointing, wished they could go together, wished life was that simple.

He opened his mouth to say something else but shook his head and shut it, waved awkwardly, and jogged off. Ess watched him run away with relief, spitting out the blood in her mouth.

—

It was morning. The headache was trying to kill her, but it was different from the earlier headaches, more wobbly and caused by too much cheap vodka. And it was her own fault. Though, she supposed the other ones had been too. A lot of bad things were her fault.

After her run the day before, she'd returned home, half listened to Joe vent about a sketchy tall guy hanging around the parking lot, and then sat at her table determined to think of a way out of her multilayered mess. Half a vodka bottle later, she'd crawled into bed full of self-pity.

Now it was a new day, and all she wanted was to stay in bed and deny the existence of the world and her role in fucking it up. But a kernel of an idea that had come last night demanded her attention. A possible alternative to running. She slid herself to the edge of her bed and put her feet on the floor, then levered her torso up. *Sea Dragon*'s radio was on. The weather report described the monster storm in the Pacific that was due to hit Vancouver Island hard. Soon.

Off the bed and two steps later, she was leaning over the sink trying not to vomit. When she looked in the mirror, she flinched. For a split second, the face from the video looked back at her. Blinking and shaking her head fixed that, but then her brain started replaying the thing her shadow had said. That she'd paid for her new life with the amnesia drug. She gripped the edge of the sink as she wondered if old her had imagined what the outcome of handing over the drug might be. Had she cared?

The nausea got worse but she choked back the saliva filling her mouth. Once she'd gained control over her stomach, she grabbed her notebook and read what she'd scribbled the night before to see if it was drunken nonsense or a plan that might actually work.

—

Her ears were ringing from the wind raging outside. The buzzer system for Hito's building was nonresponsive, so Ess caught the door as someone left and slipped in.

She stared at the numbers on the door. 502. Her face flushed as a memory from the first time she saw those digits came to mind. Putting the back of a hand to her cheek, she sank into the memory for a few seconds. A nice escape.

But she was here for Yori. She needed Yori for her plan to work. And Yori wasn't answering calls or responding to any messages.

No one came to the door when she knocked, but Ess heard a shout so she pushed it open and stuck her head in. Yori's voice bounced off the walls, flooding Ess with relief.

"I didn't ask you to put your life on hold for me, to sacrifice yourself. I can take care of myself—" Yori yelled.

"Obviously," Hito interrupted.

"Oh, your life is so perfect? Living alone, spending all your time working and working out?"

Ess stood in limbo, wanting to turn and leave, but needing to talk to Yori. She hovered in the doorway, half in, half out.

"Yeah, terrible. I don't party like you, Yori, haven't since I was twenty. Is it time you stopped? Grew up maybe?" Hito's voice stayed low and calm.

A moment of silence followed, so Ess pushed the door open and stepped in. "Hello?" she called.

"What the—" Hito said.

Yori appeared in the hallway, arms crossed.

"Hey, Yori, I need to talk to you—" Ess stopped, a darkness in Yori's expression making it clear this was not the time. "I can come back later."

"No, this is perfect, actually. Come in. We need help," Yori replied, her voice sharp.

"We really do not," Hito muttered.

Yori waved Ess over. Slipping off her shoes and walking down the hallway, Ess was confident she should be going in the other direction.

Hito left the living room before Ess got there. "What's going on?" Ess asked, looking at Yori.

Raising her voice enough to ensure Hito could hear her in the kitchen, Yori responded. "Hito has been offered and is turning down the NDRT position."

"Oh. That's, uh, that's a surprise." Ess sensed a minefield.

"Isn't it? Hito, it turns out, has been thinking of applying for the past five years. I talked to his trainer, Will, who says Hito is perfect for the team. That it's all Hito talks about."

Crouching to sweep up a broken glass on the living room floor, Hito was careful not to look at or acknowledge Ess. "Yori, it's not your business. It's a job offer. I'm turning it down. It's not the right time for me."

"Oh, yeah, the NDRT wants older people? Wait until you're thirty-eight and have back problems, then reapply? If you want this job, you should take this job; screw everything else."

"Yori, I've had a screwed-up shoulder since I was thirty. I've seen a physio about it every three months for the past four years. Which you'd know if you were ever here or cared about anyone's shit besides your own."

Stepping back, Ess glanced at the door, then Yori.

Yori's mouth opened, then closed. Lips tightened into a thin line.

Voice lowered, Hito tried to clarify. "I mean, NDRT people are never a hundred percent physically. If I wait a few years it won't hurt."

"Ask him why he isn't taking the job," Yori demanded.

A door slammed somewhere in the distance. Ess looked between Hito and Yori. Hito's posture was relaxed, but his face was flushed.

"Hito, why isn't it the right time?" Ess asked quietly, earnestly.

His eyes darted over to her, finally. He crossed his arms and shook his head subtly.

Jaw clenched, Yori was still fuming even though Hito had pulled back from the argument. "Oh, won't say it to her? Let me catch you up," she said to Ess. "Before you came, it slipped out. He needs to be here to be my safety net, to catch me when I fuck up."

Hito's lips tensed, holding back a snap response. "That's not what I said."

"I'm paraphrasing."

There was a pause as they stared at each other, and Ess wondered if this kind of fight was normal. It felt like a crater was opening between them, threatening to swallow everyone.

"Why is it wrong that I want to be here for you?" Hito asked finally. "I'm your older brother. It's what I'm supposed to do."

"Because I don't want you to live this abbreviated life and blame me for it!"

"My life is not abbreviated. I like my life," he said calmly, as if he was trying to infuse Yori with his stability. It had the opposite effect.

"You like your life, except for this job you've been dreaming about for five years that you train for every day, that Will says is super prestigious, that you're going to turn down so you can hang out here to pick me up when I fall apart again. How do you think it makes me feel? Like a perpetual loser, the basket-case sister you're always cleaning up after. It's shit, Hito."

The words washed over Ess, even though they weren't intended for her. Hito was giving up his dream job for his sister. Watching Hito weather his sister's anger at his attempt to do right by her made it clear to Ess what she needed to do about her own mess.

"Yori—" Ess put a hand on Yori's arm, but Yori pulled away.

"No, you don't understand, you don't know what it's like to look back over a life of memories of always being a failure and a disappointment. To have a perfect brother who forgives you every time you fuck up, amplifying your fucked-upped-ness because he's so goddamned not fucked up." She kept backing up, then turned down the hall, put on her shoes.

"Yori—don't go. Where are you going?" Hito called after her.

"If you reject this job, Hito, I swear, I will never set foot inside this fucking apartment again."

"Come on—"

"No, I'm serious. I won't come back."

The door clicked shut and Ess hesitated for a second, then ran, stepping around Hito and following Yori into the stairwell. She padded down the concrete stairs in her socks.

"Yori, I need to talk to you. I—"

A flight of stairs below, Yori turned her face up to Ess, eyes brimming with tears and flashing with anger.

"What?"

Ess tried to summarize her morning meeting, but it came out convoluted and confused. She tried again. "I'm responsible for the amnesia refugees. All of this is my fault. All of those people. It was me."

Yori wiped her eyes, shook her head.

"I need to fix it. I need to stop it."

Yori turned away and started down the stairs. "I need to get a drink. Call me tomorrow or next week or something."

"I'm going to fix it, Yori. I can't do it without you."

Yori's descent paused for a moment, then resumed. Her voice echoed up the stairwell. "I don't fix things, Ess; I screw them up. Go ask Hito. He'll tell you."

She didn't respond to Ess's pleas for her to wait. A metal door clanged shut below. Ess thought about going after her, trying to help in some way, but was at a loss. What advice could she offer that would be of any use? What did she know of siblings? She padded back up to the fifth floor. Standing at the door to Hito's apartment, she debated whether she should knock or slip in unnoticed to get her shoes. She was so tired of never knowing what the right thing was.

She knocked. Hito flung the door open immediately. His face fell when he saw Ess.

"Where is she?"

"She left," Ess said softly.

He walked away, leaving the door open. Ess stepped inside.

"I imagine you have good intentions in being here, but…" he said.

Ess's face flushed and her stomach gurgled uncomfortably. "Right. Sorry. I'll go." She moved to get her shoes, but he stood in the way. He shifted to block her path more.

"She wasn't surprised to see you," Hito said, mostly to himself.

Ess's headache intensified.

Hito crossed his arms. "You and Yori?" He tilted his head.

The half-formed question hovered in the air between them. Ess tried to parse what he was asking, what she should say. "We've been hanging out in the studio and—" Ess cringed as the word slipped out.

He raised a hand as if to rewind a video playback. "The art studio? You've got Yori going to her art studio?"

An awkward pause filled the apartment while Ess searched for a way out of the conversation. Lost, she nodded.

"I need a drink." Hito went to the kitchen, ushering Ess in before him.

The kitchen smelled faintly of burnt sugar and fake strawberry. Two blackened Pop Tarts sat on the counter, a bit of Yori chaos in Hito's orderly apartment.

"I've spent so many years trying to get her to consider picking up a paintbrush. It's the subject guaranteed to cause her to storm out or break something. I had to stop pushing, stop mentioning it even." Hito had his hand around a bottle of red vitamin water but he seemed to have forgotten it. "She's known you not three weeks and she's, what, painting? And letting you see it? Is she painting?"

"Exercises, not art. She says it's an important difference. Are you angry?"

"No. No. I'm mystified and confused. Whatever you've done, I don't understand it, but thank you." He turned his head to look at her, a half smile trying to form on his face. "Thank you."

She met his eyes briefly before looking at his hands on the counter. "I don't know that I did anything."

"Ten years I've been trying to get her in that studio, in the building even. She bites my head off if I mention it. You waltz in and…." He shook his head. "You are a puzzle, Ess."

Hito drank his red vitamin water and rinsed the bottle at the sink, put it in a box with other empties all lined up like soldiers waiting to be refilled.

The tension from his fight with Yori had faded, so Ess hazarded a question even though she needed to go. "Are you going to take the job?"

Running a hand through his hair, Hito slouched against the counter. "I don't know." He didn't continue until Ess took a step toward the door, thinking she'd gotten too personal and should leave. "She has to be clean when she stays here, so you've seen her during a good spell. But she never maintains this for long. She's insulted by my safety net, but she uses it. I don't know. Maybe she'd do better if there was no net. Maybe I'm enabling. Fuck." He ran his hands over his face.

"You want the job?"

His reply was immediate. "Yes." His head dropped like he was making a confession. "Yes."

The answer struck Ess with its raw honesty, and she wished she could tell him everything too. She wanted so badly to be raw and open.

"I should go," she said, moving toward the living room, then hesitating. "I'm... Giving advice isn't my thing, and you know Yori better obviously, but I believe her when she says she won't come back here if you turn the job down. So, she's kind of got you boxed in. Might as well take the job, see what happens."

Hito laughed. "Yeah, that thought crossed my mind."

He smiled and Ess let herself imagine that staying with Hito instead of going to her empty boat was an option. But the gutted, hollowed-out feeling she'd experienced when her shadow told her what she'd done came back, and while she tried to keep a neutral expression to hide her turmoil, she could tell from Hito's face that she was failing.

She made an awkward exit to escape, hyperaware that she never left him with her composure intact. Someday she would like to leave Hito's apartment without being discombobulated. Best not to think about these things. Better to focus on whatever the immediate next step was. In the lobby, she zipped her raincoat and braced herself to go out into the world.

32

THERE WAS A GIANT ASTERISK in her notebook by the part of the plan that hinged on Yori. Ess had hoped to actually go over the idea with Yori, get her assessment of it, but that hadn't happened.

She sent a message to shadow guy and her tablet rang a few minutes later, a call from a blank social profile.

"Explain," he said.

"Is it safe to talk?"

"Yes. What do you mean you aren't going into hiding?" he asked.

"I want to meet with the smugglers. Tomorrow. Before this storm hits. I want to get this done."

There was a pause.

"And why exactly are you delivering yourself to them on a platter?"

"We have no way to know that they haven't already tracked me down, looked me up in whatever systems they can hack." Ess chose her words carefully. "We don't know if there is time left to run. If I meet them and tell them some lie about how I can get more of the drug, then I buy myself time to disappear properly."

"It's too risky."

"It's not—"

"Sarah, they met you pre–memory wipe. That's why they're contacting you. They think you were a straight smuggling job. They don't know you wiped your memory, have no reason to think you would."

"So?"

"So, you were different. You are different. They'll know something's up. Even if they don't know what it is, it'll get you killed."

"Well, you'll have to help me so I can fake being the way I was before."

Another long pause.

"If you're hoping the smugglers know who you were before and will tell you, they don't. I contacted them for you. They never knew your real name or where you came from or what you were running from. They're professional in that respect; they don't ask questions."

"I'm not looking for answers. This isn't about that." She waited. He wasn't saying no outright, which surprised her. "You think they already know where I am."

He swore under his breath. "When they called me, they said they were sorry to interrupt your sailing vacation. They shouldn't know that you were planning to get a boat once in Canada. Fuck, maybe we let it slip and they remembered, but I don't think so."

Ess's fingertips tingled. She kept her voice steady, tried to adopt the authoritative tone of the her from the video. "Okay. Settled. Set up a meeting for tomorrow and then coach me on how to impersonate myself. I'll convince them I'm happy to sell them more of this stuff and have the ability to make it. Buy time."

Reluctantly, he agreed. Three hours later she was fortified with some bits of her old mannerisms and had a meeting date with the smugglers for the next day. They'd arranged to meet on their boat in Logan Bay, a small inlet with nothing nearby but a provincial park.

Contacting Yori to convey the details of the meeting so Yori could arrange her part wasn't going well. She wasn't responding to calls or messages, and her social profile had been dark since the fight at Hito's. Ess tried all day, then left a message and hoped for the best.

237

Yori, hope you're okay. Sorry if I made things worse with Hito. I feel like I did. Also sorry for turning around and asking for your help now. I think my life is on the line or I wouldn't bother you.

I need you.

I'm meeting with the people I mentioned to try and fix the trouble I caused. My plan depends on Hito showing up at Logan Bay and boarding the boat he finds there at 2:15 p.m. The boat will look like it's in distress at 2:15 to give him an excuse to board. It will be obvious which boat.

It needs to be exactly 2:15. Earlier won't work, later may be too late for me. The risk of these people wanting to kill me is high.

You know Hito best, so tell him what you need to to get him there, but don't mention me. A tip about smugglers from your refugee community contacts maybe? Just don't say anything about me being there. If all goes to plan, he shouldn't find me onboard.

I'm counting on you.

33

FROM THE PUBLIC DOCK, Ess borrowed an old boat with a worrying dent on the port side. It didn't look long for this world but it was easy to access, didn't require a key to start the motor, and there was no way to trace it to her, so she got over her guilt about stealing and motored off in it.

The sea was surprisingly calm considering they were only a few hours away from the worst storm of the century. The decrepit boat held up and got her to Logan Bay a few minutes early. There was only one boat in the area, an older pleasure fishing craft called *Bait and Tackle*, the type of thing that took groups of people on game-fishing adventures back when there was enough legal stuff left to catch to make that fun. A skinny figure stood on the upper deck, watching her as she approached.

"Sarah," he called down when she came alongside and turned off her motor.

"Hello." She wondered if she should wait to be invited to tie up. *Be curt*, her shadow had said. *Use as few words as possible. Look unimpressed.* These tidbits of guidance suddenly felt like far too little to assemble into a convincing personality.

"Wonderful to see you again, need a hand?"

"I got it." She quickly secured her boat and stepped onboard, looking around. It was a solidly mediocre boat, the kind your eyes slid past in boredom.

The rail-thin man extended a hand and Ess shook it firmly. Another, larger figure watched them from the door to the cabin a few meters away. Ess stumbled, caught off guard by an unexpected wave tipping the boat.

The thin man assisted her back to an upright position and she gave him a tight smile.

"Thanks for the ID, Frank. It's holding up well." She hoped the names the shadow had given her were right.

"Good to hear. You paid us well, so it would've been a shame if Sarah Song hadn't worked out. It has such a nice ring to it." He scanned the area around the boat, the water empty except for some cormorants floating nearby, and then gestured to the cabin. "Come in and we can discuss opportunities to work together over a drink."

Be imperious, the shadow had said. *Carry yourself tall; you're better than everyone else.* Ess smoothed her hair, a gesture she'd memorized from the warning video and went inside. The blinds were all closed, and it took Ess's eyes a moment to adjust to the darkness. It smelled of mildew and stale beer.

"You remember my colleague." Frank gestured at the figure by the door, a woman who looked like she could bench press Ess without straining. She had a gun in a holster, and seeing it made Ess question this whole plan. Knowing they would be armed and seeing an actual gun were two different things.

"Casey, wasn't it?" Ess ventured.

The armed woman nodded and extended her hand as though she expected something.

Ess had no idea what she was supposed to do. She took a breath and looked inconvenienced and unimpressed, wrapping this persona around herself like a protective cloak.

They stood in silence, frozen like a strange still life.

"Casey will need to check your bag. Precautions, you understand."

Reluctantly, Ess handed over her bag, and while Casey rifled through it, she wandered toward the control panel at the front of the main cabin, pretended to look at a photo pinned to the wall while assessing the equipment.

"Fan of game fishing, are you?" Frank asked.

Ess's stomach twisted at the random reference she didn't get. Then she focused on the photo in front of her and realized it was someone hoisting a trophy next to a massive fish. She shrugged and turned her back on the bank of electronics, crossed her arms. It was already 2:00 p.m.

"Do we need to small talk or can we get right to business?"

Frank smiled thinly. "The business is exceptionally straightforward. We want to buy more of your boutique drug. Set up an exclusive pipeline."

Ess assessed Frank instead of responding right away. He was well dressed, clean-shaven, and he carried himself with confidence. But he looked hungry, chronically undernourished. "You haven't exactly been subtle in your use of the last batch," Ess said. "It's all over the news; authorities are investigating. I'm nervous about this coming back to me. Tarnishing my new identity. Which wasn't cheap."

Casey grunted like Ess had hit a nerve. Frank shot her a look.

"Yes, well, the work to date was the learning phase." He opened a fridge and pulled out a cheap beer, offering one to Ess who shook her head.

"The drug let us skip the headache of building new identities. People still get relocated as promised, just with an added service they didn't ask for in exchange for additional payment they didn't agree to. In the end no one knows there's been a crime. The victims certainly can't file a complaint, so I think it's quite brilliant." Casey snorted and Frank frowned. They all swayed as the boat rocked on another wave.

"That was a good game, but we're looking at moving on. And for that, we need you." He lifted his beer can at Ess. "As you astutely point out, a volume-based operation like we've been running isn't sustainable, attracts too much notice. Gets Border Services all tense, our transport routes get watched, a lot of bother. A more niche but lucrative market has opened up now that people know memory wiping is a real thing. So, we need more product. And here we are." He gestured at Ess and smiled a thin, creepy smile.

"What's this new market?"

"Oh, that's not something you need to worry about."

Ess tried her best to sound bored. "If I'm supplying the drug to facilitate this new business model, then I do need to worry about it."

"People *want* their memory wiped," Casey said.

"Case!"

Eyes on Ess, Casey shrugged.

"People want *to pay you* to wipe their memories?" Ess asked, also ignoring Frank now.

Casey nodded. "They started to come out of the woodwork when the amnesia refugees hit the news and authorities confirmed it wasn't a virus. Discreet inquiries through back channels—"

"That's enough, Case," Frank said, voice tight.

"People desperate enough to wipe their memories can't possibly pay a sum that would be of interest," Ess said flatly. "If you're not going to level with me, we can end this conversation now. I'm out." She started toward the door.

Frank intercepted her and clutched her arm, fingers digging in. "Sit. Down." He pulled out a chair and pointed at it.

Casey's hand had moved to her holster, so Ess eased into the chair, sitting on the edge, back straight. She'd played it too hard.

"We don't need to give you a business plan, Sarah. We're not looking for investors. We are buying product you illegally possess. There are a number of people at the nexus of well-resourced and wanting to wipe their memories, and we have an opportunity to serve them. If you cooperate, you can participate in this bounty. Or, we can find less pleasant ways to convince you."

It was 2:05.

"Prior to getting into this line of…transportation work, we had a business deal go sideways. Our partners expressed objections at the eleventh hour," Frank said, leaning in close. "The other parties are no longer around to share their objections." He sat back, looked at Casey's face all scrunched up with displeasure at the reference, and laughed. "Casey is still touchy about it. Got blood on her favorite shirt."

Sweat rolling down her back, Ess shifted on the chair, tried to ignore what Frank was implying. She did her best to look unimpressed, keeping her hands in her lap to hide the shaking. "This new approach will be on the front-page news less. Is that what you're saying?"

Arms crossed, Frank nodded, all business again. "Yes, higher fees mean we can go that extra mile and tuck them away where they'll be less noticed, get them on their feet so they blend in better. We've trialed it already. Wildly successful."

Ess pretended to like the sound of that. "Did you bring the used vials like I asked?"

Frank signaled to Casey, who left her post and pulled a black case from under the table. She opened it to show rows of empty vials tucked under bands that kept everything neat and secure. Forty doses. A terrifyingly large syringe sat in the case along with a bottle of familiar pills.

She pulled a vial and held it to the light looking for residue. It had no markings other than a long sequence of numbers. "I can work from this. Did you use all of them?"

"Actually, there's one dose left," Frank said. "We thought that might help motivate you, knowing we had that at our disposal."

"Wiping my memory wouldn't get you what you need," Ess said, dropping into her imperious voice. Her heart skipped a few beats at the idea of starting over, going through that horror again. Her palms itched.

"True. But wiping someone you care about, is that motivating? You have a particular friend. She's a pretty, dainty thing. Japanese? Cute freckles? Do you think she'd be sad to lose all her memories? Not everyone is. For some, the idea seems to be a nightmare, for others…" He searched for the word. "Liberation."

Another wave hit. Glasses clinked in cabinets and something fell over with a thud. Ess pulled her persona tighter. "I do not appreciate being threatened," she said, voice nearly choked with anger. "And it's not necessary if you can pay. I can synthesize more of the drug using a sample but it'll cost five thousand Canadian per dose, and you will never threaten anyone I know again."

"Well, suddenly you're amenable to being business partners. Isn't that grand. Three thousand per dose and we need ten doses immediately."

Ess frowned. She should negotiate to be convincing, but the clock was ticking. "Fine. We can start there and revisit terms after the first ten. It will take time to get the equipment I need. I can promise ten doses seven days from now if you're okay with no quality control."

"A week is too long—"

"You think I can grow advanced medical-grade nanotech overnight? Do you have any idea what this drug is, how it works? It's not meth you cook up in a shed." Ess stood and marched to the control panel, muttering under her breath. She put her hands on the desk, quickly flipping the transponder and radio switches off. Then she straightened, turned, and put her hands up in front of her. "I'm sorry. I get frustrated when dealing with people who don't appreciate the technical complexity of what I do. I can get you ten doses in a week. It's not physically possible to do it any faster."

Squinting at her, Frank chewed his lip, then nodded. "Deal."

"Deal," Ess confirmed, forcing a tight smile.

They shook hands. It was 2:12 p.m.

"I need to use the bathroom," Ess said.

Casey handed over her bag and showed her the bathroom, down a narrow set of stairs. Ess stepped into the small room and shut the flimsy door behind her, a breeze on her face from the open porthole. She took out her water bottle, unscrewing the bottom in the sink and extracting a canister in a plastic bag hidden inside. Pausing to be grateful that Casey had only been looking for weapons and had overlooked the weird collection of items Ess was carrying, she took out the Pringles can and dumped the chips in the garbage, pulling a second canister out.

She'd purchased the smoke bombs from a photography shop downtown. She tied them on a string and checked the built-in timers. She programmed one to go off after two minutes and the other after six. Each one was supposed to provide three minutes of thick black smoke. She hoped it was enough. Hoped Yori had done her part. Hoped Hito had agreed to do what Yori had asked of him. The amount of hope supporting the plan made Ess's hands shake.

She tied the string holding the chain of bombs to a towel rack, then pressed start on each timer and slid the canisters out the window. 2:14 p.m. She flushed the toilet and washed her hands.

Back in the main cabin, Frank had poured three shots of vodka to celebrate their business deal. Casey drank hers perfunctorily. Ess took her glass, hands already slick with fresh sweat. A sudden vision of Hito boarding this boat and getting shot by Casey made her choke on her drink. Frank clapped her on the back, laughing.

"Not everyone grows up with vodka this foul. It's a family tradition for me so it goes down easy. Casey says she'd rather drink paint thinner." He laughed.

Ess gripped the table, her eyes watering—not from Frank's blows or the vodka burning her throat but from the sudden absolute certainty that she'd made a massive mistake. Her stomach rumbled, threateningly.

She started to move back toward the bathroom, needing to untie the smoke bombs before they could go off, to stop the whole crazy scheme, but Frank took her arm and sat her down, pressed a glass of water into her hand.

Ess had been half-drunk when she thought of this plan. That should have been a red flag.

At the moment, Frank was excited and overlooking Ess's change in mood, but Casey was watching her with a frown forming. Casey with the gun.

2:17 p.m.

Only one path out of this now. Ess straightened her back and wiped her eyes with the back of her hand. "Wait, let me try again," she said, waving at the bottle on the table, trying to look confident and relaxed.

Frank cheered like he was at a soccer game and poured her a generous new shot, sliding the glass over. Chugging it in one go, Ess felt it burn but kept it down.

"Tell me who wants to wipe their memory," Ess said, trying to keep Frank from looking out a window and seeing smoke. "Just an example. I don't understand."

This time Frank shrugged and talked freely. "The drug was a mistake, right? A dead end en route to some useful treatment. But, I mean, presumably the manufacturers kept producing it because they knew there was something useful there, but they were just too chickenshit to use it. Or maybe they are using it and keeping it hush-hush. Imagine how giddy the military would be with this in their arsenal." He let her consider that horror before continuing. "You were very tight-lipped about all this last time, wouldn't say who made it, claimed you didn't know anything about it. Want to revise that?"

Ess shook her head.

He frowned, then took another sip of vodka and continued. "Domestically, I think the number of people wanting do-overs is going to skyrocket as the world gets more and more fucked up. Lose your entire family in a Cat 7 hurricane that destroyed your city? Or in a war over water? Just wipe all that trauma and start over fresh. Give me an advertising budget, I can sell that easy. 'Reboot: the ultimate ghosting.'"

"Starting over isn't rainbows and unicorns," Ess said.

"You say that because you did it without wiping your memories." Frank laughed, unscrewing the bottle to pour himself another shot. "Can't wipe 'em now though, we need what's in there!"

Casey's head suddenly swiveled. "Do you hear that?" She ran out on deck.

Someone was shouting about fire.

Ess stood but Frank pressed a finger against her chest. "You. Stay here."

Hands up, Ess sat as Frank joined Casey outside to investigate. Ess could see that a boat had pulled alongside them. Casey and Frank were trying to understand why black smoke was billowing from their boat. Tearing the cushions off the dinette seats, Ess yanked out the life preservers and coiled hoses. She chucked the gear down the stairs and squeezed herself into the empty storage space, carefully putting the cushions back on the wood and sliding it into place as she lay down. There was one small cutout she could use to watch the cabin and to breathe so she didn't feel like she was in a coffin.

Now it was up to Hito.

—

Voices were yelling on deck, but the cabin stayed empty for a frustratingly long time. Ess shifted in place, tried to find a version of the fetal position that was less painful but still let her keep her view of the door through the quarter-sized peephole.

Frank's voice boomed in the cabin. "We're fine—"

"That was a lot of smoke. We should find where it was coming from. Have you checked below deck?"

Ess smiled at Hito's voice. Yori had gotten Hito here exactly to plan, and Ess was too full of relief to regret it.

"Thanks, buddy, appreciate the concern," Frank said, "but we're good. Probably just a joke by our friend—"

There was a pause. Ess saw Frank's feet turn in a circle. She held her breath.

"Someone missing?" Hito asked.

"No. No. We're good. You're right, I should check below. Casey, check if the skiff is still tied up."

Frank stomped down to the sleeping cabins below, and Hito took the opportunity to walk around. His feet stopped at the table, and Ess heard the case of drug vials click open. "Shit," Hito said under his breath. Another click. She imagined him counting the three shot glasses on the table. His feet went out of view. Ess allowed herself a small, slow breath.

"Hey, Steve, it's Hito. Yeah, enjoying civilian life, but I've actually got a three-fourteen. You're on duty now, yeah? Can you send a patrol…"

Ess strained to hear, but Hito's voice was too quiet. Casey came in, walking past Ess's line of sight to join Hito somewhere by the control panel. "What are you doing?"

"Oh, hey. I was checking your control panel for any errors that might explain the smoke. This rig isn't running a diesel engine still, is it?"

A long pause followed.

"Is Frank below?"

"Yeah."

"Step away from the control panel."

"Oh. Sure, okay."

Hito's feet came into view closer to the door. Sweat dripped down Ess's face. It felt like she wasn't getting enough oxygen. Shaking her head to get rid of the drowsiness settling over her, she banged her head on the back of the box and froze. Her head throbbed from the blow, and she thought for sure Casey would tear off the seat and haul her out.

Instead, Frank's footsteps returned.

"No fire. Everything's fine. Appreciate the concern but no help needed," Frank said.

"Frank, the skiff is secure. What's going—"

Frank cut Casey off. "Good. Everything's fine then."

"Smoke but no fire," Hito said slowly.

"Exactly. We'll give the old girl a look-over when we get to dock. Sorry to hold you up. I'm sure you have places to be."

Hito ignored Frank's attempt to shuffle him along and instead asked about their radar system, said he'd been thinking of upgrading, rambled on about his current unit and problems he had with it. Frank wasn't helpful, but Hito kept asking technical questions anyway. After a few minutes of this, when it became clear Frank and Casey didn't know anything about the boat they were on, Frank cut Hito off.

"Buddy, we have to get going. You need to leave."

"Am I holding you up? I didn't realize. So hard to keep track of time on the water. But you're right, weather is getting bad, we should all get someplace safe before the storm hits. They're saying it's going to be a one-in-a-thousand-year storm. Best batten down the hatches, literally." Hito laughed. "Oh, you know your radio and transponder are off, eh?"

"Oh yeah? And who are you, local harbor police? Going to write me a ticket?"

"I'm not police. But marine law does require all boats to have an operational communications device. It's basic safety equipment in case you get into trouble. A real fire, for example. Aside from the serious safety concerns, failure to have an operational comm means a third party can board to investigate and ensure the ship is safe."

Hito was speaking very slowly and being wordier and more pedantic than normal. Even Ess found it somewhat tiresome but was grateful he was sticking around. If he left, Ess knew Frank and Casey would find her quickly, and they wouldn't be offering her vodka shots.

Frank ushered Hito toward the door, but after a few steps, Hito planted his six-foot-one frame in place. To Ess, he looked vulnerable without his uniform and body armor, but his posture sent a message.

"I really can't leave until you get your systems operating. If you were to go down after I left, it would be my responsibility." Hito paused. "I wouldn't want to live with that on my conscience."

"God. Quite the Boy Scout, aren't you? We're so lucky you came by."

Ess heard Frank stomp over to the controls, where he argued with Casey in a low voice. Hito stayed near the door, glancing outside, checking his watch. She thought she saw him smile.

A booming voice over a loudspeaker crashed their party. "*Bait and Tackle*. This is Harbour Authority. Prepare to be boarded."

Casey and Frank swore in unison. Hito backpedaled a few steps as Casey rushed him, gun pointed at his chest.

"What the fuck did you do?" she yelled.

"Hey, hey, calm down." Hito put his hands out in front of him.

Frank peeked through the blinds. "Two HA patrol boats? You called HA? You motherfucker. That's really inconvenient. Casey, put the gun away. Shooting this jackass won't get rid of them."

"I'm not going away, Frank! Not after Madison. I'll never get out once they pin that bloodbath on me."

Casey turned her head to yell at Frank and her arm dropped. With a move so quick Ess missed it, Hito disarmed Casey, ejected the clip from the gun, and emptied the chamber. Placing the gun on the floor, he put a foot on it and lifted his hands as two HA agents appeared in the door, weapons drawn.

"Hito, you good?"

"Yeah. Just disarmed this one. You want to secure the weapon?"

"Let's get these two sorted first."

The second agent moved in and tried to put cuffs on Casey, but she struggled. Ess could only hear grunts and the sound of body parts hitting the floor. Then it was quiet until the dinette seating creaked as someone was dropped onto it. Frank simply extended his hands and let the agent cuff him.

"I see you're really adapting well to life as a nonagent, Hito." The agent laughed, then got serious. "What's your read of all this?"

"Not sure. Suspect there's someone else onboard though. And drugs…"

She strained to hear, but Hito's voice faded. Everything became muffled and a familiar metallic taste filled Ess's mouth.

34

ESS SPASMED AND HER KNEE slammed against the side of her box. She tried to find the little hole to see what was happening, but she was too disoriented.

"Max, over here!"

A new voice.

Ess clenched her jaw. A seizure hadn't been part of the plan.

The seat above her flew off. Ess lifted an arm to block the sudden sharp light cutting across her.

"Well, hello!" said the excited new voice.

"Holy shit," said a second new voice.

Squinting, Ess looked at the two uniformed people staring at her like she was a carnival prize they'd just won. Neither one was Hito. She tried to sit up and failed, her legs stuck under her. The uniformed woman helped Ess out and onto a seat. Ess extended her legs and got blood flowing into her feet. Her left knee was red and swelling. She was drenched in sweat, a sour odor wafting off her.

The two agents stared at each other and Ess.

"Hello, miss. Do you have a name?" the woman asked.

"Uh. I…" Ess put a hand to her temple, remembered the headache when she'd first woken up in Haida Gwaii, remembered the disjointed thoughts, the confusion. She looked around for Hito but didn't see him. "I don't… I'm sorry, I…" Her voice trailed off.

"Oh my god, Max, she's one of them."

The woman nodded, grinning.

"What's going on," Ess said, voice rising in pitch. "Why can't I remember my name? Where am I?" She moved her hand to where she'd hit her head earlier, felt a bump. "Did I hit my head?"

"Hey." The guy sat next to her, gestured for Max to go to the sink. "Look, we're Harbour Authority agents. We're here to help you. Do you have any identification?"

Ess patted her shorts but the pockets were empty, of course. She shook her head.

"That's okay. Do you know the other people who were on the boat?"

"There were others? Why am I on a boat?"

"Okay. Yeah, don't worry about that. We're going to take you to the doctor and have them check you out. But you're safe. Have some water."

Ess's hand trembled for real as she took the glass and drank. She considered vomiting for accuracy but couldn't make it happen despite the boat being bumped around by waves constantly now. No more smooth sailing.

The agents called for backup while Ess sat cradling her head in her hands. From their chatter, she learned Hito had just left with Frank and Casey in the other HA boat to give his formal statement. He'd rescued her just as she'd needed and hadn't even known she was there.

The agents ignored her while they searched the boat. The case with the drug vials was sitting on the table with a tag on it. They found another gun and a stack of cash under a mattress, Canadian and American bills.

When the next HA boat arrived, they loaded Ess on to it wrapped in an emergency blanket despite the heat. She looked at everyone in confusion, asked the new agents what was going on. They promised to explain it all at the station.

The ride back was slow, the water rough, wind gusting. The boat rising up and slamming down over and over reminded Ess of the storm she'd narrowly survived on her trip. Seemed so long ago, another life. Focusing on the horizon to fend off nausea, she studied the looming dark clouds. She asked the agents when the storm was going to hit, and they looked at her with surprise that she knew the forecast. She pointed a shaking hand at the dark clouds on the horizon. "Bad storm coming, yeah?"

Everyone relaxed.

"Supposed to be a one-in-a-thousand-year monster, hitting Nanaimo tonight. But don't worry, you'll be somewhere safe and dry. Lucky we found you. Would be a very bad day to be adrift on the ocean in some sketchy little skiff."

"Lucky," Ess repeated dully as they slammed down again. She leaned over and vomited into the water.

Someone handed her a bottle of water. "Happens to all the amnesia refugees, apparently," they said.

She nodded and looked away.

—

Once on land, they skipped the Harbour Authority station and shuttled Ess directly to the hospital. With the coming storm, they didn't want to delay.

They put her in a curtained-off area to change. Her sour, sweat-encrusted T-shirt went into the garbage, and she slipped on a blue gown, soft and fraying from hundreds of washings. Then she was escorted to a room where staff from various organizations sat across from her at a conference table, their uniforms and suits making her feel ridiculous and vulnerable in her thin gown and hospital-issue slippers.

Her request for drugs to dull the pounding headache was refused.

She had to wait for the doctor. She felt out of control of even the most basic aspects of her life in a way that made her dizzy.

Someone inspected behind her ears, lingering on one side but refusing to explain what they saw when she inquired.

They asked her basic questions that she failed to answer. She didn't know her name. Didn't know how she'd come to be on that boat. Didn't know where she'd come from. Modicum of truth in all her nonanswers. With each question they asked that revealed a new supposed chasm of blankness, Ess ratcheted up her visible frustration. Simulating this was easy and setting it loose was unexpectedly cathartic, so she didn't hold back.

Once she'd spent her anger and been reduced to messy sobbing, they stopped. The biggest challenge was hiding her anger at herself for causing others to go through this humiliating process.

The uniforms and suits left and she was carted to radiology, where they scanned her, the technicians grumbling about patients in need getting bumped yet again. Ess numbly followed instructions until they deposited her in a private room, head ringing from the MRI machine. A nurse entered with mild painkillers and said the specialist wouldn't be able to come for a while due to the storm. He advised that Ess "sit tight" and then left, locking the door behind him.

The pills didn't have the *c* logo on them the way the ones on *Sea Dragon* had, but her headache this time was a garden-variety one caused by dehydration and stress so she swallowed the pills with a lot of water and moved on.

Everything had gone to plan. Yori had gotten Hito there, and Hito had been perfect. And the authorities had slotted her in as evidence that they'd caught the amnesia refugee smugglers. Hito hadn't seen her, which simplified everything immensely, for now. If they brought in Doctor Saravanamuttoo in person, Ess had to hope the doctor was sufficiently motivated to get the smugglers behind bars that she'd keep it to herself that Ess had been a functioning amnesia patient a week ago and might not be freshly wiped smuggled cargo.

Eventually they would photograph her and show her face on the news, and whoever she did the memory wipe to get away from would know she was alive. That she could live with. Her guts twisted far more at the thought of Hito seeing her face as the amnesia refugee found on the smuggler boat and knowing she was lying. Hito would feel compelled to tell the authorities that Ess hadn't been smuggled, that she'd been walking around Nanaimo free as a bird. Yori would have to tell him things to try to keep him quiet. Things about Ess. That bothered her far more than faceless people chasing her for reasons she didn't understand.

She paced the room. The locked door made her antsy. She'd intentionally put herself here; this was the plan, but having no options still rankled.

"Suck it up," she said to herself. "You made this bed."

Turning on the TV for a distraction, she watched the reports of the storm, which had made landfall on the other side of Vancouver Island a few hours ago. The beloved seaside town of Tofino had been destroyed. The storm was quickly crossing the island eastward, and Nanaimo was already seeing swaths of drought-stressed trees topple over in the wind, causing widespread power outages. And far worse was coming. It was already the worst storm the region had ever seen, just another prediction of the climate scientists leaping off the page.

Video played in an endless loop: roofs folded under fallen trees, roads buckled due to landslides, flooding, boats smashed against the shore. Ess turned it off and listened to the wind howling outside, felt like she deserved to be out in the thick of it getting bashed around.

Tempted by the bed and a chance to rest, to escape, instead she flicked off the light and dragged the plastic chair over to the window to at least witness the storm. She watched trees bend in the wind, wondered how long they could be whipped around before they yielded. She willed them to withstand the fury. When the streetlights winked out, she closed her eyes and listened.

35

She awoke with a start. It was dark. The sounds of the hospital outside her door had gotten louder. PA calls were constant.

A dark figure moved on her left and she scrambled out of the chair, opening her mouth to scream.

"Don't scream, Sarah."

That took her breath away and she stood in her bare feet on the cold linoleum, mouth hanging open while her sleepy brain processed the voice. She recognized the voice. Her eyes adjusted. The figure was in scrubs, complete with a surgical mask and cap.

"You need to get dressed," he said, throwing a bag of clothes at her.

The bag hit her in the chest and fell to the floor. She mechanically pulled on the pants and shirt while he moved to the door to peak at the hall through the window.

Her shadow.

"What is—"

"Always so many damn questions."

"How did you know to—"

"I listened to the police radio chatter. Heard they took in an amnesia refugee case along with suspected smugglers from a boat in Logan Bay. What have you *done?*"

His tone was one of barely contained rage. Ess pulled on the rubber boots she found in the bag. "I fixed my mistake, as best I could."

"By getting caught and taken into custody."

"By being the evidence they needed to lock the assholes up."

He didn't answer right away.

"You intended to let them detain you, perform their tests. That was your plan all along, to get caught and carry on this charade?"

Fully awake now, Ess looked at herself dressed in street clothes. "You came to break me out?"

"You've given them what they need. HA agents pulled an amnesia case off the boat as stowed cargo, and they have medical records proving you're an amnesiac. They're set. Fuck. Did they take your photo?"

"Not yet. They skipped all the HA processing to get me to the hospital before the storm."

"Good. Then you slip out now; they still have their case and they can't track you. As far as they know, you don't have any memories of the smugglers. You are literally of no use in person. You won't exactly be a helpful witness."

This was annoyingly logical, but Ess hesitated.

"What about the people you're supposed to be hiding from? The whole fucking point of all this. You want them to see your face on the news as the latest amnesiac found?"

Ess shrugged, tried to make it look nonchalant. "If they see me listed as an amnesiac and still feel the need to kill me over something I don't remember..." She stood tall. "I'm done being scared. I've lost so much already. I'm not giving them any more."

He adjusted his face mask, pinched the bridge of his nose. "Fine. I won't drag you out of here." He slipped something from his back pocket, contemplated it in his hand for a moment. "You should look at this. I was meant to give it to you earlier." He held it out.

Crossing the room, Ess stayed as far from him as she could while taking the object from his hand. An old, cheap cell phone. It required a fingerprint to unlock. She tried her right index finger, and the screen blinded her as it flashed the home screen. It was empty except for a blinking text memo notification. She clicked it.

Sarah,

If you have this, then something from your past has shown up. That's the only condition where you get this device and this note.

You may need leverage to extract yourself from whatever situation you're in, so I've put the documents related to what caused this mess on a hard drive in Vancouver. The physical location is listed below. It will require your fingerprint to access.

The storage device holding the documents will format itself ninety-six hours after this phone is unlocked and this message read. Everything will be erased.

This four-day limit is to ensure you only go after these documents if you truly need them. I know you won't be able to commit to your new life if your old name and identity are sitting on a storage drive forever.

My advice: Let the documents disappear if you possibly can.

SS

"What time is it? Is the storm over? Are flights operating? Ferries to the mainland?" Ess said.

"Hold on."

Ess looked for the remote for the TV to find the weather or news but he grabbed her arm. She jerked away and he let go, backed off a few steps.

"Just wait." He adjusted his mask. "I was instructed to give you that if something from your past came up. I didn't know what was on it, didn't know if the smugglers showing up counted. So I opened it to read it, to assess." His voice had lost its bossy edge.

Ess stopped mentally tallying the steps needed to get off Vancouver Island to the mainland, to the city of Vancouver. "What do you mean, you opened it?"

"When we met the other day, while you were blindfolded I used your finger to unlock the phone so I could read the message. During your seizure."

"How many hours ago, exactly?"

He was quiet, resuming his position by the door and glancing out the window. "We met at six. I opened it not long after. It's 5:00 a.m. now. About twenty-five hours left, plus or minus."

Ess's stomach lurched. She reminded herself that Vancouver was just an hour-long flight from Nanaimo normally; twenty-five hours was plenty of time, if she wanted it.

"Should we get out of here now?"

Squeezing the phone in her hand, Ess let the possibility of answers flood her veins. All she'd wanted since she woke up in this nightmare was to understand who she was. To get that old life back. She nodded, gave in to temptation, following him into the bright hallway.

36

Ess had been secured in a quiet wing of the hospital away from emergency services, but as they moved toward the elevators, things became increasingly chaotic: hallways crammed with equipment and staff rushing between rooms shouting. Her escort, clad in medical garb, carried himself with arrogant authority, and no one looked at them twice as they passed. The smell of disinfectant and fake lemon brought Ess's headache back.

On the ground floor, he navigated them away from the primary entrance. A barrel-chested security guy by the door to the ultrasound department shifted like he was going to ask them to justify their presence. Ess lowered her head and looked away. Walking in front, her escort said something to the man in an urgent tone that sent him down the hall at a quick pace.

They continued to a side exit, dodging staff hustling on urgent business. Coded calls rang out from the PA system continuously. Ess's escort grabbed a jacket shoved behind an empty chair without slowing, shrugged it on, then they simply walked out the door.

Ess was almost pushed back into the hospital by the wind, an angry, vigorous shove. She staggered, had to lean into the wind just to stay upright. It seemed like a suggestion, a prudent one, by nature to turn back, and she did look back at the hospital, hair whipping in her face. But she didn't want to go backward. Her escort—mask still on, hood up, and several steps ahead—turned to check on her, then pointed across the parking lot to a row of low-rise office buildings on the other side of the street.

Ess dropped her chin and focused on advancing. Small steps forward.

There was no rain, which she found strange. Clearly it *had* rained—half the parking lot was flooded, cars partially submerged—but the storm in that moment was focused on wind. The air felt alive, a sensation she knew from sailing, the wind as an entity with intent, with power. It could get you where you wanted to go or snap your mast and sink you. This was a snapping, sinking sort of wind.

A street sign hurtled past them, slicing the air like a knife, smashing into a bus shelter and splintering the glass. Ess watched it happen, heard only howling wind.

Her escort moved to her side, gripped her arm, and tugged her forward. He held on as if she might fly off next, might smash against something sharp and shatter.

The weight of him anchored her, made her steps more secure. They held on to each other and moved together.

At the sidewalk Ess froze, staring at the tableau of damage in front of her through narrowed eyes. The hospital parking lot had been edged with tulip trees and they'd grown tall, unfettered by building foundations. Now it was as if a forest of giants had tumbled down, carpeting the road. Sixty years to grow a tree, and just one storm to erase it all.

He jerked her arm as rain started to blow sideways, pelting their faces, making it even harder to keep their eyes open. Ess put a hand to her left eye as debris flew into it, but she kept moving. They clambered over branches and foliage, and Ess felt brokenhearted about each tree, thought about the forests in Haida Gwaii, where each fallen tree became nourishment for the rest of the forest, still valued and full of purpose, still important.

A snapped branch snagged her leg, scraped at her skin. Her shadow tugged her forward, unrelenting, zigzagging through the obstacles. Then they were on the other side of the wide street, clear of the horizontal forest.

Suddenly the wind relented. Ess fell forward into the man. He didn't turn around, busy with the side door to the office building they were now sheltered by. Ess pawed at her eye, trying to clear the debris.

The door he was working popped open and they tumbled inside, the wind screaming in protest behind them. He shut the door and immediately moved them farther inside, into a hallway of dark shadows.

"Has it been like this all night?" Ess asked, her voice too loud in the sudden quiet.

"Was worse before."

The building creaked around them, the wood structure in argument with the wind.

He led them down stairs into a basement. Concrete, underground. He kept going, pulled her past shelves lined neatly with boxes to a corner with a soft glowing light, where Ess was surprised to find a lantern, water bottles, and an old office chair with a blanket draped over the back.

She worked the debris from her eye finally and exhaled in relief, wiping the stream of tears from her face. Felt a bead of rain or blood drip down her leg into her boot.

She glanced over at him. He kept his surgical mask on and hood up, stayed in the shadows. Ess could tell he was white, pale with dark eyes. She didn't care. Didn't need him anymore. Her answers waited less than a hundred kilometers away. She just had to get her hands on a hard drive in a café in downtown Vancouver. She wondered for the millionth time if she'd find family when she looked up her real name. Maybe Video-Her had told the truth and her immediate family was gone, or maybe she'd lied.

He picked up a backpack sitting by the chair, held it out. "I went to *Sea Dragon* and packed some stuff. Your tablet's in there, ID, cash."

Ess took the bag, grateful but irritated at the invasion of privacy.

Handing her a square of cotton from his pocket, he gestured to her cheek. "Look, you never ask for my opinion, but here it is anyway. You should leave it alone. Information about who you used to be isn't going to help. It's not who you are now. It's what drove you to do this."

She pressed the cloth against her stinging cheek. It came away bloody. "Maybe if I knew who you were, I'd care about your opinion," she snapped, tired, her patience frayed, her head pounding.

He nodded, expression hidden behind his mask.

Giving in to her frustration, she pushed on. "I'm done with you, done with your attempts to help. I don't want your help. Slink back to the shadows and stay there."

This made him frown, she could tell by the crease between his eyes. He stood straight, tugged a baseball cap from his coat pocket and nodded. "If the drive erases at six in the morning, there isn't a flight early enough to get you there tomorrow. You have to go today, tonight. You'll be safe from the storm down here." He wiped a trickle of blood or sweat from his temple with the back of his hand. "Whatever you choose, I hope it works out for you."

He walked away, swapping his hospital cap for the baseball hat, transforming into someone else, no backward glance as he melted into the dark. His boots clomped up the stairs, and she listened to the basement door open and shut.

Running after him and begging for answers was an option, but Ess preferred taking her chances with her remaining twenty-five hours. When the storm calmed enough, she could catch a plane or ferry to Vancouver, be there before the drive reformatted. She could fill the void.

She sank into the office chair, let it spin, her view shifting from

---

LISA BRIDEAU

dark to light with each rotation. Taking the phone out of her pocket she reread the message from herself. Let herself dream for a moment that it was possible to return to her old life, recover who she was. She closed her eyes and tried to imagine it.

Jerking upright, she planted her feet on the floor, realized she should let Yori know she was alive and thank her for getting Hito to the smugglers' boat. Digging through the backpack, Ess found her tablet. She saw the networks were down so she had no data, couldn't reach Yori, but she had an alert from *Sea Dragon's* security camera sent the day before, sent just after she'd left to meet the smugglers. A quick tap on the screen, and footage from the security camera played.

Yori on deck, approaching the cabin door.

A dark figure over her shoulder.

Arms grabbing her from behind.

A raindrop landed on the camera, obscuring Yori's face as the figure picked her up effortlessly, hand over her mouth, and carried her off *Sea Dragon*.

Ess pushed her tangled hair out of her face as she stood, looking frantically around the basement as though guidance would be sitting on a dusty shelf in the corner.

The pieces clicked together with sudden, sickening clarity. Frank had threatened to wipe Yori's memory. It hadn't been an idle threat to prove he knew who Sarah's associates were. He'd had someone grab Yori before Ess even stepped onto his boat. She'd been right that Frank already knew where Sarah Song was.

She watched the video clip again, saw the figure carrying Yori turn left after disembarking instead of right, which was strange; the marina exit was to the right. A tiny clue.

She told herself that Frank had seemed fairly professional and had no reason to hurt Yori, had every reason to store her safely to use as

266

leverage. When her panic subsided slightly, Ess noticed her tablet had also downloaded a voice message.

"Ess, wondering if you've seen Yori." Hito. "She's… I haven't heard from her in a while, since before the storm started, and things are getting bad. I thought she'd go home but the apartment hasn't logged her entry…" Ess heard official-sounding chatter in the background, heard Hito tell someone he'd be right over. "If she's with you, can you tell her to come home before the storm gets worse? Fuck, she might be at Jessie's. Okay, I'm going to try Jessie's but then I have to work. There are a lot of ships in distress. It's…it's bad. I hope—" He was interrupted by a muffled, urgent voice. "I have to go. Stay safe, Ess. Don't go out in this mess. It's bad and going to get worse, apparently. Hope you evacuated from *Sea Dragon* in time."

The worry in Hito's voice landed on Ess like a punch to the gut. His sister, missing. Because of her.

Ess yanked her yellow raincoat from the bag and put it on. She packed the two phones and sealed the bag shut, threading her arms through the straps and hiking up the stairs.

As soon as she cracked the basement door open, the fury of the storm hit her ears. She fell back a step, her safe basement corner calling to her. She stepped out into the hall. Rain pounded the office windows in unrelenting sheets. Something banged against the building, loud, impatient and persistent. Ess hesitated, her gut strongly advising that she retreat to the basement, but instead she ventured down the hall the way they'd come in. As she neared the door, the large pane window next to it shattered. Something big flew in with the rain, knocking her down. She crouched on the floor, holding her breath, arms protecting her head, waiting for more things to rain down.

The sound of the snapping wind wrapped around her, but nothing else came.

Opening her eyes, she saw she'd been taken out by a recycling cart, its wheels spinning uselessly above her. Pushing the heavy plastic cart aside with a shaking hand, she stood, put a hand to her chest where the cart had struck her, sucked in a few shallow breaths. Another window further away broke and Ess watched a tree penetrate the building, spreading its canopy over the empty desks, wiping monitors to the floor.

She ran for the basement.

—

She forced herself to wait a full hour before trying again. Spent the time pacing laps around the perimeter of the basement, imagining all the places Yori might be, all the states Yori might be in.

When the clock ticked over to six thirty, her heart skipped. Less than twenty-four hours to get to the drive. She immediately crept upstairs, skirted the recycling cart, and went to the side door. Nothing exploded on the way. She cracked the metal door open, bracing, expecting the wind to snatch it, but there was nothing. Rain fell and wind gusted, but compared to before, it was nothing, it was practically a summer day.

No planes would be going anywhere at the moment, but if the worst of the storm was truly over, eventually they would.

It was time to go.

37

ON THE MAIN STREET IN front of the hospital, Ess flagged down a woman in a heavy-duty off-road vehicle who introduced herself as Claire and explained she was out helping random people impacted by the storm. She agreed to transport Ess to the shoreline.

"Was the storm as bad as they expected?" Ess asked as Claire navigated a road littered with storm debris, sometimes choosing to bump over it, sometimes edging around. They were the only vehicle on the road. The city was eerie in its emptiness.

"Locked in a bunker, were you?" Claire said with a snort. She cursed a tree blocking the road and carefully navigated up onto the opposite sidewalk to get around it. "Winds hit 110 kilometers an hour, the clouds dropped a month's worth of rain in five hours. Flooding, landslides. Colliery dam failed. A truck lost control on Front Street and wrecked the Bastion. It's been wild. I've been out running a one-person rescue operation. I imagine NDRT will be on the ground soon to sort it out."

Claire's vehicle smelled of antiseptic and Pine Sol. Ess lowered her window and let rain lash her face for a few seconds to get a break from it. A gust of wind rocked them while they waited for a light to change at an empty intersection.

"It's a lot calmer and the meteorologists say it's done, but wind is still kicking up sometimes, so we're not out of it yet. You should get somewhere sheltered and hunker down for a few more hours. Flying debris is no joke."

"I've got a friend in trouble at a marina." Ess felt Claire staring at her but she kept her eyes straight ahead.

"Marinas were hit hard," Claire said softly. "You should let the authorities handle that. Don't add yourself to the people needing rescue."

Ess couldn't find the words to explain her situation, explain why Yori was in trouble, whose fault it was. A sinking dread hit her around the fact she only had a weak suspicion that Frank had stashed Yori on an empty boat near *Sea Dragon*—one of the few to the left along the dock.

It took several detours around downed power lines and flooded sections of road, but Claire got Ess to a spot on the highway overlooking the channel normally dotted with a row of marinas. The view now was of buildings missing roofs, flooded low-lying areas, broken-up docks, and boats stacked against the shoreline. It looked like an angry child had let loose a temper tantrum on their model city.

Arming Ess with a bottle of water and some granola bars, Claire tried to talk her into returning to shelter and, when that failed, offered advice. "Don't walk in moving floodwater. It'll sweep you away. Two feet of water can carry away a car. Seriously, I've seen it. Everyone gets too cocky about floodwater and then they get dead."

"Thanks." Ess put the supplies in her backpack. "I really appreciate the help."

"I hope you find your friend." Claire frowned, studied Ess as if she was forming an image to match when she had to identify Ess postmortem, then waved and drove off to rescue people more interested in safety.

"Okay. Get to the flooded shoreline without walking in any water," Ess repeated as she slid her backpack on and started down the hill.

She walked along a higher-elevation road as long as she could. Then, with only a slight hesitation, waded into the flooded street leading to the shoreline. Her rubber boots filled with water, sending a shiver through her. She tried not to think of the hazards hidden under the surface. Each step took focus, her footing unsure. Someone clad in a garbage-bag poncho going the other way pointed out the idiocy of walking toward the ocean right now. Ess didn't disagree but kept going, heart pounding, wind whipping her hair around her face. Trees made ominous creaking noises.

An unseen object bumped against her ankle and she jerked her foot back. She couldn't tell if the wind was rushing in her ears or her blood. She exhaled and edged forward.

Ess was drawn to the stomach-turning sound of fiberglass hulls grinding against rock. All the boats that had been neatly docked at Escape Marina were piled against the rocky seawall, some capsized. Cold ocean water swirled around Ess's calves while she struggled to accept what she saw—her boat, her home, the only home she knew, was in that jumble. The dock was gone. The marina office smashed to bits, each wave carrying off more debris from what had been Joe's whimsical rooftop greenhouse.

She scrambled out of the way of splintered lumber swirling in the water. Her eyes watered as she thought of Yori somewhere in this mess. She pictured Yori dead and *Sea Dragon* on the floor of the ocean, storm and circumstance having taken from her the only things she cared about, leaving her with nothing. Wiping a wet hand over her face, she reconsidered. Maybe this was a sign she was meant to go to Vancouver and fall back into her old life.

Either way, first she had to find Yori. She stood back from a fragment of surviving chain-link fence, trying to remember the shoreline as it had been before the storm. She could see where the flood defenses had failed and water had flowed in to fill the low-lying land of Nanaimo. She couldn't approach the pile of boats from land. The rocky shore and unpredictable waves made that a deadly prospect. Gathering her wet hair into a fresh ponytail, she assessed the situation. She had no one to copy, no one to mimic. Paralysis started to creep in, the fear she would make a mistake, fuck things up. She'd fucked up so many things.

The wild wind faded and the water looked almost calm, as though it couldn't possibly have caused all this damage. Among the bits and bobs kicked loose in the storm, she saw a plastic kayak wedged between a few trees not far away. Letting out an excited yell, she waded over to it and pulled it to shallow water. It took a few minutes to flip it, empty it, and assemble the spare paddle strapped to the front. She straddled the kayak, dropped her butt into the seat, and ungracefully held her feet up to empty her boots of water. Folding her legs in, she used the paddle to push off. The kayak seemed sturdy so she took the liberty of plowing through the eddies of debris she encountered, going directly to the pile of boats stacked against the shore. She had to fight to keep the kayak from slamming into the mess. She thanked the wind that the water was tame and manageable compared to what it must have been earlier. Still, her arms already ached from the hard paddling.

She saw *Sea Dragon* in the pile but couldn't get to it. It was afloat, and seemed okay, but it was sandwiched between other boats and she didn't like the look of the situation. The visceral urge to get in there and pry the other boats off, get *Sea Dragon* to safety, had her scouting for a path, but she forced herself to focus on the task at hand. If Yori was here, Ess needed to figure out where, and she wasn't on *Sea Dragon*. Her assumption that Frank's people wouldn't have risked carrying Yori far was all she had to go on. She'd thought maybe the greenhouse or a nearby boat. She paddled hard to stay in place, her sweat mixing with the rain and stinging her eyes.

"Yori!" she screamed as loudly as she could. "Yori!"

Paddling in a circle around the boat pileup, she alternated calling and listening. When she stayed quiet and the wind blew the right way, she could hear the squealing of fiberglass rubbing against fiberglass, a cacophony of halyards clanging, wood creaking—all bad, bad sounds to a sailor. Then she really listened. One banging noise was not random, it was a pattern: 1, 2, 3—pause, 1, 2, 3—pause. Nature didn't make patterns like that. She tried to source the banging and paddled toward it.

She let the waves push her against the outside boat on the pileup. She secured the paddle, grabbed a rope flapping off the nearest boat, and tied up the kayak so she wouldn't lose it.

The sailboat was partially capsized, its deck at a forty-five-degree angle to the water. Before she could think better of the idea, she hauled herself up the boat's ladder, balancing on the edge of the deck like she was walking the roofline of a barn. She held on to the lifeline with her wet and slippery hands as the boat rocked and banged against the boat it was resting on top of. She would kill for her sailing gloves.

"Yori!" The banging pattern broke, and a continuous staccato banging started. Ess's heart leaped to her throat.

She tried to pinpoint the noise, but the wind played tricks and she couldn't be sure. Her best guess put Yori on the next boat over. Which was technically below. It was the old mariner docked near *Sea Dragon*. She remembered Joe complaining about it being effectively abandoned garbage but belonging to a family friend so they had to host it. It was now partially submerged in shallow water, pushed against the rocky shoreline by other vessels. It hadn't been a great boat to start with, and Ess wasn't convinced it could survive this stress for long. It was only a matter of when it would crack apart and finish sinking. Wiping her face, she did what she always did: pretended she could do this, pretended she'd done it before. She shoved her fear into the emptiness inside and handed the situation over to her instincts.

The boat Ess needed to get to was sitting mostly level, pinned under the boat she was precariously balanced on. There was no obvious way to get there other than to slide down the sloped deck she was on and land on the deck of the doomed boat Yori was on, hoping she didn't fall into the water in the process. She wasn't keen on the idea of free sliding, so she edged her way forward and worked to untie a spare line. Her hands, exhausted from paddling and stiff from the cold water, took forever to untie the rope while also holding on for life as the boat rocked. She wanted to check her watch but resisted. She had time. She had to fix this.

Finally, the line came free. She anchored it and let the free end drop down along the sloped deck to the boat below. She took a moment to warm her cold fingers against her neck to try to get some feeling back. Then, gripping the rope in both hands, she slowly slid down until her feet hit the mostly level deck of the crap boat. It hadn't been scrubbed in years and was coated in slimy algae and streaked with black gunk.

A small wave hit unexpectedly, shifting everything. The line ripped from Ess's hands. Her feet slipped out from under her. She landed hard on the deck and slid toward the edge.

She swore loudly and repeatedly until her left hand hooked on a cleat and stopped her slide into the ocean. Her shoulder was yanked in its socket, causing a bloom of pain, but she held on. She took a breath, shifting her other hand to the cleat to take the pressure off her now injured arm.

Standing slowly, she gripped the lifeline and looked around. The sound of boats grinding against rocks grated on her. Every instinct told her to flee.

"Yori! Where are you?"

Banging. Nearby. Then she heard Yori's muffled voice from inside. "I fucking hate boats!"

Relief flooded Ess's body, countering the adrenaline. She shuffled away from the edge. "Keep banging!"

Her feet slipped on the algae-covered deck, but she recovered and made it to the cabin door, ignoring the fire in her left shoulder. The door had splintered and what was left of it lay ajar. She peered into the dark space, couldn't see anything, couldn't see stairs. She lowered herself in, landing in cold water with a gasp. The water reached her knees but didn't seem to be getting higher.

"Yori?"

"I'm in here!" Banging on the door of the sleeping berth made her location obvious. "The door is stuck. There's a lot of water in here. I don't want to drown in this shitty boat."

The boat was a glorified storage unit full of crates and useless old parts that Ess guessed were from illegal diesel engines. When the ship capsized, a bunch of stuff had fallen in front of the sleeping-berth door, including what looked like a stack of old industrial batteries, each one the size of a cinder block and about as heavy. Ess had to move them one by one. The first one was manageable, the second one harder. She hoped they weren't leaking acid or worse into the water swirling around her legs. She didn't want to know what was in the water.

"Yori, are you okay?" Ess asked, needing a distraction from the impossible task in front of her as she inched another battery out of the way.

"Fuck no. I came to see you to tell you Hito would be at the spot and to talk you out of your plan, but these dudes grabbed me and locked me in here and never came back and then the storm hit and everything went to shit. It was fucking terrifying."

Ess braced her back against the stack of batteries and planted her feet, pushing hard with her legs. The stack shifted a few centimeters, not enough.

"Did Hito show?" Yori asked.

"Hito was perfect. You were perfect." Ess took a break and tried to rotate her left arm to relieve her aching shoulder, but it refused to move properly. She resumed trying to move the batteries one at a time. Something slammed the deck above them and the boat tilted a few degrees. Ess froze, listening to the creaking, waiting for the hull to collapse. She had two batteries to go but they were underwater and she couldn't get a grip on them.

"Can you try pushing on the door on the count of three?"

Ess counted to three and pulled as hard as she could on the handle. The batteries shifted enough that the door opened a crack and she could grab it with both hands, plant a foot against the wall, and heave. It opened slowly but enough for Yori to squeeze her narrow frame through. Ess expected her to emerge but she didn't. Looking in, Ess saw her leaning against the bed, hand pressed to her side, head down, water up to her thighs.

The boat rocked and a deafening creaking, screeching noise filled the cabin. Ess reached in and pulled Yori out, ignoring her gasp of pain.

"We have to get out of here. Now." She tried to quiet the panic in her voice and failed.

Yori clenched her jaw, nodded. She stood on a crate, reached for the cabin doorframe and pulled herself out. As she neared the light, Ess saw Yori's shirt was drenched red with blood.

A snapping sound came from the port side, followed by a loud bang that shook the boat, and cold water crept up Ess's legs with increasing speed.

38

Ess TRIED TO HAUL HERSELF out of the cabin after Yori, but fell back in when she attempted to put weight on her bad arm. Waves of pain crashed over her, but she reached up to try again. Yori offered her hand, her other arm wrapped around a rail for support. Ess grabbed it, noticing Yori's involuntary intake of breath as she took some of Ess's weight. When Ess was out, Yori's hand went immediately to press against her side and she shivered hard. Ess, now soaked herself, shivered too.

The relief of escaping from the doomed cabin quickly dissipated. "You're bleeding," Ess said.

Yori nodded, teeth clenched.

Crouching, Ess looked at the spot Yori was holding, ignoring the shifting, possibly disintegrating hull underneath them. Yori's torso was sliced and three long gashes were bleeding, but the real trouble was the sliver of wood sticking out of her abdomen that she had her hand braced around. In a quick motion, Ess closed her fingers around it and pulled. She expected Yori to scream, but she just grunted and slumped in relief as it came out. The sliver was as thin as a toothpick but distressingly long.

Ess took off her jacket and forced Yori to put it on, then went aft to the ancient rubber dinghy still lashed to the deck. It was filthy, ungodly heavy, and apparently made to withstand the end of the world. The launch wasn't graceful but they got it in the water and managed to flop onboard, relieved to be off the death trap.

Ess refused to let Yori paddle, insisted she focus on applying pressure to her wound and staying in the boat. Since her left arm wasn't much use, Ess could only sort of control their approach to the shore as the flowing water pushed them in. Within a few minutes she was soaked from the rain, and every wisp of wind carried off more of her body heat.

There were a few industrial buildings nearby that Ess thought could provide shelter and hopefully a working connection to call for help.

They bumped against the shore next to a small tree. Their arrival was so gentle, it made Yori laugh; then she leaned over the side and vomited. Ess put a hand on her back to make sure she didn't pass out and fall into the water.

"You okay?" Ess asked.

Yori wiped her mouth with the back of her hand. "Uh. Great. Let's get on land. I'm really, really done with boats."

Ess dropped into water up to her knees, felt the cold draining her energy. Holding the slimy dinghy steady, she tried to offer Yori her other hand but her body refused to lift the arm high enough, so she turned to let Yori brace herself against her shoulder.

Even with the support, Yori stumbled on the hill, her legs giving out and dropping her into the shallow water. A current took the dinghy as Ess let go to help Yori.

Once they'd moved up the hill to dry land, Ess leaned Yori against a tree and took a moment to evaluate their options. The big blue warehouse straight ahead required the least walking by a large margin, so it was the winner. "We've got to get in that blue building, dry off, and call for help."

Yori looked ready to pass out, but she nodded and took a few steps up the hill.

It was slow going and Ess had to fight her desire to jog to get out of the pelting rain. She also had to fight the urge to calculate how much time she had left to get to Vancouver. But she stayed with her arm around Yori, taking it step by step. Yori's full-body tremors made Ess wonder how long she'd been immersed in the cold seawater. They needed shelter and heat. Ideally, a warm bath and some hot coffee. And whiskey.

The steep hill made for excellent flood protection but was an annoying obstacle for anyone injured and exhausted. When they finally reached the windowless warehouse, they had to walk to a small office on the far corner. Ess tried the door: locked. Without hesitating, she picked up a heavy chunk of scrap metal and threw it as hard as she could. The safety glass cracked. It took some additional work with a rock to create a hole she could reach through to turn the dead bolt. A shard of thick glass dragged against her finger as she reached through and unlocked the door.

"Breaking and entering, Ess? I'm shocked."

"Storm damage." Ess flung the door open. She resisted the urge to put her cut finger in her mouth.

They both looked in. It was completely empty. No hope of a working connection or a first-aid kit. Or even a chair. Just a pile of black garbage bags in one corner.

Yori shuffled inside anyway, leaned against the wall, and tried to wipe the rain from her face with a wet jacket sleeve. She lifted her shirt, watched blood seep out from the three long gashes and the puncture wound for a second before reapplying pressure.

Opening her backpack, Ess checked her tablet for a data signal. Nothing. No way to reach Hito or call for an ambulance. She couldn't help but see the time: one o'clock. She pulled out her favorite T-shirt, folded it, and handed it to Yori, gestured at her wound. "What happened?"

"These guys grabbed me, locked me in that crap boat. And the storm hit and shit went apocalyptic, the marina breaking up like it was made of Popsicle sticks. All this junk in the cabin went flying when the boat tipped over and something slashed me." She winced at the recollection. "I dove for the bedroom to avoid getting crushed alive by antique engine parts. I thought I was done for when the water started gushing in. I was in full negotiation with any deity willing to listen."

"But why where you at the marina?"

"I wanted to make sure you were okay before you went to negotiate with human traffickers." Yori sighed and looked away before finishing. "I was, you know, worried."

Ess paused rummaging in her bag at those words but didn't look up.

The wind rattled something on the roof, something that sounded like it was going to lift and take the roof with it. Yori, so small, so easily blown away by a storm. The thought of her going to *Sea Dragon* because she was worried about Ess didn't make sense. Ess was nobody.

Ess focused on practical matters, unwrapping and handing Yori a protein bar from the bottom of her bag, then inhaling one herself.

Yori lifted the folded T-shirt to check her wounds again. The shirt was already wet with blood. "I think I need a hospital. This isn't stopping."

Ess looked at Yori's stomach. "Do you know any first aid?"

"I'm usually in need of first aid, not delivering it," Yori said. "It's Hito you want."

"How do you feel?" Ess looked around the empty office again, wishing for a scrap of dry clothing she could give Yori.

"Light-headed. And my side is on fire. But I'm also freezing. It's not awesome. I'd like a drink. And a heaping serving of poutine."

Ess took Yori's ice-cold hand and pressed it against her neck to warm it while she considered their situation. She tried not to shiver.

"The roads to the hospital are probably a mess. And I didn't see any cars out on our paddle in. But it's too far to walk."

"That's bad." Yori nodded slowly, like she'd forgotten what they were talking about.

Ess tried warming Yori's other hand, but Yori started to slide down the wall to the floor. It was time to get moving before Yori faded any further.

39

THEY WERE IN THE SWATH of industrial land that surrounded Escape Marina, but there was a residential neighborhood a few blocks away. Ess had wandered through it before, admiring the old houses for stubbornly holding on as the city had changed around them.

"We have to walk, find a house with someone home. Maybe they'll have a working connection, first-aid stuff." Ess did her best to avoid rotating her bad shoulder as she put her backpack on. She put her good arm around Yori, who sagged but stayed on her feet.

"Can you keep pressure on it as we go?"

Yori grunted a yes. Every movement caused her pain, Ess could tell, but Yori didn't complain.

Stepping outside revealed a much quieter scene than Ess had expected. It was quiet that felt like a heavy blanket on a hot day. It was gently spitting rain but the sky was brighter, the oppressive dark clouds thinning. Turning their backs to the ocean, they started their slow shuffle inland.

"Storm is over, I guess," Yori said, her voice hollow and flat.

Ess didn't reply. She gritted her teeth and tried to take as much of Yori's weight as she could.

They carried on for half an hour down the empty street, taking slow, plodding steps together. The percussive sound of helicopter blades echoed in the distance and a plane flew overhead, making Ess's heart miss a few beats. That was surely a flight from Vancouver. She returned her focus to the ground in front of her, to taking a step. And another. As she'd done since Haida Gwaii, everything one step at a time. Never thinking that stopping was also a path open to her.

"I can't believe you got caught up in all this shit because of me. I'm so sorry, Yori. It was crazy selfish of me to involve you. You must hate me."

Yori laughed and winced, then looked over to see Ess's expression. "Really?"

Ess kept her face straight ahead. She was glad for the rain to disguise the droplets on her eyelashes.

A car drove by up ahead and Ess tried to raise her arm to wave it down but ended up gasping in pain and stumbling. She and Yori fell on the sidewalk next to each other. Ess clutched her left arm against her body and screamed in frustration. The car turned the corner and disappeared.

Yori lay on her back. She reached out her free hand and gripped Ess's arm, her frigid fingers surprisingly strong. "Listen. Only a near-death experience would compel me to say this kind of stuff, so you better fucking listen." She drew in an unsteady breath. "I haven't touched a paintbrush in ten years. Losing my art was like losing an arm. Shit, I lost myself. You smashed through all my bullshit and got me to open doors I had nailed shut. And the world didn't end. No demons came at me. Watching you take each day and each new unfamiliar thing and just get on with it helped me realize I've been a pathetic fucking baby and I needed to step it up and get on with life. Starting over is part of life." She took another ragged breath and continued, the words coming faster and faster. "Ess, you're basically the most important person in my life besides Hito. Being here for you for this fucked-up weirdness... I was relieved to have a way to pay you back."

The ground fell from under Ess. She turned her head to look at Yori, to be sure she was serious.

"Is this one of those awkward situations, like where you tell someone you love them only to get silence in return?" Yori asked, half smiling the way Hito frequently did.

Ess put her hand over Yori's, pressed her cold fingers against her face to warm them. "I don't know. I didn't know. I—"

"I assumed you just didn't like to talk about feelings. I'm not big on talking about feelings myself. This may be the last time it happens. It's very awkward. Two thumbs down. Do not recommend."

"I've been so fixated on getting back to my old life. I didn't think..." Ess caught a thought from the flow of them flashing past. "I didn't think I could matter to you. You don't even know me. There is no me to know."

"Bullshit. It's your most annoying feature, this idea that you're going to get back to your old life and suddenly be a real person. You are a real person. You're the kind of person who goes into a storm to rescue someone trapped on a boat. You're the kind of person who walks around pigeons on the sidewalk to avoid inconveniencing them. You're astonishingly, insanely trusting. I could go on, but I'm feeling kind of woozy."

Ess shook her head. She was simultaneously light-headed and anchored for the first time she could remember. "You were only on the death-trap boat because of me."

Yori laughed, winced. "Usually I'm the one who gets grief for the headaches caused by my shit, so I'm enjoying this role reversal. Bloody wounds aside."

Wiping tears from her face, Ess got to her feet.

"It's okay, Ess. Leave me here. I'll wait. I'll take a nap. Won't even know you're gone."

"Fuck that." Ess crouched and lifted Yori to her feet, legs shaking with the effort.

They traversed another block, their pace best measured using geological time scales.

A bird darted in front of them trilling a happy tune. A black-capped chickadee, Ess knew. Turning her head to follow its flight, she saw an old wooden house tucked in between overgrown abandoned lots. It had a white picket fence that had seen better days, but the house looked tidy and, more importantly, lived in. A giant oak tree in the yard had collapsed in the storm, its root ball up in the air, the thick trunk resting on splintered remnants of an arch over the walkway to the front door. Edging around it, feet squishing in the soggy lawn, Ess sat Yori on the bottom step of the porch and pounded on the front door.

"Hello?" she yelled.

She kept pounding. Didn't know what else to do.

The door opened and Ess fell forward. Someone caught her by her shoulders and put her on her feet, setting her arm on fire in the process.

"Hey! Whoa." It was an older man, pale with white hair shaved close to his head, age spots freckling his temples.

Ess stepped aside and pointed to Yori, who was hunched over on the step. "My friend needs help. She's bleeding and cold."

He didn't hesitate. He rushed down the stairs and crouched to look at Yori. "Hey, let's get you inside, shall we?"

Yori nodded, and he picked her up like she was a kid. He climbed the stairs with stiff knees. "Shut the door behind you, if you would," he said to Ess as if she'd arrived for Sunday tea.

Putting Yori on a bed in a small bedroom on the main floor and handing Ess a set of faded floral pajamas and instructions to get Yori dry, he left. When he returned, he was armed with a blanket, a large first-aid kit, worn towels, and a bowl of water. He handed Ess the blanket and gestured for her to wrap herself in it. The idea of warmth made Ess's eyes water.

Yori lifted her new floral pajama shirt, and the man cleaned the cuts as best he could with shaky hands, then quickly applied patches of foam. He held each foam bit in place, waiting for it to absorb blood and form a seal.

"I'm afraid you'll have to stay very still," he said. "This should seal the wounds, but any movement will likely tear it open and let the bleeding start again if it's inclined to. I have one spare if that happens, but then we're out." He applied tape over the foam, trying not to jostle Yori. When he finished, he laid a sunshine-yellow quilt over her.

"Thank you," Ess said. "I… Thank you."

He extended a hand, saw the blood covering his fingers and Ess's, and pulled back. "I'm Gus."

"I'm Ess. That's Yori you've patched up."

"Pleased to meet you, though I'm sorry for the circumstances."

"I don't know what we would have done if you hadn't answered your door. I'm not sure we could have walked any farther."

He smiled. "I'm always home these days. I'd offer to drive you all to the hospital, but I haven't had a car since back in the gasoline days."

"Is the network up?"

"I've got a landline, probably the last one in the city. Tends to fritz in heavy rain but I'll try, see if I can get 911."

Floorboards creaked as Gus walked down the hall. Something tapped against his deck in the breeze. Ess pulled the heavy floral curtains closed.

"Have you been through a storm like this before?" Ess asked, falling into the wicker chair next to the bed, thrilled to be off her feet and somewhere safe.

"Hmm? Oh." Yori paused long enough that Ess lifted her good arm to nudge her. "Mom said storms used to be rare here, but there have been some scary ones."

"What's the worst you remember?"

Yori was slow to reply, slow to form each word. "Hito was at university. Mom and I were huddled in the closet of our apartment, and I thought I could feel the building swaying in the wind. The sound of the wind as it whipped around our tower, god, it sounded like a herd of banshees hunting us. Scariest thing I've ever experienced. I had nightmares for months."

Yori stopped talking, and Ess looked up to make sure she was still awake.

"Do you think Hito's okay?" Yori asked.

"Of course, no way this storm could take him out."

Yori frowned. "He's only tough on the outside. You know that, right? Marshmallow all the way through."

"Really?"

"As a kid he got picked on at school for being puny, for being Japanese, so he took up boxing so he could fight back. Mom was so pissed. Hito was supposed to play piano and study, and he spent all his time in the gym instead, building his protective shell." She picked at a loose thread on the quilt covering her. "How did you come looking for me instead of Hito?"

"He went to look for you at Jessie's—"

"Not in a million years." Yori was quiet, twisting and smoothing the quilt. "But I have made a big deal of other arguments with Jessie, and I have always gone back to her, so he's not crazy to think it. It's like sport to her, bringing people down. It's easy to see that when I'm sober."

Ess didn't know how to respond to this.

Yori closed her eyes. "Did he take the job?"

"Don't know."

"He better have."

Yori tried to shift in the bed and Ess held her still. "You'll break the foam."

"My back is killing me. This mattress is basically a pile of springs. I can count them with my spine."

"Okay, Princess." Ess took a thin pillow from the armchair and slid it under Yori. She pulled back the blanket and watched the bandage for signs of fresh blood.

Yori relaxed in the new position. "Okay, I'll be still if you spill what happened. You went to see bloodthirsty smugglers who thought you were pre-memory-wipe you. What happened?"

After checking to be sure Gus wasn't nearby, Ess quietly recounted the events of the past day, to Yori's delight. She rolled her eyes at Hito arriving on time to the minute but was clearly proud of him behaving exactly to plan despite not having any idea of the plan.

"What did you say to get him there?" Ess asked.

"The usual, told him I couldn't explain but really needed him. Told him to get on the boat that looked like it was in trouble but to be careful and ready to call for backup if he found anything suspicious, anything smuggler related. He felt bad after our fight, so I knew he'd tolerate nonsense from me."

Ess continued the story, covering her escape from the hospital and her realization that Yori had been taken.

"Those fuckers were going to wipe my memory?" Yori started to sit up.

Pressing against Yori's shoulder, Ess held her in place.

Putting her hand to her stomach, Yori sank back against the pillows, eyes squeezing shut. "Your plan was clever. Risky though. Stupid."

"I know. I got you in trouble. Hito could have been shot." Ess hung her head. "I don't know how to make up for all the messes I've created. Don't know where to begin."

"Hey. Hey." Yori poked Ess's leg weakly. "This topic I know. You can't make up for the past. It'll break you to try. Just do better; that's all you can do."

They both contemplated this advice, listening to a wooden cuckoo clock on the wall noisily marking time. Ess tried not to count the chirps but couldn't help it. Two o'clock.

"The guy, my shadow, gave me something at the hospital," Ess said. When she got to the part about her previous life being detailed on a storage drive in Vancouver, with a clock ticking down, Yori grabbed her wrist, holding her in an awkward position.

"Holy shit. You have to go!"

Ess shook her head.

"Ess, you have to go! The last flight to Vancouver is normally at eight, but who knows how fucked up the schedule is from the storm."

"I know. Trust me, I know." Ess slid her free hand under her thigh, pinning herself in place.

Yori let go of Ess's wrist and pushed her leg with all the force of a summer breeze. "Well, get going. You have to get to the airport, take whatever flight is running, hijack a plane, seduce a pilot, whatever. It's all your answers, waiting."

"Yori, I'm not leaving you here to bleed to death."

"Gus will take care of me. Medical help will get here eventually or Hito will finish rescuing everyone else and come. You're totally superfluous."

"While I'm sure Gus is a nice guy, we've known him for five minutes. And medical assistance could take hours to get here. I'm sure they're overwhelmed with calls and the roads are fucked."

"Ess. This might be your only chance. If you stay here, you'll never get your answers."

The part of Ess that was constantly raw from the not knowing screamed at her to go, but a new part was getting louder. It said if she didn't want to be alone, if she wanted connections with people, it was up to her to make it happen. She had always been in control of that.

Ess smiled tentatively, unconvincingly. "I would have agreed a few hours ago, but I have to let it go. I–I've been an idiot. Such an idiot." As she said the words, the full force of her delusion struck her: all the time she'd spent on her boat, desperately alone and pining after the life she had before, a life that had only existed in her imagination. And she'd risked so much to try to get it back.

"That video I sent myself," Ess continued. "Pre-Memory-Wipe Me made a video and I could have said anything, and I chose, out of all the subjects in the universe, to talk about how alone I was. Last week I heard those words but refused to believe them. I held on to the idea that if I could just get back my old life, I'd find a web of loved ones waiting. I'd be okay. I thought knowing what pushed me to do this would be worth whatever fate was waiting. But I did this to myself, and the thing I wanted most was that in this round I would find a way to avoid being alone. Chasing after my old life… It doesn't help, it puts everything at risk."

Yori shook her head. "Regrets can consume you, poison you."

"I'll never regret staying with a friend when they need me."

Yori caught Ess's hand, gave it a weak squeeze.

They sat, holding on to each other and listened to the sound of the dying storm. The window stopped rattling, the violence spent.

"You can't ever tell anyone this, or I'll murder you in your sleep. I've never been more scared."

"Same," Ess said.

—

Ess went to get Yori some water and found Gus in the kitchen, picking up the handset of his wall-mounted phone, listening and putting it back on its cradle. He retrieved jugs of water from his emergency supply cabinet and poured a glass for each of them. "No luck yet. Heavy rain always causes problems with the old copper phone line, should clear up in a bit now that the rain has stopped."

The water was warm but tasted wonderfully of nothing, and

Ess gratefully drank her glass dry. "Should I go door-to-door, find someone who can drive her to the hospital?"

"Best not to move her, I think. The line should be good soon. We'll get an ambulance here. I'm sure they're out clearing the roads now."

Gus filled a mixing bowl with water and handed Ess soap and a thin towel decorated with sunflowers, pointing at her bloody hands. She dunked them in the warm water, the jagged cut on her finger stinging as she scrubbed with soap.

"Think flights to Vancouver have resumed?" Ess couldn't help asking.

"Oh, will soon, I'm sure. Heard on the radio that NDRT just flew in." He removed cookies from a box and put them on a plate. "You have somewhere you need to be?"

Ess made a head movement that was somehow both a shake and a nod.

"Well, I've got a scooter in the garage I could loan you if you need to get to the airport. Should be all charged."

Ess looked at Gus to see if he was serious. If the roads were clear, she could be at the airport in half an hour. Her eye darted to the clock. Her mouth opened to accept his offer but she forced it shut and shook her head. "Thanks, but no. I need to be here."

He nodded. "My late wife, she didn't accomplish big fancy things in life, but she was a rock for so many people, always there when they needed her. A beautiful thing to see. Our dinner table was always full, usually our spare room too. Hundreds of people came to her funeral, so many people I didn't know. I heard all these stories. Her getting someone a badly needed job, sending someone else home-baked cookies to let them know she was thinking of them when they were low, paying for a single mom's meal in the café with a note telling her what a great job she was doing as a parent. So many stories of her deeds. So much of her energy spent lifting others up." He was quiet for a moment. "It seems rare to find people these days who care about others that way."

Drying her hands on the threadbare towel, Ess thought about the woman who had probably purchased it long ago. She took the bandage Gus offered. "Your wife sounds incredible."

He coughed, cleared his throat. "Yes. Well, you two must be real good friends, for you to look after her the way you are. It's nice to see." He lifted the tray with water glasses and cookies. "I'll take this to your friend, make sure she stays awake."

As he walked away, Ess applied the bandage tightly around her finger. She put her forehead against the fridge and pictured the version of herself retrieving the storage drive, sitting at a computer to read the files on it, understanding dawning on her about how all this came to be, why she'd been carrying amnesia drugs, why she'd faked her own death and erased herself. How she could be okay with erasing herself. Memories would spark, come flooding back.

Her hands shook. The part of her desperate for answers was making it hard to breathe. She balled up the sweet floral towel and screamed into it until there was nothing left. She looked out the window, thought she saw a plane streak overhead, then went to make sure Yori hadn't passed out.

40

EVERY MOLECULE OF HER WAS heavy and stiff. They'd been waiting at Gus's for two hours. His phone had started working forty minutes ago, but 911 was triaging ambulance requests and couldn't say how long it would take. The network was still down, so Hito was unreachable.

Unable to stand waiting any longer, Ess got up and packed her bag with her good hand. It was time to go knocking on doors to find someone with a car so she could get Yori to the hospital herself.

At the bedroom she leaned her head against the doorjamb and listened to Gus tell Yori a story about his wife and their first rescue dog, a corgi called Stanley. He had to stop repeatedly to nudge Yori awake.

Ess's stomach twisted as she stepped over to the bed. Yori's face was gray and slack, her eyes open but trying to close.

"Yori, hey. No sleeping."

Yori shook her head. "Screw you. Long day."

"She's rather confused," Gus said.

"Where's Hito?" Yori moaned. "We're going to be so late. He hates being late."

Putting her hand on Yori's cheek, Ess's heart skipped a few beats. She was clammy, her breathing fast. Ess realized she'd have to break it to Hito if Yori died. Lost in the horror of that possibility, Ess needed a minute to clue in that her tablet was ringing. She ran for her backpack and dug the tablet out, fumbling, dropping it.

"Yeah," she said, putting it to her ear and making her way back to Yori's side.

"Are you with Yori? Is she okay? Are you?" Hito asked, frantic.

"We're waiting for an ambulance for Yori. She's injured, lost blood, but she's here, she's holding on." Ess squeezed Yori's arm as she said this, causing her eyes to slowly blink open. "Are you okay?"

Hito said a few choice swear words in relief. "Yeah, I'm in one piece. Where are you?"

Lights flashed off the hallway walls and Ess heard a siren cut out in front of Gus's house.

"The ambulance is here. It's here." Ess's knees buckled with relief. She braced her back against the wall. "Meet us at the hospital."

"Make sure they take care of her, Ess. I'm on my way."

Ess nodded, gripping Yori's hand until the paramedics moved her aside.

—

They rolled Yori directly into surgery. Straightforward and simple, they said, just needed to stitch up a small internal injury.

Watching Yori wheeled off on a stretcher, Ess thought of the fact that she'd broken out of this same hospital just shy of nine hours earlier. She was relieved to find herself in an entirely separate building from where she'd been scanned and held before. Given the chaos caused by the storm, she was fairly sure no one had time to recognize her.

A nurse took Ess to a curtained-off area and scrubbed the dried blood, salt, and potentially contaminated floodwater residue off her arms and legs. She dabbed Ess's cuts and scrapes with an antiseptic gel and properly bandaged the finger Ess had sliced during the break-and-enter. After a short period of poking and requests to move her arm into painful positions, a doctor with dark circles under her eyes instructed Ess to come back tomorrow when the hospital was less overwhelmed to get her shoulder x-rayed. She set the arm in a sling, secured it tightly, handed Ess mild painkillers and a cold pack, and rushed off to deal with other patients.

The noise of the busy hospital strained Ess's frayed nerves. She put her head in her hands, covered her ears, and wished for the quiet of Gus's house, with its ticking clocks gently portioning out time. Swallowing the drugs, she pulled together a few ghostly strands of remaining energy and got up.

Hito was in the blood donor clinic. Thankfully, it was a quiet corner of the hospital, most of the staff having been pulled into other emergency duties. Greeted by a nurse, Ess offered but was rejected as a donor given her obvious state of exhaustion. They set her in a folding chair next to Hito, who was already hooked up and bleeding.

"Hito, look, I need to apologize," she started, fidgeting with the cold pack.

His brow furrowed. "For what, saving my sister's life?"

"No, I mean, she was in that mess because of—" She stopped as a staff person came to check on Hito's progress. An image of Hito in his Harbour Authority uniform flashed, and she checked her desire to spill everything. "Did you quit HA?"

"Wait, what? Did we just change subjects?"

Ess nodded. "I need to know… Did you take the NDRT job, or are you still with Harbour Authority?"

"I quit HA two days ago."

Running her fingers along the edge of her chair, Ess thought about the choice she'd made when she turned down Gus's scooter offer. Building a new life, connecting with people; that meant trusting people. When the staff person moved on, Ess dove in. "I lied to you when I said I was from Haida Gwaii, raised by my aunt. I made all that up." She took a breath and ignored all the people milling about, forced the words out. "The truth is, I don't know where I'm from. I don't know anything about my childhood or my parents."

Even with her eyes focused on her hands, she knew Hito was staring at her.

There was still time to retreat back into her shell, to run.

Instead, she plunged into deeper water. "I woke up on *Sea Dragon* in Haida Gwaii two months ago." She mustered her courage to hold his gaze as she said the next words. "I don't remember anything before that."

Hito said the words right away. "Amnesia refugees."

"Yes." A wave of vertigo washed over Ess as Hito saw her as she was, finally. "My case was…different. I woke up with a new identity, bank account. And a note warning me not to dig into my past."

She could see Hito chewing through this information, trying to process the implications. He wasn't giving any clues on how he was taking it.

An alarm started going off down the hall, a distant emergency. Someone else's emergency.

"Why couldn't you tell me this? Why lie?" A frown creased his face in a way she'd never seen.

Light-headed, she focused on the room, tried to anchor herself to the place. It was a struggle to feel connected. It always felt like she would float away. Before, she had embraced this untethered feeling, thought it would make it easy to let go and plug back in to her old life. She'd avoided connecting. She could maybe have had a friendship or something more with Hito but had fucked it up.

"I've been desperate to find out about my past, some clue that would lead me to someone who knows me, or to some answer about how this was done, how it could be undone. I thought if you knew, you would toss me in jail like the other amnesia cases and I'd never get those answers."

"What? I—" Hito paused his protest, tucked his chin. He sat back against the chair. "I said something that scared you, didn't I? We were talking about amnesia refugees and I said something?"

"Something along the lines of locking them all up and doing medical testing. To be safe."

He grimaced. "Shit. Ess, I didn't mean—"

Ess had a strong desire to say *I know* and excuse him, but she pushed the words down. "It's fucking terrifying to lose that much of yourself, and I think about them alone, isolated. It's... I can't explain how awful it is. We should be inviting them over for dinner and reassuring them they can build a new life. To be locked away with nothing but your thoughts when so much is missing—" Ess stopped, her throat too tight to continue.

The machine collecting Hito's blood started beeping in protest as he leaned over to put his free hand on her knee.

"Ess—"

The pained expression on his face was too much. Ess stood and walked a few paces away. He didn't know the full story, didn't know her responsibility in all of it, and she didn't know how to tell him.

A nurse came over and scolded Hito, made him sit back. The whirring of machinery filled the space between Ess and Hito.

"Your stories about your aunt and your life in Haida Gwaii?" Hito prompted gently, drawing her back to her seat.

"Wishful thinking. I don't know anything about my family. It's all a blank." She struggled for a way to convey the pain of it. "My brain goes in circles trying to find the missing bits, endless circles around a boundless nothing. That's my excuse. I've been drowning in that emptiness, trying to find my way out."

Hito didn't reply to this and she was glad for it. "Just to be clear, you're not going to, I don't know, report me, arrest me, whatever one does with suspicious amnesiacs? Send me off to be locked away with the others."

"No, no. I wouldn't. Ess. No." He ran a hand over his face. "If I was still a law enforcement person, I'd note that your ID checked out, you're clearly able to care for yourself, so there'd be no cause for anyone to take you into custody. You're fine."

The words were like a balm and she wanted Hito to keep repeating them forever. Fine. She wondered if it was true. If it could be true.

A timer went off and the nurse came to disconnect Hito. He sent them to the recovery area and gave them cookies and juice. Ess looked at her glass, thinking it should remind her of some childhood experience, but of course it didn't. It was just juice. She shoved the dry oatmeal cookie into her mouth mechanically, her stomach growling. Her eyes were heavy. Hito was speaking, but he sounded far away. Blackness crept in at the sides of her vision, which she thought was strange. She felt herself tipping over.

She woke up on a cot with her feet elevated and a cold compress on her head. Hito sat next to her, a shiny new wrist comm on his arm dinging. A new dinging noise.

"Hey," he said softly. "You passed out."

"That's embarrassing."

An older woman came over to check on Ess, made her consume more cookies and juice while she watched. Hito finally responded to his wrist comm and Ess heard him telling someone he couldn't come in, that he was at the hospital with family. He had to repeat it several times. The nurse, satisfied Ess had consumed some calories, told her to stay put, patted her hand, and left.

"Are you okay?" Hito asked. His wrist comm dinged again, but he took it off and stuffed it in his pocket. "Whatever happened to make you change your mind about things, about telling me, is this good for you?"

Lights flickered in the room and everyone froze, waiting to see if the power would blink out, but everything kept humming.

"I'm facing it," Ess said. "That's a start."

Hito squeezed her arm. She moved the damp cloth from her forehead to cover her eyes, to hide the tears she was trying to fight off. Hito's acceptance of all this news with kindness made her feel foolish about her weeks of refusing to tell him. She was tempted to admit all the rest now too.

Someone came over and spoke to Hito in a low voice. His hand left Ess's arm. The breeze of the air-conditioning across her skin erased evidence of any touch. She pulled the cloth off her face.

"Surgery complications. I have to go—"

Voices down the hall were shouting. Ess tried to sit up, but a staff person held her in place with a firm hand on her good shoulder. "No, no. You need to stay here a bit longer. You can join your friend later." Ess watched Hito sprint down the hall toward his sister.

41

When the blood clinic staff let Ess go, she joined Hito outside Room 207. His hair was more asymmetrical than usual, ruffled like he'd run his hands through it a thousand times. She put her free hand to her hair but it was too encrusted with salt to fix. She tried to remember if she'd congratulated Hito on his new job. This didn't seem like the moment. Her thoughts bounced around. No walls to maintain. No facade needed. She wasn't sure what was left without those.

A pale man with gray hair and a red beard hurried from the room. He stopped, clapped Hito on the shoulder once, and continued on like he had an urgent appointment far, far away.

Hito led Ess inside, past curtained-off beds to the far end of the room. Yori was propped up with the assistance of the bed and several pillows. Her hands rested on the tightly tucked bedding as if they'd been placed there and she'd forgotten she had the ability to move them. It was a very un-Yori-like posture.

"Hey," she said, turning her head to look at them and blinking slowly.

The tension and worry that had been holding Ess up disappeared when she saw Yori with color in her cheeks. She had to lean against the wall for support.

"Dad came. Who told Dad to come?"

"I did, Im." Hito said, using his don't-argue-with-me brotherly voice.

"I think I said something rude to him. I didn't mean to. No, I did. Doesn't he have his new family to bother? Shiny wife, perfect kids?" She flopped her head on the pillow to look at Ess. "Hito says I gave them some trouble, but they sewed me back together."

"Yeah. They patched you up. How are you feeling?"

Yori nodded. "Very floaty. I was thinking, about your—" She lifted her head off the pillow and her eyes darted between Ess and Hito. "Oh."

"I told him," Ess said, not looking at Hito. "He knows about my memory loss."

"Oh, thank fuck. These drugs make it hard to filter, everything wants to spill out." She made a vomiting gesture and relaxed against her pillow.

"Oh really?" Hito stepped toward the bed. "Are you painting again, Im? At the studio?"

Yori nodded, her head rolling. "Yeah. I mean, not producing capital-A art, but trying stuff, seeing what I remember, seeing what comes out. It's like, what was I waiting for, what was the problem? It's just fucking paint and a canvas."

Hito crowded closer to Ess so he could lean over and kiss Yori's forehead. "That's amazing." When he straightened, he turned and pulled Ess into a hug, squeezing her, making her shoulder throb. "Thank you," he said, relaxing the hug and lingering for a moment before letting her go and stepping back to give her space.

"I had a thought about your storage drive, Ess, about how you could still get it," Yori said.

Ess pressed one foot on the other, pinning herself in place. She glanced at the clock on the wall, couldn't stop herself from doing the math. Two hours until the last flight. "Oh?"

"Yeah, it was a brilliant idea, but then they pumped this drug into me. It's awesome, so floaty. But I forgot the idea. Put me back in the death-trap boat. I'm useless."

Ess laid her free hand on Yori's shoulder. "It's okay. I'm choosing to not know."

"It'll come to me. Maybe if I have a quick nap." She fell asleep as soon as she closed her eyes.

Hito and Ess retreated to the hallway. The intensity of action that had filled the hospital earlier was gone now. Hito leaned against the wall next to the door, pressed his head back, and stared at the lights.

Sitting in a chair across from him, Ess adjusted her sling, searching for a position that stopped the darts of pain shooting down her arm. Watching Yori give in to sleep made Ess feel the exhaustion permeating her bones. Even the noise of the hospital wasn't making her anxious anymore. She wondered if her bed was underwater, if her *Dragon* was okay.

She jerked awake sometime later, her head on Hito's shoulder.

"Hey," he whispered.

"Oh. Sorry." Rotating her neck, she tried to work out a kink, gave up, and added it to her list of pinched, bruised, banged-up parts.

He shrugged.

She wiped saliva from the corner of her mouth and tried to have a clear thought. "Yori?"

"Nurse says she'll be out for a while."

"She's going to be okay though?"

"Yes. She started bleeding out during surgery, but they fixed it. There won't be any kickboxing workouts in her immediate future, which will make her happy."

Ess smiled, a tiny bit of guilt dissipating. "What time is the last flight to Vancouver?"

Hito looked confused but pulled his wrist comm out of his pocket to look at the time. "An hour from now. Normally."

"And earliest in the morning?"

"Seven. Normally." The half smile crept onto his face at her randomness. "Need to be somewhere?"

Ess knew Hito would take her to the airport if she asked. She could go, might make it. Her fingers tingled at the thought. She shook her head. The movement came more easily than it had at Gus's.

Hito waited to see if her strange line of questions had run its course. "Ess. Can I... Do you need more sleep? Can we talk?"

"I don't have anywhere to be." Her gut twisted as she said the words.

He took a deep breath. "I need to thank you for saving Yori, and I mean that in every sense. You brought her back to her art. I think that will change things, even if she doesn't stick with it. A demon vanquished maybe." Hito struggled to find his words. "I'm glad you and Yori... I hope I didn't make it awkward."

Ess shook her head. "What?"

"You and Yori, it's good, I'm—good."

She was about to smile and nod, her usual fallback action when confused, but she didn't. "So, part of having no memory of my lived experience is that I sometimes don't get things. I need to have them explained to me. This is one of those things. Can you spell it out for me?"

"You and Yori dating, I'm... I don't know, it's not like you need my permission. I wanted to say I'm happy for you."

Hito didn't seem happy. "Yori and I aren't dating," Ess said.

"You're not?"

"Pretty sure."

"Ah, I just assumed." He took a minute, processing, adjusting to this new reality. "She knew your secret. You got her into the studio. Going out into the storm after each other—"

"Isn't that what friends do?"

"Yes. I mean, I guess." He laughed, breaking the quiet of the hallway. He slouched, smiled. "I think maybe you've raised the bar for friendship."

They sat, staring at the wall across from the row of chairs, each lost in thought.

"You know. I did always find it suspicious that you'd never had a Nanaimo bar," he said out of the blue.

She laughed, a body-shaking laugh that set her shoulder on fire. Sitting with Hito in a hospital, laughing at her amnesiac missteps, she couldn't have pictured this. And there was a whole future ahead of things she couldn't yet picture. Good things.

"You're not like the other amnesia refugees."

He meant it as a question so Ess nodded. "Same procedure, but done for different reasons. Running from something different."

"Are you in trouble?"

Looking at Hito slouched in the plastic chair, exhaustion draped over his face, still seeking out people in need of rescuing, she smiled and thought about the machinations of the universe that had caused their ships to intersect on the vast ocean.

"Not anymore."

He didn't look convinced, but he nodded as if it was settled. "They think they caught the smugglers responsible for the amnesia cases, arrested them just before the storm hit. So that might be the end of it."

She noted he didn't say anything about his pivotal role in the capture.

"The smugglers aren't talking, from what I hear, aren't admitting any knowledge or involvement in drugs or amnesia refugees. Apparently, the FBI wants them in the States for a string of murders in Madison, Wisconsin, so don't know if we'll ever get answers."

An image of Hito on the boat, Casey pointing a gun at him,

flashed through Ess's mind. One day she'd have to tell him the rest of the story, confess the rest of her misdeeds and see if he still wanted anything to do with her. But not now.

"Do you want to get some proper sleep?" he asked. "You can crash at our place."

The thought of a dry, stationary bed almost made Ess cry. "I would like to sleep for a few days. Yes, please."

Hito stood and extended a hand. Ess took it with her good arm and he pulled her up. He grabbed her bag from the floor and they walked slowly to the exit.

The roads between the hospital and Hito's place were empty and dark, streetlights out. The flooding hadn't reached this far, and aside from some tree branches on the road that the cab took forever to navigate around, it was hard to tell the storm of the century had happened. If she'd had more energy, she would have been annoyed that her life could have shifted so tectonically and this bit of the outside world bore so little sign of it. Ess leaned on Hito at the entrance to his building while he tried to get the sensor to recognize his fob. The door unlocked after he gave the sensor panel a hard whack. "I'm going to rip this thing out and install a lock that uses physical keys."

An arm around Ess, he guided her into the elevator and to his apartment. Sitting on the bench by the door to take off her boots, she discovered she'd wrenched her lower back at some point and it was now protesting any further involvement in verticality. Placing her mud-encrusted boots on the mat, Hito effortlessly lifted her to standing. She liked knowing that if she couldn't take another step, Hito would get her where she needed to go. She started toward the couch, half-asleep at the sight of a soft horizontal surface but he caught her by her good shoulder and steered her to a bedroom.

"You have earned a bed," he said. He scooped up a pile of Yori's clothing and dumped it on the dresser in the corner. Before he could finish tidying, Ess crawled into the huge, plush bed, feeling a twinge of guilt about her filthy clothes. She lay on her back, adjusting her left arm in its sling so it didn't hurt as much. Soft warmth fell onto her as Hito pulled covers up. The light went out and the door clicked shut. Glancing at the clock before her eyes slid shut, she saw the display. Eight. She sighed deeply, exhaling and letting it all go.

42

Ess stood in Yori's bedroom in the morning sunlight, staring at the clock and letting the knowledge sink in. The search for answers was behind her, all the doors shut and locked. She'd thought she'd feel an irrational urge to try to get to Vancouver anyway, just in case the deadline had been a lie or the erasing a lie, but she actually felt… relief. It was done.

Making her way to the kitchen took an eternity. Everything hurt. She thought about giving up and mounting an expedition to return to bed, but her growling stomach pushed her on.

On the fridge was a note from Hito. "Called in to work to assist with vessels in distress. Make yourself at home." A spare fob sat on the counter.

The floor dropped out from under her. *Sea Dragon.* She needed to get to the marina. Back in Yori's room she searched for something she could wear, her own clothes, rumpled from sleep were encrusted with salt and mud and blood. Taking off her shirt and throwing it in the garbage, she thought about how glorious a shower would be but instead grabbed a sweatshirt from the pile on the desk. It was tight and said "F you" in gold letters on the front, but it was clean, so it would do. She held up a pair of pants, appraising them, and gave up on that idea. Yori was just too small. She glanced at the closed door to Hito's bedroom but decided she could make do with what she was wearing for one more outing.

In the kitchen, she drained a sports drink from Hito's supply. She found the cupboard with the absurd quantity of Pop Tarts. Ripping one open, she shoved the cardboard pastry into her mouth, chewing quickly, thinking of Hito compulsively buying them in the hope Yori would come home. Her stomach protested, demanding real food.

Her jacket had been lost somewhere on her adventures, so she picked up her bag and left without one.

The floodwaters had mostly receded, but getting to the marina was still a problem. The cab dropped her off several blocks away and she slowly walked the rest of the debris-strewn way, skirting massive puddles and a downed power line with caution tape flapping around it. Her back complained with each step, and her shoulder sent sparks of pain down her arm. Standing in the muck where the road dipped down to the unprotected shoreline, she beheld the mess that had once been an orderly arrangement of docked boats at the edge of a channel. The area was cordoned off, and a salvage boat was already there, separating the boats and tugging them away.

Joe came over, Leeloo running ahead to bump her head against Ess's hand. Ess knelt and buried her face in Leeloo's fur. She smelled of wet dog, and the familiarity of the scent made Ess's eyes water. She squeezed Leeloo tightly.

Ess and Joe stood together as the salvage boat worked on *Sea Dragon*. She was still floating, though Ess worried about her keel, seeing her in shallow water by the rocky shore. The death trap Yori had been on rested on its side, broken and submerged underneath another boat. Ess's stomach lurched as she remembered feeling it pitch over and water rush in.

Joe wasn't wearing his life preserver. He looked strangely skeletal without it, like flesh had slipped from his bones. "You're okay," he said, his voice flat.

"I guess. Still working that out."

"Yeah."

"Did everyone evacuate in time, Joe?"

He nodded. "Yeah, no one was hurt. We were lucky."

Ess adjusted her arm in her sling, thought about correcting him, telling him about Yori being sliced open, but she kept her mouth shut and held her breath as the crew shifted her boat away from the pileup.

"You have friends in high places? Harbour Authority and the salvage crew showed up first thing and went to work on the mess of boats yours is in. Normally they'd be servicing all the fancier boats before they got to us."

She looked over to see if he was serious. His slumped shoulders and frown made it clear he wouldn't be joking for a while.

"They'll tug her to the harbor and anchor her if they can," he continued. "They'll let you know when they let people access the area again. She looks okay though."

Ess breathed a bit, hearing his prognosis. "What happens now, to the marina?"

Joe made a noise that wasn't quite a laugh. "Escape is gone. It only exists on paper now."

She put a hand on his arm. "Sorry, Joe. Especially about your greenhouses."

Pulling a metal flask from his pocket, he nodded and took a long drink, then offered it to Ess. She took a sip, letting the whiskey burn her throat.

"Did you hear the big news about the smuggler boat?"

Ess kept quiet.

"Just before the storm, HA boarded a sketchy boat by Logan Bay and arrested two folks they say are the smugglers responsible for the amnesia refugees. They had another amnesia case stowed away onboard."

"Oh. That's good, right?"

He wobbled his head and they watched the ship at work in silence.

"My cousin's in a camp in India," Joe said suddenly. "Used to live in Mumbai, owned a successful tailor shop. He's a brilliant bespoke suit maker. But the ocean took everything. He lost his home and shop in the forced retreat in '32. There were a million people relocating at once. It was chaos. We applied to sponsor him to come here four years ago, but the government keeps throwing up roadblocks, delays. He's losing hope, was talking of paying a guy to get him on a cargo ship to Canada last time I heard from him." He wiped his face with a hand. "Anyway, I think I'm done with the ocean. It's just not friends with my family."

Normally this kind of personal sharing left Ess wondering how to respond. But it was suddenly clear that there was no right response. Everyone was guessing at how to make life work, how to be there for others. "Sometimes a badly needed new start lands in your lap when you weren't looking for it."

"Yeah, no kidding." He put the flask back in his pocket. "We'll see what the insurance company says about the marina. But I think I'm going to go inland, start a real greenhouse. Reinvent myself. Rise from the ashes or floodwaters or something."

The clouds overhead thinned and everything brightened.

"You did seem happiest when you were up to your wrists in dirt," Ess said, thinking about her own need for a new life plan. Starting life from scratch had seemed so daunting and impossible before. But needing to start over didn't make her that special, not really, especially not these days. Everyone was going to need to adapt.

She stayed until she saw them tugging *Sea Dragon* away, stable and upright. When her boat was out of sight, Ess clapped Joe on the shoulder and told him to message her when he got his new greenhouse going.

—

Hito's house phone rang. Ess went to the control panel, wondering if she should answer, and saw the call came from the hospital. She pressed Answer.

"Ess? Where's Hito?" Yori sounded annoyed.

"He got called into work. Some people needed saving."

"Right, of course. That's why he's not answering his cell. Can he not take five minutes off to nurse me back to health? I did nearly die."

"Are you okay? Do you want me to come to the hospital?"

"The patient across from me is having major family drama. His wife and girlfriend met each other in the hallway. There's a lot of yelling and crying. I need someone to distract me."

They listened to the drama happening on the other side of the curtain from Yori's bed. Ess studied the photographs on Hito's shelf, tried to see some resemblance to Hito or Yori in the stern face of their mother. She noticed a photo she'd missed before, one of their mom with two young kids, the boy standing properly and facing the camera, the much younger little girl upside down on her mom's lap. Mom smiling. Happy family.

When it was quiet again, Ess spoke. "I haven't told Hito I'm responsible for the amnesia."

"Well, it's been like a hot second since you found out. And who says he has to know."

"I'm supposed to be done with having secrets."

"Everyone has secrets. Look, we all do things we regret; this I am an expert in. And you were a different you. That's a compelling mitigating factor. Sometimes your regret-filled suffering will help, but usually not; usually it's suffering to no purpose."

Ess made a noise that conveyed she wasn't convinced.

Yori sighed loudly. "You erased your own memories and gave up everything and everyone you ever knew, and now you've put the smugglers who were doing the damage in jail. I say you've taken your hit for your crimes, whatever they may have been."

"Or I ran away, dropping a bomb into people's lives on my way, and then turned my back on the chaos I caused. I set myself up to live a happy life while others suffered because of me. All those amnesia refugees, Yori, my fault."

"Oh god. Is that why you walked into the smuggler's den with your half-baked plan? Guilt and a hidden desire to be punished?"

Crumpling onto the ottoman, Ess tried to catalog her own motivations. Hearing it said out loud so plainly was cutting.

Yori spoke, the usual sarcastic tint missing from her voice. "If you've chosen this life, I think you have to be all in. You can't carry useless burdens from the old life. Tell Hito or don't, but you need to make peace with it yourself."

"How?"

"That is the question. Maybe start by assuming Pre-Memory-Wipe You was trying to do the right thing. Then I think you find a way to believe you deserve to have a happy life, despite your fuckups." The sound of static on the connection filled the space for a few moments. "If you find out how to do that, let me know."

Ess was digesting that when Yori spoke, her words flowing out in a rush.

"In the cabin, I thought I was done. Bleeding, with cold water filling the room, the horrible noise of all the boats grinding together. Who was going to find me trapped in the cabin of some random boat with a storm still howling? And suddenly all the crap I've been doing all these years, I see it, like I *really* see it. Such a waste of time. If I want to paint, I should just paint. So what if I make ugly shit no one wants to look at? If I want to quit drinking, I should motherfucking quit drinking. All the rehab sessions Hito's suggested were pointless because I wanted to drink, I wanted the escape. If I hadn't had that epiphany on the boat, I don't think I could have kept up banging that stupid pipe. I would've just gone down with the ship."

Ess tried to wrap her head around the idea that Yori's experience in the storm might set her on a better path, that some lasting good may have come from it all. That good and bad were all tied up together.

The drama in the bed across from Yori flared up. They listened to hospital security escort someone out. Yori coughed, then grunted in pain.

"I went to check on *Sea Dragon*," Ess said softly. "The other boats got the worst of it, kind of shielded her. The boat you were on sank."

"Shit, that would have been my coffin. What a stupid way to die, to drown in like five meters of water. How fucking embarrassing."

"I think I'm going to sell her," Ess blurted out.

A pause. "I thought you loved that thing."

"I do, but… I think I want to try living somewhere less prone to moving. She'll need repairs, expensive repairs. It's a good time to let her go."

Yori was quiet. When she did speak, her voice wasn't as cocky as usual. "Well, if you're going to be apartment hunting, let me know if you need a roommate."

"You can stay here for free, can't you?"

"God, Hito and I would kill each other. But I think I'd like to be done with bouncing around crashing at friends' places. Traveling light lets you take off on the fly, but there are downsides."

Ess nodded. "Okay. Yeah, not being alone sounds really great."

The call ended when Yori's nurse came to change her dressing. Ess promised to visit in the morning and bring the rice soup Yori insisted she needed for her recovery.

In the sudden quiet Ess sat very still, trying to imagine what it would be like to live in an apartment, maybe one with a view of leafy trees where she could watch birds come and go. A place where she could invite friends over for dinner. A place that wouldn't get blown around by unexpected winds and currents.

43

YORI'S GALLERY OPENING WAS THAT night, and Ess knew she would be freaking out. It would be a short sail so she could go home and talk Yori down and help her get ready.

The boat was just a rental for the weekend. It wasn't elegant or familiar; it wouldn't be as nimble in the water as *Sea Dragon*. But it was her first time out since she'd sold *Sea Dragon* and settled on land, and she would happily have sailed a bathtub.

She opened her bag and pulled out *Sea Dragon*'s compass, wiped its glass dome cover with her shirt and set it on the console, the vivid memories of her days alone on the ocean washing over her. Days when she'd been so raw in so many ways. She tilted her head up to look at the clouds, appreciating how far she'd come since then. So easy to be daunted by the steps ahead and forget to acknowledge the hard path already traversed.

Her wrist comm rang, Hito's image popping up. She ducked into the cabin to answer, expanding her display.

"Have you landed already?" she asked.

"Connecting flight was delayed, they rerouted me to Calgary. Should be there by lunch. How's Yori?"

"She left for the gallery early this morning to check everything for the tenth time."

"She's coming home at night, that's good."

Ess smiled. "You always find the silver lining. She did pop by the apartment for a few hours. Reorganized the utensil drawer."

He squinted at his screen. "How's the rental boat?"

Ess looked around the cabin, shaking her head. "It's exceptionally weird to be on a boat that isn't *Sea Dragon*. It's a solid boat; it'll be fun." She showed Hito the tiny cabin.

"You're sure you don't want to wait until I get there to be your deckhand?"

Ess turned the display so he could see her raised eyebrow. "A very kind offer. I'm not sure how much help you'd be, hobbling around with your broken leg. You stick to pulling people from collapsed buildings. I'll handle the sailing."

"Aye, Captain. Can I talk you into dinner tonight, before we go get Yori down off the ceiling for her show? She has refused to eat beforehand. I already asked. She says she'll hurl for sure if she eats."

A dizzy feeling washed over Ess. "You don't have to, you know."

Hito leaned in, adjusted his earbud. "What?"

She ducked her head and studied the floor. "When you went off on your NDRT deployment, things were different. I was a mess with no idea who she was. I mean, I still don't know who I am, but—" She pushed the words out. "You might not like who I turn out to be."

"Ess, we've been talking almost every Saturday for the past six months—"

"In person is different."

Hito nodded. "Granted."

"It could be that everything you liked about me six months ago was a product of my newness…" Her voice trailed off, her throat tight.

"Hey. Can you look at me?"

She lifted her eyes to the screen, saw his half smile. She forced her shoulders down.

"You might discover you dislike *me* if you spend too much time with me. You'll find out my only topic of conversation is gruesome, very detailed stories of the injuries my teammates have suffered." He smiled, then got serious. "I get that you need to find your footing. We'll have dinner, as friends are known to do. No expectations. Okay? Just dinner."

She nodded, relaxed her grip on her forearm.

He pulled out his earbud and listened to an announcement. "That's my flight, gotta go." His gaze turned to the camera. "See you in a few hours. Be safe. Watch out for restricted zones."

She lifted her hand in a wave and Hito's face disappeared.

The National Disaster Response Team had whisked Hito away for training in Ontario a week after the storm. It would have been sooner, but they gave him a few extra days because of Yori. He returned briefly and then a string of deployments followed in rapid succession.

The easy conversations they'd had every Saturday that Hito could get to a working network connection made it possible to avoid the question of what exactly they were to each other. They'd talked about the steep learning curve for his job, about his worry around being the weak link on his team. He'd let her see that the unflappable facade of confidence she knew was mostly a front. He had as many doubts as anyone else. They talked about Yori's new sculptural painting style. And once she'd come to terms with it herself, Ess had told him what she knew about being the source of the amnesia refugees, and about using Hito to get the smugglers arrested. He'd taken a few weeks to wrestle with that, but the friendly calls had picked up again eventually. She'd been wrong about Hito's discomfort with gray.

The thing they hadn't talked about was what would happen when they were physically in the same place. Ess wondered if she had a solid enough sense of self to immerse herself in a relationship. Maybe. It would certainly be nice to get Yori to stop trying to set her up on blind dates.

~

The wind was perfect for a pleasant sail. Skipping up the steps, Ess stretched her bad shoulder and went to cast off. She found a figure on the dock by her mooring line. He was familiar, but she couldn't quite place where she knew him from; not a sensation she had often.

The man smiled. "Hi, Ess." He raised a paper bag. "I brought pastries. No icing."

The slight French accent helped her brain make the connection. "Rene?"

He nodded and stepped aboard without waiting for an invitation.

Rene from the pub in Haida Gwaii. Rene who she'd stupidly invited onto her boat after knowing him for five seconds. Rene who she'd told about her amnesia while drunk. "How?"

Resting a hand on her arm briefly before letting go, he looked around, taking in the busy dock and boats coming and going. "We need to talk. We should go inside," he said, "for privacy."

"What's going on?"

Inside, he went to the galley and arranged the scones he brought on a plate. Putting it on the table, he sat across from Ess, studying her face.

"You seem to be doing well," he said.

Her stomach churned. It was Rene, but the uncertainty in him that she'd found so comforting was entirely absent, replaced with a sharpness that made her uneasy, reminded her of someone else. "Let's skip the chitchat and get to how you could possibly know to find me here." Ess's voice was tight, quiet.

"I do dislike chitchat. Didn't mean to freak you out. Bad start."

Rene took a bite of a scone, carefully wiping the crumbs off the table and onto the plate before starting. "There's no way to say this that doesn't come as a shock. So. You hired me, Sarah. Sorry, Ess. Fuck. We made a point of calling you Sarah to avoid slipups."

Her heart skipped and her vision narrowed. He'd dropped his French accent and his intonation shifted. It was the voice from the blindfolded conversation, from the man in the surgical mask who'd taken her from the hospital. Her shadow.

"Explain," she said, throwing her sailing gloves on the table and crossing her arms to hide that her hands were shaking.

"You were clear about all of this. The deal was, if you settled into a new life, stayed away from digging into your past—then after a year my contract was complete and I was to leave you to your own devices."

It was Rene's face but the voice was wrong, the posture was wrong. How he curled his lips when he spoke was wrong. Ess felt ill.

"You seem to have a good life going. A job, friends." He picked up a piece of scone, popped it into his mouth. He pulled a folded-up newspaper page from his pocket and dropped it on the table.

Sliding the paper over, Ess saw the headline and knew the article. It was from last year, shortly after the storm. Frank and Casey had been killed in a van crash while being transported to the United States to face charges there. Ess had read every report there was about it, but there weren't many. Their deaths shuttered a triple homicide case in Wisconsin *and* the human smuggling investigation, and no one particularly seemed to care.

"Frank and Casey won't be mentioning Sarah Song as their drug source," he said. "You should be safe, so I thought I'd say goodbye in person."

Pushing the paper back at him, Ess crossed her arms. "Explain what I hired you to do."

He wiped the corner of his mouth with a thumb. "You know this story, Sarah. You were in serious trouble. We devised this exit strategy. Smugglers, new ID, etc."

"You know who was after me."

"I know."

The question lodged in her throat, nearly choking her.

He locked eyes with her. "You know you need to keep away from it. You *know* this."

Clenching her jaw, Ess looked away.

"You know this," he repeated more gently.

She wanted to punch him in the face, but she nodded. She stared at the plate of scones. She loved blueberry scones. Hated icing.

"You knew things people didn't want known," he said softly, "and you wanted to share those things. The wipe was to neutralize you as a threat and to disappear you."

Ess snapped her gaze back to Rene as he doled out this sliver of information. Her mind flipped through the things that had happened after she woke up in this new life. Annoying puzzle pieces suddenly slotted together. "You bought *Sea Dragon* in Victoria. You're Bob McDonald. You were at the boat shop in Nanaimo with me, getting it outfitted so I could sail it solo."

He didn't disagree.

"Sam at the boat shop—"

This elicited a frown. "Sam found the security footage with my face on it, and I paid her well to erase it and ghost. That footage was an oversight."

"How did you know I talked to Sam?"

"That's what you hired me to do. I watched you, made sure you were safe, made sure you weren't undoing what had been done at great cost. I was always there. In Haida Gwaii—"

"No."

"I was on a motorboat on the other side of the little island from *Sea Dragon*. Listening, watching."

She looked unconvinced. He smiled as though this was what he expected.

"I suggested to the Watchman that he check on *Sea Dragon*." Ess's expression didn't shift. "You got knocked overboard the first time you tried sailing after you woke up," he added.

"Oh god—meeting in that bar, that was not an accident."

"It was the plan to talk to you when you reached land to confirm the memory wipe had worked, find out what you were planning to do. But…"

"But what?"

Shifting in his seat, he pushed the plate and scone away like he was finished with the pretense. "I was supposed to talk to you, learn what I needed to, then back to the shadows. I went off plan."

"Why, because I was such a pathetic mess?"

"You were so much yourself, except more raw." He spoke slowly as he said this as if he was trying to explain it to himself. "You were willing to let people in, willing to let people see you weak. It was a revelation. I didn't think it would affect me, seeing you after the wipe. But it did. I wanted to tell you that you were a powerhouse, that you were thunder, but there's no way to say that to a stranger." He paused again, lost in a memory. "So yeah, being with you on the dock in Haida Gwaii, it threw me."

"And the proposal to sail off into the sunset together? Was that what I hired you to do?"

"That was a mistake." After a pause he sat back, adopted a relaxed posture. "It is what it is. My objective throughout all of this has been to keep you safe. And you're safe, so…"

Ess thought through the rest of the year. "You broke into my boat?"

"I had a key. A bug on the *Dragon* failed, had to swap it out. I also needed to check your notebook because you weren't being very chatty."

Cheeks burning at the thought of him reading her words, she pushed on. "Were you there when I made the video?"

"Yes."

"Was I going to die if I didn't do this wipe?"

"Yes."

Laughter floated into the cabin on a breeze, people on the boat in the next slip setting off.

"Who was I? What kind of person was I?" Ess balled her fists, wished she could retract the words, also desperate for an answer.

"Why does it matter who you were? You're someone else now."

"It doesn't matter. It shouldn't. But—" She didn't want to say it, she tried hard not to say it. "Not knowing, even when you've agreed to it, is like carrying an anchor—"

He waved a hand, cutting her off. He took a few seconds before he started. "You were an expert sailor. A workaholic. You were cutting-edge brilliant in your field, though you were never recognized for it, which bothered you to your core. You dedicated everything to your work, held yourself to a ridiculous standard, and were rarely satisfied. Other people were a constant disappointment for you. You found it hard to make allowances for the fact that not everyone was as smart and quick-minded as you. You were going to report the corporation for an ethics violation, but really you were furious someone was going to take credit for a breakthrough you'd made. Though you only admitted that when you were drunk."

Ess stared at Rene's mouth, watching the words form. She tried to feel some connection to the person he described. The closest she could get was picturing herself in the video message, picturing *Her*.

"She would not have given up on getting answers to be there for a friend in need," he added, his voice shifting closer to Rene's.

The cabin filled with the low hum of a floatplane taking off nearby. Ess's heart pounded as the memory of the visceral need to get to Vancouver washed over her.

"Did I really leave no family behind? No one?"

"Not even a pet goldfish."

Ess waited for more, waited for a more solid answer she could hold on to.

He met her gaze without wavering. They sat across from each other in silence, a standoff that Ess didn't know how to end. But he wasn't leaving, so there had to be more.

Reaching out, she touched his hand lightly. He pulled back and crossed his arms.

He looked away but started speaking. "Your parents rode you pretty hard for academic accomplishments," he said, choosing each word like a flower to add to a bouquet. "I understood from what little you said that friendships weren't something they prioritized for you growing up. You didn't talk about other people much around me. You were generally a closed book."

Ess nodded, heavy with sorrow for her old self.

"Your work was your world," he added. "Work and sailing."

"Was I telling the truth in the video…about my parents?"

He sighed and looked at her with an expression she couldn't read, that she wasn't sure she wanted to read. She turned away from him, regretting the question, wishing she could erase it and his look.

"I do wish the best for you, Ess." He stood and placed a business card on the table. "I don't think you'll need this if you keep your low profile, but if something from your past comes up and you need help, contact me. Otherwise, this is goodbye."

"No more spying on me?" she asked.

"It's just been an algorithm listening for key words lately. But yes, no more spying. You can do a sweep of your apartment to find and remove the bugs if you like. Check the light fixtures. The contract ends here. You're safe and it looks like you're living the kind of life she hoped for, as much as she shared her hopes with me, at least."

"Who are you?" Ess asked, moving to block his exit.

Rene shook his head.

"Rene isn't your name."

"No, it's not."

"How did I find you? Someone willing to do this for me? It's not exactly want ad, temp agency kind of work."

He leaned against the counter and crossed his arms. "I am—was—in the business of doing unsavory things."

"And I led the kind of life where I knew people like you?"

"No. God, no. Ess, I was sent by someone in the company to deal with you." He closed his lips tightly after saying this.

The temperature in the boat seemed to drop a few degrees. She backed up, stumbled on the step behind her. "Deal with?"

He watched her regain her footing, made no effort to help. "Someone thought things would be better with you out of the picture. You, clever thing, talked me into an alternative plan. Same outcome for my client, less dying for you, more money for me. I told you in Haida Gwaii that I'd recently left my job. You were the reason, the thing that made me realize I was done."

More pieces slotted into place. Scary ones. Ess didn't really want the answer but the question spilled out anyway. "Did you kill Frank and Casey? To keep them from sending the authorities to Sarah Song?" She found the courage to look him in the eye. "To protect me."

A small muscle twitched in his cheek, but he otherwise gave no hint of an answer.

"Convenient for me that they both died before they talked about where they got the drugs."

He shrugged. "Two fewer awful people in the world; I'm not crying over the loss."

Tilting her head, she studied him standing there with his arms crossed, his jaw tight. There was something in the way he looked at her, part of the puzzle he wasn't sharing. "Did we have a thing? You and I?"

This made him duck his head and move toward the steps. "I have to go. It's been a mindfuck, Ess; I'm not sure if I should thank you or not."

Ess closed the small distance between them, stepping into the personal space people reserved for loved ones. She smelled his cologne, studied his face, waiting to see if a glimmer of a memory would come to her. He held her gaze and gave nothing away.

"I don't think it will jog anything," he said. "You never really looked at me. I was like air, just there keeping you alive."

"That can't be true."

He smiled. "The fact that you think so is tantalizing." He tilted his head, studying her. "You are her and you aren't her. It's astounding."

Stepping around her, he straightened his shirt. Giving Ess a little salute, he climbed the stairs and disappeared.

She sat at the table to process what had just happened. She pulled his card across the table, a white card with an anonymous email address on it, nothing else.

"Thunder," she whispered. It intrigued her, the sense that the previous Sarah had been powerful. She could use some of that, just a bit.

Escaping the suddenly stuffy cabin, she untied her rental boat from the dock and motored off.

Once away from harbor traffic, she switched off the engine and drifted. Standing at the stern of the boat with the business card in hand, she thought about her friends, Hito, Yori, Joe, Gus, her coworkers at the greenhouse. Previous-Her had gone to extraordinary lengths to provide this chance at a full life. Fake documents. Offshore bank account. Somehow flipping Rene, then turning away from him. Letting go of her chance to set the record straight on something that mattered, mattered deeply. So much sacrificed to get away. To live. Ess had taken the past year to realize it was a gift.

Her ignorance was part of the gift and the price for the gift.

She watched the water, waves forming and bouncing off the hull, waves rippling out and dissipating, waves returning to the ocean.

Previous-Her was just one form, one wave. Now the water had

come together in another shape somewhere else. Same water, same ocean, different wave.

Her hand gripped the business card, sunlight highlighting the jagged scar on her finger from her break-and-enter effort during the storm. The hands were hers. Pulling her wrist back, she pitched the card into the wind, watched it soar before plummeting to rest on the water. She imagined it sinking, ink unforming, paper dissolving—a key she no longer wanted to a door now forever sealed. She watched it bobbing in the waves as her boat carried on.

Giving a little salute like Rene had, a sailor's farewell, she switched on the engine and moved forward.

EPILOGUE

GOVERNMENT ANNOUNCES VISA STATUS FOR AMNESIA REFUGEES

Immigration Canada has announced establishment of a visa category for the special classification of "Doe Refugees," those without documentation who show the markers of forced memory wiping. The number of confirmed amnesia cases is now thirty-four. Nineteen additional claims of amnesia have been disproven via brain scans, according to a joint statement provided by Border Services and the University of Victoria Department of Neuroscience.

Amrita Rao, executive director of nonprofit Refugee Safe Shore Network, is glad to hear something is finally being done and credits public protests and lobbying for the change. "The government's standard approach for people who are unable to produce verified identification is to keep them in detention for an extended time, sometimes years, and hope the situation resolves itself. I'm glad they're going to develop a new way to process people who run up against this documentation wall. I hope they aren't only addressing the high-profile amnesia cases, as many people with intact memories are also suffering under our current regulations and also deserve an expedient pathway to refugee status."

In addition to the visas that will allow the amnesia refugees to be released from detention facilities, the government announced another significant increase in funding for Border Services. The added resources are directed to areas where the amnesia refugees were found, presumably to identify the smuggler routes and prevent other migrants from crossing the border.

The UN Refugee Resettlement Council is calling on Canada to dramatically step up its refugee settlement efforts in light of the numerous global crises underway. As carbon levels approach 500 parts per million for the first time in geological history, the number of climate migrants is expected to soar even further, adding to existing record-high numbers. Last year Canada took in 21,100 refugees, a number that is essentially unchanged since 2025. The UN estimates there are 50 million refugees in official camps waiting for receiving countries. The prime minister responded with a statement that Canada remains committed to providing a safe home to refugees and is working to settle an additional 5,000 over the next two years. She added that immigration programs "need to be guided by what's best for Canada's interests."

Rao countered that "Canada's massive historic contribution to the climate change crisis creates an obligation to assist those suffering the devastating impacts. The response so far has been shameful, with a focus on migration pushback rather than acknowledging that migration may be the only viable way for many to adapt to a drastically changing climate. We need to have a just, humane immigration system that acknowledges that. We have an obligation to those who are suffering the impacts of what we've caused."

—

NEWS DECEMBER 2040

CORMACK BIOLOGICAL SCIENCES UNDER FIRE FOR MEMORY-WIPING DRUG

Official charges were filed this week against American pharmaceutical giant Cormack Biological Sciences for violating U.S. federal regulations on testing on humans without ethical oversight, including failure to obtain approval from a research ethics board prior to conducting testing on humans, failure to register clinical trial activities with the international database, and failure to keep unregulated Category 5 prototype drugs secure.

The surprising allegations stem from

the arrest of two alleged smugglers in Nanaimo, BC in July 2038. They were found with an "amnesia refugee" hidden onboard their boat, one of thirty-four such people found in Canadian waters near the U.S.-Canada border. Lab tests of drugs found on the boat revealed the drugs were an almost identical match to the recent PTSD treatment that Cormack Biological Services began official trials of in August. News of those trials bumped Cormack stock prices to new highs.

Research on methods to dull the triggering memories of PTSD patients has been underway for decades, but Cormack won the race to be the first company to complete human trials. A breakthrough in nanotech delivery of proprietary drugs to the brain is responsible for the leap forward, a Cormack spokesperson said at the launch. "Our ability to program nanotechnology to precisely target the problematic memory means people suffering from PTSD will finally have a viable treatment option. When approved, this will dramatically improve lives."

The challenge of passing the blood-brain barrier has thwarted the use of nanotechnology in treating conditions like PTSD for decades. The scientific community appeared to be in agreement that the developers of Cormack's nanotech breakthrough would be obvious contenders for the Nobel Prize in Physiology or Medicine.

Recent revelations, however, cast shade on whomever gets credit for the breakthrough, as charges filed claim that an earlier version of the nanotech formula—one that wiped all autobiographical memories—was developed and tested by Cormack without proper ethical oversight, including testing on humans without approval. The company is also charged with failure to keep experimental treatments secure, as doses of the memory-wipe compound were removed from the company in early 2038. A container with one of those doses and multiple empty vials is alleged to be what the arrested smugglers had in their possession. Investigators have not been able to determine how the smugglers obtained the drugs.

Cormack Biological Sciences declined to comment on the charges, citing ongoing legal proceedings.

LEARN MORE ABOUT CLIMATE CHANGE

Climate change is a global crisis, the impacts of which are already being felt in many places in many ways. Unfortunately, those who did the least to contribute to the problem are feeling some of the earliest and worst impacts.

The short form on climate change is: it's real, it's us, experts agree, it's bad, there's hope. We don't have a lot of time to cut our carbon pollution to zero to secure a habitable planet for ourselves, so every action matters, every decision matters, every fraction of a degree matters.

Here are a few good places to start if you want to learn the basics about climate change:

- NASA: climate.nasa.gov
- The Climate Reality Project: climaterealityproject.org /climate-101
- Podcast: *How to Save a Planet* with journalist Alex Blumberg and scientist and policy nerd Dr. Ayana Elizabeth Johnson: gimletmedia.com/shows/howtosaveaplanet

Action: Making changes to cut your personal fossil fuel use where you can is great—definitely do that—but the three most important things you can do when it comes to climate change are:

- Talk about it! Let others know it's important to you, that they aren't alone in caring/worrying about it. Let your leaders at all levels know you care and support them in taking real action and making real changes
- Join an organization that amplifies your voice, and
- Advocate for system-wide change and regulations that move us away from oil, gas, natural gas, methane, and coal.

To learn why lifestyle changes alone aren't enough (i.e. you can't recycle your way out of climate change), search the internet for the essay by Mary Annaise Heglar "I Work in the Environmental Movement. I Don't Care If You Recycle."

Climate Migration

Each year, collapsing ecosystems, economies, and natural disasters force large numbers of people from their homes around the world, some within their country and some across borders. These fast- and slow-moving disasters are caused or intensified by our collective burning of oil, coal, and gas. And more and more people will need to migrate as the planet gets hotter, weather gets more extreme, and sea levels get higher.

Climate change doesn't just pose a threat by causing immediate harm to people and infrastructure, it can also slowly destabilize societies and economies, making them more vulnerable to other threats.

Current systems aren't set up to handle what's coming. Climate migrants who cross borders are not afforded refugee status under the 1951 Refugee Convention, which provides legal protection only to people fleeing persecution due to their race, religion, nationality, political opinion, or particular social group. More than international migrants, though, most people who will be or are being displaced do so within their home country—there, too, they often lack protections or support from the rest of their society. In Canada, for example, more than one hundred thousand people have lost their homes over the past decade alone.

A collective effort is needed to find solutions to help climate change refugees and migrants, to ensure the humane, safe, and proactive management of climate migration flows. Wealthy, high-carbon-emitting countries have changed the planet with the carbon pollution they've produced, and we must proactively help those who will be forced from their homes as a result.

To learn more, visit: pbs.org/newshour/world/climate-change-is-already-fueling-global-migration-the-world-isnt-ready-to-meet-peoples-needs-experts-say

READING GROUP GUIDE

1. If you found yourself in Ess's position at the beginning of the book—with no memories and a dire warning about not looking into your past—would you take the warning's advice to start over or try to find out who you were and how you got there?

2. In her early days, Ess can only get into the rhythms of sailing when she's not thinking about them. If you didn't remember learning anything, which tasks do you think you could do on instinct and muscle memory alone?

3. Because of changing climates, during the events of the book, Canada has become such a popular destination for U.S. citizens who are fleeing disasters that the Canadian authorities are on high alert. In times of emergency, why do we treat refugees as threats?

4. How would you describe the relationship between Hito and Yori? How do they shape each other's decisions, whether intentionally or unintentionally?

5. How does Ess help Yori reconnect with her art when she's been avoiding it for so long? What role does art play in Yori's life?

6. Rene and Yori see the chance to leave behind negative memories and experiences as a silver lining to amnesia cases like Ess's, but Ess thinks the loss of her positive memories outweighs that benefit. Which would you prioritize?

7. The video from Sarah Song asserts that she didn't have family or close connections. Did you think that was true or just a deterrent to keep Ess from looking any further?

8. Ultimately, Ess decides against trying to get to Vancouver. What do you think she would have found there? What motivates her to accept her circumstances?

9. One of the central questions of the book is how we construct our identities, whether from memories or the expectations of the people around us or something else entirely. What, to you, is the most essential part of an identity? What do you absolutely need to know in order to define who you are?

10. Ess's story is set against one possible climate-change impacted future. What climate change impacts have you personally experienced? What positive changes have you seen in your city/state to reduce fossil fuel use or prepare for future extreme weather?

A CONVERSATION
WITH THE AUTHOR

What inspired *Adrift*? What kinds of questions bring you to the page?

The seed for *Adrift* was planted during an amazing weeklong kayak camping trip in Gwaii Haanas National Park Reserve and Haida Heritage Site in Haida Gwaii where we would pull our kayaks up on beaches and pitch tents in the forest. The wilderness there is unlike any other place; it's rich and lush and feels untouched and magical. Gwaii Haanas feels like a place that experiences time differently. A woman waking up on a sailboat there with no memory was an idea that stuck with me long after I returned home.

One thing that brings me to the page consistently is my curiosity about whether entertaining fiction can be fun and also spark conversations that we need to be having more of. I think everyone feels very alone in their worry about climate change and their desire for significant change to prevent it. Surveys in Canada and the U.S. repeatedly show that an overwhelming majority of people are concerned or very concerned about climate change, but I think we don't talk about it enough so we think we're the only one who feels this way. Maybe if we see it reflected in our stories and culture, people will talk about it more, and talking hopefully leads to action. So this theory that I can perhaps entertain AND spark conversations that lead to action keeps luring me back to my laptop, even after long days at work.

If you woke up in Ess's position, would you try to find out who you used to be or try to make the most of your fresh start?

I have a rational answer to this, but I think once one is actually in the situation, the response wouldn't be remotely rational. I imagine that the not knowing would be unbearable. I think about how frustrating it is to be unable to recall a trivial piece of information you know you know—how torturous it must be to feel like that about *everything*, to have just a giant black hole where all of your memories and experiences should be. Also, for all the silver-lining perspective of Yori and Rene regarding fresh starts, they're hard. Starting over is hard. Making new friends is hard. It's not an easy path to choose. I have great respect for all the immigrants and refugees who travel this road.

Ghosting society is a complicated proposition but one that comes up a number of times throughout the book. Would you ever attempt to go completely off-grid?

I think some people can thrive off-grid, folks who know the reality of the hard work involved and embrace it. That's not me. I like to unplug occasionally, but I'm a city person at heart. I adore downloading books to my e-reader and having video calls with friends and family who are on the other side of the planet. I love learning new skills via internet tutorials. I love having answers to questions at the tip of my fingers. But I also like to weave, make my own soap, waltz, and dream up stories. So, I guess it's a hybrid life for me.

Why did you choose to set the story in the near future? What was the most difficult part of trying to think just a few years ahead of the present?

I love speculative fiction. I love worlds that are ours but not quite. It's my favorite play space. With *Adrift*, I wanted to imagine what Canada and BC might look like if we successfully took action, transitioned off fossil fuels, prepared for sea level rise, built a team to support places suffering from extreme weather events, etc. For me, it's a fairly hopeful future in *Adrift*, given the path we're currently on with respect to climate change. (We need to keep below a 1.5°C global temperature increase and projections have us on track to a 2.8°C–3.2°C increase by the end of the century.) I admit I took a more pessimistic view of the degree to which the U.S. takes action on climate, but I was writing this between 2018 and 2021, which was not a rosy time for U.S. climate policy. The new Inflation Reduction Act (a massive investment in climate solutions) is giving me hope again.

There were two challenges for me in looking ahead fifteen years.

One was resisting the urge to be very tech heavy. Things don't change that fast, not really. Think back fifteen years—it wasn't that dramatically different from today tech-wise, aside from smartphones. So I resisted the urge to push things too far, particularly as I think we'll need to embrace slowing down if we want to be successful in climate change mitigation. We can't constantly upgrade tech, create new things we don't need, consume ever more stuff. We need to be more deliberate.

The second challenge was that the actual weather events of 2021 were more extreme than what I'd written initially (excepting the storm at the end of *Adrift*, which hasn't happened yet). In 2021, British Columbia had a heat dome in June that killed more than six hundred people. That was followed by wildfire smoke that blanketed the province for weeks with hazardous-level air quality. Then the worst flooding the province has ever seen destroyed farmland, killed thousands of farm animals, and washed out all the highways connecting Vancouver to the rest of Canada. A town called Lytton set a record during the heat dome for the hottest temperature ever recorded anywhere in Canada—then it broke that record twice. Then during the wildfires, it burned to the ground completely. It was a bad year. Now, imagine fifteen years of increasing warming of our atmosphere intensifying everything and try to write that. But leave a sliver of hope.

Ess struggles to redefine her identity without memories. How much of her pre-amnesia life did you need to plan out? How much did you keep secret even from yourself?

I actually did a surprising amount of backstory for Ess. Since pre-amnesia Ess is the one who set things in motion and built the fail-safes into the plan that you see on the page, I needed to understand her, to understand what motivated her. What would she anticipate happening? What would she anticipate she would do when her memory was wiped? And how might she attempt to keep her memory-wiped-self from undoing the plan? It was a fun puzzle.

Ess never does find out *exactly* what she was fleeing. Why did you want to preserve that ambiguity?

This was one of the most critical elements of the story for me. I wanted an amnesia story where the character does not find out who she is, does not get all that back in a neat and tidy wrap-up—and I wanted it to be their choice to permanently turn away from those answers. (And, ideally, I wanted to do it in a way that didn't result in angry readers throwing my book at my head.)

I tried to give the reader a bit more information than Ess gets to try to ease the curiosity we all have that wants to be satisfied, but for Ess, her not-knowing at the end was built in from the beginning for me. This is life—it's messy and we usually don't get the clear answers we want.

ACKNOWLEDGMENTS

I wrote most of this book in Vancouver, on the unceded territory of the Squamish, Musqueam, and Tsleil-Waututh Nations. Their long history of sustainable stewardship of this beautiful place is something we would all do well to find a way back to. A portion of the book was inspired by Haida Gwaii and the power of the Haida Nation that imbues the place; it was a gift to be able to visit.

Writing a book seems like a spectacularly solitary project until you reflect on the crowd of kind, smart people who helped make it happen. So many generously gave their time and knowledge to help with *Adrift*. My heartfelt thanks to everyone listed here and those I have inevitably left out in my rush to write this; I appreciate you all tremendously.

Massive thanks to my agent, Sarah Bedingfield, for pulling *Adrift* from a slush pile and patiently working through deep edits with me while pregnant during COVID. You turn these crazy writing dreams into reality for people, which is an amazing superpower, and I'm very glad we connected! Thanks also to the folks at Levine Greenburg Rostan Literary, including Courtney Paganelli, Kirsten Wolf, and all those who work behind the scenes on my behalf.

For loving this story and seeing additional possibilities within it to explore, for the kind and insightful edit notes, and for making this publishing process so easy, my wonderful editor, Shana Drehs, thank you. Thanks to the entire fantastic Sourcebooks Landmark team: Diane Dannenfeldt (so sorry for all the missing commas you had to fix), Jessica Thelander with your incredible eye for detail, art director Liz Dresner for the perfect cover, and creative director Kelly Lawler. Also Cristina Arreola, Anna Venckus, Elizabeth Otte, and Sophie Kossakowski, plus the sales staff and all the others working to get this book out into the world that I haven't yet met at time of composing this list. You all make book magic happen, and I'm so, so grateful.

The Raincoast Books team: Jaime Broadhurst, Cameron Waller, the hardworking sales teams, and all those I haven't yet met who are working so hard to share *Adrift* with Canadians—an effort close to my heart, merci!

Gratitude to SG̲aana G̲aahlaandaay for generously sharing cultural reflections on the Haida Gwaii portion. Haawa. (Any errors are entirely mine.) I wouldn't be here if not for all the folks who read early disaster drafts and the folks who read later respectable drafts who universally encouraged me to keep going and provided helpful insights so I could see my work more clearly: Cristela Henriquez, Ryan Campbell (and the RevPit folks), Kirstin Innes, Katie Lattari, Sarah Tanburn, Karl Henwood, Ariana Townsend, Tammy Takaishi. Also, Charlene Henwood, Kristie Tatebe, Suzy Peakall, Alison Ker, Elan Hannah. Thanks to Pat St. Michel, Daniela Lucas, and Duane Elverum for trying to explain sailing to me. Thanks to Julia Kostka for the helpful fictional medical advice and George Benson for climate migration impacts conversations. The Canada Council for the Arts financially supported my professional development as an early-career artist during the course of writing this. For reading my earliest writing efforts as a kid and telling me it was great when it surely was not, look what that little white lie led to, Mom; thank you.

And, finally, to my partner in all my life adventures, my husband, Peter Kostka, who hates being called my partner but is my partner, who I forced to work out plot problems with me without letting him read the actual story—thank you times a million; you are the best. Also, the most handsome. And, yes, you can read it now. (Sorry for the lack of pirates. Next time.)

Thanks to the following book lovers at Sourcebooks who helped to publish *Adrift*:

Publisher
Dominique Raccah

Editorial
Shana Drehs
Jenna Jankowski
Findlay McCarthy
Olivia Turner
Todd Stocke

Production Editorial
Jessica Thelander
Tara Jaggers
Holli Roach
Jessica Zulli
Bret Kehoe

Design
Liz Dresner
Kelly Lawler
Stephanie Gafron

Marketing
Cristina Arreola
Molly Waxman
Anna Venckus
Kavita Wright
Alexandra Derdall
Kacie Blackburn
Valerie Pierce
BrocheAroe Fabian

Sales
Paula Amendolara
Brian Grogan
Tracy Nelson
Sean Murray
Raquel Latko
Margaret Coffee
Elizabeth Otte
Sophia Kossakowski
Shawn Abraham
Stephanie Beard
Jiayun Yang

Copyediting and Proofreading
Diane Dannenfeldt

Kelly Burch

Contracts
Elizabeth Berrones

Operations
Sarah Cardillo

Deve McLemore

Tina Wilson

Michelle Denney

Sarah Haley

Susan Raasch

Ian Voves

Christy Droege

Lindsey Holaday

ABOUT THE AUTHOR

Lisa Brideau is a sustainability policy nerd by day and a writer/weaver/ballroom dancer by night. Originally from Dartmouth, Nova Scotia, she found herself on the west coast by accident, fell in love with Vancouver, British Columbia, and now calls it home with her husband. *Adrift* is her first novel.